MW00654175

THE
ORPHAN TRAIN
SAGA

LOYAL · BOOK 5

Enjoy the Journey

SHERRY A. BURTON

Dorry Press

* A note from the author regarding The Orphan Train Saga. While each book tells a different child's story, some of the children's lives intertwine. For that reason, I recommend reading the books in order so that you avoid spoilers.

Loyal
Book 5 in The Orphan Train Saga

Written by Sherry A. Burton

Loyal, The Orphan Train Saga Book 5 © Copyright 2021
by Sherry A. Burton
ISBN: 978-1-951386-08-5

Published by Dorry Press
Edited and Formatted by BZHercules.com
Cover by Laura J. Prevost
www.laurajprevostbookcovers.myportfolio.com

To the National Orphan Train Complex, for all they do to preserve the memories of the children who rode the trains, and to educate society on the history of the Placing Out Program.

Table of Contents

Chapter One

Cindy woke to the sounds of birds chirping merrily outside her bedroom window and lay there gathering her thoughts. Two months had passed since Frank's funeral, and she hadn't been able to shake the funk of knowing she'd never see him again. It didn't make sense, as she'd known his time to be near, but here she was still trying to find her new normal. *You're not going to find it here.* She pulled herself from the bed, tugging on yesterday's clothes.

"Good morning, Sunshine," Linda said when she slogged into the kitchen.

"What's so good about it?" Cindy groaned.

Linda looked at the clock. "Well, for starters, you're out of bed before noon. Would you like breakfast or lunch?"

"I'm not hungry."

"Lunch it is," Linda said, turning to the stove. "I thought we'd start back into the journals today."

"I'm not sure I'm ready," Cindy said with a sigh.

"You'll never be ready with that attitude. I'm going to start reading. You can join me or not, but I want to read what Slim has to say."

"Is this some kind of tough love?" Cindy said, dipping a spoon into the bowl of vegetable beef soup Linda sat in front of her.

"You know as well as I do that Frank would tell you to knock off the moping and move on with your life."

She was right, but it still didn't make his being gone any easier.

"They'll make you feel better," Linda told her.

"How can you be so sure?"

"Because they helped me after your father passed."

Oops, how could I have forgotten that? "I'm sorry, Mom."

"Nothing to be sorry about. I seem to remember a time when you had to nudge me to get on with my life. God knows I needed it. I think focusing on someone else's troubles made me forget about my own."

Her mother had a point. Besides, she didn't like the thought of Linda reading the journals without her. It was something they shared, and she was happy her mother had been patient enough to wait for her. "Okay, Mom. I'll give it a try."

They finished their soup and went to the living room, which they'd officially named their reading room, as it had both read and waiting-to-be-read journals stacked about the room. Linda went to the end table, selected two piles, and handed her one. The second she felt the weight of them in her hands, she knew her mother to be right. Tucking her feet under her bottom, she began to read.

I'm writing these journals at the request of my good friend Paddy, who, for reasons unknown, thinks someday someone will be interested enough in the children who rode the trains that they'll wish to know how we came to ride them and further wish to know what became of us. I did not have it as bad as some of the others as I had people in my life who were eager to see me succeed. Why they chose me, I do not know. A wise man—small in stature but abundant in knowledge—once told me that my mother, who'd been overly protective during her life, had somehow found a way to watch over me after she died. I found comfort in those words, which sounded as logical as any reason I could ever come up with on my own, so I like to think it to be true. Anyway, since I don't have any words of wisdom of my own, I will tell my story as it happened in my own words.

***

August 1916

Percival circled his arms around his legs, grasping his ankles to keep his legs from moving and giving away his presence to the visitor in the outer room. From the sound of things, he wouldn't have to stay hidden much longer. He ached to release his legs and use his hands to cover his ears to muffle the sounds coming from his mother's bedroom, but the last time he'd interrupted, it hadn't ended so well. His breathing increased as he remembered that evening.

His mother was entertaining a visitor, her laughter turning to screams as the man with her slurred phrases that made Percival's cheeks burn. He put his hands to his ears, but it did nothing to drown the sounds coming from outside his boxed enclosure. He knew he wasn't supposed to open the door, but when she cried out once again, he gathered his courage, pushed open the closet door, and rushed to his mother's side, his small hands balled into fists as he demanded the man leave her alone.

An image of the half-naked man came to mind, and Percival closed his eyes. A mistake, as the image gave way to the chaos that had ensued. His mother screaming for the man to leave him alone. The pain as the bottle hit him alongside the head, followed by the brilliant flash of light just before everything grew silent. He'd spent over a week in the hospital. That his mother never left his side the entire time he was there nearly made the pain worth it. She'd sobbed as she ran her slender hands alongside his bandaged head, uttering apologies for not keeping him safe. Further promising that things would change. They had for a while, but there were bills to pay, and since his mother wasn't married and he too young to work at the time,

3

things soon returned to normal. Normal for them anyway. Then one day, the landlord knocked on the door. Reeking of alcohol, the man practically drooled as he swayed in the doorway demanding the rent. His mother handed the man some bills, but the landlord shook his head, telling her it wasn't enough. His mother had insisted it was the same amount she always paid, but he smiled a wicked smile and told her he'd found someone who could pay more. He'd then sneered at Percival and said the person he was speaking of didn't have a snot-nosed kid.

Percival had taken exception to that, as his nose wasn't snotty. His mother had silenced him before turning to the landlord, asking what she was supposed to do. His smile turned menacing as he looked Percival's mother up and down, then whispered something only she could hear. His words must not have been very pleasant, as Percival saw her trembling as he spoke.

After a moment's hesitation, she'd pulled herself taller, then turned to Percival and told him she had to go out for a little while. He'd begged her not to go with the man, but she'd told him to mind his place. When she'd returned, he could tell she'd been crying. Later that day, the landlord had knocked again. This time, she'd refused to open the door. After he went away, she announced they would be moving as soon as she could find a place for them to stay.

It hadn't taken long. Within a week, they'd moved to a small one-room apartment not far from the club where his mother worked as a dancer. The room held a bed, a small round table with two chairs, and the closet, which his mother had brightly declared Percival's new bedroom. At first, he'd thought her to be jesting, but she'd lined the enclosure with blankets and given him a pillow for his head. Since that day, he'd spent a lot of time in the closet, mostly hiding while his mother entertained visitors.

The noise on the other side of the door subsided, and Percival began to relax. He listened for the click of the outer door before releasing his ankles. Shoving off the floor, he silently pushed open the door to the closet. His mother stood on the far side of the room with her back to him.

"Momma." The word came out in a whisper.

She gathered her robe together, pulling the tie into her waist as she turned, greeting him with a smile. "Percival, come give Momma a hug."

He walked to where she stood and sank into her arms, wrinkling his nose against the smell of musty cigars and unwashed bodies.

She released her hold then used her robe to wipe the sweat from his face. A frown fleeted across her face as she lifted a towel from the hook beside the door. "Your supper is on the table. I'm going to the washroom. When I come back, you can tell me about your day."

Percival felt the heat creep across his face as he stood staring after her. Had she guessed his secret? Did his mother know he'd waited long enough for her to leave before sneaking upstairs and sitting in the shade of the adjacent building? While still hot on the tar rooftop, it was decidedly better than the stifling confines of the small room.

He walked to the small table and opened the cloth to reveal a hunk of bread. Beside the bread sat a small green bowl filled with pasta and sauce. He dipped a finger into the sauce, grabbed a plump tomato, and plopped it into his mouth. It was cold, and not nearly as tasty as the food his momma once cooked, but it was food, and for that, he was grateful. There had been many days when there was nothing but a few crumbs. That had changed after he and his mother had moved. A feat, as the small room they now called home didn't actually have a kitchen. Shortly after moving in, his mother started entertaining visitors when she wasn't working at the club. Though he wasn't pleased his mother had so many guests, he was happy when they started bringing her food. She'd told him that was why she was so nice to them. He never let on that he knew the men also left her money on the bedside table.

Tearing off a chunk of bread, he dipped it into the sauce then shoved it in his mouth, enjoying the tang. Watching the door as he chewed, he waited for his mother to return.

He was nearly finished when she came floating into the room in long, confident strides. His mother was a dancer, and it showed. She even taught him to dance, something he'd been much better at before the blow to the head. Now his legs seemed to have a mind of their own, dancing even when he didn't want them to. If he wasn't holding on to his legs, they were hopping around like someone had spilled hot coals down his pants. The movements didn't hurt so much, but they were bothersome all the same. It was as if his legs were now wired into his head, matching his mood. If he was upset, they'd move all the more.

"Not much of a breeze today. I'm sorry you had to stay inside all day," his mother said, then moved to the window and grabbed hold of the curtains, twisting them into a knot to allow more air. "Someday, we will have an apartment with more than one window where the wind can flow through to create a nice breeze. You'd like that, wouldn't you?"

Percival was glad his mother hadn't looked at him as she spoke. If she had, he felt sure she would have seen the guilt on his face. "Yes, Momma."

She lowered to the floor and sat with her arms resting on the windowsill, her face staring out as if drinking in the fresh air. She sighed, her shoulders dropping as she exhaled.

"You're thinking of Papa." He knew it to be true, as she always grew sad when she thought of him.

She turned, and he could see the moisture in her eyes. "There isn't a day that goes by that I don't think of Armano."

Percival walked to where his mother sat and kneeled beside her. Sitting like this, with his legs anchored underneath, helped to keep them still. "I wish I could remember him."

Her brows knitted together, then she smiled, lifting his chin with the tips of her fingers. "You only need to look in the mirror to see your papa's face."

"You've said that before. But I wish I remembered what he was like."

She picked up the paper fan used to cool them on days such as this and moved it back and forth to create a breeze. "Your papa was a good man. He loved you so very much. He would put you on his shoulders and parade you through the streets. He'd point to all the buildings that he helped build, telling you that someday you'd be big enough to help him. He'd toss you into the air, and you would giggle when he caught you."

"And you were afraid he'd drop me and tell him to stop." He knew, as she'd told him so many times before.

"I did, but I needn't have feared. Your papa, he was a strong man with solid arms." She drew her arms into her body and closed her eyes, the sweat glistening on her face.

"But he wasn't strong enough."

Her eyelids sprang open. Instantly, Percival regretted his words. He was just about to ask her to tell him the story when she waved the paper fan and began speaking of her own accord.

"It was July of 1911, and you'd nearly reached your fourth year. The heat had been growing for days and didn't let up at night. The air…it was so thick and foul. Day or night, it didn't matter. It was so hard to breathe." Her hand went to her throat as if remembering. She swallowed, then looked out the window and sucked in another breath of air. "Horses pulling carts would fall to the ground dead, leaving their owner to walk the rest of the way home. The horse would lie where it fell, festering for days because it was much too hot to move them. Oh, the smell…I don't think I'll ever forget it."

Percival watched her face grow pale, her nostrils flaring as she spoke.

"Mothers would put their babies to bed, only to have them never to wake. Word of the deaths spread, and mothers took to taking their babies out into the night air instead of laying them in their cribs. You were older, but I was so afraid of losing you. I took you outside each night, walking the streets with the others. When we were too weary to walk, we would go inside, make our way through the stifling stairway to the rooftop, and fall asleep under the stars. It was so hot, the factories shut down. The steel was too hot to touch and your papa couldn't go to work. Nobody could.

"On the tenth day of the heat, your papa kissed us both then told me he was going to the rooftop to get some air. It was the last time I saw your papa alive. Two days later, a great storm arrived, its booms heard throughout the city as buckets of rain did its best to wash the stench from the streets. With the thunder came cooler temperatures…if only your papa could have waited a couple more days."

She'd told him the story so many times that she could tell it without tears. The pain etched on her face let him know how deeply she felt the loss, though it didn't stop him from requesting her to retell the events. He enjoyed his alone time with his mother, loved hearing her tell him stories about his papa. Even the ones that ended with his papa going up to the rooftop and never coming down. Sometimes he would imagine his father sitting all alone with the sky overhead, just waiting for Percival to come to see him. He'd often snuck up the stairs to look for the man, but he was never there.

The only memories he had of his papa were those given to

him by his mother. He liked that his mother never spoke ill of his papa. With the exception of the story she'd just told, she would smile and regale him with tales of how happy they were when his papa was alive. It was just the three of them then. There were no visitors sharing her bed, no landlords pushing them from the apartment where they had once lived with his papa, and most importantly, no closets used as bedrooms. Percival longed to remember when they were a family. Now it was just he, his mother, and countless strangers drifting in and out. He didn't mind the strangers so much. Most of them never stayed long enough to pay him any mind. What he minded was having to hide in the closet turned bedroom listening to things a child should not hear.

"It's hot. Do you want to sleep on the roof tonight?" his mother asked as she pushed the sweat away from her brow.

He studied her for a second, wondering if she'd read his mind. She hadn't. But the sadness in her eyes told him that when they climbed the stairs to the rooftop, he wouldn't be the only one hoping to find his father there.

Chapter Two

Percival stared out the window, his legs dancing with anticipation as he impatiently waited for his mother to exit the building. He trembled as she came into view, then anxiously watched as she crossed to the other side of the street. Once on the far sidewalk, she turned and lifted her hand to him—something she did each time she left the apartment without him. He returned the gesture, staying in front of the window until she was well out of sight. He had to be sure she didn't change her mind about leaving. Not that she ever did, but it wouldn't be good if she returned to discover him missing. So many times, he thought to tell her of his forays to the roof, but he was afraid, scared that if she knew, she would insist he stop. He didn't like disobeying his mother. It had started as a way to cool off, but with the small act of defiance came a newfound freedom he'd never before experienced. That he'd traded the confines of the closet for the confines of the roof didn't matter. At least on the roof, he could run and jump to his heart's delight. And, while the roof was still hot, there were no walls blocking the delicious summer breeze.

On occasion, he would have to share the space with others—mostly mothers who would sometimes take smaller children up there to play. Once, he'd been disappointed to find a woman had claimed part of the rooftop to dry her laundry. She'd not been pleased when he'd shown up, shaking her fist and warning him against bothering her clothing. She needn't have worried; he didn't have any need for her undergarments and the woman's dresses were much too large to fit his mother. Besides, his mother liked to wear more colorful clothing than those the woman had strewn across the wooden racks she'd carried to the roof. He hadn't seen the woman in more than a week and hoped the same proved true today.

Opening the door to the apartment, he peeked into the hallway, pleased to find it empty. Pulling the door shut behind him, he hurried to the stairs, taking them three at a time. As soon as he opened the door and saw he was alone, he sighed his relief. Letting the door close behind him, he stepped to the middle, spread his arms, then lifted his face to the sun and spun in slow circles. He opened his mouth and stuck out his tongue, hoping to drink in as much sunshine as possible. He loved the rooftop. It was the perfect place for a boy whose legs had a mind of their own. He could move and shake without worrying about running into anything or anyone so long as he stayed away from the edge.

As Percival completed his sixth circle, he was pulled from his fun by the sound of rhythmic thuds. He'd heard the noise before but thus far had not been able to figure out where the sound originated.

Tilting his head, he tried to ascertain where the sound originated. Oddly, it seemed as if it was coming from all directions. He walked to the side of the building and looked over the edge at the street below. While he could see movement, he could never look long enough to decipher what it was he was seeing. A wave of nausea sent him backing away from the edge. The thuds continued, and he decided to go to the other side to have another look. When he was halfway across, the thuds stopped. Undaunted, he closed his eyes, stretched his arms, and turned in place once again.

Tiring of spinning, he thought of the dance moves his mother showed him the day before. He'd tried to do as she said, but there wasn't much space in the small room, and he'd bumped into both the table and bed before stepping on his mother's toes. Cautiously, he willed his legs to move in the way she'd instructed.

Excitement raced through him as his feet drifted around the wide-open space with ease. He closed his eyes once again, picturing his mother showing him the steps and imagining her pleasure at his mimicking her actions. He stopped dancing, his excitement waning as he realized he wouldn't be able to tell her of his feat, not without admitting that he'd disobeyed her. Instantly, the jubilance he'd felt a moment earlier was replaced with guilt. While his mother always looked out for him, he'd repaid her by sneaking out of the apartment every chance he got. Closing his eyes, he heaved a heavy sigh. *I need to go home.*

He opened his eyes, surprised to see a boy standing only a few feet away. The boy was a good head shorter than he, with a mop of red hair, and seemed just as surprised to see him.

Percival's mother had once told him a story about a leprechaun with bright red hair who had appeared out of nowhere and granted the farmer a single wish. He considered this for a moment.

"Whatcha gaping at?" the leprechaun asked.

Percival swallowed his fear. "Are you magic?"

The leprechaun scratched at his head. "Magic? Why, whatever gave you that idea?"

"My momma told me leprechauns are magic." Much to his dismay, his legs started moving on their own accord. "Said they granted farmers wishes."

"Yeah, well, I ain't no leprechaun. Even if I was, you sure don't look like no farmer, so I wouldn't be granting you a wish no how." He pointed at Percival. "You're the one hopping around like a toad in the rain. Maybe I should be questioning you. What makes you think I'm a leprechaun anyhow?"

"Because you've got red hair and the door to the roof's over there," Percival said with a nod of the head.

"I got red hair 'cause I'm Irish. Least that's what my ma says. She says I take after my pop. I don't, though. My pop's an ornery soul. Drinks too much and likes to beat on me and my brothers. Ma said he's got the devil in him, said I gots it in me too on account of I have red hair."

Percival peered in the boy's direction. The boy had red hair, alright. He didn't know what the devil was, but if it was in the boy, he wanted to see it.

A frown tugged at the boy's mouth. "Now, whatcha gaping at?"

Percival shrugged. "Trying to see the devil's all."

"You can't see the devil."

Percival sighed his disappointment. "You can't?"

"No, the devil is in the actions." He scratched his head once more. "Least I think so."

"You don't know?"

"No, but when my pop gets mean, my ma says the devil's in him, so I figure that to be true."

"Do you think the devil put you here?"

"Why, I never thought of that. Do you think he did?"

"He must have, 'cause you didn't use the door," Percival replied.

The boy laughed. "Oh, that. No, it wasn't the devil. I jumped."

"Jumped?"

"Yeah, from the other roof. I do it all the time."

Percival recalled looking over the side and the wave of nausea that followed. "You do?"

"Sure, lots of kids do it, especially at night. It's safer than walking the streets. Why, a kid gets caught on the streets at night and … well, it can be real bad."

Percival was more interested in the jumping. "Ain't you afraid of falling?"

"Nah, you just have to know the ones to jump. We've done it enough, we know. Like that side there," the boy said, pointing to the spot Percival had looked over moments earlier. "Only experienced jumpers would try that. And then only the ones with long legs. You got ya some long legs, and they seem to like to move, so you could maybe make it. I wouldn't try it until you've jumped a few of the easier ones. 'Cause if you get scared, you might not jump so good, and you'd end up splattered on the street. That happens, and they'd scrape your body into a wagon with a shovel. I've seen it happen."

Percival thought of his father and swallowed the bile that threatened to come up. "I've slept up here at night. Why ain't I never seen ya?"

"We've been here, my friends and me. We know to be quiet."

Percival decided that to be true, as he had not heard the boy land on the roof. Still, he was a bit disappointed the kid was not a leprechaun. "You got a name?"

The kid rolled his eyes. "Course I got a name. Everybody's got one."

"Well, what is it?" Percival pressed.

"My name's Howard, but everyone calls me Paddy on account of I'm Irish and have red hair."

Percival wasn't sure what being Irish meant. Maybe it

was like having the devil in him. The boy knew he had the devil but said you couldn't see it. Was it the same with being Irish, or did he know he was Irish on account of him having red hair? He was just getting ready to ask the kid when he heard the thumps again. "What's that noise?"

Paddy tilted his head toward the sound, and the color drained from his face. "Nothing you need to concern yourself with."

Maybe not, but he was curious all the same. "But what is it?"

"It's Big Joe. You don't want anything to do with that guy. Why, I heard he stole a man's soul, that one. My pop said Big Joe kilt the man with just one punch. You ever see him, you run." Paddy looked around as if just speaking about it would bring evil down upon him. "I best be going."

Percival felt a pang of regret for having asked about the noise. He rarely got to speak with anyone other than his mother, and though he'd seen other kids before, he'd seldom had the chance to talk with anyone even close to his own age. "Will you be back?"

"I might. Tomorrow." The words had no sooner left the boy's mouth when Paddy took off running the length of the building, leaping just as he reached the edge.

Percival looked after him, watching with a mixture of fear and longing, as the boy ran the length of the roof, jumped once more, then continued to do so again and again. He yearned to run after the boy just to see where he was going. Fear kept him rooted in place.

***

Cindy gaped at the page she'd just read, knowing with utter certainty she'd just met the child version of her grandfather.

"You keep your mouth open, and you're going to

swallow a fly," Linda chided.

"It's really him, isn't it?" Cindy felt giddy beyond belief. "Grandpa, Howard. I knew he would be in the journals, but to read about him like this is more than anything I could've wished for."

Linda laughed. "You're telling me you're surprised to learn your grandfather was a real superman."

"Superman?"

"Leaping tall buildings."

It was Cindy's turn to laugh. "Superboy is more like it. Can you imagine his parents allowing him to play on the rooftop? He was probably no more than eight at the time."

Linda's brow arched. "Something tells me his parents had no clue what he was up to. Or didn't care."

Cindy nodded her agreement. "You're probably right. Did you catch that part about his dad hitting him and his brothers? Grandpa Howard never mentioned having brothers. All my life, I grew up thinking him to be an only child. I probably have cousins I've never even met."

"Maybe you should get one of those DNA tests."

"Maybe. Up until we started reading the journals, I thought we were a perfectly normal, albeit dysfunctional family."

Linda removed her glasses, cleaning them with the edge of her shirt. "Speak for yourself."

Cindy laughed. "Are you questioning normal or dysfunctional?"

"I'm normal. I married into dysfunctional." Linda said, returning the glasses to her face. "I have to admit, it would've been nice if Howard had actually been a leprechaun. Instead of finding journals, we could've found a pot of gold."

Cindy smiled. "I'm happy with the journals."

"And I'm happy you've found your smile again. Still, it would have been fun if Howard would have led us to the journals with rainbows instead of x's, half-moons, and mouse paws," Linda mused.

"They would've been easier to find, that's for sure," Cindy said, remembering the hours they'd spent on their knees scouring the attic in search of the hidden journals. She flipped through the stack of papers in her hand, hoping to see her grandfather's name mentioned.

"You used to do the same thing with Cracker Jacks."

"What?" Cindy said, letting the papers fall into place on her lap.

"When you were a kid, you'd tear open the box of Cracker Jacks and dump them into a bowl, searching through the popcorn and peanuts until you found the prize."

"I remember. I always hoped for a ring but usually ended up getting a paper tattoo. This is even better than a ring. Where are you going?" Cindy asked when Linda shoved off the couch.

"I said popcorn, and now I can't think of anything else. Want some?"

"I do now." Cindy ran her hand over the papers, eager to continue reading. "Want me to wait for you?"

Linda shook her head. "No, you go ahead. I'll catch up. Besides, what kind of mother would I be if I spoiled your prize?"

Chapter Three

He sat on the floor beneath the window reading from his copy of *Peter Pan*. It was his mother who taught him to read, an activity he usually enjoyed. But that was before. While *Peter Pan* had long been a favorite, he now found himself agitated while reading from the book. Was it because Peter Pan could fly out the window and experience great adventures? Or because Percival was suddenly afraid that he too would never grow up. He listened to the rain pelting against the window and sighed, knowing that he was nothing like Peter Pan. That boy would never allow a little rain to slow him down.

Percival thought of the boy he'd met on the rooftop the day prior, wondering if he would be daunted by the rain, and instantly decided the answer to be no. He looked to the ceiling. *Maybe Paddy's on the rooftop at this very moment waiting for me. If he doesn't find me, he may never come back. Don't even think about it; you'd never be able to explain away the wet clothes.*

Still struggling with his conscience, he sat his book aside and picked up another longtime favorite—a thick book with a dark brown cover and a title he'd never been able to read. In fact, neither he nor his mother had actually read any of the original content, as the book was written in another language. She'd purchased it long before he was born, using the wide margins to scribe old family recipes and script little notes to herself. He opened the book, instantly greeted by his mother's handwriting. He turned it to its side, his eyes skimming a recipe for Picnic Caramel Cake. He turned the page and drooled while reading the recipe for raisin date bread pudding. On the opposite page was a simple recipe for rice pudding, one he'd watched his mother make countless times when they'd lived in the apartment with the proper kitchen, the one they'd shared with his papa before his father had gone to the roof. He thought about what Paddy had said about not jumping some of the roofs because they'd have to scoop you up with a shovel. He wondered briefly if that was what had happened to his father, then pushed the thought from his mind. He turned the page and found his mother's recipe for spaghetti sauce. His stomach rumbled as he began to read.

*Coat the bottom of a big pot with olive oil. Add chopped onions and fresh chopped parsley. Cook on medium heat till cooked down, and then add garlic. Once the garlic starts to release flavor... add 5 cans of crushed tomatoes, 1/3 can of water, fresh oregano, and basil to taste. * A cup of red wine will help break down the acidity. Now this is important, never use a metal spoon. Use a wooden spoon to scrape the bottom and keep it from burning. Lower the flame and simmer, stirring with the same wooden spoon every 20 minutes for about 3-6 hours. The longer it simmers, the thicker the gravy gets. *Never cover the gravy with a lid, as it will cause condensation.* He read that last sentence in his mother's voice, adding, "No one wants to eat watery spaghetti sauce."

Smiling, he turned the page and found the shortened version called Poor Man's Sauce. Though he knew the recipe by heart, he skimmed the ingredients, once again hearing his mother's words. *Every Italian mother knows that, in a pinch, one could make sauce using five basic ingredients: Tomatoes, oregano, basil, onions, and garlic.* Though the recipe only called for a few cloves of garlic, his mother would always add more, insisting one could never have too much garlic. His mouth watered at the thought of his mother's spaghetti sauce.

I miss her cooking. His stomach echoed his sentiment.

Turning the page, he hesitated. Though he'd skimmed the pages countless times over the years, he saw an inscription he'd never noticed before. Perhaps it was because the color of the ink was the same as the bold lettering within the pages of the book, perhaps it was because he was paying extra attention. Regardless the reason, the note at the bottom now appeared as if it were shouting from the page. ***Thou shall not speak ill of the dead.*** Beside the sentence was another note, this one written in much smaller print. He pulled the book closer, squinting his eyes to get a better look. *Armano Barsotti 1859-1911.*

"Papa." He wondered why he hadn't noticed it before. And further wondered why she'd bothered to write it at all. His mother never said anything bad about his papa. Was this her reminder? Turning the page, he saw the recipe his mother used for meatballs. Instantly, he recalled standing in the kitchen at their old apartment, watching as his mother added the ingredients to the bowl before using her hands to mold everything into large, round balls. She'd let him help her on occasion, showing him precisely how much to take from the bowl and how to rock the mixture back and forth in his hands to form the perfect shape. Every now and then, he'd take too much, and she'd wordlessly pluck some away and nod for him to continue. He'd once asked her how she knew how much to grab, and she'd told him it was the way it fit the palm, further telling him that, in time, he'd be able to tell just by the way it rolled when he cradled it in his hand.

An image of a man approaching his mother and kissing her on the back of the neck flittered into his mind. The man looked older, but his mother didn't seem to mind. Her eyes sparkled with delight as he took her into his arms. Like Percival and his mother, the man also had dark hair and eyes. He blinked his surprise. He wasn't sure how he knew, but he was certain he'd just had a memory of his father.

Slamming the book closed, he blew out a disgusted sigh. He rose to his knees and glared out the window, angered by both the memory and the books, all of which appeared to be teasing him with things he couldn't have.

Laughter floated up from the street and he leaned out to get a better look, further chastened at the sight of children playing stickball in the rain. He stood, then sat on the windowsill, stretching his long legs out one at a time. He smiled as his legs danced against the brick building as he imagined himself running and playing with the children below. The rain streamed down his bare legs, dripping from his toes, and he thought of Peter Pan, and for a moment, he considered pushing from the sill to see if he too could fly. Remembering Paddy's words, he hastily pulled in his legs. They'd not be scraping him from the sidewalk today. Still, the discovery in his mother's book left him feeling hollow. He missed the freedom of moving from room to room in their old apartment, the joy of eating his mother's cooking, and the man whose memory was just beyond his grasp. He longed to go to the street and join the children in their games.

Dare he? Why not? He was already mostly wet.

Making a decision, he left the apartment. Only, instead of going to the street, he headed up to the roof and stepped into the rain without caring if his mother found out. The roof was empty and the rain gloriously cool despite the mugginess of the air. He planted his feet, bent his arms as he'd seen the children in the street do, and swung, connecting with the imaginary ball. He dropped the invisible bat and ran around the roof to cheers that were heard only within his mind. It was a one-sided game, but he was running. Once he'd started running, he quickly lost interest in the game and ran in large circles until at last he could run no more. He stood with his back arched, heaving heavy breaths as the rain dripped from the tip of his nose.

Laughter greeted him once more. Only this time, the laughter was the deep laugh that came from someone much larger than he. Percival lifted his gaze toward the sound and sucked in his breath. Standing on the roof of the next building over was the darkest man he'd ever seen. Wearing short pants normally reserved for boys, the man's shirtless back glistened against the rain. He lifted a gloved hand and waved, laughing once again when Percival did nothing but stare.

Undeterred, the man moved closer to the edge of the roof. For a moment, Percival thought him about to jump and wondered if he would make it or if they'd be scraping him from the street at the end of the day. The man stopped just at the edge, looked down, then seemed to decide against making the jump.

"Come on over here, boy," he said instead. Percival cast a glance at the door to the stairs, his legs dancing as if they'd made up their own mind. "Come on; I'll not be hurting you."

Much to Percival's surprise, his legs moved him closer to the edge of the roof and he found himself within feet of the man, who now stared at his legs as if he too were in awe of them. Why wouldn't he be? The legs in question continued to dance from side to side, even though Percival wasn't going anywhere. He willed them to stop, but they only moved quicker, splashing around the roof like a marionette he'd seen once when his mother had taken him to see a puppet show. His face flushed despite the coolness of the rain, and much to his embarrassment, the man laughed once again.

Percival lowered his eyes and turned to leave.

"You got a name, Slim?"

Slim? Percival pivoted to see who the man was speaking to, surprised to find he was talking to him. "That's not my name.

My name's Percival."

"Your legs got a mind of their own, don't they, Percival?"

"Yes, sir."

The man's eyes grew wide, and he rocked back on his heels. "Not often I get called 'sir'."

Big Joe. This was the man Paddy warned him about. Percival took a step backwards, recalling Paddy's words. *You don't want anything to do with Big Joe. He kilt a man with just one punch.*

The smile left the man's face. "I see you've heard the rumors."

"Yes, I heard you killed a man." He thought to tell the man it was Paddy who'd told him but decided against it so as not to get the boy in trouble. "You mean it's not true?"

"No," Big Joe replied solemnly.

"You mean Paddy lied to me?" Percival realized he'd outed his source and clamped a hand over his mouth as his legs picked up the rhythm.

"Paddy? That be the redhead boy that jumps the roofs?"

"You know him?"

"I've seen him. The boy races by so fast, I always figured he's afraid of something. Makes sense now that I know. Never seen you before. Why were you talking about me anyhow?"

The sun broke through the clouds and Percival realized it had stopped raining. "I heard a noise. A thump thump. I'd heard it before but could never figure it out. I heard it again when Paddy was here, so I asked. He never did say what the sound was. Just that it was you and you killed a man. Why would he say that if it wasn't true?"

"Why do kids say anything? A boy hears something and then repeats it regardless of if it's true or not. I'm sure you've told a lie or two in your day." He smiled. "See there, your legs're about to dance you off this here roof. I'm right, ain't I?

Come on, tell me what lie you done told."

Percival lowered his head in shame. "I come up here on this roof while my momma is at work. I'm not supposed to, as she tells me not to leave the apartment unless I have to go to the washroom."

"Your ma got a reason for not wanting you to go outside?"

"She's never really said, but I think it's something on account of my legs. We used to go more places, but now, I mainly stay inside." Percival looked up and grinned. "At least I used to."

"What happened to your legs?"

"The doctors said it is because of my head. I'm not sure what my head has to do with my legs, but they didn't dance on their own until after I got this." Percival turned his head so Big Joe could see the scar. As the man looked him over, Percival felt the heat warm his cheeks. He didn't like talking about his scar.

Big Joe blew out a long whistle. "Boy, I sure wish I had a scar like that."

Percival jerked his head up. "You do?"

"Sure do. Why, if all it takes to get your legs moving like that is a little bonk on the head, then it would be worth it."

Percival frowned. "Now you're just pulling my leg."

"I'm doing no such thing. Why, I couldn't catch your legs even if I wanted to pull them."

Percival's frown deepened and he turned to leave.

"Where are you off to?"

"I may not be too smart, but I know when someone is funning me."

Big Joe held his hand up in protest. "I'm telling you the truth, boy. If my legs moved around the floor like yours, then I couldn't lose."

"Lose what?"

"A fight. I'm a boxer."

"A what?"

"Now don't go telling me you don't know what a boxer is."

Percival shook his head and watched in amazement as the man stepped back from the edge of the roof and began hopping from foot to foot while jabbing his fist in the air. It was like a dance, but nothing as graceful as the moves his mother made.

"Well, what do you think?" Big Joe asked, punching the air with his fists.

"I think you dance worse than I do," Percival answered honestly.

"Boy, this ain't dancing. It's boxing. Only, when in the ring, I'm hitting my opponent instead of the air."

Percival remembered the man who'd hit him with the bottle and his hand instinctively went to the scar upon his head. "You mean you hit people on purpose?"

Big Joe's legs stilled. He lowered his arms and narrowed his eyes. "You mean to tell me that's what happened to your head?"

Afraid to speak, Percival merely nodded.

"You know the man that did that?" The humor was gone from Big Joe's voice.

Percival thought to tell him that his mother knew the man but decided against it. Instead, he shook his head and fought to steady his legs.

"You ever see the man, you come find me. I'll see to it he never hurts anyone again." The lines in Big Joe's face softened. "Do those legs of yours ever listen when you tell them to be still?"

"Not so much, sir."

Big Joe blew out another whistle. "Yes, sir, sure do wish my legs moved like that. Listen, kid, I've got to be going."

Percival sighed.

"Tell you what. You find your way up to the roof again and hear me hitting my bag, you come to the side and give a shout. I'll hear ya and I'll come say hello."

Percival wasn't sure why the man would be hitting a bag, but he decided it to be better than punching the air and nodded his agreement. Big Joe waved before disappearing behind a wall in the center of the roof. A moment later, Percival heard the familiar thump. He smiled picturing Big Joe hopping from foot to foot with his hands punching into the air.

Picturing Big Joe doing the awkward dance, Percival willed his feet to move from side to side. To his delight, the movement was much easier than the graceful way of his mother's gait. He pulled his arms in and knotted his hands into fists and floated around the roof with a gleeful sense of accomplishment. Just as he completed his fifth waltz around the rooftop, he stopped near where he'd last seen Big Joe. For a moment, he thought to call to the man and show him what he'd learned. The door to the stairs creaked open and his mother pushed through the doorway.

At the sight of her worried face, his swagger disappeared.

Chapter Four

His mother drew him into her arms, holding him so tight, he couldn't breathe. After a moment, she released him, clutched him by the hand, and led him toward the stairs without a word. He opened his mouth, thinking to tell her she was hurting his hand, then decided against it. Better to suffer the pain than chance irritating her further. He matched her steps, following as she yanked him down the four flights of stairs as if being chased by some unimaginable demon. How the woman walked so fast in heels remained a mystery.

They reached the doorway to the sixth floor and cut off a woman coming up the stairs. The woman shouted her annoyance, but his mother only lengthened her stride, pulling him down the long corridor and into the confines of their small room. Only after locking the door behind them did she release her grip. Leaning against the door, she fanned herself with her hand.

At first, he thought she'd been caught in the rain as he watched the droplets trickle along her cheek, then realized it wasn't rain. "Momma, you're crying."

She wiped the tears away before answering. "Percival, how could you disobey me like this? Do you know how upsetting it was when I came home, and you weren't here? I thought... I thought something bad had happened to you. I was worried sick. I don't know what I would have done if I hadn't found you...Why?"

Percival could not recall a time when his mother had ever

been this upset. It was all he could do not to run to her and beg her forgiveness. Even still, he held his ground, knowing he had to make her understand. "Because I don't want to be like Peter Pan."

She stared at him without blinking.

"I know you worry about me, but you're not allowing me to grow up."

"You're going to be nine on your birthday. You're growing up. I couldn't stop you even if I wanted to," his mother argued.

"But you are. Can't you see? I have no friends. There are boys much younger than me playing in the streets."

Her face paled. "You've been out on the streets by yourself?"

"No. But I can hear them. I can see them from the window laughing and playing. And what do I get? Books."

"You say that as if it's a bad thing. You enjoy reading."

She was watching him move around the crowded room. Deciding his legs might be his saving grace, he didn't bother trying to steady them. "I used to, Momma. But my legs need room. When I go to the rooftop, I can dance. Not the way I do in here, but the way you showed me. There's plenty of room, and I can feel the sunlight all the way down to the bottom of my feet. I need it, Momma. All of it."

His mother set her chin. "No."

"I'm not Papa!" Watching her cringe, he felt a moment of guilt, then pushed forward. "I saw him today."

She cast a glance toward the ceiling.

"Not up there." He pointed to his head. "In here. I was reading your book and saw what you wrote. A second later, I saw him. No, I saw both of you. You were cooking, and he was standing behind you. He kissed your neck. I know it was him because when he turned, he looked like me."

Fresh tears streamed down her face and her shoulders

relaxed for the first time since entering the room. Her hand drifted to the back of her neck, a slight smile replacing the frown. "You remembered?"

"I did." That she smiled gave him hope that she'd forgotten her anger.

"Did I ever tell you that my papa was furious when I told him I was marrying Armano?"

"No." He thought to remind her that she seldom spoke of her parents, then changed his mind. "Did your papa not like my papa?"

"Your grandpapa," she lowered to the edge of the bed, melancholy replacing the fear in her voice, "was a good man and would have loved you so very much. He liked your papa very much. They were friends until I told him about us. You see, your papa was very close to your grandpapa in age. If he'd been marrying anyone else, your grandpapa would have congratulated him and wished him well. But since that wasn't the case, he was furious. I still remember him pacing the floor and shaking his fist in the air. Not that he would have ever used it, but he shook it all the same. 'Margareta Louise'—he always called me by both names when he was angry—'you cannot marry Armano. I forbid it. You must find a boy your own age.' I didn't care that he didn't want me to marry your papa. I was in love, and I knew your grandpapa well enough to know that he would eventually accept the fact that I married Armano."

"If you loved Papa, why was Grandpapa mad?"

"Because Armano was triple my age and had been married three times before he set his sights on me. I didn't mind that he'd been married before. Armano was nice to me. He was such a handsome man, his words smooth, his kisses smoother." She sighed. "He loved me. I could see it on his face. We were so happy. He took care of me and I of him."

It was the first time his mother had ever told him this story, and he had so many questions. "What about his other wives?"

"Dead," she said, making the sign of the cross. "All of them."

Percival blinked his surprise. "How'd they die?"

"His first wife died of scarlet fever. The second was in a buggy accident and broke her neck. The third died in childbirth, the baby too. Your papa was so scared when I told him I was with child. He insisted we hire a private nurse near the end. I told him he needn't waste the money, but he'd set his mind to it, and that was that. He needn't have bothered. When you decided you were ready to come, there was no stopping you. You came out all wrinkled and red, with legs so long, I thought you were going to start walking right then and there." She smiled as if remembering. "Your papa was at work when you were born. He came home, took one look at you, and started crying. He carried you around the room, telling you stories about when he was a boy. He'd hold you up and tell you that you looked just like him and go on and on about how handsome you were."

Percival felt a wave of sadness. "I wish I could remember."

Margareta smiled. "Maybe you will. You remembered a little today."

"I wish he hadn't…"

"So do I," she said, cutting him off. "If not for the heat…"

He opened his mouth to speak, and she held up a hand. She closed her eyes for a moment, then took his hand in hers. "I'm not sure you're ready to be alone on the roof."

"No, Momma. It's you who isn't ready. I'll be fine. Today wasn't the first time." He knew he was risking punishment but needed to make her see it was okay. "I've been going up there for weeks. I even met a friend."

Her eyes grew wide. "A friend?"

"Yes, his name's Paddy. He's younger than me, and he gets

to play on the roof by himself all the time." He thought about adding how the boy got there but decided telling her that Paddy traveled the rooftops wouldn't help his plight.

She blew out a sigh. "This boy, Paddy. He's nice to you?"

Is that what she's been worried about? "Oh yes. He likes me just fine."

Her face softened. "He's the only one?"

Percival thought to tell her about Big Joe but decided that wouldn't make her happy. Instead, he decided to embellish the truth. "Paddy is great. We sit and talk for hours. He tells me about his family, and I tell him about the books I read. His family is so big, they can't afford books."

"You talk about books?"

"Uh-huh." He couldn't bear to repeat the lie. She started to speak, and he cut her off. "I want friends, Momma. I want to be like everyone else."

Her bottom lip quivered, and she looked as if she were about to cry again. Finally, she nodded her consent. "Okay, but just the roof. I don't want you following that boy down the stairs. Can you promise me that?"

He could. Especially since Paddy didn't use the stairs. "Yes, Momma."

"Percival?"

"Yes?"

"I'm not pleased that you disobeyed me."

So, she hadn't forgotten. "No, Momma."

She met his eyes with hers. "Is there anything else you need to tell me?"

"No, Momma," he said, shaking his head.

"Good. I'll try to remember that you are not my baby anymore. That doesn't mean you don't have to do as I say," she said when he broke into a wide grin. "We will start with allowing you to go to the roof and see how that goes."

He started to remind her that he'd already been doing that, then decided to leave well enough alone. It was enough to be allowed to go to the roof. At least for now. He nodded his head. "Okay, Momma."

Margareta moved to the bed and pulled open a sack, removing a book. She trailed her fingers over a thick book with a bright blue cover. "I stopped by the bookstore today and bought you this. But I think I'll hold on to it for a day or two as punishment for your disobeying me."

At first, he thought her to be jesting but realized she was serious when she failed to hand it to him. "Will you at least show me the cover?"

"I suppose there'd be no harm in that," she said, turning the book so that he could see a fierce gold dragon etched onto the cover.

Percival was just able to read the title, *The Book of Dragons,* and the author's name, *E. Nesbit,* before she returned it to the bag and brought out another book.

"I found this one for me," she said, holding up a purple book with a lady and man sitting on a horse.

Percival rolled his eyes.

Margareta smiled a wry smile. "You don't approve?"

Percival took the book from her and studied the cover of the Zane Grey novel. "I like westerns well enough. It's the kissing part I don't like. Why do books have to have kissing anyway?"

"Because some of us like the kissing part best," his mother said as she plucked the book out of his hand. "But that's not the only reason I like to read them."

"No?"

"Of course not. If all I wanted was kissing, I wouldn't have to read a book. I like the romance." She fanned through the book as if reading at lightning speed. "I like that reading gives me hope."

"What do you hope for?"

"I hope that someday you and I will board a train, and that train will escort us from this wretched city and deposit us in a place where we can walk the streets with our heads held high. A place where a handsome cowboy might be able to wipe away the pain."

"Are you hurting, Momma?" Percival asked worriedly.

A blush crept up his mother's face, and she closed the book. "No, Percival, I'm fine. I was just talking about the woman in the book."

He could tell she was lying, as she didn't meet his eyes when she spoke. Had she hurt herself when she was hurrying to lead him down the stairs? If so, it was all his fault. While he was happy she'd agreed to allow him to leave the room, he now regretted not asking her permission instead of having her find him on the roof. As she tucked her novel into the bag with the other, his legs steadily drummed his guilt.

Chapter Five

In the three days since his mother had permitted him to go to the roof on his own, Percival had spent nearly every waking hour on top of the building. He'd even convinced her to allow him to sleep under the stars by himself on one occasion. With his newfound freedom came an unexpected dilemma. Though he'd promised his mother going to the roof was enough, he found he now wanted more. Maybe it was because he'd yet to see Paddy or Big Joe. While he enjoyed being outside, dancing and running on the roof seemed less exciting now that he no longer had to worry about getting caught.

His mother had finally relented, allowing him the book she'd purchased for him, which he'd brought with him today. After tiring of running circles on the roof, he sat in the shadow of the building, feet crossed under his thighs to help still them while enjoying the warmth of the afternoon sun that lingered on the brick wall. The book rested on his inner thighs as he read about a dragon with claws as sharp as bayonets. A warm, stiff breeze blew across the roof, and it took both hands to keep the wind from turning the pages before he was ready. He was so engulfed in the story that he didn't realize he wasn't alone until the shadows fell over him. He looked up, surprised to see a handful of boys scowling at him, and he wondered what he'd done to raise their ire.

Closing the book, he stood and faced the lads. Though he was equal in height, he could see they were older. Their glares told him they were not interested in friendship. For the first time since he began his forays onto the roof, he wished he'd stayed in the small room he shared with his mother.

A boy with dark eyes and a crooked nose stooped to pick up the book. Percival reached for it, and the boy slapped his hand away, then smiled when Percival's legs began to move from side to side.

Crooked nose laughed a wicked laugh. "The chump thinks he's going to get away."

"The goof's not getting past us, Milo," another boy said as he and the others stepped closer, pressing Percival further into the wall.

The boy named Milo opened the book and began tearing the pages free. Holding them high, he sneered each time the wind carried them away without a sound.

Percival's legs danced him forward, and a boy elbowed him in the gut. He sucked in a breath, bending against the pain. He wanted to collapse to the ground and stay there until the torment was over, but his legs would not allow that to be. The more they moved, the more the boys took exception, pounding him each time he drew near. All the while, the boy they called Milo seemed to take great pleasure in his pain, laughing as he methodically tore the pages from the book. When at last there were no pages left, he solemnly dropped the empty shell and pressed his foot into the cover, grinding it into the ground.

Percival remembered a passage where the character named John had charged the dragon, and as if receiving the message, his feet propelled him forward. Only Percival didn't have a sword or a great collar to harness the beast. Instead, he lowered his head, hitting Milo square in the chest, sending him sliding across the ground on his backside. Before he could revel in his accomplishment, the others seized him. Though they managed to contain his arms, his legs were still free and more than willing to kick anyone that got within range. He downed two of the boys before the others managed to drag him backward.

"Get him over the side," Milo said through gritted teeth.

Over the side? I'll die. The thought had no sooner come to him than the boys veered to the left and started dragging him, kicking and screaming, toward the side of the building that faced the street.

"STOP!"

It was a lone word, spoken with such authority, the boys froze and turned to see who had spoken. Percival looked up to see Big Joe racing toward them. He wore a glove on each hand and his eyes were wild with anger. He slowed as he neared, his nostrils flaring as the veins in his neck looked as if they would burst. Instantly remembering one of the dragons in the book, Percival half expected Big Joe to open his mouth and belch flame.

"You let that boy go, or Big Joe will see you over the side along with him." His voice was calmer.

The boys released their hold, and Percival plummeted to the tar-covered surface scraping his knees and shins. He looked up, saw he was precariously close to the edge, then scrambled to his feet, bumping into Milo in the process.

The boy looked as if he were going to yell at him, then slid a glance to Big Joe and stepped to the side without a word.

Percival's head hurt something fierce. He felt something crawling on his lip, drew the back of his hand across his mouth, then pulled it back, surprised to see deep rich blood coating his fingers. He sucked in his breath and moaned against the simple task. He'd not felt this bad since the beating that had sent him to the hospital. He wiped the blood on his pants, then lifted a trepid hand to his head, half expecting his scalp to be split open. It wasn't, but that knowledge did little to ease the pain.

Big Joe stretched a finger, showing his knuckles were wrapped in dirty white bandages, not gloves as Percival had initially thought. He used the finger to beckon Percival forward. "You move on over here, Slim."

Percival limped to where Big Joe stood. Hiding behind the man like a shield, he glared at the boys whose sneers were now replaced with arched brows and wide eyes. One of the smaller boys had a puddle under his feet. Percival stifled a gasp as he realized the boy had wet himself. Apparently, Paddy wasn't the only one afraid of Big Joe.

"We weren't really gonna throw him off the roof. We were just having some fun with him." Milo said.

"Is that why he looks like he's been three rounds in the ring with me?" Big Joe snarled.

"Wasn't me. I didn't touch him." Milo said, and the color drained from the faces of the others.

Big Joe pulled himself taller, the muscles on his arms bulging as the sweat dripped from his elbows. When he spoke, his voice was cold. "This sorry bonehead is who you're loyal to? You were ready to kill this boy on that one's say, and he can't even own up to his word. Does that sound right to you? If I'm going to follow a man, I want to know he's ready to put his life on the line for me. If you're going to be loyal, you will do well to expect that loyalty in return and not have your leader make you the patsy."

Percival blinked his surprise as the others stepped away from Milo, who tossed his head from side to side like a horse after an annoying fly.

"Come around here, Slim," Big Joe said and waited for Percival to step forward. "I'm going to leave it to you what's to be done with those boys."

"Me?" The word came out in a squeak as blood dripped from his busted lip.

"Yes, you. You're the one wronged. You decide the punishment. You can send them over the side like they were going to do to you, or you can show mercy."

Percival looked up at Big Joe. The man was staring at the boys, leaving little doubt he meant what he'd said. He looked at each boy in turn. Though they'd once looked menacing, each boy now quivered with fear. The boy who'd wet himself even had tears trickling from his face. For the first time, he realized that even though the roof was hot, none of the boys wore shoes to protect their feet and what clothing they wore appeared to be little more than rags. They weren't just dirty but covered in deep grime as if it had been months since any of them last cleaned themselves. He wondered why their mothers hadn't insisted they wash, then remembered his mother telling him about the motherless children who roamed the street. For a moment, he wished she were there to ask if these were the children she spoke of. He licked his lip, tasted blood, and pushed his sympathy aside. These weren't kids, they were dragons, and it was his job to banish them from the kingdom. Scratching his head, he winced against the pain of the simple movement. They needed to pay for what they'd done, but could he really send them to their death?

He thought about how much he missed his father and wondered if the boys had anyone that would miss them if they fell from the roof. He further wondered what his mother would think of him if she ever learned he'd been responsible for their deaths. In the end, it was his own conscience that won out. Regardless of what they did, he could never live with himself if he said yes. He looked at Big Joe and shook his head. "No, they'll not be scraping them from the sidewalk on account of me."

"If it were up to me, I'd toss each of you from the roof. You're all living to see another day on account of this boy and this boy alone. But you better remember this," Big Joe clamped his hands on Percival's shoulders, "Slim here is under my protection. You spread the word. Anyone even so much as looks at him menacingly, and he'll have no say in the matter. Big Joe will find them. Understand?"

The boys readily nodded their agreement.

"Good. Now beat it!" The words had no sooner left his mouth than each of the boys took off running across the roof, leaping to the next building without a word. Only when they'd disappeared from sight did Big Joe release the hold on his shoulders. "We'd better get you cleaned up before your ma sees you."

Percival sighed.

"Regretting your decision already?"

"No, sir."

Then what's the problem?"

"My momma's never going to let me out by myself again." Not that he was in a hurry to come back to the roof by himself. "She was afraid I'd get hurt, and now I have."

"She'll let you," Big Joe said with conviction.

"How can you be so sure?"

"You just leave it to me," he said, then began to unwrap the bandage from his right hand.

Percival winced as Big Joe used it to dab the blood from his busted lip. "Why do you have a bandage if your hands aren't hurt?"

"The wraps help protect my hands from the bag."

Percival still wasn't sure how a bag could hurt anyone's hands. If Big Joe noticed his confusion, he didn't let on.

"You okay to walk, or do you need me to carry you?"

The thought of being carried down the stairs by the big man was unsettling. "I can walk."

"That's what I like about you, Slim. You're tough."

"I am?"

"Sure you are. Most boys get a beating like that, and they'd send those boys over the side without a moment's hesitation. It took a lot of guts to let them live."

"It did?"

"Sure. How do you know those boys aren't going to come back and finish the job?"

Percival gulped. "Because you told them not to?"

"I did, but not until after you saved them. Yes siree, Slim. You're a tough one."

Suddenly, he wasn't so sure letting the boys go was a smart choice. It was one thing to be brave when Big Joe was around, but what if he hadn't shown up?

They'd be scraping me from the sidewalk by now. What if they come back?

Percival licked his busted lip with the tip of his tongue. No matter, once his mother got sight of him, she'd never allow him back on the roof by himself. Instead of being disappointed, the thought of staying inside now comforted him. Big Joe might think him tough, but he wasn't in much of a hurry to grow up.

Chapter Six

"Where're you going, Big Joe?" Percival asked when the man started for the stairwell.

"Home."

"But you don't live in my building."

"No, I live in the next building over."

"You're not going to jump?"

Big Joe chuckled. "Not when I have perfectly good stairs to use."

"You jumped before," Percival reminded him.

"That's because I didn't have time to be scared. Those boys were going to toss you off the building."

"You get scared?" Percival gasped.

He laughed. "Sure, everyone does."

The thought of Big Joe getting scared was beyond belief. "But you're so big."

"That don't mean nothing. Why, I'm scared of plenty."

"Like what?" Percival asked, following him down the stairs. Typically, Percival would have attempted to match the man's stride, but he was too sore to try to keep up.

Big Joe cast a glance over his shoulder and slowed his pace. "Well, for starters, I was scared that you were going to tell me to drop those boys off the side of the building."

"You wanted to do it. Why would that scare you?"

"Just because I said I would do it doesn't mean I would. I was bluffing."

"You were?"

"Course I was. I didn't know if they would have really dropped you over the side. If I'd done that to them, then that would have made me a murderer. Do you know what they do to murderers?"

"Put them in jail?"

"Mostly. Only they'd have done a lot worse to me."

"Why?"

"It's just the way of things, son."

Percival couldn't help noting a touch of sadness in the man's voice and wondered at the cause of it. "Are you okay, Big Joe?"

"Are you my friend, Slim?"

Friend? Did Big Joe honestly want him to be his friend? Except for Paddy, who he'd only seen the one time, he didn't have any friends. But if Big Joe wanted him to be his friend, he'd say yes and be grateful for it. "Yes, sir."

"Then I'm gonna be just fine."

"I promised my momma I wouldn't go down the stairs," Percival said, stopping at the landing to the fifth floor. "Course after she gets a load of me, she'll not allow me back to the roof either."

"Don't you worry about your ma. I'll get her to let you out."

"You said that before. You don't know my momma. She's gonna be pretty sore that the boys beat on me. She's also going to be mad they tore up the new book she bought me. I'm pretty mad about that too. I wasn't finished with it." He started to add that he wasn't in any hurry to return to the roof but decided against it. Big Joe had called him tough, and he didn't want to prove otherwise.

"You said your momma was afraid to let you go off on your own 'cause she was scared you'd get hurt, right?"

"Yes, sir. And she was right too. Those boys hurt me something fierce."

"I'm sorry for that, but it works in our favor. That's the reason she's going to allow you to leave again."

Percival scratched his head. "It is?"

"Sure. Not only that, but she's going to let you come see me."

Percival laughed. "My momma is not going to let me out of the room, much less let me leave the building."

"What say we put a little wager on it?"

"I don't have any money." Too bad, as he was sure to win.

"Don't need no money. We are going to trade services."

"What kind of services?"

"If I win, I'll teach you to fight so you'll never have to worry about being beat up again."

"Never?" Not that it mattered, since he didn't have anything worth trading.

"Not so long as it's a fair fight," Big Joe promised.

"I don't have anything to trade."

"Sure, you do. You have something I need very much."

"Like what?"

"I want you to teach me to read."

"Now you're just funning me."

"Am not."

"You're all grown up, and you're telling me you don't know how to read."

"When I was growing up, there was no need for book learning. Why, I ain't set foot in a school a day in my life."

Now that, Percival could believe. "Neither have I."

Big Joe's eyes widened. "I thought you said you could read."

"I can. Very well, in fact. My momma taught me. She said my papa used to read to me all the time before he… I don't remember my papa reading to me, but I can remember my momma teaching me to read."

"Then it's settled," Big Joe said. He pulled open the door to the fifth-floor hallway and waved Percival ahead. "Lead the way, Slim."

"You're coming too?" Percival asked when Big Joe let the door shut behind him.

"It'll be difficult to speak with your momma if I don't see her."

"She's not home."

"I can wait. Best have a go at her before she has a chance to worry herself into making you stay inside." Percival opened the door to their room, and Big Joe grasped his shoulder. "Is this where you live?"

Percival looked around the small room and nodded.

"Why, it's no more than a bedroom," Big Joe replied. "Where does your momma cook?"

"She don't. Least not anymore." Percival stepped inside the room, expecting the man to follow. "Aren't you coming?"

"Naw, it wouldn't look right if your momma were to come home and find me in there with you. "I'll wait right out here for her. Be better that way."

Percival walked to the mirror, took in his wounds, and sighed.

"Those boys sure did a number on you. You sure you're okay?" Big Joe asked from the hallway.

"I'll do," Slim replied. He stepped back into the hall and closed the door behind him. He liked Big Joe well enough, but he didn't think the man had any chance of persuading his mother to give him his freedom. Though he stood in place, his legs moved as if he were practicing a jig.

"What's troubling you, Slim?"

"I was thinking of my momma."

"Don't you worry; I told you I'd talk to her. She'll let you out."

No, she won't. "That's not what I was thinking about."

Big Joe settled on the floor. "No?"

"I was thinking that if those boys had tossed me off the roof, my momma would have thought I did it on my own, on account of what my papa did," Slim said, sitting beside him.

"What did your pop do?"

"He jumped." The words came out in a whisper. Though Percival and his mother often spoke of his papa, they never went so far as to say the words, always preferring to say he went to the roof.

"Takes a lot of courage to do something like that," Big Joe said softly.

"No, not to the other side. He jumped. They had to scrape him from the sidewalk," Percival said firmly. Though his legs were stretched in front of him, they continued to jump about. He leaned forward in an effort to still them.

"I know what you meant. Something like that got to be hard on a man. How could it not?"

Percival's legs twitched something fierce. "I don't think it took courage."

"Oh, but it had to. It's one thing to think it, but another to do it. There's no coming back from something like that," Big Joe replied.

"Momma said it was because of the heat. She said it was awfully hot, and she had to walk me in the street at night to keep me cool. Said the whole city was so hot, people were dying."

Big Joe nodded. "I remember. I lost my mother during that."

Percival stared at the man. "Did she jump from the roof?"

"No, she died peacefully in her sleep. I guess it just got too hot for her to breathe."

"Did you cry?"

"Of course."

"Sometimes I get mad at my dad for doing what he did." Percival hung his head and sighed. He'd never told anyone that.

"Anger's to be expected, but you've got to find a way to let that anger out. You keep it inside of you, and it'll fester. Rots a man's soul, it does. I've seen it happen."

"You've seen a man's soul rot?"

"Big Joe's seen lots of things, Slim," he said ruefully. "There's a lot of ugliness in the world. You'd do best to remember that. A man can only take so much before they too become ugly. Now I'm not talking about looks, son, but what's in their heart. That boy up on the roof, the one in charge."

"Milo?" Percival said, cutting him off.

"That's the one. You take him. He keeps on the way he is, and there'll be no hope for him. He'll end up dead or in prison. Prison is no place for a man and even less for boys. Some of those following him might get out before it's too late. Especially after what happened up there today. They saw him for what he is."

Percival wiped the sweat from his face with the bottom of his shirt. "What is he?"

"A coward. And yet, somehow, he was able to get the others to follow him and do his bidding. His time's coming. You'd do best to remember that. And don't you go joining no gangs. They're not any better. You decide to follow a fellow, you make sure he's worth following. If he isn't going to have your back, then don't give him the privilege of your loyalty. You going to pledge your devotion, you make sure he does the same. A man is only as good as his word. You remember that, Slim."

"Boy, Big Joe, you sure do know a lot. You sure you ain't never gone to school?"

"Not the kind of school you're thinking of, Slim."

"What other kind of school is there?"

"Life."

"That's not a school."

"It most certainly is. When I was little, my ma cooked and cleaned for a family that made her use the back door anytime she came or went. I was a quiet fellow, so she had them agree to allow me to come along. Those folks had a little boy, and we became good friends, only he said how we wasn't supposed to let anyone know we were friends. Now, Stephen, he didn't mind that my skin was darker than his, but he knew if his folks found out, there would be a big to-do about it."

"What was wrong with the color of your skin?"

Big Joe smiled a broad smile. "That's what I like about you, Slim."

Percival started to ask him what he'd meant, but Big Joe started talking again, and he didn't want to interrupt.

"Stephen had a tutor come in every day. That's a teacher of sorts," Big Joe explained. "I would hide in the drapes and listen to all the things the woman taught him."

"Didn't she teach him how to read?"

"She did, but since I was hiding in the drapes, I couldn't see the words. I learned enough to sound like an educated man, but never learned to read or write. I get by not writing, as I can just make my mark, but I'd like to know a bit about what I agree to. You're lucky you had your momma to teach you to read. My ma couldn't teach me."

"Why not?"

"On account of she didn't know how. Even if she'd known, she was too busy to go about it. Then she got sick. After that, she spent all her time in bed too tired to even lift her head."

"What about your papa?"

"My pop died a long time ago."

"Are you mad at him?" Percival asked when Big Joe grew quiet.

"Yes, but not for the reason you think. Pop was a mean man. He liked to hit me with his fist. So I wasn't mad at him for dying. I was mad that he left me to take care of my ma. With her so sick, it was up to me to keep us fed and some semblance of a roof over our heads. We lived in a tenement with five other families, but I still had to work to pay the room fees and put food in our bellies."

"You were just a boy. What kind of work did you do?"

"I tried begging at first, but there were so many kids running the streets that people were more inclined to boot us in the backside than hand us money. I ran coal for a few years."

"What's running coal?"

"I walked with the coal wagon, and when someone asked for a bucket of coal, I'd run it up the stairs. That's a lot of work for a few pennies here and there." He smiled. "But those coal buckets were heavy, and it gave me some mighty fine muscles. I was already big for my age, and carrying coal made me bigger. One day, I brought a bucket of coal to a man, and the man asked me if I wanted to make some real money. I asked him what I had to do, and the man said that I had to let a fellow hit me."

Percival's legs drummed against the floor. "What did you say?"

"Why, I told him no. Told him I'd had enough of being hit."

Percival nodded his understanding.

"You know what he said?"

"No, what'd he say?"

"He told me to go on and keep hauling those buckets like someone's…well, he told me to keep it up. Said he would find someone else who wanted to earn a dollar."

"A whole dollar?"

"Yes siree."

"What'd you say?"

"Why, I said yes, of course. What I didn't tell him was that

I didn't have any intention of getting hit. I'd already had enough of that from my pop."

"You mean you lied to him?"

"Not really. You see, when I answered, I told him I'd be willing to let someone take a swing at me for a dollar. I just left out telling him that I didn't plan on standing still while the guy did it."

"Did he get mad when he figured out you lied to him?"

"At first. Then, when he saw how good I was at not getting hit, he paid me that other guy's money to hit him."

Percival glanced at the welts and scrapes that covered his arms and legs. "Did you like hitting him?"

"Before the fight, the man had some pretty mean things to say about me. I didn't mind that so much as I'd heard it all before. But then he started saying things about my ma and, well, she'd never done nothing to nobody. It's not right to talk about a man's ma. So, when the time come to hit him, I enjoyed it just fine."

"Oh." Percival knew he shouldn't be disappointed. He wouldn't like anyone talking bad about his momma either. But he was still suffering at the hands of the boys, so he didn't like the thought of being hit.

"I know what you're thinking, but it's not like that. What happened to you was wrong. Ain't nobody got the right to hit on a fellow for no reason."

"What if Milo would have paid the others to do this?"

"Nope, still wouldn't be right."

"It wouldn't?"

"No, it wouldn't. Boxing is different. Legal boxing, anyhow. It's the only kind of boxing I do because it has rules."

"What kind of rules?"

"Well, for one, I only fight men who agree to fight me. A fellow steps into the ring with me, and he knows there's a fair chance he'll get hit. We tap gloves and proceed to see who's the better fighter. We stop fighting when the bell rings and sit in the corner until it rings again."

"Then what happens?"

"We start fighting again."

Percival thought about this for a moment. "I don't think I'd be able to go back and let someone hit me if I had time to think about it."

"You would if there was a big enough purse involved."

Percival laughed. "I'm no sissy. I don't carry a purse."

"It's not really a purse. That's just the term for a big payout. There's some big money in boxing. Most is made by the fellows who do the betting, but I get my share. Why, I was able to bury my ma in a fashion like the rich folks on 5th Avenue. Yes, sir, Slim, she had a fine hearse pulled by six white horses. She's resting in a proper casket in a real cemetery with a grand stone that has her name etched for all to see instead of rotting in a pauper's grave. No one never paid my ma no mind when she was living. But they stopped and lowered their hats to her that day. Yes siree. So, when you think about why I do what I do, you remember that."

"I will, sir." Percival didn't want to think of his momma being dead, but if she were to die, he would like to think he'd be able to give her a proper send-off. "Big Joe?"

"Yeah, Slim."

"Thanks for telling me about your momma."

"You're welcome, Slim. And don't you go worrying about yours. When it comes to mommas, I know a thing or two."

Chapter Seven

The clacking of heels echoed in the stairwell. Percival jumped to his feet and stood looking over the railing. A few moments passed before he saw his mother making her way up the stairs. He jerked his head back then quietly joined Big Joe in the hallway.

"She's coming," he whispered, though she couldn't have heard him.

Big Joe pushed to his feet. "Remember what I told you to do?"

According to Big Joe, the best way to get his mother to agree to allow the man to train him was to let her see them in action. The plan was to have Big Joe pretend to take a swing and have Percival dive out of the way. They would then explain what had happened on the roof, further telling his mother of the plan to have Big Joe train Percival in exchange for his teaching the man to read. They'd practiced several times, with Big Joe punching in slow motion since Percival was sore from the skirmish with the boys.

Percival nodded, then waited for Big Joe to move into position. Time ticked by as they waited for the sound of the heavy stairwell door. Finally, as Margareta stepped into the hallway, Big Joe doubled his fist, pulling back his arm as if ready to take a swing.

Suddenly, his mother's screams pierced the air.

Percival watched in abject horror as his mother tossed the purse and bag she was carrying aside, kicked off her heels, and raced toward them, eyes blazing. She lunged at Big Joe, who turned to ward off her attack. Unwavering, she straddled his back, beating her fist against the man's bare shoulders and screaming obscenities, the like of which Percival had never heard. While Big Joe had warned she would be upset when she saw the cuts and scrapes on Percival's face and arms, from the bewildered look now plastered across the man's face, he'd gotten more than he'd bargained for. If not for the fact that Big Joe looked as if he were about to fling his mother against the wall, Percival would have laughed.

Several doors opened, and their neighbors filed into the hallway. While they'd never bothered to pay him or his mother any mind in the past, their faces now held a mingled look of humor and horror. Maybe it was because his mother's dress was hiked to her bottom, her long bare legs gripping the dark man like a saddle.

Two men started toward them, and a third stepped forward, blocking their way.

"It's Big Joe," the man whispered.

"Big Joe?" one of the men repeated. "He'll kill her for sure."

"Perhaps we should help her?" the other man suggested.

"What, and get ourselves killed in the process?" the original man replied. "From where I stand, the woman seems to be holding her own."

As the men weighed their options, his mother kept clawing at Big Joe, who danced around the hall like a horse trying to buck an unwanted rider. Percival realized it wouldn't be long before the gawkers overcame their fear and joined in to help his mother bring down the big man.

"Momma! Mom! Margareta Louise!" Percival called out as the men inched their way closer. His mother stopped her assault, staring at him as if seeing him for the first time. "It's alright, Momma, Big Joe wasn't hurting me. He was teaching me how to protect myself."

His mother loosened her grip, slid from Big Joe's back, and hastily yanked at the hem of her skirt. Having regained her poise, she walked to the end of the hallway to retrieve her purse and bag.

One of the men grumbled something about the crazy woman, then ushered some of the onlookers back inside their rooms. Two others studied them for several moments before taking their leave.

"You mean he wasn't... then who did that to you?" Margareta's voice trembled as she spoke.

"No, Momma, Big Joe didn't hurt me. He helped me. There were some boys on the roof. They got mad at me for reading, and he made them stop hurting me," Percival assured her. He left off the part about nearly getting tossed off the roof, as Big Joe had told him that might be too much for his mother to bear.

"I told you you'd get hurt. That's it. You're never to go onto the roof again." She shook her head. "No, that's not enough. You will go to work with me from now on. I'll find a closet for you to stay. Yes, that's it. You'll not leave my sight. Not ever again."

A closet? He knew she'd be upset, but he hadn't expected her to take it this far. "No! I won't."

Margareta jerked her head about as if he'd slapped her. "Excuse me?"

Big Joe had remained silent until this point. "That's not the solution."

Margareta turned her anger on him, causing him to take a step back. "And just who are you to be telling me what's best for my son?"

"This is Big Joe, Momma. He's a boxer," Percival said and watched as the color drained from her face.

"Big Joe, the boxer. I...I've heard of you." This time, it was she who stepped away from the man.

Big Joe sighed. "People say things that aren't true."

Margareta jutted her jaw. "You're going to stand there and tell me you didn't kill a man?"

Another sigh. "Not in the way that makes me a murderer."

To her credit, his mother stood quietly, waiting for him to explain.

"I was in the ring with the man, and we both gave as good as we got. Only I must have given a little better, as I was declared the winner. We both went home, and sometime later that night, the man I fought died. One of the doctors said it was something inside his head and that it could have happened even if he hadn't been fighting. But the reporters blamed me. News like that sells more papers, you know. The boxing people didn't mind the reporters saying things. 'Cause people, they read that stuff and pay more money to see me fight. I figure they hope they too get to see me kill a man."

To Percival's amazement, his mother smiled.

"I know a thing or two about being judged improperly. I have so many questions, but I'll start by thanking you for helping my Percival. His father...well, he isn't around to teach him the way of things. I try, but the only thing I know is to keep him close so that I can protect him."

Big Joe ran a finger across one of his scratches and grimaced. "I wouldn't want to fight you in the ring."

His mother blushed. "I'm sorry. I just saw you with your hands in fists and then saw my boy's face and thought you were about to hit him again."

"I never intended to hit the boy. I just wanted to show you that Slim could duck out of the way. I thought it might be easier if you saw what Slim here is capable of."

"So, you knew I was there?" She laughed a carefree laugh

that Percival hadn't heard in a long time. "Then, in that case, I'm not sorry. You should know better than scaring a woman like that."

"Yes, ma'am," Big Joe agreed. "But I tell you, the boy shows great promise."

Margareta blew out a sigh. "Percival can't stand still long enough to comb his hair. What makes you think you can teach him how to fight?"

"His legs give him the advantage. Why, if I had legs like that, wouldn't no one be able to lay a hand on me." Big Joe's voice was full of excitement. He scratched the side of his head then tilted his head in Percival's direction. "You talk about keeping the boy close, but there ain't a momma bird I've ever seen that keeps their babies under their wing once they get old enough to feed themselves. As soon as that happens, Momma Bird's going to push them out of the nest and watch them fly."

"And if they don't fly, it's a long way to the ground," she said bitterly.

"I'm not Papa," Percival blurted before Big Joe could respond.

Big Joe patted the top of his head then turned his attention to Margareta once more. "Slim here told me what happened to his pop, and I know that must scare you something fierce. But we all have to make our own way. Your heart is in the right place, but you can't keep on punishing the boy for what his pop did."

"The only reason I'm standing here is what you did for my boy today. I owe you the courtesy to listen to what you have to say. That doesn't give you the right to lecture me on how I raise my son."

"I was there. I saw the fear in his eyes, and know from experience that you won't always be there to protect him. Don't you owe it to your son to see that he can protect himself instead of living a life of fear?"

His mother's lip trembled, and Percival felt a pang of hope.

"My husband had such high hopes for our son. He wanted him to learn to read and write and earn a respectable wage."

"Big Joe can't read, and he makes lots of money. Why, he even had enough to give his momma a proper burial. She had white horses and everything. Wouldn't you want that, Momma?"

Big Joe cleared his throat. "I believe we are getting ahead of ourselves. I only wish to teach the boy to protect himself, not step into the ring. Even if he decided to take up fighting, it would be years before he's ready for something like that."

"But you said you said…"

"I never said I would train you to be a boxer. I said you have an advantage. Those legs are nothing to be ashamed of. They will take you places most wouldn't be able to go."

"Do you really believe that?" his mother asked softly.

Big Joe nodded. "I wouldn't lie about that."

Margareta opened her purse. "How much for lessons?"

"The boy and I already have worked out a deal."

Margareta narrowed her eyes. "Just what is it you want from my son?"

"I'm going to teach Big Joe how to read," Percival said proudly.

Her eyes widened. "To read?"

"Yes, ma'am," Big Joe agreed. "I never had much need for book learning before. But sometimes the man puts a paper in front of me and tells me to sign it. I think it's time I learn what it is I be signing."

Margareta smiled. "If you think it's a fair trade, then I give my permission."

"Oh, boy! When can we start?" Percival asked.

"Next week," Big Joe said after looking him over.

Percival's enthusiasm waned. "Next week? I want to learn now."

"Next week," Big Joe repeated. "You'll be mostly healed by then. That bag packs a mighty punch. You try hitting it with those bruised ribs of yours, and you'll quit before we even get started."

Percival still wasn't sure how hitting a bag could hurt. That Big Joe's tone hadn't left room for argument and that he was, in fact, terribly sore kept him from protesting. "Yes, sir."

"If your mother doesn't object, you can come over tomorrow and start learning me to read."

It was better than nothing and would keep him from spending the day with his mother. Margareta hesitated to answer, and for a moment, Percival thought she was going to object. Finally, she nodded her agreement.

"Good, it's settled. I've got to be going," Big Joe said, then started to leave.

He was almost to the door to the stairs when Percival realized he didn't know where the guy lived. "Wait, what's your apartment number?"

"I'm in the next building over, number 309," Big Joe replied, then ducked through the doorway.

Percival gulped then slid a sideways glance towards his mother. The paleness of her face showed that she too had been unsettled by the fact that though it was a different building, 309 was the number of the apartment they once shared with his papa.

Chapter Eight

Percival's feet drummed the floor as nervous energy coursed through his body. A week had passed since the incident on the roof, and while he didn't mind teaching Big Joe to read, he was eager to learn to box. He'd spent the week helping Big Joe sound out words while the man had taken great pride in showing him posters and photos from his time in the boxing ring. Several times at the end of the day, he'd drifted off to sleep and dreamt about being in the ring.

"I'm finished dressing. You may turn around now," Margareta said at last. "We'll need to get going soon, or you'll march right through that wall."

Percival turned and gulped his surprise. Though he'd seen his mother every day of his life, he barely recognized her. Normally, when heading to work, she dressed in gowns with a mixture of lace and beads. She'd once told him she showed just enough skin to entice the men to dance and make women on the street blush while hauling their husbands to the other side of the road.

Today, she'd successfully transformed herself into one of the women from the posters that littered Broadway and promised a titillating show. Her face was freshly painted, and her dark hair sat piled on top of her head save for one long ringlet draped suggestively over her right shoulder. Her dress, what little there was of it, was white as freshly fallen snow and showcased her barely covered bosom. Then again, maybe it was because it clung to her waist, cinching it so tight, it made everything else stand out. The bottom of the fabric was adorned with matching feathers that did little to hide her buttocks. She wore matching stockings cut in a way that allowed the flesh of her legs to peek through. She'd brought the outfit home several days prior, placing it in the closet while telling him about her upcoming audition. He felt the heat in his cheeks and turned to hide his embarrassment.

"They need to see my legs," she said, drawing his attention once more.

They're going to see more than that. He watched as she slipped a stocking foot into a pair of tall heels and had a momentary image of her toppling forward. He shook off the image. "You're not going to walk with me the whole way, are you?"

She smiled. "I thought I might."

"Momma, you've walked with me every day for a week. I know the way, and there hasn't been any trouble. Besides that, today, we are meeting on the roof. Why, you'll have to walk all the way down our stairs and then back up six flights and back down again. How will you dance with all that walking?"

She hesitated, and he could see she was considering his words. Finally, she sighed her consent. "It would be a lot of walking. And I have that audition this morning before work. The one I was telling you about."

He remembered. "The one on Broadway."

"That's right, *The Century Girl*. Now I know they aren't going to give me the lead, but there'll be other parts. If I can get a good role, I'll be able to spend more time with you. There'll be enough money for us to move out of the city once the show ends. We'll go someplace new. Someplace without memories. We'll get a real home with a proper kitchen, and you'll have a bedroom with a bed." She spoke with such conviction that even he believed it possible. "Who knows, someday I might even open my own restaurant."

"You've been working so hard, and the can is stuffed with paper money. Surely there is enough."

She shook her head. "No, not yet. I know you're making great sacrifices, but houses cost a lot of money. I need to make sure I have enough so that I won't have to…I want to make sure we don't need to have evening visitors. You'd like that, wouldn't you?"

Percival knew the men that came to see his mother weren't visitors. Not the real kind anyway. He wasn't the only one making sacrifices. "Yes, Momma."

Margareta checked her lipstick in the mirror, picked up her clutch, then hesitated. Walking to the closet, she pulled out a thin overcoat. Pulling it on, she tied it at the waist, sighed, then untied it once again. "It's too hot for that," she said by way of explanation. She smiled, then nodded for him to open the door before continuing their conversation.

"Yes, Percival, you and I are going to have a fine house one day. Why, I hear they are making houses with lavatories right inside. Now you wouldn't believe it, but some houses have little sheds outside for doing your business. We're not going to buy one of those houses."

How his mother could manage the stairs at such a pace in shoes that made her a good head taller impressed him. He lengthened his stride to keep pace. "We're not?"

"Of course not. We're city people. And as such, we are way too civilized for that. We will have indoor plumbing. And we're not going to haul our water from a stream like folks in those books I've read. No, Percival, that would never do. Windows. I want lots of those. Why, I want windows in every room. Wouldn't that be grand?!" She continued without waiting for a reply. "We will open them all each and every day to let the breeze flow through. It'll be so cool in the summertime, I'll have to throw a shawl over my shoulders just to stay warm. We'll have a front porch to sit on, and you'll have to tip your hat to the neighbors as they pass by. You'll have a yard with real grass to cradle your toes as you walk. My kitchen will have a real icebox to keep food cold and a window over the sink so I can look out at the birds while I'm doing dishes. I'm going to order a complete set from the Sears catalog. Dishes, that is. Blue. Yes, they must be blue. Don't you agree?"

He'd never given any of it much thought. While his mother had spoken of them leaving the city often enough, she'd never discussed her plans with such detail. Could it mean they were close to having enough money to go? How would it even feel to walk barefoot in the grass? He wanted to ask a million questions, but they didn't have time. His mother had to get to her audition, and he needed to go up to the roof to see Big Joe. *Will I still be able to go onto the roof if we live in a house?* He looked at his mother, thinking to ask the questions, then decided only to answer the question at hand. "Blue would be nice, Momma."

"And your bedroom, you'll have to decide what color you want for it."

"Color?"

"For your quilt and curtains. You must have a quilt and curtains. Maybe we can even get some paper for your walls. Something bright and cheery. No, that won't do at all. You need blue. Stripes. Yes, that's more like it."

His mother was nervous. She always grew chatty when worried. He wasn't sure if she was anxious about his going to the roof with Big Joe or about her audition; maybe a bit of both. "Don't be scared, Momma."

"Why would I be scared?"

"Of your audition. You're a good dancer. You must be; you taught me. With my legs, that's some doing."

Though she kept walking, her hands flew to her coat, pressing out imagined wrinkles with trembling fingers. "Does it show?"

Percival laughed. "Your mouth runs as fast as my legs when you're nervous."

She giggled and slowed her pace. "That's very astute of you. I am nervous. This could be our big break. Our chance to have a normal life."

"You'll get the part, Momma. I know you will." He didn't know what part she was trying out for but hoped his vote of confidence would lift hers.

"You're a good boy, Percival," she said as they reached the bottom of the stairs.

"You're a good momma," he said, and she stopped.

"Am I, Percival? I know I do things that...I do things mothers shouldn't, but I only do them so that you can have a better life. We have but a small space to call our own, but we are together. So many of the ladies I work with have had to take their children to the asylums. I would too if there were no other way to keep you safe. You don't know what it's like out there, with so many children running the streets. I do what I do for you. Everything I do is for you."

Her eyes filled with tears. She looked at him as if begging his approval. He wanted to tell her that he didn't need to leave the city. Nor did he need a fancy house to make him happy. He wanted to beg her to use the money she'd earned to get a small apartment near Big Joe so that the man could teach him how to box, and he could make enough money to take care of her. He was all she had left, and he was the man since his papa wasn't around. He wanted to tell her that it was he who should be taking care of her. Instead, he smiled, brushed his fingers against her hand, and repeated the words she most needed to hear. "You're a good momma."

Tears trickled down her cheeks as she gathered him in her arms and kissed the top of his head. "It won't be long, Percival. Things are going to change, this I promise."

He wasn't sure what to say, so he remained silent and let her shed her tears.

After a moment, she released him, then reached into her clutch and drew out a handkerchief, cautiously dabbing at her eyes. "Oh, Percival, I have been so unfair to you all these years. I ask so much from you and allow you to do so little."

He thought to ask her what she'd asked of him, then decided against it when she started speaking once more.

"If you're man enough to be there when I release my burden, you are man enough to go out on your own. You run on up to see Big Joe, and we'll talk about giving you a little more freedom tonight."

More freedom? Did that mean she was going to allow him to go out into the streets? He dared not ask. "Yes, Momma."

She bent, kissing him on the cheek. He knew without looking that she'd left the imprint of her boldly painted lips. He moved to wipe it away then decided against it, knowing Big Joe would take great pleasure in seeing it. "Good luck with your audition, Momma."

"I'll see you tonight. We'll celebrate." She sniffed.

They walked out the door, each going their own way. He turned when he reached the door to the neighboring building and saw her watching him from the other side of the street. She blew him a kiss then waved for him to go inside. He did so without hesitating, running up the stairs, thinking of nothing but his lesson with Big Joe and his impending freedom. His mother had promised to open her wings and let him fly. It was at this moment that he knew this to be the best day of his life. One he'd remember for years to come.

Chapter Nine

Percival pushed through the door to the roof expecting to find Big Joe waiting for him. Instead, he found the space empty save what looked to be a small room on the far side of the building's roof. He took a few tentative steps toward the enclosure then quickened his pace. As he neared, he discovered it to be more of an open shed, with a roof and three walls. He peeked inside, expecting to see Big Joe, but instead saw a long, round cylinder hanging from a chain attached to a beam in the roof. *The punching bag.* He recognized it from one of the photos Big Joe had shown him. He took a step closer, placing his hand against the warm leather. Big Joe called it a bag, but it didn't look like much to him. He cast a glance over his shoulder, then turned back toward the bag. Big Joe hadn't told him not to hit it. On the contrary, he'd said this was precisely what they'd be doing today.

Percival smiled, doubled his fist, and thrust it forward. To his surprise, it was much like hitting a brick wall, not that he'd ever been foolish enough to hit one. The jolt of the punch vibrated through his body, and he knew why Big Joe had insisted he wait a week before starting his training. He rubbed the fingers of his right hand and wondered if he should beg off entirely. While he was eager to learn to defend himself, Big Joe was right; that bag packed a mighty punch.

Maybe I should leave before he arrives. No, that won't work; he's probably already on his way up. I could jump.

He walked to the edge of the roof that overlooked his

building. The distance across didn't seem all that great. It was the distance to the ground that scared him. One slip, and he'd be done for. *Paddy does it all the time. Even Big Joe jumped it with ease. Yeah, because he was scared.* He was still contemplating jumping when he heard agitated voices behind him and chided himself for being allowed to be caught unaware yet again. Hoping they would pass him by without incident, he tried to remain frozen in place, something that proved difficult to do since his legs refused to stay still.

"Slow down. The man's not out here."

The voice was that of a child, who was obviously worried about coming face to face with Big Joe. *If not Big Joe, then who? Have the boys come back to finish the job? Big Joe told them to leave me alone, but he's not here. What if they don't listen?* At the thought of another beating, Percival's mouth went dry. *I'll not allow it. I'll fight back.* He pulled his right hand into a fist, the effort reminding him of the leather bag. His legs twitched something fierce as he looked at the street below and emitted a nervous giggle. There was no use attempting to jump the roof. He'd need a running start to ensure he made it. Even if he somehow managed to reach the other side, the boys would follow. They did it all the time. Unless he was willing to save them the trouble by leaping to his death, he was about to get pulverized.

A tear slid from the side of his eye. Big Joe was right about his Papa. It took a lot of courage to do what he'd done. Courage he did not possess. If he were going to go off the roof this day, it wouldn't be of his doing. Another tear trickled down his cheek, and he laughed at his own cowardice.

"What's so funny?"

Paddy! Percival breathed a sigh of relief. He swiped at the tear and turned to see Paddy and three other boys. Two of the boys looked to be of identical height with the same dark hair and eyes. Percival closed his eyes, then opened them once more, yet still couldn't see anything that set them apart. Though all the boys studied him with wary caution, none looked inclined to pound on him. The two that looked the same had red-brimmed eyes and looked as if they'd been crying. The tallest of the group, a boy with dirty blonde hair, kept looking over his shoulder as if expecting someone.

One of the smaller boys sniffed and rubbed his nose with the back of his arm. "You know this kid, Paddy?"

"Yeah. I don't know his name, but we've talked some."

"The name's Slim," Percival said, using the name Big Joe called him.

"This is Tommy, Jacob, and Joshua. Don't worry if you can't remember their names; we can't tell them apart, so we just call them both twins." Paddy's brow slid up as his eyes fixed on Percival's cheek. "You been smooching a dame?"

Percival remembered his mother's kiss, suddenly wishing he would've removed the lipstick. "Nah, it was my momma doing the smooching."

Paddy blew out a low whistle. "Ain't no ma I never saw that wears paint like that."

"We best be g'tting. I don't wanna be round here no more," the tall boy said, casting a nervous glance over his shoulder.

"Don't worry," Paddy said. "Big Joe's not gonna be up here anytime soon. I saw him and a bunch of others in the crowd. They'll all be busy gawking for a while yet."

Has something happened to Big Joe? Is that why he isn't here? Percival hesitated to ask questions, knowing the boys were afraid of the man.

"That dame was messed up," he said with a shudder.

"Shut up, Tommy," Paddy said, silencing the kid.

"You were scairt too. That's why you ran. Not that I blame ya, seeing sumptin like that…"

"I wasn't scared," Paddy countered. "I just didn't want to stick around, is all. You know what my pop will do if he finds out I didn't go to school."

Percival couldn't resist any longer. He had to find out what had happened to Big Joe. "What happened?"

The boys all looked at each other, fidgeting as if deciding who would tell the tale. Finally, it was Paddy who spoke. "The boys and I were fishing in the grates when we heard someone whistle. We looked up and saw a dame coming down the street. Now, this wasn't any dame. She was a real looker. And those legs, they were fine gams, to be sure."

"She was a looker for sure," Tommy agreed. "Downright shame."

One of the twins elbowed the kid. "Pipe down, Tommy. Let Paddy tell it."

"She was wearing a coat, see. And that's what caught my eye, it being so warm and all." Paddy said, wrinkling his brow. "Nobody wears a coat this time of year, 'specially on a day like today. So course I'd be watching to see why she'd be needing such a coat."

As he listened to Paddy talk about the woman in the coat, an uneasy feeling crept over Percival. He wanted to yell at the boy and tell him to hurry up with his story. Instead, he bided his time while his legs drummed their concern.

"When she passed by, I could see right up under that coat and how all she had was feathers under there. She saw me looking and smiled." As Paddy spoke, the color on his cheeks took on a rosy tint. "She had the prettiest smile and those lips. Why, I do believe they were the color as what's on your cheek."

Feathers? Momma! Percival's stomach turned as fear crept over him. It was hot out. He couldn't imagine anyone else wearing a coat. "This woman, what happened to her!?"

Paddy looked at the others before continuing. "Someone

whistled at her. Calling her by name and yelling. Said as how they'd like to…well, if my momma heard me say what the man said, she'd wash my mouth out with soap for sure. So, the lady yelled back at the man, saying how she was a lady and all. Only she never stopped walking. I'll be danged if she didn't step right off the curb. Her ankle turned and sent her sprawling out into the street. Those heels were so tall, it's no wonder she fell. It wasn't the driver's fault. Why, he couldn't have known she was going to fall. He didn't have time to stop."

Percival swallowed the bile that threatened. "What was her name?"

"Drug her down the road he did, feathers flying everywhere," Tommy said sadly. "Kilt her dead."

"WHAT WAS HER NAME?!" Percival yelled. Every part of his body vibrated as his legs danced in place.

Tommy's eyes bugged. "Mary."

Percival was just about to apologize for his behavior, when Paddy shook his head.

"No, Tommy, that wasn't it. He called her Margareta."

The other two boys nodded their agreement, and Percival felt the sorrow welling up inside. He remembered the shoes. They were new. He recalled his mother slipping her foot inside and the vision he'd had of her falling. *It's my fault. I should have insisted she take them off!* Unable to contain his emotions any longer, he crumbled to his knees, oblivious of his screams filling the air.

"What's wrong with him?" someone asked.

"Maybe his legs were hurting. They were jumping sumptn' fierce."

"Nah, I think maybe the story made him sad."

Though he wished he could stay there bawling out his sorrow, he willed himself to his feet. While he didn't doubt the woman they spoke of was his mother, his heart couldn't accept that she was dead. Wiping his eyes, he faced the boys. "The woman, she's my mother."

Each of the boys sucked in their breath, and Paddy blew out a long whistle. "Of all the dumb luck."

Percival wasn't sure if he was speaking of his mother's accident or his finding out this way. He looked into Paddy's worried eyes. "I want to see her."

"You can't," Tommy said, shaking his head. "It ain't right a kid seeing his momma that way."

"Not right," the two smaller boys agreed.

"I've got to make sure," Percival said. He stared into Paddy's eyes, silently pleading for him to understand. "Please show me."

"I don't know. Maybe you should get your pop to take you," Paddy said nervously.

Percival narrowed his eyes at Paddy. "My papa's dead."

"You got any other family?" Paddy asked.

Percival shook his head. "Mamma has kin in Italy, but that's not around here."

Paddy looked at the others then narrowed his eyes at Percival. "You don't tell no one else that. They find out you don't have any kin, and they'll take you to the asylum."

"Or in prison. That's where they took Buster, remember?" one of the smaller boys said.

"Buster was different," Paddy said, shaking his head. "He got caught dipping pockets. They wouldn't throw Slim in the big house for being an orphan. They'd toss him into the asylum."

Orphan? Is that what I am? Peter Pan was an orphan. Does that mean I can fly?

"I heard tell it ain't so bad. At least they'll feed ya," Tommy said, pulling him from his thoughts.

Percival felt tears well in his eyes and furiously wiped them away. "I'm going. With or without you."

"I'll go with you," one of the smaller boys said, stepping forward. "I don't want to, mind ya, but ain't no one should see that alone."

"I'm coming too," Tommy said, and the other boy nodded his head.

"I'll go," Paddy said at last.

"What about your pop?" Tommy asked. "He nearly kilt you last time."

"I ain't afraid of him," Paddy said, jutting his chin. He turned to Percival, hesitating before he spoke. "Just in case it really is your ma, I want you to know I didn't mean to look under her coat. I was on my knees fishing for dimes at the time, and well, I just couldn't help it."

Percival wasn't sure what to say, so he didn't say anything.

The boys took off running, leaping to the other side as Percival looked after them. They were nearly ready to jump to the next building when they realized he wasn't with them. The others remained on the other side while Paddy returned.

"I thought you wanted to see if she's your ma," Paddy said when he approached.

I do. "Can't we just take the stairs?"

"Sure, when we get closer. This way's faster."

"I'm scared. I've never jumped the roof before." Percival knew he sounded like a baby, but at this moment, he didn't care.

"You don't live in this building. How'd you get over here?"

"I used the stairs. I was coming to see…"

"It don't matter," Paddy said, cutting him off. "We've got to get going before the meat wagon comes to take your ma away. They do that, and they'll not let you see her."

Panic rushed through him. "I've got to see her. I need to be sure."

"Then you need to come," Paddy said gently.

Percival looked to the others and nodded his head. The worse that could happen was he'd fall to his death. *Would that be so bad? If Momma's dead, she's probably with Papa.* The thought calmed him. He took off running and sailed to the other side with ease. As his feet connected with the roof of the neighboring building, a piece of him wished he'd missed. Still, a larger part gave thanks that he didn't. If his mother found out he was jumping rooftops, she'd wallop him a good one. If that were to be the case, he would welcome his punishment with open arms. Because he knew for her to punish him, she'd have to be alive.

Chapter Ten

After the initial jump, Percival's confidence grew, and the ones that followed were a breeze. If not for the circumstances, he would have relished the adrenaline rush that came with each leap. The boy named Tommy led the way as he and the others trailed behind. No one spoke, which was okay with Percival, as it was all he could do to keep from throwing up. It seemed the thoughts in his head were now also connected to his stomach. Every time he thought of his mother being dead, tears sprang to his eyes. Not only was he worried about being alone, but he kept thinking about what Big Joe had said about giving his mother a proper burial. At the time, he'd thought it a nice thing to do. He never imagined having to worry about it so soon, especially since he didn't know the first thing about burying anyone.

Tommy's stride increased, and Percival wondered why the sudden change. He got his answer seconds later when he realized the building looming before him spaced further than those they'd jumped thus far. If he'd had time to think about it, he might have reconsidered. As it was, he gathered his feet and jumped. Suddenly, he was Peter Pan flying through the air, an image he angrily shook off. *I'm not an orphan.* He landed on the roof with a jolt, his arms flailing, then sighed his relief when Paddy and the smaller boys made it without issue. That none of their faces showed any sign of distress let him know this wasn't their first time making a jump.

Tommy hurried to the door to the stairwell, racing down the

stairs as fast as his legs would carry him.

"They'll catch up," Paddy assured him when the twins fell behind.

They raced past an elderly woman who shook her fist, telling them they should be in school. If Percival hadn't been in such a hurry, he would have told her he didn't go to school. Tommy stopped when they reached the bottom, and Percival assumed he was waiting for the twins to catch up. While it felt as if they'd been running forever, he was eager to continue and to confirm his mother wasn't dead. "How much further?"

"Just on the other side of this door," Paddy said as the two smaller boys joined them.

Not able to contain himself, Percival pushed through the door and found himself amidst instant chaos. A group of men stood with their backs to him. To his right, a cluster of ladies stood fanning themselves. Shaking their heads, they spoke of the horror they'd just witnessed.

Unable to see, Percival pushed his way through the crowd. His breath caught as he saw the size of the truck parked just in front of him. As he stepped off the curb, a man grabbed him by the shirt collar.

"They have enough to do without kids out there gawking," the man scolded.

Percival shrugged out of the man's grip, hurrying to the front of the truck. An open cab Rolls-Royce ambulance idled just in front of the truck. Between them stood two men dressed entirely in white. Tall and in no hurry, they stood over a body lying on a long board covered with a white sheet. The boys had told him his mother would be taken away in a meat wagon, and for a moment, Percival felt a surge of hope. The motorcar clearly said ambulance, not meat wagon. Looking closer, he realized the sheet was covering the person's face. *It's too hot. The person must truly be dead.* The men bent, grasping the board at each end. As they lifted the body, feathers fell to the ground like rain.

"Wait," Percival said, pushing past the officers.

One of the policemen grabbed him by the arm. "Hold on there, lad. This ain't no place for kids. Go on now, get out of here."

"No, I have to see," Percival said, struggling to break free.

"This is no place for gawkers," he said, holding firm.

"I'm not gawking. That's my mother," Percival's voice broke as he spoke. "At least I think so. Please, sir. I must know if it is truly her."

The man who held his arm loosened his grip. "Are you sure, son? She doesn't look so good."

"Yes, sir," Percival whispered, and the man let go of his arm.

"Let the lad have a look." The words were no sooner spoken than the men in white pulled the board from the back of the ambulance, leaving just enough inside to support the end.

One of the men took hold of the sheet and leveled a look at Percival. "You ready, son?"

Unable to speak, Percival nodded his readiness. The crowd behind him held their tongues as everyone waited for his reaction. It took him a moment to be sure; then, suddenly, he was leaning across the gurney, holding on with all his might. He wasn't sure how long he stood there before someone peeled his fingers free.

"There, there, lad," the police officer said. "Come along with me and let the men take care of your ma."

"Where are they taking her?" Percival sniffed.

"Ah, they'll be taking her to the city morgue. Now tell me, son, where be your pa?"

Percival felt the bile rise in his throat. He tried to stop it, but it was no use. He turned, heaving the contents of his stomach on the ground where the stretcher once lay. As his stomach lurched for a second time, the officer stepped to the side to avoid the spatter. The second he stopped heaving, Percival gathered his legs under him and sprinted off. Pushing his way through the throng of onlookers, he continued running until, at last, he could run no further, then bent heaving sobbing breaths, wondering who'd stabbed him in the side. Slowly, the pain eased, allowing him to stand upright. As he took in his surroundings, it dawned on him that nothing looked familiar, and he had no clue how to find his way home.

Home. Do I still have one? The landlord won't allow me to stay if I can't pay the rent. He was on his way to a major panic attack when he saw Tommy, Paddy, and the twins running toward him.

Tommy was the first to reach him. "Boy, you're sure fast. I thought we'd lost ya. Ya didn't have to run so far; that policeman didn't even try to follow you."

"Why'd you come all the way over here?" Paddy asked, catching up to them.

Percival shrugged. "I just couldn't stop running. When I stopped, I didn't know where I was or how to get home. Then I wondered if I still had a home. With my momma dead and all."

"Not for long," Paddy said. "I've seen it happen. Soon as the landlord figures out she's dead, he'll take what he can sell then toss the rest on the curb. If there's anything you want, you'd better get it quick. It happened to someone in our building, and the landlord had another family in there before sundown."

Percival looked at the sky as his feet mimicked his agitation. "Where will I sleep?"

The boys looked at each other. Finally, it was one of the twins who spoke. "Maybe you should let them take you to the asylum."

The second twin nodded his agreement. "I hear they have beds for you to sleep in."

Paddy shook his head. "Maybe the landlord hasn't heard the news yet. You should go back home, see if there's anything you want to keep."

Percival walked around the small room in his mind. Aside from her dresses and a spare set of clothing for him, his mother had sold all their belongings when they'd left the larger apartment. She'd tucked all the money she'd received into the money can. The money can! *I have money to pay for a proper burial. Unless the landlord has found it.* His mother had told him never to tell anyone about the money she kept in the can. Until now, he didn't have anyone to tell. He looked at his new friends and tried to keep the urgency out of his voice. "Can you show me how to get home?"

***

Percival sat under the windowsill, finding comfort in the light of the full yellow moon. He was too afraid to turn on the overhead light as it would show him what he already knew. He was alone. His eyes remained dry, indicating he'd finally emptied all his tears. His stomach growled, reminding him for the umpteenth time he hadn't eaten in nearly a day. He'd never had to worry about eating before, as his mother always furnished his food.

He circled his arms around his knees to still his legs. It didn't work. His legs always mimicked his worry and this night was no different. He reached for the tin can, dumping the contents. There seemed to be a lot of money, but while his mother had taught him to read, she hadn't taught him about the value of a dollar. Still, if it was nearly enough to buy the house she'd dreamed of, surely there was enough to pay to give his mother a proper burial. He'd find his way to the morgue in the morning and beg the man to let it be enough.

He picked up the small picture frame that held the picture of his mother. Though the photo lacked color, his mind filled the void. He could easily visualize the creaminess of her skin, the black within her hair, and the deep rich brown in the eyes that stared back at him.

He studied her smile and wondered about the color of her lips. Were they the fresh pink that she often wore that matched the shade of her cheeks or the deep red like what she'd worn this day? He touched his cheek, remembering the kiss she'd placed there moments before hugging him and bidding him goodbye. If he'd known it would be the last time he'd see her alive, he would have insisted she hold him a little longer.

His stomach grumbled once more, and he dismissed it. His need for food was no greater than the ache that filled his heart. He curled into a ball, staring at the empty bed, as if doing so would bring his mother back.

***

Cindy pulled the journal to her chest, as if doing so would ease Percival's suffering. She slid a glance toward her mother, grateful to still have her in her life.

"I'm not going anywhere," Linda said as if reading her mind. "And even if I do, you won't be rid of me."

Cindy raised an eyebrow. "Planning on haunting me, are you?"

"I am," Linda said, nodding her head. "It'll be your penance for not giving me a grandchild."

"And if I give you a grandchild before you die?" Cindy asked.

"Oh, no. You should've thought about that years ago. You've waited too long now. You see, now I'll have to come back just to get to play with the little darling."

"Fine by me," Cindy said, lowering the pile of papers she

was holding.

Linda looked over her glasses. "Let me guess. You'll call in one of those exorcists and have them banish me."

"Only if you come back as a hateful ghost," Cindy replied.

"So, it's alright if I come back?"

"Sure, it'll cut down on the daycare bill." Cindy bit her lip to keep from laughing, even though it felt good to be happy again. "Just let me know your schedule, and I'll get someone to work on the days you want off."

"It'd be just like you to wait until I'm dead to give me a grandchild." Linda pouted.

Cindy sighed. "I'm sorry I've been such a disappointment."

"It's not your fault. I'm the one who pushed you to be a teacher." Linda sniffed.

Cindy had often blamed her profession for not wanting to have children. The truth of the matter was she'd been having second thoughts since they'd begun reading the journals. Not about having children of her own but adopting. Surely things hadn't changed so much over the years. There had to be older children in need of a home. She was just about to confess her thoughts to her mother when she spoke.

"If I had it to do over again, I'd do things differently."

"It's not your fault, Mom. You didn't force me to be a teacher. I did that on my own."

"Oh, I know it's not my fault. I blame your grandmother."

Cindy leaned forward. "And just how is my not having children Granny's fault?"

Linda let out a wistful sigh. "Because of the way she raised me, of course. It's her fault I have values. Why, if not for her instilling me with them, I would have lost my virginity at Woodstock along with everyone else."

"The horror of it all." Cindy laughed.

"Laugh if you will, but this is my cross to bear. If I'd have been a loose woman, I could have had more children. Odds are one of them would have given me a grandchild."

Cindy was about to remind her mother that she'd suffered two miscarriages before becoming pregnant with her but decided against it. Some things were best left unmentioned. "Mom, you know there are no such things as ghosts."

"And just how can you be so sure?" Linda said, crossing her arms.

Cindy smiled. "Because if there were, Granny's ghost would be chasing you around the room with her willow switch."

Chapter Eleven

Cindy stood in the shower watching driblets of rain trickle in from the half-moon window, chiding herself for never having the window fixed. She yawned, still tired from an exhausting night of tossing and turning, revisiting what she'd read in Percival's journal at each turn. She thought of Percival seeing his mother after the accident, and began to cry. Not only had he witnessed the horror, but now he was alone. Something she'd struggled with most of the night.

Turning off the water, she dried herself then dressed, hoping to snag a cup of coffee before her mother woke—no such luck. The aroma of coffee greeted her the moment she opened her bedroom door.

"Good morning," Linda greeted the moment she entered the kitchen then held up a box of toaster pastries. "Chocolate or strawberry?"

"Chocolate. You're awfully chipper this morning," Cindy said, slipping into an empty chair.

Linda placed the pastry in the toaster then sat a coffee cup on the table in front of Cindy. "Rough night?"

"The worst. Oh, while I'm thinking about it, remind me to call someone about the window in my bathroom. I keep forgetting."

"You shower in there every day, and you're asking me to remind you?" Linda laughed. She waited for the toaster to release, then retrieved the pastries, handing one to Cindy before topping off her coffee cup and joining her. "It's all I can do to remember my name sometimes."

"Why didn't Big Joe go check on Percival?" Cindy asked, jumping straight into something that bugged her during the night.

"I admit to wondering the same thing myself. Is that the only thing that kept you awake?"

It didn't surprise Cindy that her mother picked up on her distress. She took a sip of coffee before answering. "No...maybe. I don't know. I mean, I know all the kids will become orphans at some point. I just don't like them being alone."

"I've known you long enough to know that it's more than that," Linda pressed.

"It's the whole adoption thing."

Linda's eyebrows arched. "You don't think Percival and the others should be adopted?"

"Of course I do. I'm talking about me. I'm not sure adoption is the best option for me."

"You love kids," Linda said, peering over her cup. "Besides, I'm here to help."

Cindy closed her eyes momentarily, trying to choose her words. Finally, she just spoke her mind. "That's just it. You won't always be here."

"I told you last night I feel fine."

"I know, but no one lives forever."

"Speak for yourself, Lady." Linda chuckled.

"I'm not going to live forever either. What happens if I adopt a child, and something happens to me? Then the kid will end up right back in the system."

Linda drained her cup and walked to the sink to rinse it. After placing it in the dishwasher, she returned to her chair and slapped her hand on the table. "You want to talk what-ifs? What if you never try? What if the child you could have never gets adopted and spends the rest of his or her childhood in the system being sent from home to home, never knowing a mother's love even for a moment? What if I die and you are all alone for the rest of your miserable life?"

"That a lot of what-ifs," Cindy said dryly.

Her mother narrowed her eyes. "I'm not finished. Now, what if you adopt a child? Then what if we both live to see that child grow up and have a family? What if they have, say, two or three children? Now, I'm not only a grandma, but I get to be a great-grandma. You get to be a mom and a grandmother, and then when I die at a hundred and fifty, you won't be all alone. You'll have a family to love you and help take care of you in your golden years. Why do you have to be so negative all the time?"

Cindy liked the thought of having family around in her later years, but she also knew better than to rush into the decision. "You forgot to say 'what if'."

"Does that mean you're going to adopt a child?" Linda's voice was hopeful.

"What if I think about it a little longer?" Cindy replied.

"Don't think about it too long. I'm an old woman."

"You're going to live to be a hundred and fifty, remember? You've got a good seventy-eight years ahead of you." Cindy said, throwing her words back at her.

"One more thing, as long as we are on the subject," Linda said, leaning against the counter. "It's as if you don't believe you deserve to be happy. You're a good person, and you're healthy. I'm doing better too. I had a rough go of it after your father died, but I'm good now. Sometimes I feel as if we've traded places. I'm ready to live, and you are the shut-in."

"I go out," Cindy objected.

Linda waved her off with the back of her hand. "You leave the house, but you don't go out. Not on dates and not with your friends. I'm not a child you have to keep an eye on twenty-four seven. You need to put yourself back out there. I promise not to wander off or leave the stove on."

Her mother was right. She'd declined multiple invitations since Linda had moved in with her. At first, it was because she'd been worried about leaving her mother alone, but that wasn't the case any longer. She'd become complacent, but the truth of the matter was she was enjoying the renewed friendship with her mother. "I rather enjoy your company."

"Be that as it may, I want you to promise me you'll find some time for you. Even if it's just sitting in the coffee shop drinking a cup of coffee," Linda encouraged.

"I promise," Cindy said, suddenly wondering if it were her mother that needed some time apart.

Linda smiled. "Good. How about we go see what Percy's up to?"

"Okay, but I doubt he'd appreciate being called that."

"I'm counting on that," Linda replied.

"On him not liking it?"

"Sure. He can come back and tell me to stop."

"Mom, where did this sudden fascination with ghosts and hauntings come from?"

"I watched a television show the other day. Only the woman's ghost was boring, just kind of appeared and disappeared without doing anything. I thought that if I can get myself a real ghost, maybe one of those producers would want to make a TV show about me. They pay lots of money for things like that, you know. Just think of the inheritance I could leave for my adopted grandchild."

"You sure are something, Mom," Cindy said, following Linda to the living room.

"That's me," Linda said, tapping at her head with her index finger. "Always thinking."

Cindy gathered the copies of the journals and tapped them on the coffee table to straighten them. Once settled into place, she waited for her mother to get situated then began to read.

***

I woke in the same position I started in, took in my mother's unused bed, and pushed my grief aside. I needed to find out where they took my mother and see to getting her put into a proper grave. My pockets weren't deep enough to hold all the money in the money can, so I emptied the contents into one of my mother's stockings, tied it into a knot, and stuffed it into the front of my pants to keep it from being stolen. I didn't know how much I had, but I knew better than to let anyone take it from me. I opened the door to the apartment and checked for the landlord, only letting out my breath at not seeing him. I started walking down the stairs and realized I had no idea where I was going. Paddy might know, but I had no clue how to find him. I wanted to go find Big Joe and ask him what to do, but the problem was I was mighty sore at the man. Paddy and the others said he was in the crowd when they saw my momma get hit. That meant he knew my momma was dead, and yet he never came to check on me. That didn't sit right with me. If he really was my friend, he would've come. I was halfway down the first flight of stairs when I reconsidered. He might not be my friend, but he knew something about burying. I decided to go see him just this one time and ask for his help.

Cindy breathed a sigh of relief that Percival was going to ask for help. All through the night, she had imagined Percival handing over all his mother's money and getting nothing in return. As she continued to read, the story took over.

***

Making up his mind, Percival hurried up the stairs, pushed through the door to the roof, and continued running, leaping to the next building without hesitation. Even before landing, he heard the familiar thumps and knew Big Joe to be on the roof. His heart drummed heavily in his chest as he approached. He stood unnoticed for several moments, watching the man throw his fists at the heavy bag over and over. Remembering how he'd felt his punch all the way to his shoulders, he winced each time the man's fists connected with the leather. His legs jerked from side to side, and he realized he couldn't even watch without it hurting. He wanted nothing more than to turn and run away, but he needed the man's help. Anger fueled his legs as he watched Big Joe hit the bag in several quick successions without so much as flinching. He wasn't sure where the anger came from, but it boiled inside him like a bubbling cauldron.

Big Joe's fist slammed into the bag one last time, and then he tapped the bag as if calming a horse. A moment later, he reached for a towel, wiping it across his face as if he didn't have a care in the world. He tossed the towel aside then turned, smiling a broad smile upon seeing him.

"I hate you!" Percival wasn't sure who was more surprised, Big Joe, at hearing the words or him having said them. He hadn't planned on saying it but felt better for having done so.

Big Joe eyed him carefully and rocked back on his heels. "I suppose that's why you didn't come up for your lesson yesterday."

Percival couldn't believe his ears; the man knew his mother had been killed, and he expected Percival to act as if nothing had happened. He opened his mouth, only this time, his words held more meaning. "I hate you!"

"Yes, you made yourself clear the first time. Care to tell me why you don't want to be my friend anymore?"

Either the man was daft or pulling his leg. Either way, Percival was in no mood for games. "You said you were my friend, but you don't care about me. It was just a trick to get me to teach you to read. Well, I'm not going to teach you no more.

I wish I hadn't even started. You can read a little, and I got nothing. But that's okay. I don't need to know how to hit. I need to know about something else."

The smile returned. "What do you need to know about? Whatever it is must be something to get you so riled."

"I need to know about burying my momma. You buried yours, so you gotta know something about it. I got some money but don't know if it's enough."

The smile was gone in an instant. "Is your momma sick?"

Percival's legs now moved so fast, he thought he was going to take off. "No, she's not sick. She's dead, and you know it! You were there. Paddy and the guys saw you."

"Dead? How?" Big Joe's eyes widened, and Percival wondered if the boys had been mistaken about seeing him there.

An image of his mother lying on the board flashed before his eyes, and he swallowed the bile that threatened. "The truck. You were there. Paddy said so."

Big Joe scrubbed his hand over his face. "That was your ma? I swear to ya, Slim, I didn't know it was her."

The man sounded sincere. Could he be telling the truth? Was that the reason he didn't come see him? Percival's voice shook when he spoke. "But you were there. You saw her."

Big Joe shook his head. "Me and a bunch of others. All we knew is a woman got run over. We didn't see her face."

So Big Joe hadn't forgotten about him. A sob escaped as he tried unsuccessfully to keep the tears at bay. "I'm sorry for what I said. I didn't mean it. I was just...I didn't mean it."

Big Joe stepped forward and clasped a hand on Percival's shoulder. "I understand your pain and I'll help you see your momma has a fitting place to rest."

Unable to speak, Percival nodded his understanding.

Chapter Twelve

Hands wrapped to protect his knuckles, Percival danced around the small enclosure jabbing his fists into the bag as Big Joe had instructed. Though it had taken a while to get the hang of it, he could now hit the bag without feeling as if it hit him back. An image of his momma dressed in her costume telling him of the grand life they would soon have flittered before him. She turned to check her reflection, and when she faced him once more, her image was grossly distorted. Anger fueled his training. He connected with the bag and, for the hundredth time, wished he had a face to put with the punch. He hadn't, so his anger was focused on the truck instead. Each time he threw a punch, he pictured the truck, pounding his fists against the steel. Occasionally, his fists would pummel an imaginary windshield, his feet dancing fiercely to avoid the glass.

"Stay calm, Slim. Don't let the anger take over," Big Joe said over the top of the bag.

Percival liked the way Big Joe called him Slim and not Percival—that name was reserved for his momma. Thinking of his momma lying under the ground, he slammed his fist into the bag once again. "But I am mad."

"Of course you are. You have every right to be," Big Joe agreed.

"But you just said I shouldn't get mad."

"No, I said you shouldn't get angry."

Percival scrunched up his face, wondering if the man had gotten hit so many times that it had jarred his brain. "Isn't that the same thing?"

"Some would think so."

"But not you?"

"No."

Percival lowered his fists and faced the man. "What's the difference?"

Big Joe sat on a weathered old bench and patted the spot beside him. "Sit with me."

Percival sighed. "So you're not going to teach me to fight after all?"

"You've learned a lot in the last couple of days. There's a lot more to fighting than pounding someone."

"Like moving out of the way so I don't get hit."

Big Joe nodded. "That's a large part of it."

Percival sat and looked up to Big Joe, watching as the sun glistened off his dark skin.

The man saw him looking and took out a handkerchief, wiping his face before he spoke. "Getting mad is a normal reaction to being done wrong, and lord knows you've been done wrong. You get mad, and you deal with the situation."

"You mean like we did with burying Momma?" Percival's voice cracked as he spoke.

"Yes, we dealt with the situation at hand, but now comes the hard part."

"Harder than burying Momma?" Percival didn't know what could be harder than that and wasn't sure he wanted to find out.

"Yes, harder than that."

Percival gulped. "Like when the landlord finds out my momma is dead."

"There's that. He'll find out soon enough. When that happens, you'll have some decisions to make."

"Like if I'm going to the asylum or living on the streets," Percival said softly.

"That's right. You know I would take you in if I could, but that wouldn't be right. Even if folk wouldn't put up a fuss, I have to go on the road soon, and that's no life for a boy. Why, you'd do better living on the street than following me around. If you were older, maybe, but not a boy of your size."

"You could watch out for me," Percival said.

"Not all the time. And that's not the thing of it anyway. I bring you with me, and people would think, well they'd think wrong, and I'd be in a heap of trouble. Men like me are not supposed to spend time with boys like you." He put up a hand to stop further questions. "I know you don't understand now, but there'll come a day when you do."

Percival's legs bounced their disappointment.

"See," Big Joe said with a nod to his legs, "you're mad, and that's okay. But you let that madness build up inside, and it becomes anger. Anger can rot a man's soul. You...why, you're just a small boy. You don't have that much soul, so it won't take long for it to fester into something dark and ugly."

Percival glanced at Big Joe's arms, and the man laughed. "Big Joe's dark, alright, but I'm not ugly. At least my momma didn't think so. It's not that kind of darkness anyhow. It's a darkness inside. One that eats at a man and keeps him from living a good life."

"You beat people up. Is that living a good life?"

"Beating people up is my job. It's no different than any other job."

"It's not?"

"Nope. I go into the ring, do the best job I can do, then collect a wage like anyone else that goes to work. It's a job, see. I do the work and leave feeling good about what I've done."

"Like beating people up and winning the fight."

"Like doing the job. The job is to entertain people. People come to see a show, and I give them one. Sometimes I like the job more than others, but in the end, I do what I do for the money."

"My momma used to say the same thing. That she just did the things she did for the money. She was going to buy us a house and never have to work again," Percival said and wiped a tear that pooled in his eye.

"Your momma was a good woman, Slim. Remember what I said about your pa? Well, it's the same with your ma. It took a lot of guts for her to do the things she did. She was doing that for you to have a better life." Big Joe was quiet for a moment. "You sure you don't want to hold on to the rest of the money?"

Percival shook his head. "No, sir. It wouldn't be right, my spending Momma's money.

"It's your money now," Big Joe reminded him.

"I have enough to keep me fed for a while. That money was to get us a house. I want you to hold on to it for a while. At least until I'm old enough to buy one," Percival said.

"You change your mind, you just come see me. I'll see to it you get your money. I'm an honest man and will do right by you."

"Big Joe, how do you keep from getting angry when someone's hitting on you?" Percival asked, returning to the original subject.

Big Joe laughed. "First off, I try not to get hit. And if I do, I don't let myself get angry. Anger is fuel, but that kind of fuel burns out real quick. It makes a man tired and sloppy, and when a man is sloppy, he loses. I let all the other guys do all the work. Let them get angry. Getting angry takes up way more energy, and it tires a man out quicker. I focus my energy on my legwork, and when I do that, I don't have to throw as many punches. That's what I'm going to teach you. You get the legwork down, and they'll have to chase you. Don't you worry about looking like a coward. It ain't nothing like that. It's all about drawing in your opponent. Get them close so you can concentrate on delivering the right punch. You do that, and it'll only take one. We'll work on that first, and then I'll show you what to do if you find yourself facing more than one."

Percival blew out a sigh.

"What's the matter, Slim?"

"I sure wish I would have known how to beat up all those boys that hurt me."

"There were too many to get all of them."

Percival frowned his disappointment. "But you just said you'd show me what to do."

"Close your eyes for a moment."

Percival did as told.

"Now, I want you to think back to that day on the roof. No, keep your eyes closed," he said when Slim opened one. "Can you see the boys?"

"Yes."

"Okay, now find the leader. What was his name?"

"Milo."

"That's right. Can you see him?"

"Yes."

"What's he doing?"

"He's tearing the pages out of my book," Percival said bitterly.

"Okay, let it go, Slim. Remember, if you get angry, he's got you. Stay calm and breathe through your anger. He's going to expect you to lose control or shake in your boots, but you're not going to give him the satisfaction."

"That's because I'm not wearing any boots."

"No, it's because you're going to wait." Big Joe said, ignoring the quip.

"Wait for what?"

"For the right moment."

"How will I know?"

"Come on, Slim, concentrate," Big Joe said firmly. "Milo's tearing out the pages of your book. What are the others doing?"

"Laughing."

"And?"

"Hitting me."

"Why aren't you ducking?"

"I tried. They hit me anyway. Each time I go forward, they hit me."

"Did you mean to go forward, or did your legs move on their own?"

"They moved on their own. The boys thought I wanted to run."

"Then we've got to train your legs to do what you want them to do."

"My legs never listen."

"That's why we have to train them."

"How do we do that?"

"Remember those moves I showed you before when we were trying to get your momma to agree to let you fight?"

A sadness washed over him at the mention of his mother.

"Come on, Slim, I know you miss her, but we got to stay focused. You're on your own now, and you're gonna need to know how to defend yourself."

"I remember."

"It's like that. We'll practice jab and duck. Before long, your legs will know what to do without even stopping to think about it. Then if anyone takes a swing at you, you'll duck out of the way before they can connect."

"Won't that make them mad?"

"Probably, but by remaining calm, you'll be one step ahead of them. That gives you the advantage. Stand up, and we'll give it a go."

Percival did as told, squaring off against Big Joe.

"Okay, try to hit me."

Percival leaned forward and threw a punch. Big Joe connected a soft jab as he ducked out of the way.

"Now, let me show you what you did wrong," Big Joe said. "You forgot to let me come to you. By leaning forward, you opened yourself up to getting hit. Not only that, but you're putting all your weight on your front foot and taking a chance of losing your balance. What's the number one rule?"

"Let them come to me?" Percival asked.

"That's right. Let's try it." Big Joe said, getting into position.

Percival stood and squared his shoulders once more. Just as Big Joe threw out his fist, Percival leaned backward.

Big Joe tapped Percival's chest, sending him back, arms flailing. He smiled when Percival scrambled to his feet. "Do you know what you did wrong?"

Percival shook his head.

"You leaned back. You have to stay in your frame to keep your balance. Right now, you're afraid of being hit. We'll work on that. Don't worry; I'll teach you to block the punch and come around with a left jab. Don't look so glum, Slim. I know what I'm doing, and soon you will too. I might not be the smartest man, but this I can do."

Percival wanted to argue that Big Joe was the smartest man he knew but decided against it. Instead, he squared his shoulders and nodded his readiness.

Chapter Thirteen

August 9, 1916

"Do you really have to go, Big Joe?" Percival knew the answer but couldn't help himself from asking.

"Yes, I know you're worried you're not ready, but you are. If you were older and a little bigger, I would say you're good enough for the ring."

"Aww, you're just fun'n me."

"I'm not either. If you had someone your own age to fight, you'd come out the winner. Why, I would stake my name on it. You've got time for that. If that's the direction you decide to go."

"Yeah, well, if Milo and his friends come around here, I'm going to pulverize them," Percival said, narrowing his eyes.

Big Joe sat his bag on the ground with a sigh. "Seems I didn't teach you everything you need to know."

"Does that mean you're staying?" Percival asked hopefully.

"No, I can't miss my train. I have to be in Detroit this weekend to start training for the fight. After that, I move on to Chicago, Louisville, then back to Detroit. It'll be a while before I make my way back here."

"But we've already been training," Percival replied.

"Not the kind of training I need to win a fight. Now listen, there's something I forgot to tell you. Knowing how to fight is good. But knowing when not to fight is just as good. I've taught you how to defend yourself and I'm confident that you'll be okay. But just because you know that you can win a fight don't mean you should go starting them."

"But I need to settle the score."

"I can see why you feel that way, but you start fighting and you're going to draw attention to yourself. You don't want the landlord to kick you out any sooner than need be."

Percival nodded his understanding. That was why Big Joe had insisted he take some of the money for food and to give it to the landlord when he came to collect the month's rent. Percival had told the landlord that his mother had stepped out for a bit. If the man knew him to be lying, he didn't let on— simply counted the money, mumbled something under his breath, and left. Percival had enough to pay until time for Big Joe to return. After that, he'd need to make his decision on what to do next.

"Now another thing," Big Joe continued. "You start fighting and you'll get a reputation of being a fighter."

"What's wrong with that? You're a fighter."

"The problem with it is there'll always be people who want to fight you."

Percival shrugged. "So, you said I'll win."

"Most likely you will—if it's a fair fight. But people, they don't like to lose. Someday, you'll find yourself up against someone like that and they'll want to win at any cost. You find yourself up against someone like that, then it'll be bad."

"Do you think Milo's like that?"

"He might be. My guess is Milo is a coward."

"If I don't fight, people will think I'm a coward."

"You'll know the truth. It's best not to draw attention to yourself."

"By being a coward," Percival repeated.

"By not letting on you know how to fight, you'll have the advantage." Big Joe took his index finger and lifted Percival's chin. "It doesn't matter what anyone else thinks of you. What matters is what you think of yourself. You're a good boy. You want to honor your momma's memory; you remember the values she taught you. Your momma wouldn't want you to go around starting fights now, would she?"

It made sense when he put it like that. "No, sir, my momma wouldn't like it at all. She'd want me to be safe. Big Joe, how can you tell Milo's a coward?"

"Because he gets others to fight for him. That isn't the kind of person you want to be around. Not being able to fight and having someone help defend you is one thing. But telling someone to hurt a person while you stand there and watch is another. That boy's nothing but trouble. Kids that follow him will be too. You remember what I said about following a person. You only pledge your loyalty to someone worthy of your trust."

"How will I know?"

"Because that person will give something back. A trade of sorts."

"Like money?"

"Perhaps. Or kindness. It's good to be loyal to a friend. But make sure that you surround yourself with real friends."

"How will I know if they are real friends?"

Big Joe studied his feet for a moment then smiled. "Remember my friend Stephen?"

"The little boy whose house your mother cleaned?"

"That's the one. Well, his dad didn't want us to be friends, but we liked each other just fine. One day, we heard voices out in the hall, and Stephen knew one of those voices belonged to his dad. So he opened the blanket chest at the end of his bed and pulled all the blankets out, shoving them under the bed. Stephen told me to get in and he closed the lid."

"Were you scared?"

"No, on account of I trusted Stephen and knew he wouldn't

leave me in there. Stephen's dad came in and wanted to know what Stephen was doing and Stephen lied and told him he'd been studying. Stephen's dad must have looked around and not seen any books on account of his dad took off his belt and laid into him right there for lying. When he was done, he asked Stephen what he'd been doing again and Stephen lied once more, telling his dad that he'd been taking a nap and hadn't wished to get in trouble for sleeping during the day."

"Your friend was a liar?"

"Not usually, but Stephen knew if his dad had found out he was playing with me, that he would have whipped me really bad, on account of I wasn't supposed to be in Stephen's room. Then his dad would've fired my momma for bringing me to work and letting me out of her sight. So Stephen lied to save me from that whipping and my momma from getting into trouble. That's when Big Joe knew Stephen to be a true friend. You get someone who'll sacrifice for you and that's someone worthy of your friendship." Big Joe placed his hand on Percival's head and ruffled his hair. "I've taught you what you need to know; now it's up to you. You remember that number I gave you?"

"Yes, sir," Percival said trying his best not to cry.

"You need anything, you call that number. They'll know how to get in touch with me." Big Joe picked up his bag and heaved it over his shoulder and left without another word.

***

August 16, 1916

Percival woke in a pool of sweat, knowing the moisture had nothing to do with the heat. Nightmares plagued his sleep. He'd seen his mother's face over and over in his dreams as he begged her to return to him or at least come back and take him away with her as she'd promised to do so many times.

Still unwilling to disturb his mother's bed, he rose from his place on the floor and sat with his legs draped over the windowsill, watching people milling around in the street, oblivious of his misery.

In the week since Big Joe's departure, Percival had only left the small room a handful of times to go to the corner to get something to eat. While he'd sometimes gone places with his mother, they hadn't gone far, and he was afraid of getting lost and not being able to find his way home. He was also scared the landlord would find a reason to return, further afraid the man would discover the secret he was keeping. Though he'd paid the rent, he doubted the man would allow him to stay if he found him living in the room alone. Big Joe had warned him not to draw attention to himself, but he hated being in the room alone. At least when his mother was alive, he knew there would eventually be an end to the loneliness.

A woman walked past with a young boy at her side, and his heart ached at the sight. *It's not fair!* Not able to stand the loneliness any longer, Percival pulled in his legs and left the stifling room—the relief was instantaneous. As he reached the stairwell, he stood trying to decide where to go—a decision made for him when he heard voices drifting up from below. Hurrying to the rooftop, he welcomed the sunshine—closing his eyes as the warm rays of early morning sun spread over him like a well-warranted hug. He longed to hear the familiar sounds of Big Joe pounding the punching bag or see his mother rush through the door, the worry lines on her face easing at seeing him. He didn't realize he was crying until his nose began to run. He sniffed his sorrow several times before finally allowing the tears to run their course. The rooftop that had been his sanctuary for so long now felt as empty as his heart, and he wanted nothing more than to stop the pain. He stood teetering dangerously close to the edge of the roof without even knowing how he'd gotten there, hands stretched to their fullest as his legs jumped in place as if begging for one final leap. He smiled. Thinking to give them their wish, he lifted his leg.

The next thing he knew, he was lying on the ground staring into Paddy's worried face. Percival pushed the boy off and jumped up, pressing the tips of his fingers tightly into his palms.

Paddy rose and brushed the soot from his knees. "Don't go getting all flustered; I was just trying to stop you from jumping."

"I wasn't going to jump," Percival lied.

"No? Well, your legs were. Why, if I hadn't stopped you, you'd be flat as a flapjack by now."

Percival gulped and relaxed his fists. "What business is it of yours anyhow?"

"You're my friend. I don't want to see them scraping you off the sidewalk."

"If you're my friend, then why haven't I seen you around?" Percival said heatedly.

Paddy lowered his eyes. "I thought to come by, but I didn't know what to say. I get mad at my ma, but I wouldn't want to see her dead. My pop maybe wouldn't be so bad, but seeing my ma like that, that's not something a boy should see."

Percival sighed, knowing he wouldn't have known what to say either.

Paddy looked over the side of the building. "Were you really going to jump?"

Percival answered with a shrug, and Paddy blew out a long whistle.

"You must be some kind of sad," the boy said softly.

"Yep," Percival replied.

"The landlord letting you stay, then?"

"He doesn't know my mom...is not here," Percival replied.

"What about the rent?"

"I paid it."

"You?" Paddy's eyes went wide.

"My momma had a bit of money saved up."

"So you live there all alone?" Paddy smiled.

"It ain't so good." Percival sniffed.

"What if you had someone to share it with?"

"Like who?" Percival asked, scratching his head.

Paddy yanked his thumb to his chest. "Like me."

"You?"

"Uh-huh, seems that just this morning, my pop told me how I've become too big for my britches and how I need to move out."

"Why don't he just buy you some new pants?"

Paddy laughed. "My pop would rather see me naked than buy me new pants, but that's because he's as ornery as a stubborn old mule."

"Won't your momma be sad when you don't come back?"

"My momma has enough mouths to feed without worrying about me. The only thing she'll be sad about is when I don't bring her the dimes I fish out of the grates."

Percival remembered Paddy saying something about fishing in the grates the day of his mother's accident. If Paddy and the others hadn't been there that day, he might never have known why his mother hadn't returned. He figured he owed it to the boy to let him stay with him. Besides, he didn't relish the thought of spending another night alone. He nodded his acceptance. "Alright, you can stay, but we have to be quiet so the landlord don't send us away."

"Haven't you eaten nothing?" Paddy asked when Percival's stomach rumbled.

Percival shook his head.

"Got money?"

This time, he nodded.

"Come on, then. What's the matter?" Paddy asked when

Percival hesitated.

"I promised I wouldn't let the landlord see me."

"Promised who?"

Before he could answer, Paddy's eyes went wide, and he sucked in his breath. Percival turned to see what had caused his friend's face to pale. Just when he was about to ask, he saw the reason. Milo and two of his friends landed on the roof only steps in front of them.

Milo smiled at seeing him.

Percival returned the smile as Paddy tugged on his shirt, begging him to run.

Milo nodded, and the boys wavered. "What about Big Joe?" one of the boys asked.

"Big Joe's gone," Milo sneered. "Word on the street is he came into some money and left for good. Cleared out his apartment and everything."

Percival was about to correct the boy when the other two jumped him. He went down then scrambled to his feet. Remembering the moves Big Joe taught him, he ducked out of the way of the next blow and delivered one of his own. A second later, both boys lay on the ground gasping as Percival turned toward Milo, fists at the ready. Milo looked to the boys for help, then fled in the opposite direction as his friends hurried after him.

Percival swelled with pride, then turned to see Paddy staring at him with his mouth agape.

"Where'd you learn to fight like that?" Paddy asked, bending to pick up his cap.

"Big Joe taught me."

"You mean the murderer?"

"I mean my friend, Big Joe," Percival corrected.

Paddy blew out a long whistle. "Well, if that don't beat all. You sure are something, Percival."

Percival froze. It was the first time anyone had called him by his given name since his mother had died. He leveled a look at Paddy. "My momma called me Percival. My friends call me Slim."

Paddy nodded his understanding.

Chapter Fourteen

Percival stared in awed fascination at his stomach, which pooched from his midsection, looking as if he'd swallowed an entire watermelon. Never had he experienced such a glut of food as what he and Paddy had managed to inhale in that single sitting. Their consumption must have impressed the waiter as well as the fellow kept scratching his head and returning to the kitchen to bring more food until at last Percival shook his head, insisting he would explode if he ate another bite. Percival wasn't sure what amazed him most, that he'd eaten so much or that Paddy had matched him bite for bite.

The waiter approached, eyeing the empty plates as he placed their bill on the table. He stacked the plates on the edge of the table and looked down his long nose, holding Percival's gaze. "See that you don't leave without paying your tab."

"No, sir, I wouldn't think of leaving without paying." Percival pulled the sock he'd hidden his money in to prevent it from being stolen from his waistband, fumbled with the knotted string, then removed the money Big Joe had left with him.

Paddy let out a low whistle. "How much you got there?"

Percival shrugged.

The waiter smiled, then removed several bills from the fold. "This will do. Now put that away before anyone sees what you have. You should know better than to be flashing that in public. Did you steal it?"

"His papa's rich," Paddy said before Percival could reply.

The waiter's brows rose as his eyes darted from side to side, "You boys need to keep that information to yourselves. There are unscrupulous people in this city that would kidnap you and hold you for ransom for half of what's in your hand."

"My papa's not rich, he's dead. So is my momma," Percival said without looking at Paddy. He stuffed the bills into his sock, tied the string into a knot, and shoved it back into his waistband.

The waiter searched the room once more before leaning in close and lowering his voice. "You paid what's owed and that's all I care about. But I'll leave you with this advice: check over your shoulder to make sure you're not followed. If you are, find yourself a policeman. Don't go home unless you are certain you're alone. Next time you go out, put a spot of money in your front pocket so that you don't have to show what you have. Better yet, find a place to hide the rest so no one takes it from you."

"What'd you go and tell the truth for?" Paddy asked once the waiter had left. "He could have taken the money and there'd not be a thing you could do about it."

"Why would he take it if it wasn't his?" Percival asked.

Paddy snatched his cap from his seat, placing it on his head as he pushed away from the table. "Boy, Slim, for a smart kid, you sure are dumb."

Percival didn't like being called names. He recalled what Big Joe had said about not being loyal to someone who didn't give something in return. He stood his ground, refusing to follow Paddy, who made it halfway across the room before realizing he was alone. Paddy nodded for him to come. Impervious to the attention he was attracting, Percival held his ground.

"What's the matter, Slim?" Paddy asked when he returned.

Percival narrowed his eyes. "I'll not go with you if you don't respect me."

Paddy reached up and clapped his hand on Percival's shoulder. "I respect ya just fine, Slim."

"You called me dumb."

"Well, on account of you are about some things. Come on, people are staring at us. Let's get out of here."

"Momma said I'm smart because I can read and write," Percival said, reluctantly following him outside.

"Yep," Paddy agreed as they started walking down the sidewalk. "But you're dumb when it comes to the streets. Knowing how to fight is good, but there's more to living on the streets."

"Like what?"

"Like knowing how to find your way home, what grates are best for fishing, and what streets to avoid so the gangs don't pulverize you. And knowing not to let a waiter take whatever he wants from you. It was way too much. I didn't say anything on account of he could have taken it all. How much dough do you have anyway?"

"Big Joe left me with about twenty dollars, but I've spent some of that," Percival replied.

Paddy blew out another whistle. "You see, that's what I'm talking about right there. Someone asks you how much money you got, you don't tell them."

"But you're my friend."

"Don't matter," Paddy said. "Friends and enemies are all the same when it comes to money. Enemies will steal it and friends will bum it or get you to spend it on them."

"Like when you got me to buy your supper?"

Paddy shook his head. "No, see, I was taking payment."

"Payment for what?"

"For teaching you all I know about the streets." Paddy laughed. "Don't worry, Slim, you got yourself a bargain. When I'm through with you, you'll know all you need to know."

Percival remembered what the waiter had said and cast a glance over his shoulder. "There's a lot of people out here. How are we going to know if anyone is following us?"

Paddy looked over his shoulder then scrunched his face as if considering the question.

"What?" Percival asked when he smiled.

"We run!" Paddy said and took off like a shot.

Not wishing to be left behind, Percival began running. Though his stomach protested, he caught up with Paddy in no time, racing down the street, ducking through an alley, then back into the street before entering a building and racing up three flights of stairs. Toward the end of the third flight of stairs, Paddy stopped.

"Good to know your legs are good for more than jumping in place," Paddy said, rubbing his midsection. "I shouldn't have run after eating so much."

Before Percival could respond, Paddy placed a finger to his mouth and then pointed down the stairs as a door slammed shut below.

"Someone's coming. Maybe more than one. I'm going to puke if I run anymore. We're going to have to fight," Paddy whispered.

Percival nodded. He too was feeling the effects of running on an overly full stomach. He braced his legs the way Big Joe had taught him and made ready to defend himself. The pattern of the footsteps let them know whoever was coming was in a hurry.

"Are you scared?" Paddy asked when the movement in Percival's legs increased.

"Only wish I knew who it is we're going to be fighting," Percival answered as the footsteps grew closer.

"Won't be long now." Paddy's voice shook as he spoke.

"Wait up!" The plea drifted up the stairs.

Percival turned when he heard Paddy let out a relieved sigh.

"It's Tommy," Paddy said to Percival's unasked question. "The twins are probably with him."

"Who's chasing you guys?" one of the twins asked as they came into view.

"We thought you were." Paddy laughed.

"We saw you running and thought there was trouble, so we figured we'd come help," the boy's mirror replied.

"You didn't see anyone following us?" Paddy asked.

Tommy grinned. "Way youse was running, no one could have caught you even if they tried. We only found you 'cause we know'd which way you was a going. Knew you'd be jumpin' roofs the rest of the way. Who ya running from anyhow?"

"We thought we saw Slim's landlord a coming," Paddy lied.

The twins looked at Percival with newfound curiosity. One of the boys cocked his head. "Slim? I thought your name was..."

"It's Slim," Paddy said, cutting the boy off.

"Fits him," the other twin replied.

"Fits him just fine," Tommy said, wiping sweat from his brow. "I figured you'd be running from your pop. I heard him yelling at you this morning. Heck, I think the whole building heard him. What'd you go and do to get him all riled like that?"

"I didn't do nothing," Paddy said, starting up the stairs.

"Well, you'd better stick a pillow down yer pants afor you get home. Your brother said yer pop gonna lay into you the minute he sees ya."

"He ain't going to see me," Paddy said once they reached the rooftop.

"He gonna see you sumtime," Tommy argued.

"Nope, my pop's done giving me whoopings, on account

of I'm not going home," Paddy replied.

"You're not?" both twins said at once.

"Nope. I'm a man now. Just like my pal Slim here."

"I'm a man?" Percival asked.

"Sure you are. You pay a man's rent, don't you?" Paddy said in return.

Percival was shocked. *Is that all it takes to be a man?* "Yeah, but that's only because my momma's not here to pay it."

"Don't matter the reason. Just matters the doing. You have man responsibilities, that makes you a man."

"Where'd you git dough to pay?" Tommy asked.

"Big Joe gave it to me?" Percival said, knowing it was only half true.

Tommy gasped. "Big Joe? You mean the…"

"Leave it be, Tommy. Big Joe is Slim's friend," Paddy warned.

"Friends?" Tommy said, ignoring Paddy's warning. "Why ya wanta be friends with someone who kilt a man, much less a…"

Percival had Tommy pressed against the stairwell wall before he could finish the sentence. "He's not a killer. He's not any of the things people say he is. Big Joe's my friend, see. I'll not have you talking bad about him. Got it?"

"Sure, Slim, whatever ya say," Tommy sputtered.

Percival released him then turned to the twins, who each gave a nod of their own. Satisfied, he waited for them to take the lead then followed them up the stairs.

***

"This is it?" Paddy asked when Slim opened the door. "Why, you don't even have a kitchen. How'd your momma cook your supper?"

Percival's hand hovered over the light switch, debating

turning it on. It was late and highly unlikely the landlord would stop by. Making the decision, he lifted the switch. "She brought me food."

"Didn't she know how to cook?"

"Sure she did. My momma was a fine cook. I used to help her when we had a kitchen. She even has a book where she wrote down all her recipes." Percival went to the side table, picked up the book, and thumbed through it, showing Paddy his mother's notes in the margins.

Paddy glanced at the pages then sat on the edge of the bed. "At least you have a proper bed," Paddy said, testing its soundness.

"That's my momma's bed," Percival said evenly.

Paddy stopped bouncing and looked around the room. "Where do you sleep?"

"On a pallet of blankets under the window. It's cooler over there."

Paddy leaned back on the bed. "It seems a shame to sleep on the floor when there's a perfectly good bed right here."

Percival knew his friend was right. He'd had the same internal conversation each night before finally settling onto the floor. "Go ahead if you want."

Paddy sat up and stared unblinking as if he didn't believe him. "You want me to sleep in the bed?"

"No, but I'll not stop you." Percival pressed his mother's book to his chest briefly before returning it to the table and opening the closet door to retrieve the pile of blankets he used for his pallet.

Paddy heaved a wistful sigh before rising from the bed and helping Percival spread the blankets on the floor under the window. "I've never slept in a real bed before. I guess there's no need to start now."

Percival walked the short distance, turned off the overhead

light, then returned to the window and lowered to the floor. He turned, lying on the pallet so that only his head was directly under the window. Paddy took a position opposite him, positioning himself under the window so that their heads nearly touched. Percival rolled slightly so he could see a few stars in the darkened sky. "I had a real bed before we moved here. Had my own room too."

Paddy yawned. "Why'd you move?"

"Had to when my papa died," Percival said then produced a yawn of his own. He and his mother had often traded yawns. He smiled at the memory.

"How'd he die?"

The smile faded. "Jumped from the roof. Big Joe says my papa was brave for what he'd done on account of most men don't have the courage to go through with it."

"You were thinking of jumping today." Paddy grew silent as if waiting for a reply. When Percival didn't answer, he spoke again. "Are you brave, Slim?"

"No. I can't do what my papa did."

"I don't want to speak ill against your friend, but I think it takes more courage not to jump," Paddy said softly.

"You think so?"

"Well, if you jump, your pain is gone the moment you hit the ground. But if you stay, then you have to face your pain a lot longer. I think that makes a fellow who chooses to stay a lot stronger."

Funny, he didn't feel strong. He felt sad and weak. Percival closed his eyes. Just as he was drifting off to sleep, he opened them once more, thinking to ask Paddy how he knew so much about pain. Just as he was about to pose the question, Paddy's soft snores let him know his friend was already asleep. He lay there for a while staring out the window and listening to Paddy's easy breathing. He didn't know if staying made him weak or strong, but he sure was grateful not to have to endure another night alone in a room that was so full of memories.

Chapter Fifteen

"Slim, wake up. Someone's fiddling with the door," Paddy said, shaking him awake.

Percival was up in an instant, standing in front of the door, fists at the ready. The door squeaked open, and the landlord's bloated face snaked through the opening.

"Where's your ma, boy?" His words floated into the room, reeking of stale alcohol.

"She's at work," Percival lied.

"That ain't how I hear it," he said, pushing the door open. The man was grossly overweight, and bubbles of saliva pooled in the corners of his mouth whenever he spoke. "I hear you've been giving my nephew Milo a hard time."

"Milo." The name escaped before Percival could stop it.

"That's right. He's my nephew. Ain't right to be messing with a man's family," the landlord said, breaching the doorway. "Now tell me where your momma really is."

"She's at work," Percival repeated.

"You wouldn't be lying to me now, would you, boy?" the landlord said, stepping closer.

Percival swallowed.

"The way Milo tells it, she's dead and has been that way for some time."

"What's it matter to you? You got your rent," Percival said, trying to sound braver than he felt. Even though he knew how to throw a punch, he was smart enough to know he was no match for a man of this size.

"It matters on account of I don't rent to no kids." He moved around the small space as if looking for something.

"You've no right to be in here," Percival said as the man rounded the bed. It was only a matter of time before he discovered Paddy, who'd rolled under the bed to prevent detection.

"My building," he replied, then lifted the edge of the mattress. Frowning, he lifted the box springs, pushing them against the wall and exposing Paddy's hiding place. The landlord bent and clamped his hand around the back of Paddy's neck, lifting him high enough so that the boy's feet barely scraped the floor. Paddy flailed his arms and legs, but the man managed to hold him at arm's length, batting his hands away whenever they came close to scratching his arms.

Percival took a step forward, and the man looked to the window and narrowed his eyes. "Take another step, and this one goes out the window."

Judging from the sneer on the man's face, Percival thought he meant what he said. Percival took a step back. The landlord lowered Paddy to the floor but held firm to the back of his neck and turned his attention to Percival. "Where's the loot, kid?"

Loot? Was the man here to rob him? "I already paid you the rent for this month."

"I'm not looking for a measly ten dollars. I want the jewelry. I know what kind of dame your ma was. Lookers like that always have jewelry. Now tell me where it is, or the boy goes out the window."

The man was right. His mother did have jewelry. But not the kind the man was looking for. Sure, men had given her baubles, but his mother had always sold them to add to the money in her can. The only thing she'd kept was a necklace belonging to her grandmother, given to her by her mother on her wedding day, and the ring she'd used to wed his father. The landlord was not getting those. Percival shook his head, and Paddy's eyes grew wide with fear.

True to his word, the landlord dragged Paddy to the open window, pushed him through the opening, and held the screaming boy as he squirmed for something to grab hold of.

Tears pooled in Percival's eyes as he struggled with what to do. If he said no, Paddy would surely die. If he said yes, he would lose the two things that had meant the most to his mother.

"Tell me, or I let him die," the man growled.

Not wishing to be responsible for his friend's death, Percival pointed a trembling finger toward the cabinet where he'd placed the jewels.

The landlord smiled and pulled Paddy toward the windowsill. As soon as Paddy clutched hold of the sill, he let go. Percival raced to help his friend, but as he neared, the landlord pushed him into the wall. Caught off guard, Percival lost the upper hand, and the man hovered over him. "Don't you get up, or you'll be lying on the sidewalk with your friend."

Percival looked toward the window. Paddy was gone. Guilt washed over him. If only he'd given the man what he'd come for when he first asked, his friend would still be alive. Fresh tears rolled down his face as the landlord opened the cabinet and pulled out the cup that held the necklace that had once been laced around his mother's neck. As he scooped up the ring that once encircled her finger, something in Percival snapped. He scrambled to his feet and, knowing his fists would have little effect on the large man, focused his aim much lower. He delivered a solid uppercut. The landlord let out an *ooph* of air, dropped the jewelry, and toppled to the ground, clutching his own family jewels.

Percival gathered his mother's jewelry and stepped around the still groaning man to grab the book that held his mother's writings along with the money he'd stashed there the night before. He ran from the room and was halfway down the first flight of stairs when he changed his mind and ran to the roof, deciding he couldn't stomach seeing his friend spattered on the street.

As he pushed open the door to the rooftop, tears spilled from his eyes like rain. Not only had he lost his friend, but he had forgotten to bring the number Big Joe had given him in case he needed to call for help. For the second time in his short life, he was truly alone. No friends to show him the way and no roof to cover his head. He shrank to his knees, clutching his mother's belongings to his chest. A part of him knew he was in danger of being found, but grief kept him planted in place as his tears developed into long, mournful sobs.

Percival felt something touch his shoulder and scrambled across the roof like a spider.

"Hey, Slim, I didn't mean to scare ya."

Percival recognized the voice and spun around in awed disbelief. "Paddy?"

"In the flesh." The boy grinned.

"But you're supposed to be dead," Percival whispered.

"Says who?"

"Says me. Are you really a leprechaun, then?"

"Again with that? No, I'm not a leprechaun."

"Then how?"

"I climbed up the side of the building." Paddy grinned.

Percival wanted to call the boy a liar, but how else could he explain his being alive? "Weren't you scared?"

"Only of what that man was going to do to me if I stayed. Besides, I do it all the time."

"Get thrown out of windows?"

"No, ya dope, climb buildings. We all do it, Tommy and the twins, though not so much since they are almost too small to reach some of the footholds. But lots of us kids do it, all hoping to be famous like the Human Fly."

"You want to be a fly?" Percival was getting more confused by the moment.

"Not a fly, the Human Fly. Don't tell me you never heard of him?"

Percival shook his head.

"His real name's Harry Gardiner, but they call him the Human Fly. He goes all around the world buildering. That's what they call us folk that climb buildings. Course, the most I've ever climbed is five stories, but not the Human Fly. That guy climbs skyscrapers. There's a guy around here named George who's pretty good. I think he's gonna take Harry."

"Take him where?"

"He's going to beat his record. That's what he says anyway. Hey, how'd you get away?"

"I hit the guy," Percival said and felt his face grow red.

Paddy blinked his surprise. "You must have clocked the guy pretty hard if you were able to get away."

"Caught him with an uppercut," Percival said, bringing his fist up in demonstration.

"No kidding? And you were able to clock him in the jaw?"

"Not exactly," Percival said and stared at the area where the punch landed. From an early age, most boys knew what it felt like to get hit below the belt. Paddy obviously had some experience in the area, as he shifted uncomfortably and blew out a long whistle.

"So if you know the man's going to have it out for you, why didn't you get outta here?"

"I didn't know where else to go. I couldn't go to the street." Percival's legs beat a drum underneath him.

"Why not?"

"On account of I thought you to be lying on the street, and

I'd know it was me who put you there."

"I can't say I blame ya. I wouldn't want to turn over my loot neither," Paddy said, pushing at the ground with his foot.

"It wasn't the loot. It was the memories. Those things belonged to my momma. But in the end, he almost got them anyway," Percival said.

Paddy lifted his head. "Almost?"

"Yep," Percival said, patting his pants pocket.

Paddy rocked back on his heels. "Then I expect you owe me a debt of gratitude."

"I do?"

"Sure, on account of I helped you keep your momma's jewelry."

"You did?"

"Course I did. I kept you from jumping off the roof, didn't I? If you would've jumped, your landlord would have cleared out your room and taken the jewels. The way I see it, I saved you and your momma's jewels."

His friend had a point. "How much do I owe you?"

"I don't want your money," Paddy said, waving him off.

"What do you want?"

"I think I'd like to hold on to that in case I need something from you later. Right now, we have bigger problems. I can't go home, and you don't have a home, so we'd better find us a place to spend the night. What's wrong?"

"I thought I'd stay here," Percival answered.

"We can't stay here. It's too dangerous. The landlord will be looking for you. He's probably already sent Milo to find ya."

"I ain't scared of Milo. He's scared of me. I fixed him a good one the other day."

"That explains it."

"Explains what?"

"If he was sore at ya, that's why he told your landlord about your momma. Milo and his boys prefer the rooftops, so best thing we can do is go to the ground and get Tommy and the twins to help us."

"Help us what?"

"Put Milo in his place, of course."

"Big Joe said I shouldn't go looking for trouble."

"We ain't looking for trouble. Trouble found you. Now, I could just walk away on account of they think I'm already dead, but I'm willing to stay and help you. You'd like that, wouldn't you?"

Percival nodded his head.

"If we don't let Milo know we mean business, then he'll make big trouble for you. You don't want that, do you?"

Percival shook his head.

"We don't have to pound on him none. We just have to make him think we're ready to pound on him if he don't leave you alone."

"Aren't you worried about him making trouble for you?" Percival asked.

"Yep, I'm taking a big risk. You know why?"

"Why?"

"Cause we're pals, you and me. I wouldn't let you face Milo alone any more than you'd let the landlord drop me out the window. Well, you almost did, but you came through." Paddy looked from side to side then leaned in close. "Now, Milo, he'll be surprised. You see, if you were to show up by yourself, he would send one of the boys to go get his uncle. But if Tommy, the twins, and me are with you, then he'll know you mean business."

"I don't know. Big Joe said—"

"Big Joe's not here," Paddy interrupted. "Besides, didn't Big Joe tell you that if trouble came looking for you to do something about it?"

"How'd you know that?" Percival asked, scratching his head.

"Because Big Joe's smart, and that's the smart thing to do."

Percival couldn't believe his luck. Not only was Paddy willing to help make sure Milo and the others didn't bother him, but he talked a lot like Big Joe. And just like a true friend, Paddy was willing to put himself at risk just to help him. Percival smiled.

"So, it's a deal?" Paddy asked, spitting into his palm. "Now you do the same."

Percival swished and spat into his hand as he just watched Paddy do. "Now what?"

"We shake on it, and that makes us blood brothers. Some people become blood brothers by cutting their hands, but we'll use spit 'cause I don't have a knife."

As Percival shook hands with Paddy, he wondered at the events of the day. He'd gone from thinking he'd lost his friend to gaining a brother. While he no longer had a place to live, he wouldn't have to make his way in the world alone. The best part was he didn't even have to cut his hand.

Chapter Sixteen

Late August, 1916

"I'm hungry," one of the twins grumbled.

"We're all hungry," Paddy said, sliding his eyes in Percival's direction.

Percival knew what the boy wanted; he and Paddy had already had several private discussions on the matter. Paddy thought since Percival had been willing to give the landlord his mother's jewelry to prevent the man from sending him plummeting to the ground, that he should be willing to sell them to help feed them all. Percival disagreed. While he and the boys were indeed hungry, they were not yet to the point of desperation, at least not that desperate. He stood his ground, shaking his head in response to the unasked question.

Paddy sighed and turned toward the others. "We'll have our supper; we just have to go fishing for dimes."

"I saw someone else by the grates earlier," Tommy replied.

"Then we'll go somewhere else. It's time we moved on anyhow. Been two weeks and not a sign of Milo and his gang." Paddy started walking. "Tells me we don't have to worry about him no more."

The twins looked at Tommy, who merely shrugged and fell into step behind Paddy. Not having anywhere else to go, Percival did the same.

"But we always fish around here," one of the twins said, tugging on Paddy's shirt.

Paddy whirled on the boy. "You want to stay, then stay. But

I say we go and be done with this place!"

The twin's lip began to quiver, and Paddy looked to Percival and the others to chime in. When they didn't, he softened his approach. "It's not safe for us on this side of town. We can't even jump the roofs without worrying if Milo and his friends are going to come after us."

"You said he would protect us," Tommy said, looking at Percival. "Said that's the reason you asked him to come along. That and on account of he had money."

"I asked him to come because he had no place else to go," Paddy countered.

"But you said…"

"He's with us, and that's the end of it," Paddy said, glaring at Tommy.

"It's not the end of it. We can't even find enough for us," Tommy argued.

Percival's legs showed his agitation, and he started walking to ease the jitters. He'd only gone a few steps when he saw a boy on the opposite side of the street. The boy was close to Paddy in height, but the thing that caught Percival's eye was the way he moved in and out of the crowd, as if he didn't have a care in the world. The boy inched up beside a man and dipped his hand into the man's pants, retrieving his wallet without as much as a sideways glance. A few steps later, he relieved a woman of her coin purse. His mother had told him to be wary of such people, but he'd never witnessed one in action. Unlike Paddy and his friends, the boy was well-dressed and fit in with the folks around him. Fascinated by the kid's audacity, Percival followed, staying back so as to remain unnoticed. They'd walked nearly two blocks when the boy removed his empty hand from a man's pocket and retreated into a nearby alleyway.

Percival scanned the crowd to see what had captured the boy's attention and got his answer. *Milo!* Surely he was mistaken, as the boy had appeared so self-assured. He scanned the crowd for another threat. While there were scores of people hurrying to their destinations, nothing seemed amiss. Had the boy simply got his fill of picking pockets? Percival didn't think so. Not given the ripe atmosphere for someone who knew what they were doing. Milo stepped into the street and skirted his way around traffic. As he neared the side of the street where Percival stood just out of view, he was joined by several other boys. Milo nodded his head toward the alley, and the boys took off in a run with Milo close on their heels. So, he hadn't been mistaken. Percival knew it was reckless to follow, but he also knew what it was like to be outnumbered, and this boy was undoubtedly in for a beating if Milo and his gang caught up with him. He wasn't sure what it was about the boy that pulled him forward, but he found himself drawn into the alley, picking his way carefully around barrels and garbage, all the while praying he could sneak in undetected.

"Slim, where the devil are ya going?" Paddy's voice rang out when he was near the end.

Percival stepped out of the shadow and put a finger to his lips to silence the boy.

"What is it?" Paddy whispered when he and the others caught up.

"Milo," Percival said and watched their eyes grow wide.

"What ya doing following him?" Tommy looked like a rabbit making ready to run.

"They're up to no good," Percival whispered.

"They're always up to no good," Paddy replied. "Let's get out of here."

Percival blinked his confusion. "What do you mean get out of here? We've been looking for them all week."

"We didn't actually mean to find him," one of the twins explained. "Paddy said how you can fight. He wanted to make sure Milo didn't pound on us if he saw us."

"Why would Milo pound on you?"

"Milo pounds on all the kids," the other twin replied.

"Except you." Tommy grinned. "It's all over the streets how you whooped him. Ain't that right, Paddy?"

Before Paddy could answer, shouts filled the air.

"Sounds like Milo and his friends found who they were looking for," one of the twins gulped.

"Where you going, Slim?" Paddy asked when Percival started toward the noise.

"To help."

Paddy caught him by the arm. "What's going on back there ain't our business."

"That boy wasn't no bigger than you," Percival said, pulling his arm free. "Those boys are likely to hurt him bad. What happened to all of us standing up to Milo?"

Paddy gulped and kicked the dirt with the toe of his shoe. "I don't know, Slim. They sound pretty worked up."

Percival thought about what Big Joe had said about not looking for trouble, then considered what Paddy had said about trouble finding him. He recalled the look on the landlord's face when he said Milo had told him about Percival's mother being dead. He could almost picture the look that would have been on the boy's face when he delivered the news—gloating in the telling as if his mother's demise were something to be happy about. His legs showed the anger that now coursed through his body. Paddy and the boys might be scared of Milo and his gang, but he had a score to settle. He turned, ignoring calls from his new friends. The second he rounded the corner, he saw the reason for the ruckus. Milo and his boys had formed a circle around the boy, who had his hands balled into fists, daring the boys to come any closer. He had to give it to the kid. He had grit. A lot more than the friends he'd just left. Still, spunk wasn't going to keep him from being pummeled. Percival counted six boys, including Milo. He doubted he could take them all, but if he could keep moving, he had a chance at getting a few licks in before they overtook him. Besides, there was only one he really cared about.

"Milo!" The second he got their attention, the boys lost interest in their prey and focused on him instead. Percival pointed at Milo. "My beef is with you."

Milo laughed. "You'll have to get through them first."

Percival scanned the group, singling out the biggest kid. According to Big Joe, if he took out the boy the group thought to be the strongest, the others would scurry away like rats caught in the light. The boy rushed forward, and Percival sent him to the ground with a single blow to the kid's jaw. Percival looked to the group once more and resisted a smile. True to Big Joe's words, the others had lost their bravado, each looking nervously at the next for directions.

"Who's next?" Percival asked, bouncing around with his fists in front of his chest.

"Take him, Mic," Milo said, pushing the boy forward.

Percival quickly moved out the way. He danced from side to side, looking at the boy, who was a good head shorter than himself. "I don't want to hit ya, but I will."

"Now, Mic," Milo encouraged.

Mic sprang forward, and Percival sent him to the ground next to the first guy. Milo nodded his chin again, and two boys stepped forward. Before the boys could attack, the kid they'd been harassing pushed past and stood at Percival's side. Percival smiled. The boy might be small, but he wasn't a coward. It saddened him that the same could not be said for his friends.

Percival leaned in for the boy to hear. "Aim for his nose."

The boy nodded and, to Percival's surprise, crooked a

finger, beckoning the boys forward. The boys' eyes went wide, and they raced off in opposite directions. Laughter filled the air. Percival and his new companion smiled at seeing Paddy, Tommy, and the twins a few feet behind them, their fists at the ready. Percival turned back in Milo's direction, took a step forward, and Milo bolted like a rabbit.

"You look like you enjoyed that," Paddy said, coming up behind him.

Maybe a little. "Not at all," Percival replied.

"You didn't even get to punch Milo, and you're smiling," Paddy said, looking at the kids who were starting to pick themselves off the ground. "So you must have enjoyed it a little."

"Maybe a little," Percival admitted.

"What about Milo?" Paddy said, looking after the boy.

"That's the second time I disgraced him in front of his friends. He won't bother us again."

"How can you be so sure?"

"I can't. But if he does, we'll take care of him together." Percival lowered his eyes. "I thought..."

"That I'm a coward? I am, but I figured if that boy could stand with you, then so could we. Who is he anyhow?"

Before Percival could answer, the first guy he'd punched approached, hat in hand. He looked over Paddy and the others before directing his comments to Percival. "If you're looking for people to be in your gang, the boys and I wanna join ya."

Paddy coughed, and Percival ignored him. "I don't have a gang. These boys are my friends."

"All the same, I wanted to let you know that me and the boys don't have any beef with you." He jerked his chin toward the others, and the boys scrambled to their feet, following at a close distance.

"Why'd you send them away for?" Paddy's voice showed

his disappointment.

"I don't need a gang," Percival replied.

"Boy, Slim, you sure can be a dope," Paddy said, shaking his head. "You're living on the streets now. You need all the help you can get."

The boy that had stood by his side waved him over. "Where'd you learn to throw a punch like that?" he asked when Percival approached.

"A friend," Percival answered.

The kid looked at Paddy, and Percival laughed. "A different friend."

The kid kicked at the dirt with his shoe. "Knowing how to throw a punch like that sure could come in handy. I'd pay good money if you'd be willing to show me how."

Percival looked the boy over. Unlike Paddy and the boys, this kid looked as if he had a family to care for him. He was clean, and his clothes looked brand new. "Maybe your pop should teach you how to fight."

The boy narrowed his eyes. "My papa's dead. Serves him right since he killed my momma."

Percival felt instant regret and lowered his eyes.

"So you'll do it, then? Teach me how to throw a punch?" the boy asked hopefully.

"I'll teach you."

The boy pulled a wallet out of his pocket. "How much is it going to cost me?"

Percival waved him off, heard an audible sigh, and knew without looking it was Paddy. "Put that away."

"Ah, I should have known you were putting me on," the boy grumbled.

"I'm not, but a friend told me not to give something without asking for something in return."

"He tried to pay you, ya dope," Paddy said, coming up

beside him.

"I don't want his money," Percival replied.

"I do," Paddy said. He reached for the wallet, and the boy slapped his hand away. Not deterred by a boy of his size, Paddy doubled his fist.

The boy matched his stance, and Percival stepped between the two. "Stop it, the both of you."

"Who put you in charge?" Paddy fumed.

"I'm not in charge of nothing, but if I'm going to teach you both to fight, then you'll have to listen to me."

"Will you teach us too?" the twins asked, stepping up.

"Me too," Tommy asked.

"I'll teach him, and everyone can watch. That way, you'll learn too," Percival said.

"Why you going to go and teach him for?" Paddy asked.

"On account of he's going to teach us something in return."

"He is?" Paddy and the others asked at once.

"I am?" The boy seemed just as surprised as the others.

"You're going to show us how to dip pockets."

The kid rocked back on his heels. "Who said I know how to dip pockets?"

"I did. I saw you doing it just before you ran from Milo and his pals. I saw you," Percival repeated when the boy started to protest.

"You got a sharp eye," he said, looking Percival over. "Do those legs ever stop?"

"Not for long."

"Didn't think so. Might be a problem with the dipping, but we'll try."

"Good," Percival said. "This is Paddy, Tommy, and the twins."

"Ain't they got names?"

"They do, but we just call them the twins since no one can

tell em apart. My name's Percival, but my friends call me Slim."

The boy took off his cap, ran a hand through his hair, and then returned the cap to his head. "My name's Tobias, but my friends call me Mouse. You're a real smart fellow, Slim. I think we're gonna get along just fine."

Chapter Seventeen

Percival and the boys spent the next few weeks following Mouse around and learning the basics of dipping pockets. While Paddy had been upset when Percival had first declined Mouse's monetary offer, even he soon realized the value of being able to fish for something more than dimes. Though Paddy and the boys could ease through a crowd unnoticed, Percival was not so adept, as his legs were quick to give him away.

Percival slid up next to his mark, a stocky man wearing an expensive suit who'd just returned his wallet to his hip pocket. As Percival matched the man's pace, his legs moved from side to side as if he were trying to keep steady on heavy seas. Just as Percival decided to make his move, the man blew out a disgusted huff and moved away. He knew the others were watching and didn't want to end another day empty-handed, so he surveyed the crowd for a new mark. He spied a woman of formidable size, deciding she was in no shape to run after him if she caught him rooting through her purse. He followed at a distance for several moments before moving in to make the dip.

"Oh, you poor thing, what on earth is the matter with your legs?" the woman asked just as his hand neared her purse.

"I got smashed in the head," Percival said, jerking his hand away.

The lady slapped her palm to her chest. "Oh for heaven's sake, are you afflicted, then?"

"Afflicted?"

"Crippled? Do your legs not work properly?" the woman said through heavy breaths.

"They work alright enough. I can walk and run." *It just makes it hard to dip pockets.* He kept that part to himself.

"Can you not work, then?"

"Work?" *He didn't think of that.* "Why, I never tried."

"And just why aren't you in school?"

What's with all the questions. "I've never been to school."

"Never been? My heavens, where are your parents?"

"Dead, ma'am." The woman frowned, and he decided to take Mouse's advice and play on her emotions. Sucking his stomach in, he managed a tear. "Both of them. I've been out on my own for weeks. I'm mighty hungry."

The woman gasped. "My sister told me about you."

Percival frowned. "About me?"

"Your kind," the woman corrected.

"My kind?"

"Homeless. Why, I came into the city just today; traveled all the way from Nebraska for a visit. It was terribly warm in Sara's, that's my sister, apartment. I told her I was going to go out for some fresh air. Though truth be told, I'm having a mighty hard time finding anything fresh about the air here in the city. I'm a country girl myself. We don't see a lot of motorcars where I live."

"You don't?"

"Oh no, we're simple folk mostly, but some in our town have motorcars. We might not have many cars, but our houses have windows. And big yards covered with tall trees that have branches so large, you can sit in the shade underneath. Why, I told my sister that just today. Her being so smart and all telling me her Joshua, that's her husband, you know. Well, Sara, she was going on about Joshua this and Joshua that and how he was a good provider. Well, I knew she was going on because I don't have me a man, and well, I got tired of hearing her boast, and that's when I said it."

"Said what?" Percival asked when the woman finally stopped to catch her breath.

"Told her if he was such a good provider, why couldn't he provide her with a house with decent windows. Why, a lady can't gather a breath in a room like that. And I told her so too."

"Do you have curtains?" Percival asked.

"What?"

"On your windows? My momma always said she wanted a house full of windows, and each of those windows would have curtains."

"Oh yes, I have beautiful curtains. Made them myself, I did. With my own hands." The woman beamed.

Percival sighed. "I wish my momma would have gotten her curtains."

"What happened to your momma?" the woman asked, wringing her hands.

"I don't really like talking about it," Percival said, lowering his eyes.

"No, I suppose you wouldn't," the woman agreed. She pulled out a hand fan, waving it frantically in front of her face. "My, but it is dreadfully hot out today, isn't it?"

"Yes, ma'am," Percival agreed.

"Why, I don't know how people manage here in the city, all these buildings blocking the breeze. And all these people, why, I've had people bumping into me all morning."

"You might want to check your coin purse," Percival said, nodding at the woman's purse, which dangled from the crook of her arm.

The woman blinked her confusion. "Why, whatever for?"

"Dippers."

"Dippers?"

"Pickpockets, ma'am."

She clutched her chest once more. "My heavens, I completely forgot what my sister said. Do you think there are some in the crowd?"

"Yes, ma'am. They are probably right under your nose." Percival said, resisting a smile.

Her eyes darted from side to side as she clutched her purse to her large bosom and peered inside. Her eyes grew wide. "It's gone."

"What's gone?"

"Why, my sister's coin purse. The one she insisted I put inside my purse when I hid mine in my inner pocket. The jokes on them, you know."

No, he didn't know. "How so?"

The woman leaned close and kept her voice low. "My sister may be rowdy, but she's cunning. She told me about pickpockets and insisted I hide my coin purse in my inside pocket. Since I'm from the country, she thinks that I'm simple-minded, but she forgets she and I have the same blood. Beings we're sisters and all. Well, I'm not, simple-minded that is, but I guess I'm still no match for the varmint who stole my sister's coin purse. And right under my nose at that."

"What's a varmint?" Percival asked, cocking his head.

The woman laughed a jolly laugh. "It's what us country folk call rats and coons and just about any critter we don't have a use for. They are good for nothing and will steal you blind. Ought to be shot, the lot of em."

A varmint? Is that what I've turned in to? I can't even steal properly, so I must be worse than a varmint. Even if I had managed to get hold of her purse, it would have been the wrong one. It's true; I'm the worst of the varmints.

"Oh, my, but your legs are fidgeting. Are you sure they don't pain you none?"

Percival shook his head. "No, ma'am. Not so much." *The only pain I have is the ache in my heart at the moment.*

"You look so sad all of a sudden. I do wish I could take you home with me. No, Sara wouldn't approve." The woman frowned. "Well, she can't stop me from giving you something."

"She can't?"

"No, my money is mine to do with as I please." She looked from side to side before pulling a small coin purse from the waistband of her skirt. Dipping two fingers inside, she withdrew a bill, placing it solidly into Percival's palm.

"This should keep you for a few days. Make sure to get yourself a decent meal."

Percival struggled with his conscience. While he'd been more than ready to steal from the stranger, the thought of accepting money from a woman who'd been nothing but nice to him seemed wrong.

"Why, you look as if you are about to cry," she said, lifting his chin. "Tell Miss Virginia what's troubling you."

"No trouble," Percival lied. "Just appreciate your kindness."

"Yes, well, it's the least I can do now, isn't it? A boy of your age living on the streets."

Percival looked past the woman and saw Paddy, Mouse, and the others inching closer to where he and the woman stood. If any of them saw what she had in her hand, they'd see that it did not return home with her. He pushed his guilt aside and smiled at the woman. "You best be putting that coin purse away before someone sees it."

"Oh, my. There I go again, forgetting my surroundings." She hastily tucked the purse into her waistband. "You're such a nice fellow. A boy to make a mother proud, to be sure."

"Yes, ma'am," Percival said, not believing it. He couldn't remember anything he'd done of late to make his momma proud. "I'd best be going."

"What? Oh yes, remember to eat some vegetables with your supper."

"Yes, ma'am," Percival said. He tucked the bill deep inside his front pocket then pushed through the crowd to where his friends were standing.

"Boy, Slim, we were getting worried," Paddy said, handing him his cloth bag that held all his belongings. "What did the woman talk about for so long?"

"She was sad that I was living on the streets." Percival tied the bag around his waist. "I guess she's never seen a kid living on the streets before."

"She must not get out of the house much. There are kids all over the place. We thought she was gonna rat ya out," Paddy said.

"Rat me out?"

Tommy nodded. "She caught ya, didn't she?"

Percival shook his head. "I didn't steal anything."

"Oh." The disappointment on Paddy's face was evident.

"But she gave me this," Percival said, producing the bill Virginia had given him. "On account of I told her I was hungry."

Paddy blew out a long whistle. "You mean to tell me all we have to do is give a sap story, and people will hand over the loot?"

"It works sometimes," Mouse agreed. "Mostly with the dames. The men aren't so gullible."

"She must be loaded to have given you this," Paddy said, holding it up to the sun. "Come on, boys, let's go see if we can get her coin purse."

"NO!" Percival shouted. His friends turned, and he lowered his voice. "Some chump has already taken everything; this was all she had left."

"Why'd she give it to you if it was all she had?" one of the twins asked, scratching his head.

"Maybe 'cause she had more at home." Percival relaxed when the boys seemed satisfied with his answer.

"Too bad we don't know where that is," Paddy said, heaving a sigh. "At least it's enough to pay for a room at the Lodging House tonight."

Paddy started walking, and the others fell in behind him.

Mouse sidled up beside Percival and kept his voice low. "They bought it. But tell me something. How come you didn't tell them about the wad of dough the dame had in her waistband?"

It didn't surprise Percival that Mouse had seen the loot. The boy didn't seem to miss much of anything. Still, he was glad Mouse hadn't ratted him out to his friends. He shrugged his shoulders. "She was nice to me."

Mouse elbowed him slightly. "You missed your shot. Dames get all sappy and forget to pay attention. She would have been an easy mark."

"Mouse?" Percival hesitated.

"Yeah, Slim."

"I don't want to dip pockets no more."

"I know you don't like it, but we all have to pull our weight."

"I know," Percival said, trying unsuccessfully to still his legs.

"You'll get used to it. Sometimes you just have to build up your courage."

"I'm not a coward."

"I know you're not a coward. You proved that with Milo. You're just built differently."

"I'm not stupid."

"Never said you were. You're not a dope neither. Your

friend calls you that one more time, and I'll punch him in the nose," he said with a nod toward Paddy.

"Paddy's okay. He doesn't mean anything by it," Percival said.

"That's not the point. The thing is, we have enough people calling us names. It is not right when our so-called friends do it. I know those boys are your friends, but keep an eye on them. There's something about Red that rubs me the wrong way."

"Red? You mean Paddy?"

Mouse nodded. "Maybe it's just the color of his hair, but I've got a funny feeling about that boy."

"Aww, Paddy's okay."

"He said something about you guys staying in the Lodging House? Is that always where you stay?"

"No, we've been living in a shed on the roof next to my old building, but Paddy is worried the landlord might find us. Paddy thinks we need to find a new place. Said that if we had money, we could stay at the Lodging House."

"There's plenty of room where I stay, and you can save your money for when the weather cools. Then you'll really need a room."

Paddy stopped walking and waited for them to catch up. "You guys coming or what?"

"We're coming." Percival jerked his thumb toward Mouse. "He said we can stay at his place."

"You got a place?" Paddy said, wrinkling his nose. "Why didn't you tell us before?"

"I wanted to make sure I could trust you first." Mouse said, taking the lead. "A fellow don't just invite anyone into his home."

A short time later, the group stopped in front of the iron gates leading into St. Paul's Chapel.

Percival and the boys stared open-mouthed at the enormous

church looming on the other side of the black gates.

"You live here?" Tommy gulped.

"Around back," Mouse said, sneaking through the bushes. He led them to the graveyard, dropping to the ground in front of a massive monument. This is where I sleep. You boys can take your pick from the rest. Find a big one. It'll hide you if someone comes and will help keep the rain off you some."

"You live here!" Tommy repeated, only this time, his words held fear. "Aren't you afraid?"

"Nah, the caretaker doesn't mind as long as we don't make a mess of the place. Just make sure to stay out of view when people come to pay their respects to the dead."

"I weren't talking 'bout the caretaker," Tommy sputtered. "I hear'd there are ghosts in places like this."

"I ain't never seen a ghost," Mouse said, waving him off. "The way I hear it, if you don't speak ill of the dead, the dead won't bother you none."

Percival's mouth dropped open, and he quickly closed it once more. He placed his hands on the bag that rested at his hip, his hand tracing the outline of his mother's book. *I guess it's my book now. Don't cry. Please don't cry.* He swallowed to keep his composure. The last thing he needed was for his friends to think him a baby. "My momma used to say the same thing."

"I don't know." Paddy's voice was hesitant.

"Listen, I don't give a rat's tail where you go. The caretaker don't bother me, and I don't bother him. You just have to make sure you're back here before it gets dark. He closes the gates then, and if you aren't inside, you're in big trouble."

"Cause of the ghosts?" Tommy asked, sliding his eyes from side to side.

"No, I told you there ain't no ghosts, but there are gangs, lots of them. The caretaker shuts the gates at dark so they don't come in, not that they would."

"Why not?"

"Cause they're scared of the ghosts."

"You just said there aren't any ghosts," Paddy reminded him.

Mouse smiled. "I know that, and you know that, but they don't know that. Sometimes, when I hear them coming, I make some noises and watch them run away."

"Aren't you staying?" Slim asked when Paddy turned to leave.

"Na, I've got some things I need to do."

"Want me to come with you?"

"No, I'm going to go see my momma and my pop. He don't like me bringing strangers around the place."

"You make sure you're off the street before dark," Percival said.

"I thought I was the one who was teaching you about the streets." Paddy laughed. He lowered his voice. "You make sure to keep an eye on Tommy and the twins. I don't trust your new friend so much."

Percival thought to tell him that Mouse didn't like him so much either but decided against it, figuring doing so would only make Paddy mad. He didn't know why the boys had taken such a disliking to each other. It seemed to him a boy on the streets could use all the friends they could get. "I'll watch out for them."

"Good," Paddy said, racing toward the front gate without another word.

Paddy was hiding something, as he hadn't mentioned anything about his mother in weeks. *He's scared.* Percival ran toward the gate, thinking to catch his friend and ask him for the truth; however, when he looked out into the street, Paddy was nowhere in sight.

Chapter Eighteen

Cindy heard grunting as she passed by her mother's bedroom. Concerned, she knocked on the bedroom door.

"It's open," Linda said breathlessly.

Cindy opened the door, relieved to see that her mother's distress was simply because she was wrestling to change the bedsheets. "Want some help?"

"I want a maid," Linda grumbled.

"Will you settle for a schoolteacher?"

"Only if you're smart enough to get this on the bed without it slipping off the other end."

"I think I can manage," Cindy said, grabbing hold of the end.

"Your father used to help me," Linda mused.

"Dad?"

"That's the only father you have."

"I can't picture him changing the linens."

"Picture it or not, it happened. Every Sunday, we'd get up and strip the bed. Then he'd help me put the clean set on. He never did the laundry, not that he wouldn't have if I'd asked him." Linda smiled. "The man was colorblind; I didn't want him anywhere near my delicates."

"I didn't know Dad was colorblind."

"Sure was."

"I miss him," Cindy said softly.

"With all my heart." Linda agreed. "Hand me one of those pillowcases."

Cindy tossed one across the bed then picked up the other,

shimmying it onto the pillow.

"I agree with Mouse," Linda said, changing the subject.

"About?"

"Paddy. He's up to something."

"You know you're talking about Grandpa, don't you?"

"I do. I always knew there was something about the man."

"Why, on account of him having red hair?" Cindy laughed.

"His hair had long turned white by the time I married your dad. But it always seemed as if he was hiding something."

"Technically, he was. The journals in the attic," Cindy reminded her when Linda looked up.

"I think there's more to it."

"Of course there is. He's a kid. Kids are always hiding something," Cindy said, helping Linda pull the quilt over the bed.

"I think I'm going to go to the cemetery this morning. I want to put some fresh flowers on your dad and Frank's grave. Want to join me?" Linda asked, smoothing out a wrinkle.

No. Cindy kept the thought to herself. "How long before you want to leave?"

Linda added the decorative pillows then gave the bed a once-over. "I'm ready now if you are."

"Let me grab my purse."

It took more time to retrieve her purse, help search for misplaced keys, and for her mother to empty her bladder for a second time than it did to drive to Greenwood Cemetery, which lay just outside the edge of town. Linda turned in to the first entrance, skirted around a parked car, and stopped at the southwest corner. They visited Frank's stone first—Cindy stayed back to give her mother some alone time at her father's graveside.

"Well, since I'm here, I guess I should say something," Cindy said, staring at the newly etched stone. "Sorry I haven't been by much. I've started toward the facility so many times, only to stop after remembering you aren't there. I know you weren't much of a conversationalist in your later years, but it felt good knowing you were still around. Mom's doing much better. Her driving scares me, but I insist on driving when we go very far. She's still nagging me about those grandchildren. I never pictured myself as a mother, but lately…" She paused and checked to make sure her mother wasn't within earshot. "I don't know; something in me seems different since I've started reading the journals. I still don't have a desire to give birth, but I now find myself wondering what it would be like to be a mother. I've looked, you know. There are a lot of older children in need of homes. I like kids, and I think they like me. It's just a thought, but I'm considering it. Do me a favor. Don't tell Mom. I'd never hear the end of it."

"Who are you talking to?"

Cindy turned, surprised to see a small girl standing behind her. The child, who looked to be between six and eight, was wearing a pink dress and had her hair pulled back into a high ponytail. Cindy scanned the area, didn't see anyone else and, for the briefest of moments, wondered if the child were indeed real. *All that talk of ghosts in the cemetery.* "Where'd you come from?"

"Over there," the girl said, pointing. "Who were you talking to?"

Cindy smiled. "I was talking to my Uncle Frankie."

"I don't see anyone."

Cindy hesitated, then decided if the girl was in the cemetery, she should have some concept of death. "No, he died a couple months ago."

"Oh," the girl said, glancing at the headstone. "Are you sad?"

"Sometimes." Cindy didn't recognize the girl. If she went

to the local school, she should have at least seen her in the halls at one time or another. *Quit playing detective. It's not like you know every child in the school.* "Does your momma know you're here?"

The little girl shrugged.

"Maybe I should take you to see her." Cindy reached for the girl's hand.

The girl's eyes bugged. She jerked her hand back, her terrified screams filling the air as she backed away.

"It's okay. We don't have to hold hands. I'll just walk beside you to find your mom." Cindy said, trying to calm the child. Instead of comforting the girl, her words seemed to have the opposite effect as she ran off toward the middle of the cemetery, sobbing. *Great, now she'll go tell her mother I was trying to abduct her.* Not wishing to be misunderstood, Cindy followed the girl, not difficult to do since she was wailing loud enough to wake the dead. *So much for kids liking me.*

A man ran to meet the girl. Cindy watched as he scooped her up. The child threw her arms around his neck, burying her head in his broad shoulders. The way he glared at Cindy, she could only imagine what the child was telling him. Hoping to explain herself, she continued forward. "I'm afraid I may have upset her," she said as she approached.

"You think?" He'd pulled a cell phone from his pocket and began speaking into it, giving his location.

Not wishing to interrupt the man's call, she turned to leave.

"She's leaving," the man said into the phone.

She? "Me?"

"The cops are on the way. She said to tell you not to leave."

"Me?" Cindy repeated.

"Yes, you. You're the one that threatened to kill my daughter," he said, keeping the phone up to his ear.

"Excuse me?!" Even though she could hear sirens in the

distance, Cindy couldn't believe her ears. Before she could say anything else, her mother pulled up behind the parked car.

Linda blared the horn and waved for Cindy to come. When Cindy didn't respond, Linda lowered the window and stuck her head out. "Something's going on in town! Sounds like every cop in the county's involved. They're coming this way; hop in, and we'll follow them."

"Give it a moment, and you'll have a front-row seat," Cindy groaned.

***

"I've never been so humiliated in my life," Cindy said, draping her purse over the kitchen chair.

"How were you to know her mother was dead?" Linda said, closing the door.

Cindy watched her mother flip the deadbolt. "Mom, it's the middle of the day."

"Yep, but I don't want any reporters walking in on us."

"What reporters?"

"It's a small town. Once the paper gets word of this, they'll be beating on the door begging for the scoop. I can see the headline now: local teacher threatens to kill student."

"Oh, good grief. I didn't threaten to kill anyone."

"That ain't the way they'll tell it. They'll say you made her an offer she couldn't refuse," Linda snorted.

"You're enjoying this, aren't you?"

"Most excitement we've had in this town in ages. It looked like every cop in the county was there."

"Why wouldn't they be? They thought they were about to catch a killer. It's probably all over town by now," Cindy said, tapping her forehead against the door frame.

"It's a pity."

"That I'll be the laughingstock of the school?"

"No, that you made such a bad first impression. That guy

was pretty nice-looking."

He sure was. "I hadn't noticed."

"That's because you were too busy trying to convince the chief of police that you weren't trying to kill the kid."

"Very funny. He knew who I was. Heck, I have had half their kids in my class at one point or another."

"Lucky for you. That's probably the only thing that kept you out of jail. It kept me out of jail too."

Cindy raised her eyebrows. "Why would they take you?"

"For sneaking in a cake with a file in it. Can you imagine me going to prison at my age?"

"Mom?"

"Yes?"

"You have one heck of an imagination."

Linda smiled. "It keeps me young."

***

Sleeping in the cemetery wasn't as creepy as Percival had thought. On the contrary, knowing the gates were locked and that his friends, most of them anyway, were near put his mind at ease. He fell asleep the moment he closed his eyes. Sometime later, he woke to voices yelling in the distance. Opening his eyes, he pulled his legs to his chest in an effort to keep them still.

"It's one of the gangs," Mouse whispered. "They're close, but they won't be bothering us here."

"How do you know?"

"I hear them all the time."

"Don't you ever get scared?"

"I did at first," he admitted. "Now, not so much. Are you scared?"

"Of this place? No. Of what's outside those gates, you bet. How long have you been on your own, Mouse?"

"Too many days to count," he responded. "How about you,

144

Slim?"

"The same," Percival said. "Mouse?"

"Yeah, Slim?"

"Have you ever thought about running away? I don't mean from home or anything, 'cause we don't have no home to run away from."

"I know what you mean," Mouse said. "I went away once, but I came back."

"You did? Where'd you go?"

"I lived with a nice lady with a simple mind. I used to think that maybe I dreamed it, but she was real. But they took her away, and then they took me away. I'm back here now, and I guess this is where I'll stay. Besides, I've got me a girl now."

"A girl?" Percival said, pulling up on his elbow. "What are you going to do with a girl?"

"I'm going to marry her someday. She doesn't know it yet, but I will."

Percival rolled onto his back and stared up at the stairs. He'd never thought of getting married before. He'd never even kissed a girl besides his momma, and mostly, she was the one that did the kissing. He touched the place on his cheek that his mother had kissed the last time he'd seen her and sighed.

"You okay, Slim?"

"I was just thinking about my momma. She would always talk to me about the house she was going to buy someday. She wanted windows and curtains and a proper kitchen to cook in. I don't think I believed her."

"Was your momma a liar?"

"No."

"Then why didn't you believe her?"

"I don't know. I guess it just seemed like one of those stories she told. Maybe because some of the things she said seemed too good to be true. Then today, when I was talking to that lady in the street, she was telling me about her house, and she reminded me of my momma."

"That lady reminded you of your mom?"

"No, not the lady, the words she said. I closed my eyes for a moment, and it was like my momma was there. Then I thought about what I was getting ready to do, stealing from her and all, and knew my momma would be mighty sad if she knew. I can't do it, Mouse. I'll leave in the morning, but please don't make me go tonight."

Mouse fell silent for a bit before answering. "You don't have to go."

"I don't? But what about pulling my weight?"

"Remember when you asked if I was scared?"

"Yes."

"I lied. I go to sleep scared every night. Sometimes when the gangs wake me up, I'm too scared to go back to sleep."

"You don't seem scared."

"I'm not. Not tonight anyway."

"Why not?"

"I think it is because you're here. I've never had a friend before. Not ever."

Percival thought of Big Joe and how good it felt knowing the man was around after his mother died. He then recalled how Paddy kept him from jumping when he thought he didn't have anywhere else to go. He sighed. While he knew Big Joe could take care of himself, he worried about Paddy.

"Don't go telling the others I'm a scaredy baby," Mouse said, pulling him from his thoughts. "It wouldn't do for anyone to think I'm soft."

"I won't tell." The streets grew quiet. A short time later, Mouse's breathing showed he had gone back to sleep. A star fell across the darkened sky. Percival smiled and closed his eyes.

Chapter Nineteen

October 1916

Over the next couple of months, several other boys came to stay in the cemetery. It wasn't as if they were recruiting members—more like collecting strays along the way. On occasion, a kid would look out of place, and upon speaking to them, it became apparent they were in need of protection. That was where Percival came in. While the others grew adept at dipping pockets, Percival ended up serving the group in another way. It became his job to shadow the boys, watching over them to make sure they were safe as they collected what was needed in the form of money, food, and pilfering the occasional shirt or coat from an unattended clothesline. With Percival hanging back and surveying the area, the boys were free to concentrate on their marks without worrying about being nabbed by the police. If the boy doing the dipping was unfortunate enough to get nabbed, Percival would swoop in and create a diversion to allow the boy a chance to escape. Percival thrived in his new role, and the boys were happy to share a part of their earnings with him. They also gave a cut to Mouse, as he'd become the small group's unofficial leader.

Percival followed after the boys, who moved through the crowd filling their pockets. Percival spotted a police officer in the distance and whistled a warning to his charges, who casually changed course and joined him.

"It's getting near dusk. We might as well head back to the church," Percival said, scanning the sky. The boys muttered their agreement and fell into step beside him, chatting merrily as they told of the treasures they'd collected during the day. As they approached St. Joseph's Cathedral, Percival saw a boy standing next to the gate. At first, he thought Mouse had returned, as the kid was of equal size, until the boy removed his hat to reveal a mop of brilliant red hair. *Paddy!* Percival broke into a run, and the others followed.

"Where ya been?" Tommy asked the second they reached him.

"Around," Paddy said, scanning the group. "Where's Mouse?"

"He's doing his thing," one of the twins said. "Boy, will he be surprised to see you."

Paddy arched his eyebrows. "I'll bet."

"We best get inside," Percival said, searching the street. He looked at Paddy. "You coming?"

"May as well; I ain't got no place else to go." Paddy pushed away from the fence, waited for the others to go inside, then stepped up beside Percival. "I see you picked up some more boys. I thought you weren't interested in starting a gang."

"Not a gang," Percival replied.

"They seem to listen to you."

Percival shrugged. "No one else stepped up when Mouse is away."

"He away a lot, is he?"

"Sometimes," Percival replied.

"Where's he go?"

"Can you believe it? He's got him a dame."

"A dame?"

"A girl," Percival clarified.

"I know what a dame is, ya dope."

Percival snatched Paddy by the arm and pulled him back. "Listen, Paddy. I know you don't mean nothing by calling me that. But Mouse, see, he don't like when people disrespect us. He ain't going to be so happy about you coming back, but I can handle him, so you don't have to worry about that. But you got to stop with the names, or he'll boot ya right back out of here, see?"

"Yeah, I see how it is," Paddy said, jerking his arm away. "I thought we were pals."

"We are pals, Paddy. Don't you go getting all sore on me. You never liked Mouse no how and he don't like you none either, so it's best to play it straight and follow the rules. And the rules say show respect."

"So you're loyal to Mouse now, I get it." Paddy sounded hurt.

"I'm loyal to my friends," Percival said with a nod to all the boys who now sat in the middle of the graveyard sorting their loot. "Unless something's changed, that means you too."

"What's he doing here?" Mouse said, causing both boys to jump.

"Jeesh, Mouse, you about scared me to death," Percival said, stilling his legs. He took in a breath and looked down at Mouse. "Paddy's going to be staying with us."

Mouse and Paddy stared at each other for several moments without blinking. Finally, Paddy turned his attention to Percival. "Want to introduce me to the gang?"

Percival looked to Mouse, who gave the slightest of nods. He sighed his relief; the last thing he wanted was to have to choose between the two.

***

November 1, 1918

The worst part of the weather cooling was the days were getting shorter. In the summer months, the boys would return to the cemetery near dark, weary and ready for sleep. But now that the skies grew dark earlier, it was difficult to keep busy until time to go to sleep. While most of the gangs didn't grow restless until later in the evening, Slim and the boys felt safer if behind the gates by dusk. They spent their evenings reminiscing about the good old days when the boys had homes, though the stories often changed during the telling, leading Percival to think that some of the memories might be fabricated. The boy doing the talking tonight was spinning a grand tale of how his family came to New York from Boston via train. Percival figured the story was bogus, as the same kid had once said he'd never set foot out of the city. Still, a good yarn helped to pass the time, and no one ever bothered to question the authenticity of the tale. Just as the kid declared himself finished, a roar the likes of which Percival had never heard echoed through the air.

The boys all sprang to their feet, each looking in different directions in an unsuccessful attempt at identifying the sound. Percival ran to the front gate searching the street for anything amiss. People filed out nearby buildings, their murmurs filling the air. A wail of a siren sounded in the distance. Soon others joined in.

"Something's mighty wrong," Paddy said as he and the others reached the gate.

"It's the train," someone yelled. "My sister lives on Flatbush and phoned to tell me about it just now. Said how it shook all the china off the dinner table."

As word spread, people raced in the direction of the crash.

"I ain't never seen a train wreck," Paddy said.

"What about the gangs?" Tommy asked.

"It's still early." Paddy surmised. "Besides, they'll be too excited about the train to pay us any mind. What do you think, Slim?"

Percival had to admit he was just as curious as the others. "I think Paddy's right. But I don't think we all should go."

Paddy nodded his head in agreement. "Tommy, Slim, and I will go."

The boys grumbled their disappointment but stayed put as Percival, Paddy, and Tommy used their coats to climb over the spiked fence. By the time the three reached Malbone Street, there were so many people, the boys couldn't get close enough to see the train. Hordes of bystanders held lanterns high to help illuminate the scene—the boys hopped up and down trying to see over their heads.

"It's no use," Paddy grumbled. He turned toward Percival and smiled. "Let me on your shoulders so I can have a look-see."

The request wasn't unusual, as they'd used this technique on multiple occasions to judge a crowd suitable for picking. Percival squatted, and Paddy hoisted his legs over his shoulders.

"Move to the left," Paddy called from his new vantage point. "Okay, a little more. Ah phooey, let me down."

Percival obliged, and Paddy slid off his shoulders.

"Well, what'd you see?" Tommy asked.

"Nothing. Because there's nothing to see. The whole tunnel is blocked. If there's anyone left alive, I don't know how they're gonna get 'em out."

A horn blared behind them. Percival turned, raising his hand against the truck's lights. Police and firemen poured from the back of the truck shouting and ordering those in the crowd to move out of the way.

"My husband has not come home," a woman wailed. "I've got to see if he's alive."

"Yeah," several others chimed in, each naming the person they were looking for.

"Yeah, well, you better move back and give us room to work," one of the new arrivals said, pushing his way through the crowd.

The people moved to allow the officials in, and Paddy managed to slip in alongside them. Percival and Tommy moved to the side to wait for Paddy. More emergency trucks arrived, and men went to work setting up spotlights to help illuminate the area. Minutes turned into hours as the workers began the tedious task of clearing away debris. A hush fell over the crowd. Percival and Tommy jumped to their feet and stood on their toes, trying to see what was going on. The crowd parted, and a man emerged, helped on either side by two of the workers. The man's clothes were in tatters; he was covered in blood and wore only a single shoe. He was led to a nearby ambulance, which took off into the night—the wail of the siren lingering.

After that first rescue, the injured started trickling out, some walking on their own and others carried by men and nurses whose eyes told of the horror they'd seen. Some of the bodies were covered with burlap and laid in rows near the street. Though they were dead, their faces were left uncovered to allow the crowd to search for their missing family members. Another group of workers arrived and pushed the onlookers back even further. They then motioned the motorcars forward, their headlights aimed at the tunnel to give the workers more light.

Percival searched the crowd for Paddy, but his friend was nowhere to be seen.

"If we can't see anything, we should just dip pockets," Tommy suggested.

Percival shook his head. "It don't seem right."

"Why not? It'd be easy pickings," Tommy argued.

Percival struggled to control his legs. "We're not going to take advantage of their worry."

"Who put you in charge?"

Before Percival could answer, he saw Paddy barreling toward them, eyes wild, and his face looking as if he'd seen something too horrible to speak of.

"We've got to go!" he said the second he reached them. "It's Mouse; they're taking him to Ebbets Field. I think he's dead."

Though Percival's heart raced, he didn't think Mouse was dead, as they hadn't put him with the others. Still, it worried him that they hadn't loaded him in an ambulance. He followed behind Tommy and Paddy, praying with each step they would find their friend alive.

The ballfield was brightly lit and littered with bodies, most of which appeared to be alive. Nurses and doctors floated around the field working on the injured, too engrossed in their work to pay any mind to the small group of boys who weaved around the wounded in search of their friend.

They'd just finished searching the second row when Percival spied Mouse sitting by the fire. He was covered with blood but appeared to be alive. "He's not dead!" Percival said, running toward the fire.

"Is he dead? He looks dead," Tommy said, cocking his head from side to side.

"Don't be ignorant. Dead people don't sit up," Paddy said, letting out a long sigh.

Percival was glad Paddy sounded relieved. It gave him comfort to know that though the boys hated each other, they didn't wish the other dead.

Tobias opened his eyes, blinking several times.

Percival smiled. "I told you he weren't dead."

Paddy leaned in close. "He don't look much better than dead. Look at all that blood."

"Yeah, that's a lot of blood," Tommy agreed. "You were on the train, huh, Mouse. We heard it all the way to the chapel.

Climbed over the fence to come see. Sumptin makes that kind of noise be worth g'tting a stake in the belly."

"Are you hurt, Mouse?" Paddy's concern seemed genuine.

"Naw, most of this blood ain't mine," Mouse said, looking at his shirt.

"It's a good thing. I don't think you'd be livin' if it was all your'n," Tommy said.

"Leave him be," Percival said, shooing Tommy away. "What happened, Mouse?"

Mouse closed his eyes then opened them once more. "Someone said the conductor was driving too fast. The train took the curve like the driver was late for a Thanksgiving feast. It all happened so fast, I saw a man fly through the air and then the lights blinked and everything went dark. When I woke up, I had a dead man sleeping on me."

Sleeping? Percival frowned his surprise. "Woke up? How could you sleep with all that noise?"

"I didn't know dead men could sleep," Tommy said, scratching his head.

Tobias shrugged. "All I know is a man caught me dipping in his pocket and told me he was going to take me to jail. Next thing I know, I'm waking up and he's on top of me, but he ain't moving. I think his eyes were open staring at me, but I can't be sure 'cause it was dark."

All three boys' eyes grew wide, focusing on the unbelievable.

"You got caught?" Percival whispered.

"Ah, don't be looking at me like that. It wasn't my fault. The train was going too fast, and the whole train was in an uproar. Someone yelled about it, and when he did, the man turned to look. That's when he saw me with my hand on his wallet."

Tommy blew out a slow whistle. "Bet he was mad."

Loyal

Mouse's face paled and he closed his eyes. Opening them once more, he vomited.

"Boy, Mouse, you don't look so good," Paddy said, taking a step back.

"Just a little headache from the crack on the head," Mouse said and tilted his head toward the fire so the boys could see.

"So it is your blood," Paddy said. Apparently, blood trumped vomit as he inched forward to take a closer look. "Would you look at the size of that lump! You got a melon on your melon!"

Tommy moved in for a closer look. "Wowzers, Mouse. Someone done went and sewed your head shut."

Percival cuffed Tommy on the side of the head. "Well, they couldn't let his brains spill out now, could they?"

"Now why'd you go and pound on me? I didn't do nothing wrong. I just ain't never seen anyone with their head sewn up is all."

"I need to get out of here before they take me someplace." Tobias stood, studied each boy in turn, then motioned to Paddy. "Give us a minute, guys."

Percival watched as Mouse spoke to Paddy. At first, Paddy eyed him with suspicion. Then Mouse pulled some coins from his pocket and Paddy agreed to whatever it was Mouse was asking. As Paddy walked away, Mouse waved him over.

"You okay, Mouse?" Percival asked, watching Paddy walk away.

Mouse placed a hand to his head. "I'll do."

"Where's he off to?"

Mouse swallowed. "I asked him to do a job for me."

Percival struggled to keep the hurt out of his voice. "What kind of job?"

"I asked him to watch over my gal."

"I could have done that." This time, he wasn't as successful

155

at hiding his feelings, as his words jittered nearly as much as his legs.

"I know you're the best guy for the job, but your legs will never let you. Aside from me, Paddy's the best at shadowing. Slim," Mouse clamped him on the shoulder, "there's no one in the world that I trust more than you. If it wasn't for your legs..."

"I know, Mouse," Percival said, jumping in place to calm his legs.

"I need to go off so I can get some rest. I may be gone a while. I told Paddy if he needed anything, he's to come find you. That's alright, isn't it?"

"Sure, Mouse," Percival replied halfheartedly.

Mouse let go of his shoulder and started walking toward the gate. Percival and Tommy followed Mouse to the entrance where Mouse took his leave. Percival began to follow Tommy then hesitated.

"Do you know the way back to the chapel?"

Tommy nodded.

"Straight there. I don't think you have to worry about the gangs tonight but stay on the main streets to be sure. If you see a crowd stay with them, you'll be safer that way."

"Where are you going?"

"I'm going to follow Mouse to see that he gets where he's going. Tommy," Percival said when the boy turned to walk away, "keep an eye on the others until me or Paddy returns."

Chapter Twenty

November 1918

Percival followed at a distance so close that if Mouse had been in his right mind, he would have easily been discovered. As it was, though Mouse turned in Percival's direction several times, his face showed no sign of recognition. The streets were filled with people, most of whom were going in the opposite direction, but the trolleys were still full. Mouse made several attempts at finding a seat on a trolley before finally catching a ride on the back.

Percival wasn't as lucky and ended up running behind the car. Just as he feared losing sight of the trolley Mouse was clinging to, the car would roll to a stop, allowing him time to catch up before rolling off once again. During one such stop, Mouse lost his grip, only to regain his footing and hop back on seconds before he reached him. Percival wanted to jump up next to him and ask him where he was off to, but Mouse hadn't asked for his help, and he didn't want his friend to be mad at him for following. A space opened on the opposite side of the outer trolley, and Percival climbed onboard, maneuvering to where he could keep Mouse within sight.

When at last the trolley stopped and Mouse dropped to the ground, Percival thought his friend had lost his grip once more. But when Mouse began walking, he knew the boy had reached his stop. Percival gulped his surprise. *Why here?*

Though he'd never been there at night, Percival recognized the neighborhood, as Mouse had taken him and the boys there on several occasions. Each time they'd pilfered clothes without tatters, and Mouse had insisted they use a public bathhouse so they would look more presentable to the folks he had dubbed the "do-gooders." Upon seeing everyone dressed as if going to church in the middle of the week, Percival and the others quickly understood why Mouse had insisted they clean up. And clean up they did, each boy returning to the churchyard with enough money to keep them living large for weeks. Percival looked down at his clothes and sighed. There'd be no fitting in this night.

Mouse turned onto Park Avenue and Percival followed at a close distance. It was obvious that Mouse's injuries were taking a toll on the boy because he'd long since let down his guard. Furthermore, anyone who didn't know better would think the boy to be drunk, as he swayed from one side of the street to the other. *Does he even know where he's going?*

Percival got his answer a short distance later when Mouse slowly climbed a small flight of stairs and clanged the knocker of a grand apartment. On the third clang, Mouse crumbled to the ground. Percival started forward, quickly changing his direction when the door opened. He stayed out of view, watching as a woman dressed in a long white robe bent down to Mouse and yelled to someone inside. A moment later, a man appeared in the doorway, lifted him into his arms, and closed the door behind them.

Percival was still staring at the building when a light appeared in a window of one of the upper floors. While he couldn't see Mouse, he could see both the man and woman moving in and out of view.

Are they his parents, then? Mouse said his parents were dead. These people obviously know him, as the woman had called him by name. His real name, not the one he uses on the streets. These people did not look dead. Had Mouse lied?

Percival settled on the steps of the apartment across the street so that he could keep the window in view. Soon after settling in, a motorcar raced down the street and came to a halt in front of him. A man dressed in a black suit carrying a handled black bag exited the motorcar, crossed the street, and raced up the stairs, clanging the door knocker in quick succession. Percival had seen such a man before and instinctively touched the scar upon his head. The door to the apartment opened and he, too, soon became visible in the upstairs window. Percival wasn't sure how much time passed between the doctor's entrance and exit, but when at last he returned to his motorcar, he was in no hurry.

"Please, sir, could you tell me how the boy is?"

"Your friend?" the man said, looking down his nose.

Percival remembered how he was dressed and shook his head. "No, sir, but I saw he was injured, and I thought to inquire as to his condition."

"The boy is walking with the dead," the doctor said, looking up at the second-floor window.

"He's dead!" Percival gasped.

"No, I didn't say he was dead. I said he was walking with the dead," the doctor corrected.

"What's the difference?"

"Well, if he were dead, he'd just be dead. But as it is, he has a chance of recovering. Do you know who stitched him up?"

"Someone at the ballfield. He was hurt real bad from being on the train when it crashed and all," Percival added when the doctor scowled.

The doctor's eyes bugged. "A train, you say? Whereabouts?"

"You mean you didn't hear it?"

"No, I didn't hear a thing. Why, I was sound asleep in my bed when the good folks called and asked me to come have a look at the boy. Where'd you say the crash was again?"

I didn't. "Flatbush, jammed the whole tunnel. I never seen the likes. Someone said the train was going too fast to make the curve."

The doctor pulled out his pocket watch and shook his head. "I guess I should make my way over there. Explains why they sewed him up at the ballpark."

Percival reached under his cap and scratched his head. "It does?"

"Sure, half the hospitals in the city are filled to capacity with the influenza."

Percival was well aware of the influenza. One of the new boys had been sick with it when he arrived. Died right there in the cemetery that very night. Paddy and Tommy had begged the caretaker to bury him there, but the man had merely shaken his head and told them that wasn't the way things were done. Later, Mouse had explained that they would be taking him to a pauper's grave and went on to describe the burial in great detail. Percival shuddered at the memory.

"You okay, boy? Your legs," the man said when Percival looked at him.

"Oh yes, sir. It's because of this," he said, removing his tattered cap.

The doctor placed his hand on Percival's head and felt the scar. He grew quiet for a moment, then removed his hand. He walked to the motorcar, and for a moment, Percival thought he was about to leave. Instead, he turned on the machine's headlamps, returned to the front of the motorcar, and began rummaging through his medicine bag. "It's in here somewhere."

"What is?" Percival asked.

"Hang on. Yes, here it is." He pulled out a small vial and offered it to Percival.

Percival threw his hands up. "Oh, no, sir, I don't need any medicine."

"It's not medicine. It is tea. You're to place a spoonful into a cup of hot water and drink it once or twice a day." He smiled and pressed the vial into Percival's hand. "I think you'll find that it helps with the twitching."

Percival looked at the vial, then back at the doctor. "Will this really make me normal?"

The smile disappeared. "There are those in the world that will sell you a potion and promise you miracles. Mostly, they are just getting you dependent on the dratted elixir so they can sell you more. No, son, this will not cure you, but I do believe you will notice a significant difference."

"There's not much in there," Percival said, sliding the vial into his front pocket.

"No, there's not, I'm afraid, but a week's worth if you only use it once a day." He opened the bag once more and pulled out a pad. He scribbled something and handed Percival the sheet. "Take this to the drugstore, and they will get you more. Can you read?"

"Yes, sir," Percival said, bobbing his head.

"Good." The smile returned. "You memorize what I've written down, so you can get you some more when you need it."

Percival glanced at the paper. *Lavender Tea mixed with Kava Root.* He blinked back a tear then shoved the paper into the pocket with the vial.

"No need to look so glum, son. I'll not be charging you for the tea."

"Yes, sir, but that wasn't what made me sad."

"No?"

"It's my mother, sir."

"Your mother? Is she ill?"

"No, sir, she's not sick. She's dead." The doctor started to speak, but Percival cut him off. "When she was alive, she used to bring me lavender tea."

"Your mother was a smart woman. Now, make sure to have them add the kava root as well. That's where the magic lies." The doctor pulled out his pocket watch once again, sighed, then returned to his motorcar. He closed the door and motioned Percival close. "Your friend should be okay, but he's not going anywhere soon. Do you want me to take you home?"

I don't have a home. "No, sir. If it's alright by you, I think I'll stay for a while."

The doctor sighed. "It doesn't matter what I think. It's what the good folks living on this street think. And they'll not react too kindly to seeing a boy such as yourself in their neighborhood. As I said, he'll not be going anywhere anytime soon."

Percival looked toward the window and saw that the light no longer glowed in the room. The doctor was right; even Mouse had made them bathe and change, even though they were only coming to steal. "Okay, sir. I'll have you take me home."

"It's my assistant who told me of it, you know," the doctor said the moment Percival slid onto the seat.

No, I don't know. "Told you of what, sir?"

"Kava root. She's a fine botanist. Stumbled upon the profession, she did. Her father was part of some commission in the Philippines after the war. Viola, who's now my assistant, would often visit him. Growing bored on the first visit, she volunteered at the local medical clinic, where she learned of the root and its healing properties. She tells me that trip helped to ignite her passion for herbs. So, where are we going?" the doctor asked when Percival didn't respond.

"You said you are going to Flatbush."

"Yes, but where am I dropping you?"

"I can walk home from there," Percival said, staring out the window. Try as he might, he still couldn't get Mouse out of his mind. Why would his friend choose to live the way he did when he had a family who loved him? The woman's voice was frantic when she yelled for her man. Was that Mouse's father? *I'd give anything to have a momma and papa.*

"Do you actually have a home? A place with walls and a roof?"

No. "Me and some of the boys sleep in the cemetery." He might not have the kind of home the doctor was asking about, but he had a place. Not for long, he reminded himself. The days and nights were growing colder. It wouldn't be long before he would be forced to find another place more suitable to spend the winter months. Mouse was supposed to help with that, and now he was injured. "Will he live?"

"Your friend? Yes, I think so." The doctor said, pulling the motorcar to a stop in front of a large building. "You live close, do you not?"

A few streets over. "Yes, sir."

"Do you know what this building is?" he asked and pointed toward the gated structure.

Yes. All the street boys knew about the asylum and tended to stay well away from the place for fear of being captured and stuck inside. "Yes, sir."

"They take in kids like you and give them a bed to sleep in and food to eat. They see to it they get an education and help them find real homes. If you were in here, I could see that you continue to get the special tea for your legs. My name's Dr. Todd. I'm the doctor here, see."

"You work here?"

"I work many places; this is just one of them."

Percival looked at the fence. "Nah, the place has a gate to

keep kids in."

"The last time I looked, St. Paul's had a similar fence," he said dryly.

Percival whipped his head around. "How'd you know where I'm staying?"

"Deduction."

"St. Paul's gates are for keeping the gangs out. Not keeping us in."

"What if I told you this building here has a program that would allow a boy such as you to leave anytime he wanted?"

"That's not what the boys say. They say once you go inside, you never come out."

"Are you going to believe boys who have never stepped a foot inside the building or myself who goes there several days a week?"

The man had a point. "Anytime?"

"I want you to give it some thought. I give you my word that if you end up inside and decide it is not for you, I'll see to it you find your way back outside again."

"How can you do that?"

"They have work programs for the older children. A child who has a job is permitted to leave unchaperoned each day. There's nothing to keep that same child from not returning."

"I don't have a job."

"You find yourself inside, and I'll find you a job, even if I have to hire you myself."

"Why would you go and do that?"

"Because I like you. You have a good heart."

"I do? How can you tell?"

"Because you followed your friend to make sure he was okay."

I didn't tell you that. "How'd you know?"

"Deduction," Dr. Todd repeated. "You knew that young

Tobias was injured, and you know about the train."

"Big Joe, he's my friend, says I'm loyal."

"Big Joe is a great judge of character. He's sent many boys my way."

Percival couldn't believe his ears. He turned in the seat, pulling his legs underneath to quell their excitement. "You know Big Joe?"

The doctor chuckled. "I do, and I would have known you sooner if you had called."

Chapter Twenty-One

January 1919

Percival sat huddled under a pile of tattered blankets with Tommy, the twins, and several other boys, as they'd taken to doing since Mouse and Paddy had yet to return. The skies were grey, and the sun hadn't shone in days. A shiver ran through him. Percival pulled the end of the blanket closer.

"I'm cold," one of the twins said through chattering teeth.

With the main leaders gone, Percival and the others stayed close to the church, only going out to dip pockets for a few hours at a time then returning and huddling together to stay warm. If Mouse or Paddy had been there, they would have long abandoned the graveyard, but as it was, they were still there— cold and scared and looking for someone to make decisions. While both Mouse and Paddy seemed to enjoy the role, being in charge wasn't something Percival was comfortable with. Neither Tommy nor either of the twins had tried to take the lead, not that any of them were worthy of his loyalty. Since no one else was going to make a decision, he knew he had to step up. "It's time to go to the Lodging House."

The boys all cheered.

"When we leaving?"

"Now," Percival replied. "Tommy will take you."

"Aren't you coming?" one of the twins asked.

"No, I'm going to stay here and wait for Paddy and Mouse."

"They ain't coming back," Tommy said.

"Yes they are," Percival said hoping it to be true. It had been over a month since the wreck and they'd not seen or heard from either Paddy or Mouse. "I'm not leaving until they know where to find us."

"You can't stay here alone. You'll freeze," Tommy argued.

Percival narrowed his eyes at Tommy. "Take the boys and go while there's still enough daylight."

Tommy looked to the sky and nodded his head.

"Leave me all the blankets. You'll each have your own bed tonight, so you won't need them. I'll be okay," Percival said when the boys frowned. He wasn't entirely sure that was true, but there was no sense in them all freezing to death. He watched as each boy reluctantly gathered their belongings, each offering a weak smile before turning and heading out of the gate.

Percival pulled the blankets around him and pushed his back against the large headstone.

***

A chill ran through him and he wasn't sure it was entirely from the cold. It wasn't being alone in the graveyard that bothered him so much as just being alone. Not for the first time, he regretted not going with Tommy and the others.

Shouting and laughter filled the air, and he curled into a ball and pulled the blankets over his head in a feeble attempt at hushing the noise. It was a gang, to be sure. The way they were carrying on left no doubt they'd caught some unlucky soul on the streets. His legs started jerking, and Percival regretted that he'd used the last of the tea Dr. Todd had given him. It had worked too, calming his legs so that they were manageable.

The streets grew quiet again. Percival lay there staring up at the night sky, wondering for the hundredth time about the whereabouts of Paddy and chastising himself for the same amount of time for not having thought to ask Mouse where he'd sent him. He only knew he'd gone to look after Mouse's gal. Mouse sure was lucky to both have a family and a gal. *If he's so lucky, then why is he living on the streets?* It was a question that had plagued him for days and the main reason he wasn't in a hurry to leave the cemetery. Mouse would return, either to the cemetery or to wherever it was he'd sent Paddy. If he went to Paddy, Percival was sure Paddy would then return to the graveyard.

***

Percival sat on the roof of his apartment building contemplating his next move when he heard the first thud. A wide smile stretched across his face as the thuds continued. *Big Joe, he's come home.* He leaped to his feet, eager to see his friend and tell him of all that had happened since he went away. He made the easy leap to the neighboring building, and another smile crossed his face. To think he used to be scared of such jumps. This one was nothing compared to some of the others he'd crossed since learning the art. Thinking to surprise his friend, he climbed up the side of the shed, crawled across the roof, and dropped down in front of the opening without a sound. Big Joe turned the second his feet hit the ground. Only it wasn't Big Joe. It was Milo—the scowl on the boy's face clearly showed he wasn't in the mood for company.

"We've been looking for you," Milo growled. "Since you like sleeping in the graveyard so much, we thought we'd make it permanent."

Hands grasped Percival's arms, holding him in place.

"Throw him off the roof," Milo said, then turned, thumping the bag.

Percival squirmed to get away, but the hands that held him were strong. He tried dragging his feet, only to have his shoes stripped as his toes continued to dig into the tar roof. They approached the side of the building. Percival knew this time he would meet his demise. As he fell from the building, he closed his eyes and concentrated on the steady drum of Milo's hands against the bag.

Percival opened his eyes, sucking in his breath as the soft rhythmic thuds continued. The thuds were not fists but steady raindrops beating down on the tattered blankets that covered his head. *It was only a dream.* Gathering his things, he raced through the graveyard, seeking shelter under the front of the chapel roof. It was still dark, so it would be some time before the caretaker unlocked the gates. Wrapping the blanket around him, he sat with his back to the brick, pulled his knees to his chest, and waited for the rain to pass. He was still sitting in that position when the caretaker exited the chapel. Wearing a long black overcoat and wide-brimmed hat, the man jumped at seeing Percival sitting so close to the door. The black ring of keys clanged to the ground in front of Percival, who retrieved them, handing them to the man without a word. The caretaker took them, scanning the area before turning his back on him, mumbling to himself as he fumbled to open the gate. He'd ended the one-sided conversation by the time he returned.

The caretaker took off his hat and beat it against his knee. "The others gone?"

"Yes, sir."

"You'll be going too, then."

"No, I need to wait for my friends."

"Thought you said they were gone?"

"Not them, Mouse and Paddy. If I leave, they won't know where to find me."

Still holding his hat in hand, the man glanced off in the distance. "Rain's not going to be letting up anytime soon. Suppose it'd be alright if you waited it out up here on the porch. You see someone coming through that gate, you skedaddle. People see enough of your kind out begging on the street. They don't need to trip over ya when they come to pray."

Percival thought to ask what the people prayed about but

decided against it. There wasn't any sense knowing if he couldn't do it. He was a street urchin, Arab, Rat, or worse; what had the lady said? *Varmint, yes, that was the word she'd used.* Even if he knew what to pray about, they wouldn't let him inside. Percival nodded his understanding.

The caretaker stomped the water from his feet before going inside and closing the door behind him. Since the man told him he needn't leave, Percival stretched his legs in front of him, watching as they vibrated against the concrete. He closed his eyes, retracing the events of the night Mouse got hurt, picturing the woman in her long, flowing robe and the way she cradled him in her arms. His memory drifted to another similar scene, only the woman was his mother and he the boy. She too had been screaming, but by then, his papa was gone, and there was no one to come help. She'd carried him into the hallway, ran down the stairs, and into the street all the while begging for someone to help. He didn't remember how he'd gotten to the hospital, only that his mother was there each time he'd opened his eyes. The memory was so vivid, he could almost feel her eyes on him at that very moment. He opened them, saw he was alone, and closed them once more. The door clicked open. Percival lifted his eyelids as the caregiver stepped onto the porch. He carried a plate covered with a bright white towel. Percival caught a whiff of fresh baked biscuits as the man lifted the cloth.

"I figured you could do with a bite to eat," he said, offering a plate with two fluffy white biscuits with golden brown tops to Percival. His hands shook as he extended the plate. "Go on, take it. Best eaten while the honey's still warm."

Percival took the plate, his mouth watering at the sight of honey oozing out the sides. Picking the top off one, he gulped the welcomed treat in four greedy bites.

"Slow down, boy. A fellow should at least take the time to

taste the food he's putting into his mouth."

"Oh, I'm tasting it just fine," Percival said between bites.

"There's a difference between tasting it and tasting it." He put up a hand when Percival picked up the next layer. "Slowly. One bite at a time. Let it rest in your mouth for a second, then chew slowly to get the full flavor of the honey."

Percival did as told, resisting the urge to gulp it down as he had the others.

"There, see how much better that tasted?"

No. It tasted the same as before. "Yes, sir," Percival said, shoving the remaining half into his mouth.

"Someday, if you're lucky, you'll learn the difference." He walked to the opposite end of the covered porch, retrieving a chair. Placing it near Percival, he sat staring out at the rain. "What's your story, boy?"

"My story?"

"How'd you end up here?"

"Oh that, Mouse. He said how you didn't mind so long as we stay out of sight." Percival realized that he hadn't actually followed that rule and smiled a sheepish smile. He shrugged. "It was raining."

"Where are the others?" His right hand shook as he spoke, and he covered it with his other hand to still it.

Percival mimicked the action by crossing one leg over the other. "Gone."

Instead of asking for details of their whereabouts, the caretaker rephrased his question. "Why do you not have a home?"

Percival considered his answer. If he told the man the truth, he might call the police to take him away. Still, he hadn't done anything wrong, so he doubted they would send him to prison. "My momma's dead."

"And your papa? He dead too?"

"Yes, sir."

"You know," he said, directing his comment to the rain, "there are places for boys like you. Now, I know what you're thinking. I'm sure the boys have told you those are places to stay away from, but believe me when I tell you, they're a far cry better than sleeping in a cold graveyard before your time. There'll be time enough for that after you're dead."

"You're talking about one of those asylums, ain't ya?"

"I am."

"I met a doctor just the other day that said the same thing."

"Did he also tell you that if you go in, they might be able to find you a new home?"

"I thought the asylum would be my new home."

"It will, at least for a while. But getting kids off the street is only the half of it. Those asylums serve a purpose."

"What kind of purpose?"

"To help those kids find a new family."

"After my mom died, Paddy and I spit in our hands, and we became family. He said we're blood brothers. Only we didn't use blood on account of neither of us had a knife."

The man smiled for the first time since joining him on the porch. "Yes, but wouldn't you like a real family? One who sticks with you and doesn't leave you sleeping alone in the cold?"

I don't like being alone. "Sir, where do they come from?"

"Who?"

"The families."

"Oh, I suppose they are from everywhere. But most folks looking to adopt a child want the right one. Some folks don't take too kindly to kids roaming the street. Think maybe they're damaged in some way and suppose that's what got them on the street in the first place. They prefer to select their child from the asylum, thinking at least they've had some form of discipline and doctoring to make sure they're not afflicted."

"What's afflicted?"

"Sickly or suffering in some way. Some want strong boys that can help them out with daily chores or a girl to help the women in the kitchen."

"Only girls? I wouldn't mind helping in the kitchen. I used to help my mother," Percival said, remembering. He thought of his mother's book, which he had hidden in the wooden box at the back of the chapel, and made a mental note to collect it before he left.

"Oh, I suppose there are people who'd let a boy help out in the kitchen if he were so inclined."

As the man continued to talk about the benefits of going to the asylum, Percival hung on every word. Why, between the caretaker and the doctor, he now wished he'd have gone there right after his momma died. *Then I wouldn't have met Mouse.* Only Mouse had lied. Percival was sure of it. He wasn't sure exactly what his friend lied about, but he was going to find out before going into the asylum.

"You'll think about it, then?"

"Yes, sir. But not until I talk to Mouse and Paddy."

"I guess if you're going to hang around, I could give you a bit of work to keep you busy. Just you. Your friends show up and then you'll find another place. Understood?"

"Yes, sir," Percival agreed.

Chapter Twenty-Two

The next few months were filled with indecision. While the caretaker treated him well, he was not much company. He'd tell Percival what he wanted done then leave him to do it. Percival swept floors, wiped down the benches inside the chapel, washed windows, and on one occasion, helped with a burial. Well, not with the actual burial, but he helped move the barrels to the gravesite and watched as they lit a fire to help thaw the ground. In exchange, the caretaker would give him a small plate of food and allowed him to sleep on a pallet of blankets on the floor near the woodstove. If anyone came into the church, Percival knew to stay out of sight.

While Percival appreciated having a roof over his head, he missed his friends. Now with the weather warming, he knew it was time to move on, which was why he was currently clinging to the back of a trolley on his way to Park Avenue with the sole purpose of knocking on the door of the grand apartment and demanding to see Mouse. If Mouse didn't want to come with him, that would be his choice, but he at least wanted to find out why the boy had lied to him. And press him to find out where he'd sent Paddy.

The trolley stopped at the intersection of 5th Ave and Broadway. Percival craned his neck to see the Flatiron Building. If not for fear of losing his position on the trolley, he would've jumped off to get a better view of the massive triangle-shaped building. Just as the trolley began to roll, he caught a glimpse of a young boy in dandy clothes. Percival smiled, thinking how much the kid looked like Mouse. As if knowing he was being watched, the boy turned and looked directly at him.

Mouse! Percival dropped from the back of the trolley and dodged out of the way of a passing truck. An image of his mother lying on the road came to mind, causing a wave of nausea. When he regained his composure, Mouse was nowhere in sight. Percival began walking in the direction he'd just come. If Mouse were heading back to the graveyard, he'd catch up to him before long. Percival was glad Mouse had been on foot instead of riding the trolley or he might never have seen him. Still, he couldn't help wondering why Mouse was walking when he knew how to hitch a ride without paying.

Percival moved through the crowd, scanning the sidewalk for his friend. Three men in dark suits and rounded hats ambled down the sidewalk in front of him, blocking his way. He thought to push through them, remembered how he was dressed, and skirted around via the street instead. The second he stepped back onto the sidewalk, he spied his friend walking ahead of him. He was just about to call out to him when he saw Mouse move in close to a woman carrying a parasol. He knew without seeing the deed that his friend was dipping pockets— which explained why Mouse was on the move and not riding the trolley. Percival followed at a distance, watching how easily Mouse could strip his marks. While dipping wasn't for him, he couldn't help but admire the skill with which Mouse could dip into pockets and purses without getting caught. *It's not true. He did get caught. He'd said so himself. The man on the train had grabbed hold of him before the train crashed. What would have happened if the train hadn't crashed?*

Percival gulped. He'd always thought his friend to be infallible. *But he'd been caught. What if he and the boys would've been with him? Would they have been so lucky? Or would they have perished like so many others on the train?* A shudder raced through his body.

"Hey, get a load of that kid," a voice called from behind.

"Ain't nothing but a street Arab. Filthy animals should be put into cages with all the other rats." A different man this time.

"No, not the one in rags. The sharp-dressed kid in front. Didn't you see him? He just reached a hand into the woman's purse."

It's Mouse. He's been caught again! Instinctively, Percival fell to the street, yelling and wallowing around as if in terrible pain. He jerked his arms from side to side to help garner attention. His legs needed no help, as they were dancing of their own accord. Percival chanced a look at the men who'd been walking behind him. As hoped, each of the men stood over him as if trying to decide if he was worth saving. He closed his eyes and continued his performance for several more minutes, after which he pulled his arms in and rose to his feet as if nothing had happened. Mumbling his apologies for blocking their path, he darted off, pushing his way through the people that had stopped to gawk. Wanting to be sure he'd gotten away with it, he ran an entire city block before stopping. Within seconds, Mouse was by his side.

"That may have been your best performance yet," Mouse said, matching him step for step.

"Those men saw you. I had to do something," Percival said, leaving out the fact that his friend had nearly been caught a second time.

"I'm just a bit rusty is all," Mouse glanced over his shoulder. "Where are the others?"

"Gone. I haven't seen Paddy since you got hurt. Tommy and the others, they took off a few months later."

"They left? I've only been gone a few days."

Percival stopped and stared at him. "You've been gone

months."

"It's my head," Mouse said with a shrug. "I've been forgetting sometimes. The doctor said I should be fine with time."

Percival thought of his own scar and nodded his understanding.

"You didn't go with them?"

"No, I was waiting for you."

"Don't look like you were waiting." Mouse nodded to the pillowcase tied to Percival's waist and raised an eyebrow. "I'd say it looks like you're leaving too."

Mouse's head must not have been too damaged—he was still smart. Too smart, as he always seemed to know what a person was thinking. Percival shook his head. "I was coming to find you."

Mouse rocked back on his heels. "How you'd know I was here?"

"I didn't. I just happened upon you. I thought you were still at your mom and pop's house."

Mouse narrowed his eyes. "My momma's dead. What do you know about my pop?"

Dead? "Then who was that lady who took you in the night you got hurt. She looked like a mom to me."

"They ain't nobody to me."

Percival could tell Mouse was getting irritated, but he wanted to know the truth. "They seemed mighty upset that you were hurt. Come on, Mouse, I just saved your hide. You can tell me if you have a family. I won't tell the others."

Mouse blew out a sigh. "Felisha and Adam are no more family than you are. I hoodwinked them a few times, and well, I guess I wasn't in my right mind, so I went to them."

"They looked like they cared," Percival shrugged. "I figured you might need help, so I followed you the night you left. Don't be mad, Mouse. You were hurt real bad. I was worried."

Mouse smiled. "I'm not mad. They cared. At least they used to. Adam wasn't as gullible as Felisha. He saw the way I was dressed and got suspicious. Said he talked to Paddy."

"Paddy?" At the mention of the name, Percival's heart started pounding. "Do you think he squealed on you?"

"I dunno what he said. Adam said he told him about the train, so maybe."

"I know Paddy; he might not like you, but he wouldn't rat you out on purpose."

"What's done is done. I didn't want to live with no do-gooders anyhow. My head's good—better, anyway—so it's time to move on."

Though Mouse's words sounded tough, Percival detected a hint of sadness in his voice. He hated to add to the boy's troubles, but since he was already sad, decided to tell him what was on his mind. "Mouse?"

"Yeah, Slim?"

"I don't want to live in the graveyard no more." He decided not to tell his friend that he'd been sleeping inside the church for the last few months.

Mouse shrugged. "Yeah, I think it's time we find someplace new."

Wow, that was easier than he thought. "We can go to the asylum. I hear they'll give us a bed and food and schooling. They might even find us a new family to live with."

Mouse grabbed hold of his shoulder and turned him to face him. "The asylum? Did you hit your head again?"

"No," Percival said, shrugging his hand off. "But I've been talking to people, and I think that's the best place for me."

"What kind of people? I know it weren't Tommy or the boys who put that nonsense into your skull."

"No, it was the doctor that fixed my legs," Percival replied again, leaving out his conversation with the caretaker.

Mouse laughed. "They don't look so fixed to me."

"I run out of the medicine. But Doctor Todd—I met him the night you got hurt—said he works at the asylum and can get me more if I go in." Percival decided not to tell him that he could get more on his own even if he didn't. "Doctor Todd said how he could get me out if I didn't want to stay in."

"That's a lie," Tobias spat. "They get you inside, they'll keep you."

"It's not a lie. Doctor Todd swore and everything. He took me to the asylum. You know, the one we sometimes walk past with the big iron fence? Said how if I were to go in there, he would see to it I have a job, and if I have a job, how they'll let me out. Said how there's nothing stopping boys from not returning at the end of the day."

Tobias tilted his head as if considering. "Boys and girls or just boys?"

What did it matter? "I dunno, both, I guess."

Mouse began walking once more.

"And those fences for keeping people in don't bother you none."

"Doctor Todd said they were for keeping people out. You know, like the gangs and all."

"And the doctor, he takes care of sick people and all?"

"He must, on account of he's a doctor. He took care of you. That's how I met him. He was coming out from looking after you. I asked him how you were. He said how he supposed you were gonna live. I guess he was right 'cause you're standing here right now."

"I guess he's good at fixing people alright." Mouse stopped and looked around. "Where's Paddy?"

"You sent him to look after your girl, remember? I haven't

seen him since you left."

"You didn't go look for him?"

"Look where? You sent him away and then left. I've been at the church waiting for one of you to come back. Until today. Lucky for me, I saw you walking down the street or I never would have known where you went."

"You're a good friend, Paddy."

"I'm not Paddy. I'm Slim."

"I know who you are. I'm just funning you," Mouse said and began walking once more.

As Percival followed, he realized that while Mouse looked okay on the outside, things were still a bit messed up on the inside.

Chapter Twenty- Three

September 1, 1920

Percival stood near the building, watching as Paddy, Tommy, and the others moved through the crowd dipping pockets.

"The weather will be cooling soon," Mouse said, slipping up beside him

"Mouse? What are you doing here?"

"My girl and her mom are staying in more these days," Mouse said. "It's going to be cooling off soon."

Percival slid a glance to Mouse, wondering if he was having memory issues again. "We've still got a couple of months."

"There's no sense waiting until the last minute," Mouse replied.

"So, what, you want to start sleeping at the Lodging House?"

"I was thinking of something different this year," Mouse said, digging the toe of his shoe into the concrete.

Percival started to get an uneasy feeling in the pit of his stomach. "Come on, Mouse, we're friends. Just say what's on your mind."

"It's my gal. Her momma doesn't look so good these days."

"Is she sick?"

"Seems to be. She's coughing a lot and they aren't staying out very long."

"What's to be done about it?" Percival knew Mouse had a plan. Mouse always had a plan.

"I'm going to see about talking to her mother about putting her into the asylum."

Percival wasn't sure what surprised him more, that Mouse was going to approach her mother after being so careful to stay out of sight for the last couple of years or that his plan included putting her into an asylum. He opened his mouth and asked a simple question. "How?"

"That's the problem. This girl don't know me none, not yet anyway, and I don't know where they'll take her if her momma dies. So, if I could get her inside beforehand, then she'd be taken care of. At least until I can find a way to take care of her on my own."

"How are you gonna get her inside if she don't know you?"

Mouse set his jaw. "I'll find a way. But first, I need you to go inside."

Percival took in a breath of air. "Me?"

"Sure; you said you wouldn't mind."

"I did, but that was before when I was tired of being all alone. Now I've got you and Paddy." Percival shrugged. "Even Tommy and the others came back once they found you were here."

"I know I'm asking a lot of ya, but I need someone on the inside to make sure it's like the doctor said."

Suddenly, Percival was even less sure. "You think the doctor lied?"

"I don't know. Do-gooders sometimes say things, so I need to make sure my girl will be safe inside."

"What if he lied?" Percival's legs started drumming the sidewalk. "What if I can't get out?"

Mouse laughed. "You can climb a fence better than anyone I know. I'll bring you a coat. Five coats if need be. You don't like it inside; I give you my word I'll find a way to get you out."

Percival frowned. "Boy, Mouse, I'd feel a whole lot better

if you were going inside with me."

"No, that place isn't for kids like me. Besides, if I'm in with you, I won't be able to get you out."

"Oh yeah. I forgot about that. Why me?" he asked. "Why not Tommy or one of the others?"

"Some of the kids have this thing with asylums. Besides, I trust you," Mouse said softly. "This is my girl. I've tried to think of another way to keep her safe, but I can't. I'll pay you. It'll be the same as when you're out here."

"Does she really mean that much to you?" Percival asked.

"She does. I know it don't make sense, but I knew it the moment I saw her."

Percival had never been in love before, but if he had been, he would have done anything he could to keep his girl safe. The only person he'd ever loved was his momma. *I wish I could have kept her safe.* "Okay, Mouse, I'll do it."

Mouse heaved an audible sigh. "Don't tell any of the others. I don't want them to know about our deal."

"Okay," Percival agreed, knowing Mouse had a point. All of the kids had said something bad about asylums at one time or another. He was already feeling a little nervous about his decision. The last thing he wanted was for the others to gang up on him. Besides, he knew it wouldn't take much to make him change his mind.

***

September 10, 1920

Percival and Mouse waited on the corner while Paddy and the others went inside the bathhouse to get cleaned up. Mouse had even given Paddy an extra dime so he could take his time. Paddy had followed Mouse's girl the previous day and Mouse insisted it was payment for watching over his girl. While he knew his friend to be grateful, Percival was certain there was more to it. "What's the deal, Mouse?"

183

"What do you mean?"

"You're being too nice to Paddy. What's up?"

Mouse shrugged. "I've been thinking about what you said about going into the asylum. I think it'd be a good fit for you. Still, I'd feel better if you had someone inside with you. What about Paddy? Do you think you could convince him to go along?"

So that's it. He's trying to get Paddy to let his guard down. Percival shook his head. "Not Paddy. Least not willingly."

"Not even if you told him what you told me?"

"I don't think so. Not after the way he's talked against them."

"Then we'll have to find another way to get him in," Mouse said under his breath.

"You mean lie to Paddy?"

"No, we won't lie to him. We just won't tell him the truth is all."

"Not telling sounds a lot like lying."

"Listen, Slim, the doctor's right. You boys will be safer in there. If he gets inside and don't like it, he can come back out. You said so yourself."

"That's because Dr. Todd said he'd get me a job. What if Paddy doesn't get a job?"

"If I can find a way to get Paddy inside, I will be able to find a way to get him out. You trust me, don't you, Slim?"

I want to. "You okay, Mouse?" Percival asked when Mouse closed his eyes for a moment.

"I'll do," he said, opening his eyes. "It's just following them around and then worrying about what might happen has got me tired. My head still hurts sometimes, and I haven't been able to really relax. I was tired even before the wreck."

Percival remembered how bad he'd felt after getting hit in the head. He couldn't imagine how much worse he'd have felt if he'd been injured in a train wreck as well. Mouse hadn't talked much about the wreck since that night. "Did you really have a dead man lying on ya?"

Mouse closed his eyes briefly before answering. "I did."

"And he'd caught you stealing?"

"If the train hadn't wrecked, I expect I'd be in prison right now."

Percival shook his head. "Boy, Mouse, you sure are lucky that train crashed when it did. But how'd you get caught in the first place? You never get caught."

Mouse shrugged. "I supposed everyone gets caught if they're not careful enough."

"You're the most careful person I know. Why, your name says it all. You're a mouse."

"I didn't get caught because I wasn't careful. I got caught on account I was tired. I was following Mileta and her mom all day then decided to do a big score so I could take a break for a bit."

If Mouse could get caught, then it was only a matter of time before he and Paddy were caught as well. What if the police decided to take them to prison instead of the asylum? *Why, I'd be doing Paddy a favor by getting him put into the asylum before he was carted off to prison.* Mouse needed a break. He couldn't watch over them if he was in prison or worse. What could be worse than prison? *Dead.* Percival locked eyes with Mouse. "Paddy won't go in on his own."

The corners of Mouse's mouth curved ever so slightly. "You leave the doing to me. I'll see to it that you both get inside."

***

September 22, 1920

As Percival walked down Vesey Street, it was all he could do to keep from looking over his shoulder. Today was the day.

Mouse had woken him in the middle of the night and told him he'd arranged everything. Percival was to go with Paddy, supposedly to watch over the boy as he dipped pockets. Paddy wouldn't be the wiser as they'd often worked together. The difference was they'd head straight down Vesey Street, and a police officer would snatch them up just as they passed the far end of the St. Paul Building, which sat on the corner just across the street from St. Paul's Chapel. What Mouse had said to the officer to get him to cooperate, Percival did not know.

"Man, Slim, your legs are really going today. You got something on your mind?" Paddy asked.

"No," Percival said, trying unsuccessfully to still his legs.

"Just the same, you'd better stay away once I start dipping or you'll draw too much attention. Maybe you should just go back to St. Paul's. I'm not sure you'll be of any help today."

"I'm supposed to be a distraction, ain't I?"

"Yeah, but you're not supposed to scare everyone away. Heck, even I'm afraid you're gonna kick me." Paddy laughed.

Percival saw the policeman standing in the shadows near the corner of the building. He knew if Paddy saw him, he would insist on crossing to the other side to give them an edge. It didn't matter that they hadn't done anything wrong yet; police often snatched up street kids and took them away for no apparent reason. He pointed at a motorcar, hoping to focus Paddy's attention away from the officer. "I'm gonna have me one of those someday."

Paddy gave the sleek black motorcar a long look. "A person'd have to dip a lot of pockets to get that kind of dough."

"I'm going to buy it legit. Gonna get me a real job," Percival said, shaking his head.

"What kind of job are they gonna give to a boy like you? Ya can't work at the glass factory on account of those legs of yours. Why, you'd break everything around. Can't sell papers neither. A person gets near enough to pay for a paper would get a foot to the shin."

"Sheesh, Paddy, why are ya being so mean? I thought you were my friend."

"I am your friend. That's why I'm giving it to you straight. You have to find a job where your legs don't matter."

"Big Joe told me that my legs would be good for boxing. Said if he had legs like mine, he'd never lose a fight."

"I'd think Big Joe would know a lot about fighting and you're good at punching, so that might just work," Paddy agreed.

Percival was so caught up in the conversation, he completely forgot about the police officer until the man grabbed them both up by the shirt collars. At first, he followed his instincts and struggled to get free, then he remembered and slowed his resistance. Paddy, on the other hand, wiggled around like a cat caught in a burlap bag. For a moment, Percival thought his friend was going to break free, then another officer stepped up, gripping Paddy by each arm.

"Off to jail with these two?" the new officer said.

Percival was about to shout his objection when Paddy beat him to it. "We didn't do nothing worth going to jail for."

"He's right. We'll take them to the asylum instead," the original officer said. While this didn't sit well with Paddy, who continued to drag his feet, Percival breathed a sigh of relief. Good ole Mouse, he'd done what he promised.

"Haven't you heard anything I've told you about asylums?" Paddy sneered.

"Sure I have," Percival said as the policeman ushered him down the sidewalk.

"Then what are you smiling about?"

"Cause tonight we'll be sleeping in a real bed," Percival said with a grin.

Chapter Twenty-Four

It didn't take long to get to the asylum. Paddy stopped resisting after a few blocks but resumed struggling as they passed through the iron gates to the asylum. Finally, the police officer kicked his feet out from under him, dragging him the rest of the way. Percival, on the other hand, practically danced up the sidewalk. While growing a bit apprehensive when the building first loomed in the distance, he'd since reined in his fears and now found himself excited at the thought of getting through a day without worrying about gangs, meals, or sleeping in the cold and rain. Most of all, he was eager to see the doctor and get the medicine to calm his legs. He only wished he could find something for Paddy to be equally thankful for. As it was, each time he looked in his friend's direction, the boy gave him the stink eye as if he somehow thought Percival responsible for his current predicament. While it was true, there was no way for Paddy to know of his involvement.

Still holding on to Percival's neck, the officer lifted the knocker and clanged on the massive door several times. Percival wanted to tell the man there was no need to restrain him but didn't wish to further infuriate his friend. After several moments, the door swung open, and they were greeted by a tall girl in a blue gingham dress.

"Good morning, Miss Clara. We've got two more for you," the officer said, pushing them inside. "Be careful with the redhead. He's got fire in his belly to match his hair. Put up a fight the whole way, he did."

Clara pressed her hands along the white apron that covered

her dress, and the simple action helped to quell any misgivings Percival might have had. The asylum must be a grand place if the girl could stay clean enough not to soil the apron with her hands. She saw him studying her, a blush crept into her cheeks, and she turned her attention to Paddy. "You'll do as you're told in here or the headmistress will call these men back to haul you off to prison. Mark my words. I've seen it happen."

Paddy must have believed her, as the fight left him.

"That's more like it," the policeman said, releasing him. "You go for the door, and Miss Clara here won't have to bother chasing you. I'll shoot you myself. And don't think about running out that door after we're gone, as we'll be on the other side."

Percival didn't think the man serious, as he winked at the other officer. Still, he hoped Paddy believed him enough not to take the chance.

"I'll take you to the headmistress. Mind your manners; the woman has no patience for hooligans. She'll use the strap on you first, and if that doesn't settle you, she'll send you off to prison. I've seen it happen," Clara repeated. She turned and began walking down the long hallway.

Percival looked at Paddy, who shrugged and followed the girl. The hallway was as white as Clara's apron. If not for bright red crocks evenly spaced throughout the hallway, it would be hard to tell where the walls stopped and floor began. Halfway down the hall, they stopped and Clara knocked three times on the door before opening it and stepping inside. A second later, she retreated and told Paddy to go inside. Percival started to follow; Clara put up a hand to stop him. "One at a time in the intake room. You'll wait here until the headmistress is finished with your friend. You're not going to run off, are you?"

Percival shook his head. Clara studied him for a moment then followed Paddy into the room and closed the door.

Percival had wondered why she'd sent Paddy in first, then deduced it was because she didn't trust him enough not to leave. Not inclined to go anywhere himself, Percival leaned against the wall, waiting to see what happened next. It wasn't long before the door opened and Clara stepped into the hallway with Paddy following close behind.

Clara glanced at Percival's restless legs, then nodded to the door. "Headmistress will see you now."

Percival pushed off the wall. Paddy shrugged then followed Clara down the hall. The room turned out to be a wood-lined office with tall windows. A stern-faced woman sitting behind a large wooden desk motioned him forward.

"Come in, and take a seat."

Percival sat in a chair on the opposite wall and tucked his feet around the chair legs in a fruitless attempt at steadying them.

"Oh my. Is there something the matter with your legs?" she asked, peering over the large desk.

"No, ma'am, there is something wrong in here," Percival said, pointing to his head. His answer didn't seem to please the woman as she frowned and jotted something down on the clipboard on her desk.

She pointed her pen at him. "Are you slow, then?"

"No, ma'am, I run real fast."

The headmistress smiled for the briefest of moments. "I'm sure you can."

Percival put his hands on his knees to help still them when the woman's gaze went to his legs again. She didn't seem to like all the jumping, and he didn't want her to think poorly of him. "Doctor Todd has some tea to help them stop jumping."

Her eyebrows lifted. "You know Doctor Todd?"

"Yes, ma'am. Met him, I did. He gave me some of that tea and it worked mighty well. Told me as how he works here and could give me some more should I find myself inside." Percival thought to tell her that the man also told him he'd get him out if he didn't like the place, but something told him he should keep that bit of information to himself.

She wrote something on the paper in front of her then addressed him once more. "What is your name, son?"

"My friends call me Slim."

She scribbled on the paper once more. "And, your parents, what do they call you?"

"They don't call me nothing on account of they're dead."

The headmistress frowned. "What did they call you when they were alive?"

"Percival."

"And your last name?" she said, jotting on the paper.

"The last name my momma called me was Percival."

The headmistress blew out a sigh. "What were your mother's and father's names? Please don't tell me Momma and Papa."

"My momma's name was Margareta Louise, and Papa's name was Armano."

"And their last name," she said, touching pen to paper. When he didn't answer, she looked up. "If someone were going to speak to them, they would call them Mr. and Mrs. what?"

"Barsotti," Percival said, remembering.

The headmistress added that to the paper. "Do you know your birthdate?"

"December 8, 1908."

"Any living relatives? Grandfather, grandmothers?"

"Momma used to talk about my grandfather, but he doesn't live in this country, and I've never met him."

"What about anyone else? Aunts, uncles, brothers, or sisters?"

"Paddy."

"I'm afraid, for legal purposes, blood brothers don't count," the headmistress said dryly.

Percival felt his jaw drop open. "How'd you know?"

The headmistress leaned forward, her eyes staring into his. "I'm the headmistress. It's my job to know everything about you. You get into any mischief, and I'll know it. So I expect you to be on your best behavior. Understand?"

"Yes, ma'am," Percival said, pressing his back into the chair.

The woman pointed at his waist. "What's in your sack?"

"A few things that belonged to my mother."

She frowned. "You'll have to leave that with me."

"Oh no, ma'am," Percival said, clutching the bag. "These are the only things I have left of my mother."

The frown turned into a smile. "You misunderstand. I do not wish to take them from you permanently. I merely wish to keep your mother's things safe. There are those in here that will take them from you the first chance they get."

"I expect they'd have a fight on their hands if they tried," Percival said firmly.

"Therein lies the problem. If you go starting fights, you will get kicked out. They'd haul you off to prison, and I know they would not allow you to keep your mother's precious memories. Wouldn't it be better to allow me to keep them for you? I will lock them in my room here," she said, pointing to the door behind her. "They will remain there until it's time for you to leave the asylum, and then I would return them to you. How does that sound?"

"I guess it's alright." Percival untied the string that held the bag closed and pulled the book free. He clutched it to his chest briefly before handing it over. "I expect you to take good care of that book."

"I expect I will," she said, taking it from him. Anything

else?"

Percival reached into the sack and retrieved his mother's necklace and ring, holding them and feeling the coolness of the jewels before reluctantly handing them over."

Her breath caught when she saw them. "These are lovely."

"I expect you'll take good care of those as well."

"Of course." She ran a finger along the necklace. "Percival, how long have you been on the streets?"

He shrugged. "A couple years, I suspect?"

"And you've had these all that time?"

"Yes, ma'am."

"Didn't you know you could have sold these for a lot of money, which would have paid for food and someplace to stay?"

"Of course I did. Some of the kids wanted me to, but I wouldn't let them."

"I've not met many like you, Mr. Barsotti." She wrote something on the paper and turned and showed it to him—*one book, necklace, and ring.* "I will add a number to it and keep them on file so that it shows they belong to you."

"Do you do that to everything kids bring in?"

"No. I'm afraid we do not have the space to keep everything a child thinks sacred. However, we do our best to make exceptions when it comes to family artifacts."

Percival wasn't sure what an artifact was, but he was glad she'd allowed him to keep his mother's belongings. If not, he would have had to chance running away.

"Enter," the headmistress said when someone knocked.

Clara entered. Percival expected Paddy to be with her, but his friend was nowhere in sight.

"Clara will take you to the washroom. You'll have a bath and delouse. And then you will be shown to your room."

Clara closed the door and started down the hall. "You've

never been deloused, have you?"

"No. How can you tell?"

"Because if you had, you wouldn't be smiling," Clara said, stopping in front of a door labeled "washroom." "Don't worry, they usually only do this when you first arrive."

"Do what?" Percival asked nervously.

The door opened, and Paddy came out wearing a fresh set of clothes and shoes that shined in the light. His ears were bright pink, and he wore a new cap that did little to hide the fact that someone had done a poor job of clipping his hair. Upon seeing Percival, his face grew as red as the hair that once crowned his head. "You know what's good for you; you'll run. Prison has to be better than that!"

"What happened to ya?" Percival gulped.

"Come now, we don't want to ruin the surprise, do we?" Clara said, stepping between the two. "You go on in now. I'll get Paddy situated and come back for you. If I'm not here when you get done, wait. I'll come to collect you shortly."

When Percival made no move to open the door, Clara opened it for him, practically shoving him inside before closing it behind him.

A heavyset woman with a thick German accent yelled for him to come. Percival hurried to where she stood, wondering why they had a stove burning when it was already too hot to breathe in the room.

"Off with the clothes." Percival gulped, and she laughed a hearty laugh. "Seen it all before."

Yes, but not mine. Percival's feet drummed the floor as he was standing there contemplating his next move, a decision he didn't get to make as the woman stepped forward, ripped his shirt from his body, and threw it into the belly of the stove. He curled his fingers into his palms, then remembered Big Joe's warning. *Never hit a lady.* Not that the woman in question was acting very ladylike. Still, Big Joe had been adamant that it never be done. She reached for the waistband of his pants. Percival slapped her hand away, and she came back with a backhand of her own. Never having been hit by a woman before, he stood there dumbfounded as she stripped away the rest of his dignity. Percival stood covering himself with his hands as the woman picked up a pair of scissors and began clipping his hair. He now knew the horrors of which his friend had warned. Percival looked about the room, hoping to distract his mind. Six tubs, each of which appeared to be filled with water, skirted the perimeter of the room. There were two other women, each just as large as the woman standing before him. All three wore white aprons over their dress, none of which looked as clean as the one Clara had on. The lady at the back of the room stood fussing over shelves lined with neatly folded clothing and shiny black shoes. The other sat on a stool peering at the closed door as if waiting for the next victim. While the woman near him fussed over him, the other two women were too absorbed in their tasks to bother to look in his direction.

"Better keep those legs still afor' I cut off your ear," the woman cutting his hair warned.

Unfortunately, this only added to his worry, causing his legs to jump even more. When at last she returned the scissors to the counter, Percival was pleased that while she'd managed to rid him of most of his hair, both ears were still firmly attached to his head.

"In," the woman said, pointing to the tub. When Percival didn't move fast enough, the woman brought her hand around. She gasped as Percival caught it just before it made contact with his bare skin.

Percival narrowed his eyes at the woman, who, though larger in circumference, was nearly equal in height. "I'll not be hitting you, but I'll not be allowing you to hit me either.

Understand?"

The woman swallowed and nodded her head.

"Okay, then," Percival said. He released her hand and kept an eye on her as he climbed into the tub, lowering himself into the water. If not for her watching, he would have closed his eyes and enjoyed the deliciousness of the water. He saw movement out of the corner of his eye and whipped his head around.

The woman held up a brush and bar of soap and pointed in his direction. He nodded. She returned the nod, then rubbed the bar across the brush. Percival jumped when the harsh bristles rubbed across his back, causing the woman to drop the brush into the tub. He held up his hand when she looked as if she would search for it, opting to retrieve it himself. She reached for it, and he shook his head.

"I can wash myself," he said, jerking his thumb to his chest.

For a moment, it looked as if she were going to object. Instead, she sighed and handed him the bar of soap.

"Thank you," Percival said. The woman's eyes widened, her mouth dropped open. "I'm not a bad kid. I just don't wish to be hit."

Closing her mouth, she lifted a bottle from the counter. "For hair. For bugs. Best if I do."

Percival nodded and the woman poured some liquid into her palm then began rubbing it into his scalp. She rinsed her hands in a bucket then told him to close his eyes, demonstrating with her own as she spoke. Percival did as told, sucking in a breath when the hot water hit his skin. The woman placed the bucket on the floor and handed him a towel.

"You do. Yes?"

"I do," Percival agreed.

After he finished drying off, the woman pointed to the back wall. "Go."

Percival did as told and stood with the towel wrapped around his waist as the woman in the back of the room used a tape measure to size him up. She pulled black shorts and socks and a white shirt from the shelves, handing them to him. He thanked her and hurried to dress. Though he'd had showers at the bathhouse, it was the first time since leaving home that he'd truly felt clean.

The woman turned and said something he didn't understand.

Percival shrugged and she pointed at his feet then to the shelf with all the shoes. Percival thought the woman to be asking if he wanted some shoes, so he nodded his head. The woman frowned, then lifted her foot. Returning it to the floor, she pointed at Percival's foot, smiling when Percival mirrored her actions. She placed a board against the bottom of his foot, then went to the shelf, plucked up a pair of shoes, and handed them to him. Percival thanked her. She, too, seemed surprised by his manners, leading him to wonder what kind of kids they had in this place. The woman pulled a new cap from the shelf, then handed it to him. He rewarded her with a smile.

"Go now," the woman said, pointing at the door.

Percival placed the hat on his head and bid the ladies farewell. As he walked to the door, he chided himself for not having come to the asylum sooner. Except for the stripping of clothes and that he'd had to bathe in front of strangers, he was happy with his current situation. He had on a new set of clothes, socks without holes, and shiny new shoes. The best part, he'd not had to dip pockets or steal from a clothesline to get them. He wasn't sure why the kids on the street thought the place so bad. He was squeaky clean, his head didn't itch, and he had a roof over his head for the first time in months. He might feel differently in the days to come, but at the moment, he couldn't be happier.

Chapter Twenty-Five

Two days had passed since the boys had entered the asylum. While Percival was thriving in his new environment, the same could not be said for Paddy, who'd yet to accept his new surroundings.

"Does it hurt much?" Percival asked, looking at the bruise just under Paddy's eye. There were more, but his eye looked the worst, as it was nearly closed shut.

"I've had worse," Paddy said, waving him off. "The doctor said I'll be okay. I don't think that kid's gonna mess with me again as long as you're here. Boy, Slim, you really clocked him a good one."

That was what he was worried about; he'd hit one so hard, he'd knocked him out. "Do you think they're going to send me to prison for fighting?"

Paddy frowned. "You didn't start the fight. Besides, the kids were bigger than both of us."

"Most kids are bigger than you," Percival reminded him. He blew out a sigh. "I don't think it matters. Fighting is fighting."

"If they're going to send you to prison, I'm going with you."

"Boy, Paddy, you'd do anything to get out of this place. But no, there's no sense both of us going to the joint."

"I guess I don't mind it here so much as I did at first. I felt like I was in a cage, but not so much no more."

"Yeah, I like it here just fine. I wonder if I will like prison?"

"Probably not. I've heard some pretty bad things about it."

"You heard some pretty bad things about asylums too, and I don't think it's all that bad."

"Prison's worse," Paddy assured him. "They have murderers and rapists in there. Even a boy like you don't have a chance with the likes of them."

"Gee, Paddy, you sure know how to make a guy feel better."

"Just telling you like it is, Slim. It's gonna be bad for us in there."

"Us?"

"Sure, I told ya I'm going with you."

The door to the headmistress' office opened. She stuck her head out and motioned them inside. Percival and Paddy walked into the room as if they were indeed heading to the gallows. Each took their time to walk the few short steps, then stood in front of the desk to await their sentence.

"You may be seated," Headmistress said, taking a seat behind the large desk.

Percival sat, but Paddy remained standing. He took a breath and began to speak. "If it's all the same with you, Headmistress, I'd prefer to get it over with. I hear prison is bad, and well, if we are going to go, I think we should do so now."

Headmistress leaned back in her chair and pressed her fingertips together. "If you know how bad prison to be, why would you insist on going now?"

Percival sighed. *It's true; she's going to send us away.*

"On account of we just ate," Paddy replied.

"Go on," Headmistress said.

"To prison?" Paddy asked.

"No, with your explanation. What does eating have to do with prison?"

"On account of they don't feed you in prison. If they aren't

199

going to feed us, I'd at least like to arrive with a full stomach. Then it won't be as bad. Well, not at first anyway. If I were to go to prison hungry, then it would be much worse on account of I'd just be thinking about eating until the murderers and rapists came along."

"I see," Headmistress said. "You may have a seat now."

As Paddy turned to sit, Percival studied the headmistress' face. *Wait? Is she smiling?* Not a full smile, but Percival was sure he'd seen the hint of one before the woman realized what she'd done. Could he dare hope that she wasn't going to send them both away?

"Do you have anything to add, Mr. Barsotti?"

Percival gulped. No one had ever called him by his papa's name before. He stood and approached the desk. "If you please, ma'am, Paddy shouldn't have to go to prison with me, as he didn't do any of the fighting. Not much anyway. He was too busy being pulverized. He knows how to fight okay, at least for a little guy. But it's hard to fight when people are pounding on you like that. That's why I got so mad. You see, before I learned something about fighting, I had some boys try to throw me off the roof. I know the boys weren't going to throw Paddy off the roof, but I was afraid they were going to hurt him real bad. So I helped."

"You nearly sent a boy to the hospital."

Percival looked at his shoes. "Yes, ma'am. I'm real sorry about that too."

"I spoke with Dr. Todd. He said the boy will be fine."

"Dr. Todd's here?" Percival knew the man worked here, but though he'd asked, he'd yet to see the man.

"He's in the building. Came in this morning to tend to some children, and instead, he's spent his time fixing your mess. I suspect you'll want to see him now that you know he is here."

"No, ma'am," Percival said, shaking his head.

"No? Why, I've been told by more than one person that you've asked to see the man."

"Yes, ma'am, but I guess I've got no cause to see him now."

"Why on heaven's earth not?"

"If they're not going to feed me in prison, I doubt they'd allow me to drink tea. Besides, if I'm gonna have to run from the murderers and rapists, I suppose I'd like my legs to move as fast as they can. Paddy, he can't run so fast, so I suppose it wouldn't be good for him to go to prison."

"I can run almost as fast as you," Paddy objected.

"Quiet, ya goof, I'm trying to keep ya out of the joint," Percival whispered over his shoulder.

"Mr. Barsotti," the headmistress said, drawing his attention. "Is it true that on the day of your arrival, you laid your hands on one of the mistresses in the washroom with the intent of hitting her?"

"Oh, no, ma'am," Percival said, shaking his head.

"You're telling me you did not grab the wrist of Mistress Eleanora?"

"Oh, yes, I grabbed her alright. 'Cept I didn't intend on hitting her." He looked the headmistress in the eye, mentally begging her to understand. "Only, I didn't intend on her hitting me neither."

Paddy snickered, and headmistress narrowed her eyes at him.

"The lady ripped my clothes off and threw them into the stove," Percival continued.

"Mine too," Paddy agreed. "Then she rubbed my skin raw with her brush."

"Now, I might not have liked getting undressed in front of the woman, but I would have done it if she told me why. She didn't. She just started tearing my clothes off. I thought about hitting her. Thought real hard on it, but Big Joe—he's the one who taught me how to fight—told me how I should never hit a dame."

The headmistress' face paled. "This Big Joe you speak of, is he a..."

Paddy cut her off. "Slim here don't take too kindly to people calling him names."

"He's my friend," Percival said heatedly. "I'll not have you speak ill of him."

"You don't have to be all sore about it," Paddy told him. "I didn't let her call him the other word."

"I was going to say boxer," the headmistress said dryly. The color had returned to her face. She picked up a small bell from her desk and clanged it twice. The door opened, and Clara hurried in.

"Yes, Headmistress?"

"Clara, see this young man to the Meeting Room," she said, pointing to Paddy, "and then take Mr. Barsotti here to see Dr. Todd."

Clara's brow furrowed. "You're letting them stay?"

"Do as I told you and be quick about it," Headmistress said sternly.

"Yes, ma'am," Clara said. She turned and motioned the boys to follow, then hurried down the hallway, never once checking to see if they were following. Only after turning the corner did she speak. When she did, her words came out in a whisper. "How come the headmistress didn't send either of you away?"

"Maybe she likes us," Paddy offered.

"Doubtful. Headmistress doesn't like anyone."

"She seems to like you well enough," Percival replied.

"She only likes me on account of I've been here longest," Clara responded.

"How long ya been here?" Paddy asked.

"All my life." There was a touch of sadness in her words. Paddy blew out a low whistle.

"Dr. Todd told me if I'd come inside, I might could get a new family. You seem okay," Percival said. "How come no one has adopted you?"

"Maybe I don't want a family," Clara retorted. "You know Dr. Todd?"

"Met him once," Percival said, glancing at Paddy.

"Maybe that's why she let you stay."

"You never told me you know a doctor," Paddy said.

"I've met a lot of people I haven't told you about," Percival replied. He relaxed when Clara stopped and opened the door to the Meeting Room to allow Paddy inside.

"You're hiding something from him," she said when they began walking once more.

"What makes you say that?"

"I've been in here long enough to make a fair assessment of the kids I meet. So what is it?"

"Paddy's my friend. Just trying to keep him safe is all."

"Those boys deserved what they got. There are others that steal food, but those boys take it too far. They've sent their share of kids to the infirmary." She turned and offered a brilliant smile that Percival felt deep inside. "Your friend is lucky you were there. I like you, Mr. Barsotti. Not many boys would risk getting thrown into prison just to help a friend. I even heard Mistress Eleanora say she likes you."

"Likes me enough to tell the headmistress I was going to hit her. I told her that I wasn't planning to hit her. I was just stopping her from hitting me."

Clara laughed. "Is that what she told you?"

"She did."

"That's not at all what Mistress Eleanora said. She said she'd grown impatient with you and was about to slap you when you prevented her from doing so. She even told Headmistress that you were very polite about it. Hmm."

"Hmm, what?"

"Maybe that's why she didn't send you and Paddy to prison. On account of you didn't lie to her."

"I don't know, but I'm glad for it."

They stopped in front of a door marked "infirmary," and Clara offered another smile. "Whatever the reason, you caught a lucky break." Her smile faded. "Headmistress is fair, but she's also firm. Best you remember that. Can you find your way back when you're finished?"

"I can," Percival said, bobbing his head. "Clara?"

"Yes?" she said, hesitating.

"My friends call me Slim."

"Slim it is." She turned and left without another word.

Dr. Todd was standing with his back to the door when Percival entered.

"Is it an emergency?" he asked without turning.

"No, sir," Percival answered.

"Good. I don't have no time for those today," the man said. "Have a seat in one of the chairs. I'll be with you directly."

Percival took a seat near the door and watched as the doctor moved about a small table, doctoring a boy with a badly skinned knee. Though he couldn't see his face, he knew the child to be too small to be one of the boys he'd tussled with earlier in the day. A good thing, as he felt bad enough already without bearing further witness to the pain he'd inflicted. An older girl with light brown hair stood next to the boy, holding his hand as the doctor dabbed some purple liquid on the wound. The boy whimpered, and the girl wrapped her arms around him to console him. The scene reminded him of his mother and the many times she'd stopped what she was doing to hug away his pain. The image tugged at his heartstrings. For a moment, he envied the child.

"He's all finished now," Dr. Todd said, turning away.

The girl let go and helped the boy down. At first, Percival thought her to be older than Clara, but looking closer, he realized she was just more filled out than the girl. She caught sight of Percival watching and batted at the wisps of hair that had fallen into her face. Percival blushed and dropped his gaze to his legs, which were showing his nervousness.

The girl took the boy by the hand and walked toward the door. As she neared, she looked over her shoulder then paused. "You the boy they call Slim?"

"Yes."

She cast another glance over her shoulder, "I'm Dorthia. Mary wants to speak to you."

"Who's Mary?"

"She'll find you tomorrow in the Meeting Room." Before he could ask any questions, she gathered the boy in her arms and left.

Percival was still watching the door when he heard Dr. Todd's voice.

"Well, look who decided to join us," he said, extending his hand.

Percival stood and gripped the man's hand, pumping it up and down.

"How are those legs of yours?"

"Jumpy, sir."

"Did that tea I gave you work?"

"Yes, sir. Settled them right down."

The doctor frowned. "They don't look so settled at the moment."

"No, sir, I ran out of the tea."

"No need to worry, son, we'll get you fixed up." The doctor walked to a cabinet and removed a small bottle. He began measuring some into a flask. "How long have you been in here?"

"Two days, sir."

He paused and lowered the flask. "You wouldn't know anything about some patients I had earlier, would you? They told me they were attacked by a new kid."

"Yes, sir. But I didn't attack them. Not exactly anyway. They were beating up a friend of mine. I couldn't abide by that none." Percival sighed, then went on to tell the doctor the details.

"Yes, I saw your friend. He was lucky you came along when you did. You're still here. Just how was it you were able to get Headmistress LaRue to allow you to stay?"

"I don't know, sir. Even the girl, Clara, seems baffled about that. She thought maybe it was because when Headmistress asked me a question, and I didn't lie."

"Not likely. Tell me about the conversation with Headmistress."

Percival repeated all that he remembered. When he finished, the doctor laughed. "What's so funny, sir?"

"It seems you saved your own hide without realizing it."

"I did, sir? How?"

"By name dropping."

"Oh no, sir, I didn't call anyone any names. Paddy didn't either; he was just trying to tell the Headmistress that Big Joe was black, not the word he thought she was trying to say."

Dr. Todd laughed once more. "I didn't say you were calling people names. I said you were name-dropping. Meaning you used both mine and your friend Big Joe's name."

"Did I get you in trouble?"

"No, but you got yourself out of some."

"I don't understand," Percival said, scratching his head.

"Big Joe knows I donate my services here at this asylum.

Before he left town, he gave me some money to make a donation to the Headmistress to help keep the asylum running. I gave her the money, and when she asked where it came from, I told her it came from Big Joe. I also said he might be sending over a boy and, if he did, that Big Joe would be much obliged if she looked after him and sees that he's well taken care of."

"That's nice, but what's it got to do with me?"

"Why, everything. Big Joe told me about you and said he was going to give you my number. Said that if you called, he wanted me to try to get you to come here because he knew if you did, I'd be better able to watch over you." He clamped a hand on Percival's shoulder. "It was a sizeable donation. And now Headmistress knows you are the boy I was speaking of. How would it look for Headmistress LaRue to accept that money and then turn around and send you to prison?"

"Not very good?"

"Indeed. You, my boy, have a meal ticket. Why, you could do just about anything and not get pushed out of here. But don't you go and use that information to cause any trouble. Big Joe put his good reputation on the line for you. You wouldn't want to ruin that, would you?"

"Oh, no, sir. Big Joe's my friend. Why, aside from Paddy and Mouse, he's 'bout the bestest friend I got."

"He's a good friend to have, boy. He'll do right by you. Just think about it; he's not even here, and he's already kept you from going to prison. What's the matter, son?" Dr. Todd asked when Percival frowned.

"I don't think Big Joe would be as happy with me as you are."

"Why not?"

"Because I hurt that one boy pretty bad. I'm afraid I let him down."

Dr. Todd considered this for a moment. "Did you mean to

hurt him that bad?"

"No, sir, I just wanted to stop him from hurting my friend."

"I think Big Joe would understand that. Besides, I think he'd have done the same thing. I know I would've."

"You would?"

"Sure, you acted on instinct, and because you did what you did, your friend is still up and walking around. Let me tell you something you may not know."

Percival leaned closer.

"Those boys have been causing quite the fuss around here. But no one could do anything about it."

"Not even the headmistress?"

"Not even her."

"Why not?"

"On account of she couldn't prove it. She had her suspicions but couldn't very well send them off to prison for no good reason. The kids they pick on are too scared to tell on them. So, they keep getting away with it. Until now. Your friend's lucky you're in here with him."

Percival nodded his agreement, letting the doctor think his words had reached him. It didn't matter what anyone else thought. Percival knew the truth. When he'd first come upon the boys whaling on his friend, an image of Milo and his gang had come to mind. For a second, he was in Paddy's place, and fear had nearly made him turn and run in the other direction. Then he'd remembered his lessons with Big Joe and further realized that Paddy wouldn't be in the mess in the first place if not for him. He'd started swinging and driving the boys away from Paddy. Only he wasn't led by the lessons from Big Joe; he was fueled by the guilt of betraying his friend.

Chapter Twenty-Six

"Are you awake?" Paddy's voice called in the dark. Though they were supposed to be asleep, as long as they kept their voices low, the late hours of the evening were the only time the children could converse without being reprimanded.

"Yes," Percival replied.

"Something seemed different today."

Percival rolled onto his side. "What do you mean?"

"In the common room. I had kids coming up to me and talking to me like I was their friend."

"That's because you're likable."

"No, I'm telling you it was different. If you'd have been there, you'd have seen it too."

Percival had spent the better part of the day with Dr. Todd, further enjoying a leisurely dinner with the man in the infirmary, during which he found out the man enjoyed reading as much as Percival. As such, he hadn't even seen Paddy until he and the others were led up the stairs for the night. "It's on account of your face. Maybe everyone feels sorry for you because it's pretty messed up."

"Nah. I think it's because I'm friends with you. Everyone's talking about you, and there's this gang."

"I'm not interested in no gang," Percival said, cutting him off.

"This is different."

"We never joined one on the outside and we're not joining one now."

"I'm telling you this gang is different 'cause it has both boys and girls. And get a load of this, it's run by a girl named Mary, who's pretty ducky for a dame."

"Mary?"

"Yeah, you know her?"

"No, but there was this girl in the infirmary named Dorthia who told me Mary wanted to talk to me. You think it's the same girl?"

"Must be. I've only heard of one Mary. They want me too, but I think that's only on account of I know you. You'll talk to them, won't you, Slim?"

Percival sighed. He had no desire to join a gang, but he owed it to Paddy to at least talk to the girl. "Yeah, Paddy, I'll talk to her."

"I knew you would. Thanks, Slim, you're the greatest."

Percival rolled onto his back and closed his eyes. As he drifted off to sleep, he wondered if Paddy would still think him the greatest if he knew he was the one that helped get him into this place.

***

As news got around about the fight, Percival realized Paddy was right. Like it or not, it seemed as if everyone knew of him or had at least heard what he'd done. In the play yard, boys sought him out, mostly to have him recount the fight or retelling what they'd heard as if he'd not been privy to first-hand information. Even Paddy, who'd been elevated simply by being Percival's friend, seemed to be accepting life in the asylum. Even though Percival enjoyed the company, he wasn't sure what to make of his new celebrity status. He certainly wasn't as happy with it as Paddy, who didn't seem to mind reliving his moment of weakness to demonstrate how Percival had jumped in to save him from sure death. His friend was so animated in the telling that Percival was certain Paddy could have charged

210

a penny a person and gotten it.

Percival brought up the rear of the line as the boys were led to the Community Room. The girls had yet to arrive, so the boys spread out exploring the different activities. Four boys dropped to their knees in the corner of the room, pulling out marbles and positioning them on the floor. One of the boys waved them over.

Paddy elbowed him when he hesitated. "Come on, Slim, they're gonna let us join in."

"Nah, you go on," Percival said, "I want to wait for this Mary girl and see what she wants to talk to me about."

"Don't be a wet blanket. We'll be able to see her when they come in."

"Okay," Percival said, reluctantly following his friend. Paddy slid to his knees next to the other boys, and Percival leaned against the wall to watch.

"Want to shoot?" one of the boys asked, ignoring Paddy and offering a marble to Percival.

Percival shook his head. The truth was he was probably the only boy in the room that didn't know how to shoot marbles. While he'd seen the game being played, he'd never actually held a marble in his hand.

"I'll play," Paddy said, reaching for the marble.

"I guess we've got enough players after all," the boy said closing his hand over the glass ball.

Paddy turned his head to hide his disappointment, and for a moment, Percival thought to tell the boys he'd changed his mind. Before he could do so, the main door opened and the girls filed inside. All dressed in the same blue and white gingham dress covered by a white apron, Percival found it difficult to tell them apart at a distance. Finally, he caught sight of Dorthia, the girl from the infirmary, and smiled. The girls broke into smaller groups, moving around the room to different play stations.

Dorthia and several others moved to the center of the room, grinning as some of the boys joined them. Paddy pushed to his feet, his disappointment obviously forgotten as he hurried to join the small group. They were talking about him; this he knew because all eyes turned in his direction. Percival felt the heat in his face and lowered his gaze, pretending to be interested in the game of marbles.

Percival heard footsteps and looked to see Paddy hurrying toward him. "Mary wants to see you."

"Did she say what she wants?" Percival asked, scanning the group and trying to figure out which girl was Mary.

"No, only that she wants to talk to you."

Percival pushed off the wall and casually followed to where the others stood. Once there, he didn't have to ask which one she was, as all the others turned toward a dark-haired girl with crystal blue eyes. Percival tilted his head in her direction. "You wanted to speak to me."

"I did. I thought to ask if you'd like to join our little gang."

"Not interested." Apparently, they were not used to being told no, as several in the group gasped.

Mary pulled herself taller and squared her shoulders. "May I ask why not?"

"I survived the streets without joining a gang, so I guess I don't see any need to join one in here."

"Oh, but you're wrong," she said, and the others nodded. "We look out for each other."

"All the gangs I've ever known are bullies who build themselves up by putting others down," Percival replied.

"Mary's gang isn't like that," Dorthia said, fluttering her lashes at him. "When I first came inside, none of the other kids would talk to me. Oh, they'd talk about me to be sure, but they thought since I looked…older that I was promiscuous."

"You are promiscuous," one of the girls said, causing the

others to laugh.

"Yes, but they didn't know it at the time." Dorthia pouted. "I just wanted to be treated like a normal person. Mary understands that."

Percival remembered his mother, recalled her yearning to fit in, and wavered. Then he remembered his conversation with Big Joe and how he should be careful of pledging his loyalty to the wrong person. How did he know that the reason they wanted him to be one of their group wasn't because of what he'd done? It had to be. It was the reason the boys in the play yard invited him to play and the reason the boys in the corner wanted him to shoot marbles. Maybe he should have agreed to play their silly game instead of letting his friend down. Paddy so much wanted to fit in that he was willing to relive his own misery to do so. Maybe he himself would feel that same need to belong if he hadn't been left to his own devices for most of his childhood. As it was, while he preferred to have people near, his happiness didn't depend on it.

He decided to test Mary's motives. "Does Paddy get to be part of the group?"

"He already is," Mary replied. "Didn't he tell you?"

No, he left that part out. "And if I say no, does Paddy get to stay?"

Mary frowned. "What does your decision have to do with him?"

"I thought…"

"You thought we were using your friend to get to you? It doesn't work that way. I'm not trying to force anyone to do anything they don't wish to do. We," Mary spread her arms to include those standing around her, "are family. We might not be a real family with the same mothers and fathers, but we're family all the same."

"I like you better than my real mother," one of the girls said.

Several of the others nodded their agreement.

Mary shrugged. "I guess I act like their mother sometimes. Giving advice and reminding them to tie their shoes. When I first came in, there were some older kids who weren't very nice to me. So I started finding kids like me that didn't fit in with the others, and it kind of grew from there. Now I try to greet kids as they come in and let them know they have a friend if they want. Most end up gravitating to their own kind. Those who need the feel of family stick with our little group, and bullies go with the bullies. 'Tis the way it is in here."

"I think it's the way it is everywhere," Paddy agreed.

"We don't have to worry about the bullies no more, 'cause your friend took care of them." One of the boys grinned.

"There are still those that like to push kids around." Mary directed her comment to Paddy. "They will tease you or steal your food if you don't eat fast enough, but that's not as bad as what those boys did to you."

There was something about the girl that Percival liked. Though she didn't command it, everyone in her little clutch appeared to look to her for guidance. It dawned on him that he'd just met the female equivalent of Mouse. Still, just because she reminded him of Mouse didn't make it so. He looked about the small group, his gaze landing on Paddy. "I'll be your friend, but I'm not interested in joining no gang."

Paddy nodded but refrained from commenting. When Percival stepped away, Paddy stayed with his new friends. The instant he stepped away from the group, his insides churned much the way they did after his mother died. So much for doing the right thing. He'd done what Big Joe had said, and instead of feeling good about his decision, he felt even worse than he did after the man had left. Suddenly, in this room full of kids, he felt utterly alone. He looked toward the boys who'd invited him to play marbles, but nothing had changed. Even if they agreed to let him join, they'd soon figure out he had nary a clue how to play. Better they think him unwilling to play their silly game than to be laughed out of the circle. He tried talking to some of the other kids, but each interaction felt hollow. Finally, he walked to the bookcase and pulled a book free, wishing instead for the book he'd brought with him when he came. The simple act of remembering the book reminded him how much his life had changed since his mother had died. He longed to go back in time to when his mother kept him inside, hoping to protect him from the ugliness of the world. He hugged the new book to his chest, wishing with everything he had to have those moments back—no, he wanted to have his mother back.

Percival moved to the table, opened the book, and tried to read. It was no use; the words blurred as his tears dropped onto the page. Unable to stop the flood of tears, he pulled the book close to hide his face and let them flow. When at last they'd finally run their course, he wiped them from his cheeks and lowered the book. He surveyed the room to see if anyone was looking and discovered only one witness to his anguish. Across the room, surrounded by her small circle of friends, Mary's eyes locked with his. There was no malice in her face, no sneer that said I told you so. Percival looked beyond her to see Paddy laughing and chatting with his new friends. No, they'd called themselves a family. Suddenly, he was reminded of Peter Pan and Peter's longing for a family. For the first time since he'd entered the asylum, he wished to be back in the graveyard with Mouse, Paddy, and the gang. *Gang? Is that what we were?* They hadn't called themselves a gang. *No, we called ourselves family. Just like Mary. Mary!* The reason he was in here was to see if it was safe for Mouse's gal. While he couldn't keep an eye on the girl when they were separated, Mary could. If he said no, he might have trouble convincing her to watch over Mouse's gal, but if he was part of the gang, he might have a say. He looked in Mary's direction once more and found her still staring as if patiently awaiting him to reconsider. He nodded his acceptance, and she smiled.

Chapter Twenty-Seven

The decision to join Mary's gang provided instant relief. Percival started toward the group, stopping when Mistress Gretchen came into the room, clapping her hands to signal the boys to gather in preparation for heading upstairs for the evening. Not wishing to be reprimanded for dawdling, he fell into line with the others. All was quiet as they climbed the stairs to the third floor and saw to their showers before finally settling into bed. The instant the lights dimmed, Percival pulled himself up on his elbow, whispering to get Paddy's attention—calling his name several times before the boy answered.

"Leave me alone; I'm tired."

Percival knew him to be lying, as he'd never seen him too tired to speak. "Come on, Paddy, I just wanted to tell you I changed my mind about joining Mary's gang."

"You did?" Paddy was instantly up, his words coming way too loud before he lowered his voice. "Why didn't you say anything?"

"I was gonna, but Mistress Gretchen came in and I didn't have a chance to tell you. Mary knows."

"How does she know if you didn't tell her?" Paddy asked on a yawn.

Percival rolled over on his back and whispered to the ceiling. "She's a lot like Mouse, ya know."

"Who, Mary? She's a girl."

"I know, but something about her reminds me of him. Like how she just seems to know things."

"It's his fault we're in here," Paddy replied.

"It is?" Percival gulped.

"Sure, he's the one who told us where to go. We've never gone that way before. Why then?"

"It's my fault too," Percival said and felt better for having admitted the truth.

"It is?"

"Sure, if I hadn't been looking at that motorcar, I would have seen the policeman and could have warned you." *Okay, so only partial truth.*

"I'm glad you didn't see him."

"Seriously? You're not mad?" Percival struggled to keep the excitement from his voice.

"I was sore enough at first. But it's not so bad in here. Not since you took care of those boys. I was afraid you wouldn't. I mean, I knew you'd help on account of you always do, but then I was afraid you'd run away. I know I would have. Maybe not, but I think I would."

Percival stilled his breath.

"You still awake?"

"Yes," Percival admitted.

"I saw your face, and you looked really scared. But then you jumped in and showed them."

He'd spent so much time spent racked with guilt over harboring the secret and Paddy had known all along. "I don't know what happened. I saw you getting beat up, knew it was you, but all I could see was Milo and his gang."

"I didn't think you were afraid of Milo and his gang."

"I'm not, or at least didn't think I was. But there was a time when they did to me what those boys did to you. When I saw you with them, it was like I was getting beat up all over again. I'm sorry, Paddy, I really am."

"Is that why you pounded them so hard? Cause you thought

it was Milo."

"I think maybe."

"Slim?"

"Yeah?"

"I don't care the reason. I'm just glad you did what you did."

"Me too. Paddy?"

"Yeah, Slim?"

"I'm glad we're still friends."

"Course we are. Why wouldn't we be?"

"I guess if you're not mad at me for taking my time to start fighting, I won't be mad at you for choosing Mary and her gang over me." The truth of the matter was he was more hurt than mad.

"I didn't pick them over you."

"Sure you did. You stayed with them when I walked away."

"That's because I knew you'd be back."

"How'd you know when I didn't know?"

"Remember that time when Mouse led everyone to the cemetery?"

"Which time?"

"The first time. When I didn't stay."

"Yeah."

"I knew I should go in 'cause I really didn't have anywhere else to go, but I was kinda sore on account of Mouse didn't ask if we wanted to go. He just kind of took us there and told us it was to be so. You know Mouse rubs me the wrong way, and well, he sure got me mad with that one. I have to level with ya, Slim. I had a devil of a time finding a place to sleep at night. The more I thought about it, the more I knew I didn't want to be alone, even if it meant answering to Mouse. The thing is, I don't even know why I get sore at Mouse. My momma used to say there's some people you meet and just don't like for no good reason. I guess it's one of those things between me and Mouse. Anyhow, I know you, Slim. I saw your legs jumping and knew you were upset. I knew I had to be patient. My momma always said time is all a person needs to learn what's good for them."

Paddy was right; while the tea helped to settle his legs, it did not take the jitters completely away, especially when he was upset. "I guess your momma was right, Paddy."

"About some things," Paddy agreed. "Good night, Slim."

"Night, Paddy," Percival said, closing his eyes.

***

November 20, 1920

Percival raced up the steps heading to the infirmary. Dr. Todd had decided it best for him to have his tea twice a day, further arranging it to be dispensed by either the doctor himself or a nurse if the doctor wasn't in the building. He'd also managed to convince the headmistress that Percival was trustworthy enough to venture to and from the infirmary on his own. Percival liked the added freedom and often ran up the stairs, something that wasn't allowed when supervised by any of the mistresses. He rounded the second flight of stairs and nearly ran smack into Dorthia, who was on her way down at the time. The girl jumped out of the way and lost her balance, landing on her backside.

"Why you," she started, then softened her voice. "Slim, I didn't know it was you. Where are you off to in such a hurry?"

"I'm going to the infirmary to see Dr. Todd," Percival said and started to leave. Dorthia touched his arm and he wondered why he seemed to feel the warmth of her touch deep inside.

"I just came from there. He's with a little girl with a terrible toothache, so I have no doubt he'll be another few minutes yet. Your face is all red." She skimmed his cheek with the tip of her fingers. "Are you feeling alright?"

"Yes," he gulped.

"Slim," she wrinkled her nose and trailed her fingers around to the back of his neck, "what's your real name?"

Another gulp. "Percival."

"Have you ever been kissed, Percival?"

"Only by my mom, but I don't think that counts." His voice squeaked when he answered.

She laughed a flirty laugh. "No, I'm talking about a real kiss."

Too afraid to speak without showing his fear, he shook his head. She leaned forward, her lips meeting his, and she moved her hand to the back of his head, keeping it there for some time before releasing her hold on him. His skin grew clammy and his heart beat as if it were going to jump right out of his chest. The second she let go, he bolted up the stairs like a rabbit being chased by a hungry dog. Pausing at the next landing, he leaned over the rail to see if she was following him. She wasn't and he wasn't sure if that pleased or disappointed him. As he entered the infirmary, the heat of her hand still lingered on the back of his neck and his lips tingled where hers had pressed against his. He wiped the sweat from his temples with the back of his hand as Dr. Todd came around the corner of the room.

Dr. Todd cocked an eyebrow. "If I didn't know better, I'd think you were being chased."

Percival resisted the urge to look over his shoulder. "No, sir. Just stretching my legs is all."

"Don't make a habit of fooling around on the stairs. If the headmistress gets wind of you behaving that way, she'll see to it you have a chaperone anytime you're in the hall."

Wonder what she'd do if she found out what I was really doing. "Yes, sir."

"You look pretty chipper," Dr. Todd said, looking him over.

"Does that mean you're settling in?"

"Yes, sir, I like it here just fine." Percival felt a blush creep over his face and was glad when Dr. Todd turned toward the counter and began pouring his tea.

"So, I don't need to find a way to get you out of here?" Dr. Todd asked without turning around.

"I'd be obliged to get one of those jobs you told me about, but only for the money. I expect I'll stay in here for a while yet." After what just happened in the hall, he was in no hurry to leave.

"Good. That gives me a bit of time to decide what kind of job would best suit you," Dr. Todd said, handing him his tea. "That Dorthia girl just left here. I tell you, she sure likes to kiss."

Percival's hands started to tremble. "What?"

"I said that Dorthia girl just left here. She sure likes the kids."

Percival held the cup with both hands, willing his nerves to settle.

"With the girls, it's easy, as they can work with the babies, help in the laundry, and in the kitchen. But boys are harder to place. You got to figure out just the right job to keep their mind from wandering. A wandering mind can get a boy in trouble. We wouldn't want you to get into any trouble now, would we, son?"

"No, sir." Had his mind wandered when Dorthia kissed him? *If anyone should get in trouble, it should be her, since it was she doing the kissing.*

"You give me some time and I'll find the right job for you." The door opened and an older girl came in holding the hand of a boy whose other hand was clutching his stomach. Dr. Todd pointed her to a thin bed on the far side of the room, started to join them, and paused. "When you finish with your cup, set it on the counter."

"Yes, sir," Percival said, draining the cup.

"Slim," Dr. Todd said when he reached for the doorknob. "You behave yourself in the hallway. We wouldn't want you to do anything to give the headmistress a reason to punish you."

***

Still shaken by Dorthia's kiss, Percival decided to fill Paddy in on what had happened. The problem was finding a chance to speak with the boy alone. In the days since arriving, Paddy had made lots of new friends, which meant someone was always nearby. He'd thought to speak with him today during their time in the play yard, but thus far, the boy seemed content to run around yelling and whooping it up with his new friends. It was nearly time to go inside when Paddy finally broke away from the group and ran to the far side of the play yard. Thinking he'd finally found his moment, Percival followed. As he neared, it was clear that Paddy was speaking with someone. Percival sighed. He really wanted to talk to his friend in private.

"Hey, what are you doing over here?" he said, hiding his disappointment.

"He's talking to me. Got something to say about it?"

Percival recognized the voice and his spirit lifted as Mouse stepped into view. Paddy didn't seem upset, so he knew Mouse hadn't let on about getting them thrown inside. *Better stay with the ruse.* "Mouse! I knew you'd come. Have you come to bust us out?"

"Are you kidding? Paddy was just telling me how much he likes it here."

Percival feigned shock. "Give a kid a real bed to sleep on and he's a goner for sure."

Mouse raised an eyebrow. "Are you telling me you don't agree? I can get you out."

Mistress Gretchen clapped her hands.

"Got to go." Paddy turned to go inside. "You get her in; I'll find someone to watch over her when I can't."

Percival realized they'd been talking about Mouse's girl and felt a bit hurt at being left out of the conversation. *Is Mouse sore at me?* He wished he had time to talk with Mouse and maybe tell him of his encounter with Dorthia and about the boys he'd fought. At least let him know he'd dealt with that situation and the boys no longer bothered anyone. He looked to the door. It was only a matter of time before Mistress Gretchen called him out for dawdling. He shrugged. "Naw, it ain't so bad. None of the boys mess with me, and I don't miss sleeping on the cold ground. I was never good at dipping pockets anyhow."

"Don't you worry about picking pockets, Slim. Your talents lie elsewhere. Now go before you get in trouble. I'll check in on you boys from time to time to see if you need anything."

Percival turned to walk away when Mouse called to him once more. "Yo, Slim? Paddy said something about a girl that causes trouble in there. Do me a favor and get me some information on her. I'll be around in a day or two to see what you come up with."

"You got it, Mouse," Slim said. As he hurried to the door, he wondered which girl Paddy was speaking of: the new girl who liked to steal food or Dorthia who preferred to steal kisses.

Chapter Twenty-Eight

Percival made several attempts to talk to Paddy, but his friend kept avoiding him, so he had to bide his time until they got to the Common room. As soon as Mistress Gretchen released them, Percival cornered his friend. "I need to talk to you."

"So go on and talk," Paddy said sourly.

"Not here," Percival's legs were bouncing from side to side.

"What's the big secret?" Paddy asked when they'd walked out of earshot of the others.

"Mouse wants to know about that girl you told him about."

"Sheesh, is that what this is all about? I was trying to find out before you pulled me away," Paddy grumbled. He started toward the others and Percival grabbed him by the arm.

"No, there's more. That girl Dorthia, she caught me on the stairs alone this morning and she kissed me!" He hadn't wanted to tell him here, but the boy had left him no other choice. If he didn't tell someone soon, he'd surely burst.

"Jeepers creepers, Slim. You got kissed this morning and this is the first I'm hearing about it?"

"Pipe down, ya dope. I don't want the whole world to know. I tried to tell you earlier, but you wouldn't listen." Percival glanced around the room to make sure no one was listening.

"What kind of kiss was it?" Paddy whispered.

The comment caught him by surprise. "Ya mean there's more than one kind?"

Paddy laughed. "Sure there is. You've got the kind your ma

does. Where she kisses you on the cheek to let you know she cares."

My momma's kisses never scared me. "Definitely not that kind," Percival said, shaking his head.

"Then you got a quick peck on the lips, a longer peck on the lips. Sometimes the girl even puts her tongue in your mouth."

"Why in blazes would she want to do that?" Percival said, wrinkling his nose.

"I don't know why they do it, but they do," Paddy replied.

"How come you know so much about kissing?"

"I know a lot about a lot of things," Paddy said proudly. "So tell me, what kind of kiss was it?"

"I guess it was somewhere in the middle. Definitely not a peck, but there weren't no tongues involved either." He was rather happy about that.

"Did you like it?"

Maybe. "I don't know. It kind of surprised me is all."

"What did you say after the kiss?"

"I didn't say anything. Like I said, she surprised me, so I ran."

"Are you going to do it again?" Paddy pressed.

"How would I know? I didn't plan on doing it the first time."

"You know, it's not a bad thing that she likes you."

Percival elbowed Paddy in the gut and pointed to Dorthia, who was busy chatting with Cecil, another of the boys in Mary's gang. She saw them looking and smiled. "I think she likes everyone."

"Well, she likes you and that's what's important. Pretend to like her back and ask her to tell you about the new girl," Paddy said, speaking of Anastasia, an older girl who stole food and made trouble for a lot of the smaller kids. "You've seen how she acts. I suppose she's the one that would be making trouble for Mileta."

"Who? Oh, you mean Mouse's girl."

"I told ya, just because Mouse calls her his girl don't make it so," Paddy said tersely.

"Mouse wouldn't like it if he found out you're sweet on his gal," Percival said, even though he was fairly certain that Mouse did indeed know.

"Mouse don't need to know everything," Paddy said, then nodded toward Mary's group. "Now's your chance. Dorthia is looking at ya. Go talk to her and get her to spill the beans."

Percival glanced in her direction; sure enough, Dorthia had finished her conversation and was indeed staring directly at him. "What if she wants to kiss me again?"

"Even if she does, she ain't gonna do it in here," Paddy assured him. "Now go talk to her."

Percival knew Paddy was right, that it was highly unlikely Dorthia would chance kissing him with so many eyes in the room, but that knowledge didn't help ease his fear. Though he'd had his afternoon tea, his legs told of his nervousness as he and Paddy approached the small group. Paddy immediately moved away from Dorthia, speaking loudly to draw the others' attention. Percival sidled up to Dorthia and whispered in her ear, "Sorry I ran off today. I didn't know you were gonna kiss me and it took me by surprise."

"You telling me a good-looking boy like you has never been kissed before?"

"Not by no girl."

Dorthia's eyes grew wide.

"I mean, I've only been kissed by my momma, until now."

She smiled. "I bet your momma didn't never kiss you like that."

Percival grinned. "No, she did not. Hey, what do you know

about the new girl, you know, the one who steals food?"

Dorthia's smile disappeared. "Anastasia? What do you want to know about her for?"

"I don't. I got a friend who's asking about her is all."

"Who? Paddy?" she asked, focusing her gaze on the redhead.

"No, someone I know who's still on the outside. He's pretty interested in her and I promised I would ask round."

"I'm not sure why anyone would be interested in the likes of her," Dorthia said, wrinkling her nose. "I don't know much about the nasty wretch other than she's mean, except when it comes to those babies. I suppose she likes them well enough. She's only been here a little while, and when she's not on the fourth floor, she hangs around with Clara most of the time."

"What's on the fourth floor?" Percival asked.

"The babies, of course. Wait, Chalkie might know something." Dorthia pointed across the room to the boy who was well known for running his hand down the blackboard and sucking the white dust from his fingers.

Percival saw fresh handprints on the blackboard and realized the boy was in the midst of having an afternoon snack. "Him? Why would he know anything?"

"On account of no one pays him any mind. I expect people think him feeble-minded on account of the chalk and all, but he's not. I've seen Clara and Anastasia talking and him being only a few feet away. Maybe he overheard something."

"I'll have a chat with him," Percival said, then waved to get Paddy's attention. "Thanks, Dorthia. Let me know if you find out anything else about the girl."

Paddy caught up with him just as he reached the boy whose face and clothes were dusted with chalk. As they approached, the boy pulled a finger from his mouth with a plop and stood staring at them, as if trying to decide whether or not to run.

"Look at you; don't you even care that you're a mess? Why do you eat that?" Percival asked.

"I dunno. I can't seem to stop. I even wake up thinking about it," the kid said, pressing his hand against the blackboard once more.

"I can think of a lot of things I think about eating, but chalk ain't one of them," Paddy snorted.

"What do you want?" the boy said, licking his index finger.

"I want to know what you can tell me about the new girl," Percival said, keeping his voice low.

The boy had been in the process of sucking on a finger. He removed it and looked at Percival. "Which one?" he asked and returned the digit to his mouth.

"Anastasia, the girl with the scar that likes to steal food," Percival said, sliding his index finger down his cheek to mimic the scar.

Chalkie produced a nervous giggle. "No way. She finds out I'm ratting her out, and she'll claw my eyes out."

"She ain't gonna do no such thing," Percival countered.

"I'm telling you she's a mean one," Chalkie stammered. "How do you think she got the scar? I hear she 'bout killed the girl who done it. I suppose it was on account of them teasing her about having a baby."

Percival exchanged glances with Paddy then addressed the boy once more. "If she has a baby, why ain't I never seen her with one?"

"How would I know. You asked me what I know and I'm telling you what I heard. Only reason I'm telling ya is on account of you beat up those boys and I don't want you to pound on me too. Do you think I'd lie to you knowing what you did to those guys?" Chalkie asked, wiping at the beads of sweat that had replaced the chalk.

The kid had a point and he did look scared enough to tell

him what he knew. Percival leaned in closer. "I need you to tell everything you told us to a friend of ours."

"Who?" Chalkie asked, looking about the room.

"He's not in here," Paddy replied.

"What do you mean he's not in here? How am I going to talk to someone on the outside?" he asked nervously.

"We talk to him through the fence in the play yard. He'll pay you for the information," Percival said, hoping to calm him.

Chalkie laughed. "What am I gonna do with dough in here?"

Percival looked to Paddy for help and his friend smiled.

"Here's the deal. You can tell our friend what you just told us or Slim here will beat you up. After my friend finishes beating you, we'll tell Anastasia that my friend here is sweet on her, and the reason he beat you up was to protect her reputation. My money says she will be so mad that she'll whale on you too."

Chalkie gulped. "You said your friend will pay me for the information?"

"Yeah, you tell him what you told us and he'll be good for a coin or two," Percival assured him.

"You make sure he gives me enough to buy some chalk, we've got a deal," Chalkie said, turning his attention back to the blackboard. "Oh, and you might want to ask Dorthia about Anastasia. The way I hear it, the girl likes to sneak out at night, and your friend Dorthia has gone with her a time or two."

Something about the way Chalkie looked at him when he called Dorthia his friend caused him concern. "Dorthia is both our friends."

"Yeah, but I hear she likes you specially well." Chalkie giggled. "She told Clara you kissed her."

Percival pressed the boy into the chalkboard. "I didn't kiss nobody, got it?"

"Sure, Slim, whatever you say, but you might want to tell Dorthia that 'cause that's what she's telling everyone. News like that might get you sent to the headmistress's office."

"I'll tell her alright," Percival said, releasing the boy. "And you stop repeating everything you hear."

"Cept to your friend, right, Slim." Chalkie snickered.

"That boy's got a big mouth," Percival said as they walked away.

"Sounds like your friend Dorthia's got a bigger one," Paddy replied. "She keeps that up and you're going to get in a heap of trouble. What ya gonna do about it?"

Before he could answer, the door opened. Mistress Gretchen stepped inside and clapped her hands for the boys to gather. Percival fell into line behind Paddy and the others, resisting the urge to glare at Dorthia when he saw her looking in his direction. Why would she go and tell everyone that he'd kissed her when it was she who'd done all the kissing while he'd just stood there. Even his legs stilled when her lips touched his. He might not have hated the kiss, but he didn't like it enough to risk getting kicked out of the asylum. Big Joe told him not to hit girls, but he didn't say anything about pushing them away. It might not be suitable to hit her, but he sure as heck could keep her from kissing him again.

Chapter Twenty-Nine

Percival lay in the dark thinking about the events of the day. Something was wrong. He wasn't sure what it was, only that something wasn't right. He'd done everything that was asked and yet Mouse had run off without so much as a goodbye. Percival dug at his memory, trying to find a clue as to what had upset his friend. Even though Chalkie had agreed to talk to Mouse, he and Paddy nearly had to drag him to the edge of the fence. Mouse had balked at paying him for his information, but that wasn't enough to cause his hasty departure. And he hadn't just bolted; he'd actually turned white as a sheet before fleeing. It just didn't make sense. Something touched Percival's arm. He jumped, pulling it away, then realized the something was a hand.

"Sorry, I didn't mean to scare you," Clara said softly.

He braced himself, ready to shove her away if she too had come to steal a kiss. Not that he'd mind kissing her, but rather decided it wouldn't be the prudent thing to do, knowing her to be the headmistress's favorite. "What are you doing on the boys' sleeping floor?"

"I came to find you."

Percival gulped. "Why?"

"It's Dorthia; she sent me to tell you that she had the information you wished to know. She wants you to meet her in the stairway."

Instantly, he struggled with wanting the information to pass on to Mouse to fearing that Dorthia had waited until the middle of the night in order to catch him alone. *Would it be so bad? Only if the headmistress were to catch you in the stairway with her.* "I'll talk to her in the morning."

"No, Dorthia said she needed to speak with you tonight," Clara insisted. "Give me a few moments and then go to the stairwell. If she's not there, sit on the stairs and please try and control your legs or you'll wake the whole building."

Clara was right to comment on his legs, as they danced his distress. Not only did he not wish to be alone with Dorthia, something was telling him to proceed with caution. Maybe it was just he hadn't known Dorthia and Clara to be such good friends.

The stairwell was quiet when he entered. Silently, he peered up the stairs then craned his head over the railing to check the lower stairwell. Seeing nothing amiss, he took a seat on one of the lower steps and waited. A short time later, he heard the door to the upper stairwell open and trembled as footsteps sounded on the tile floors. Just as he started chiding himself for being afraid of a girl, the footsteps turned into an array of moans and whimpers as the person tumbled down the stairs, coming to an abrupt halt directly near his feet. As he began to reach for her to see if she was alright, he realized the person heaped in front of him was not Dorthia but Anastasia. As the realization set in, he wasn't sure what terrified him more, her steady stream of tears or that she was between him and the door to the third-floor dorm. He remained as still as his legs would allow, watching as she pulled her legs into her chest and wept. Something about the helplessness of gesture pulled at him, as he remembered countless times being folded in the same position on the roof of his old apartment building. He leaned closer, wishing to ask if she were alright, yet afraid to let on he was there.

"It was I who sent for you. Though I didn't expect you to see me this way," she said tersely.

Something told him the bite in her tone was more from the embarrassment of being vulnerable than anger at him. "You hurt?"

"Just a few scrapes."

Liar. "That was a mighty lot of tears for just a few scrapes."

"Sometimes, when you cry, it's hard to stop the tears." She shrugged. "I guess that's a stupid thing to say."

He shook his head. "Nah, I get it."

As she attempted to stand, her face scrunched, showing her discomfort. Without thinking, he gathered her into his arms, lowered her to the stairs, then sitting next to her, took her ankle in his hands, attempting to rub away the pain.

"Where'd you learn to do that?" she asked, closing her eyes.

"My ma was a dancer. She'd come home and have me rub her feet."

"What happened to your ma?"

He hadn't expected a full conversation and wasn't sure how to respond. Every experience he'd had with the girl up to this point had been negative. Other than Clara, no one in the building seemed to like her. *Clara. She hadn't come to tell me Dorthia wanted to speak with me; she'd come to send me into a trap.* If Anastasia hadn't fallen, they'd be having a totally different conversation right now. He doubted it would be nearly this civil. Still, she seemed agreeable at the moment, and if he played his cards right, she might tell him what it was he wished to know. Deciding to continue with the ruse, he started rubbing her foot once more. "She went to work one night and didn't come home."

"And your dad?"

He'd already given her enough information about him and saw no reason to give her anything she might be able to use against him later. "Ma never told me who my pa was. I don't think she really knew."

"They weren't married?"

Great, she knows I'm lying. He pushed her foot from his lap and stood, all the while trying to figure out what to say. "No, they weren't married. Go ahead and call me names. I've heard them all before. Don't make no difference to me."

"Ow," she said, rubbing her ankle. "I wasn't going to call you anything."

"No?" *So she wasn't onto his lie?* "Then why'd you make a big deal about it?"

"I didn't know women could keep their baby if they weren't married is all."

"Sure they can. They do it all the time." At least he thought that to be the case. His mother hadn't had to give him away after his papa died, even though she wasn't married anymore.

Anastasia lowered her eyelids briefly. "Your momma was lucky to have you."

Momma used to say that all the time. "What makes you think so?"

"Sometimes mothers aren't given a choice," she said softly.

The situation seemed under control, so he took a seat beside her. "You seem nicer than I thought."

"Yeah, well, you'd better not tell anyone," she said, narrowing her eyes. "Why were you asking questions about me?"

"Maybe I liked you and wanted to know more." *Why'd I go and say I like her? What if she wants to kiss me now?*

"What do you want to know?"

Whew. Percival studied her face, staring into dark eyes that seemed to peer deep inside of him. He decided her to be attractive even with the scar that marred her face. No, not with it, because of it. With all the girls in the building dressed the same, the scar helped set her apart from the others. "The scar? How'd you get it?"

"I was in a knife fight. Some girl cut me, and I beat the snot out of her. Haven't you heard?"

"Sure, I've heard. We've all heard. We've heard lots of things. I'm just trying to find out if they're true." He didn't believe a word of it. Her words seemed rushed, as if she thought if she spilled them quickly enough, they'd be believed. Wait? Did that mean he really did like her?

"What's it to you if the things you've heard about me are true or not?"

"Maybe I just don't like seeing people get a bum rap." *Like Dorthia telling the whole asylum I kissed her when it was she doing the kissing. Could the same be the case with Anastasia? She doesn't seem to be the horrible person everyone makes her out to be.* Still, he'd seen her in action, pushing kids around and stealing their food. There had to be some truth to the accusations.

"What kind of things have you heard?"

"I've heard you hit some of the kids," he said, looking at her hand, which now rested on his knee.

"I have. Come to think of it, I've heard the same about you," she said.

"I ain't never hit anyone that didn't deserve to be hit," he said firmly.

"Neither have I."

"I saw you hit a boy the other day. He was minding his own business and you clobbered him. You saying he deserved to have you smack on him?"

"He did."

"What did he do to you?"

"Why does it matter?"

"It matters a lot. You say he deserved to be smacked. What'd he do to deserve it?" Percival didn't want to like her, but there was something about her that tugged at his heartstrings. Something he couldn't quite put his finger on. Maybe it was the dark strands of hair that had pulled free from her bow and tried unsuccessfully to hide the lengthy scar, the vulnerability in her eyes when she looked at him, or maybe it was just how she pretended to be fierce when she'd let her guard down enough for him to see otherwise. Whatever the reason, it was the first time he'd felt comfortable around a girl other than his mother.

"He told me I was ugly," she said, pulling the strand of hair close to her face.

You are a lot of things, but ugly isn't one of them. "Well, are you?"

"What?"

"Just because someone calls you a name doesn't make it true. Are you ugly?"

She took a moment to consider his question. "I guess if you get told it enough, you start believing it to be true."

Percival took hold of her hand and placed it on the side of his head, pressing her fingers to feel the long, raised scar that ran from above his ear to the back of his head. "You're not the only one with scars."

"What happened?"

"Ma would bring men home, and sometimes those men didn't like the thought of having a kid around while Ma conducted business." So much for not opening up to her.

"I thought you said your ma was a dancer?"

"Ma had a lot of jobs." He knew he was telling her too much but couldn't seem to stop. "Anyway, one time, one of those guys was drunk and hit me upside the head with a bottle. Split my head open in the process."

She let out a sympathetic sob and he leaned against her shoulder.

"Now don't go crying on me again. The pain's long gone

from that. Besides, something good came out of it. One of Ma's regulars was a boxer, a pretty good one at that. He showed me how to duck and move so that no one could hit me no more. He said I was a natural. Can you imagine that? Someone like him telling me I was good? It was almost worth being clubbed upside the head. He came around a lot there for a while and even taught me how to throw a punch." Okay, so he hadn't told the truth about Big Joe, but he didn't wish to detail how he'd met the man or answer any of the follow-up questions that would lead to questions about his mother's accident. The last thing he wanted was to start blubbering.

"Is that why your legs move all the time?"

"Nah, that started after I got hit in the head. The doctor said the bottle must have broken something more than my head."

"My papa used to hit me. He beat my momma mostly, but he beat me too. He just used his belt and fists. I'm glad he never used anything else."

"Is that why you ran away?"

"I didn't run away. My momma told me to leave. I guess she decided she loved my brothers Ezra and Tobias more than she did me."

Tobias? The shock of the news vibrated through his body. *She's Mouse's sister?! It had to be true. That would explain why he'd run when Chalkie had told him all the nasty things about her. Was he running because he was ashamed or because he hadn't wanted them to know?*

"Are you all right?"

"Yes...I guess what you said surprised me. It must have been hard leaving your brothers. Wouldn't you like to see them again? Either of them?" *I'm sure Mouse would like to see you. Maybe. I know I would if I had a sister.*

She looked him in the eye. "No, I wish never to see or hear of my family again."

Mouse is sure to come back at some point. Then what do I tell him? "Are you sure?"

"I am. I couldn't bear it. I'm thinking you have more questions. You best be getting on with them."

His knees drummed a rapid beat. Mouse wanted him to get more information, but the question he was about to ask was not for Mouse. It was he who wished to know. "They say you came here to have a baby. Is that true?"

"No, I did not come here to have a child. I had my son before I arrived."

"So you gave him away?" He saw the pain in her eyes and instantly realized his question sounded more like an accusation.

"I did not," she said heatedly. "I was sent to a home where they send girls like me. I wanted to keep my baby, but they wouldn't allow it. The mistress told me I would have to spread my legs in order to keep him and told me all the bad things that would happen to him if I did."

"Maybe you shouldn't have spread them in the first place." Her hand struck his face even before he had a chance to regret his words, a well-deserved smack he'd never seen coming. Anger bubbled inside, not at her for striking him, but at himself for judging her. Though he'd held back, she'd answered each question honestly. Filled with self-loathing, he sprinted up the stairs, racing all the way to the next floor and into the hallway before realizing he was on the wrong floor. Knowing better than to be caught in the corridor and further realizing there was no other way to reach the boys' floor, he returned to his stairwell. To his surprise, she was still standing there as if awaiting his return. He approached and sat next to her, fully expecting her to demand he leave. He was out of line, and if he were in her place, he'd do just that. When she failed to speak or banish him from the stairs, he pried further into her life.

"Did you know the baby's father?"

"I did."

"Did you love him?" *It's none of my business.* And yet a part of him wanted to know of the man who'd captured her heart.

"I think so. We were to be married. It hurt me very badly to watch him die," she continued, and he wept along with her as she told of the fire that had taken the boy's life and that of his mother.

He sighed a heavy sigh. "You're not what I thought you to be."

"Is that a bad thing?" she asked, batting away the tears.

"It's not a good thing or a bad thing."

"I know someone put you up to the questions. Dorthia told me you have a friend on the outside that wants to know. Is it my papa?"

"No, it's no one who knows you." He hated lying to her but decided he would not add to her pain this night. "The only reason my friend was asking about you was that he'd heard you made trouble for some of the kids inside. He has a girl he's been protecting, and her mother is very ill. He knows the only way he can keep her safe is to place her inside a home. He paid me to come in so I can help protect her."

"You must love your friend very much to come into a place such as this for him. I hope he appreciates your loyalty."

"He does." *Besides, it's not all that bad.* "Can I tell my friend you'll help watch over this girl?"

"Talk to Mary. If she agrees to watch over the girl, I will see that no one bothers her."

He had to admit to being surprised when Anastasia agreed so readily and hoped the same to be true for Mary. "Mary will agree."

"Slim…" She hesitated. "I'd prefer you not tell anyone what I've said to you."

He laughed. "And sully your evil reputation? Why, I wouldn't think of it."

Percival bid Anastasia goodnight and went back to the boys' dorm. As he sank into his bed, he realized he'd gotten all the information he'd been after and was fairly certain he could see to it that Mouse's gal would be safe if he were able to get her inside. As he drifted off to sleep, he decided he would tell Mouse what he needed to hear as long as it didn't betray Anastasia's trust.

Chapter Thirty

Anastasia leaned over the art table, intimidating a young girl who appeared to be around six or seven. It was apparent the girl had recently arrived at the asylum, as her blonde hair was haphazardly cropped close to her scalp. Her eyes darted from side to side as she blinked back tears.

"One of these days, she's going to meet her match," Paddy said, watching. "Too bad you have such a thing about hitting girls, 'cause if not, you'd sure give Anastasia a what for."

"Yeah, too bad," Percival agreed. Though he felt bad for keeping secrets from his friend, both he and Anna agreed it was best not to tell anyone of their friendship. Not only did Percival not wish to be shunned, he hadn't wished to further tarnish Anastasia's reputation. Clara knew they'd become close; however, she was wise enough to know of the trouble it would cause if the headmistress were to find out.

"Maybe I should do it," Paddy grumbled. "I could just walk over and punch her right in the nose, 'cause I ain't afraid of hitting no girl."

Percival wasn't worried about his friend's threat, as he'd made similar statements before and never acted on them. While Paddy wasn't afraid of getting into scrapes, Percival had never known the kid to actually start a fight. "I think you should just leave it alone. It's on account of the girl is new—Anastasia doesn't usually mess with the same kid for long."

"That doesn't make it right."

"I'll talk to Mary, make sure she knows," Percival said—

he'd been looking for an excuse to talk to her, and this was as good as any.

"I'll come too."

"Na, you keep an eye on Anastasia and make sure she don't push the new kid too far." Not that he felt she needed watching; it was just his way of keeping his friend busy, so he could talk to Mary alone.

Just before he reached Mary, Dorthia stepped in front of him, blocking his way. "You've been avoiding me."

"No, I haven't," Percival said, looking over her shoulder.

"Sure you are. You're doing it right now." She pouted.

He was, but he didn't like admitting to it. "I need to talk to Mary."

"Then I'll come with you."

"I need to talk to her alone."

"What's the big secret?"

"No secret; I just don't want anyone else to hear," Percival said, ducking around the girl.

"She likes you," Mary said when he approached.

"She likes everyone."

"Some people need attention to feel loved."

"I'm not ready for that kind of attention," Percival said, casting a glance toward Anastasia.

Mary raised an eyebrow. "'Tis a lot of trouble that one, I'd think you'd be safer with Dorthia."

"I was coming to talk to you about Anastasia," Percival said, ignoring the accusation. "I have a friend on the outside who wishes to send in a young girl whose mother is terribly ill—he wants to see her safe."

"He cares about the girl, and yet he's sending her here." Mary's words were uncharacteristically sharp.

"You don't like it here?" Percival asked with sudden doubt.

"It's a place to live, but 'tis not a proper home."

This time, her words were filled with such yearning, they pulled at the pit of Percival's stomach. "I've heard some of the children get adopted. Maybe you too will have a home one day."

"This girl you speak of, what is it you wish from me?" Mary said, brushing off his comment.

"I can keep an eye on her at times," Percival continued, "but I cannot watch over her when they keep us apart. I was hoping you'd take her under your care and watch over her. My friend would pay you for doing so."

"I reach out to all the kids that come inside and expect nothing in return. If they wish to stay close, we do what we can to see them settle in. I will not require payment for something I will do anyway. Just know that it's up to her if she wishes to join our little family. You'll also know I'm no match for that one," she said with a nod toward Anastasia.

"You'll not have to worry about Anna...Anastasia," Percival said, covering his misstep. "I've already spoken to her."

Mary sighed. "Tell me the girl's name. I'll do my best to keep her close."

"Her name is Mileta. I'm not sure how soon she will arrive. My friend...he prefers not to let the girl know of our involvement."

"Don't fret, I'll greet her when she does." Mary touched his arm. "Percival, please be careful who you give your heart to. I do not wish to see you hurt."

Percival wasn't sure what unnerved him more, that Mary seemed to know about his growing affection for Anastasia or that she'd called him by his given name. Something about the way she said it—perhaps it was because some of the younger children often referred to her as "Momma" when they were alone in the tight little group—sent a shiver throughout his body.

***

Anastasia was at the piano when he entered, banging away at the keys, playing simple tunes she'd learned from the boy who once had her heart. She wasn't very good, but she was the only one in the building who played. Of course, that could be because no one else dared touch the piano for fear of incurring her wrath. He observed her from a distance, then closed the gap, sliding onto the bench beside her. The only hint of surprise she showed was in missing a key to a song he'd heard her play many times before.

"Someday, you'll tell me how it is you are able to move through the halls without being reprimanded," she said without taking her eyes off the keys.

"I'll not give away all my secrets," Percival said, watching her fingers strike the keys with frustration. It wasn't any great secret—at least not one of his making. According to Dr. Todd, upon learning of his arrival, Big Joe made another donation to the asylum. After testing his theory several times, Percival learned he could pretty much go anywhere and do anything he wanted without anyone saying anything to him. He used his newfound privileges to walk the halls after lights out and to have alone time with Anna. On occasion, there'd be a simple kiss; on others, it would lead to more. Mostly, they would talk about their past and dare to dream about a future beyond the walls of the asylum. Percival spoke of the house in his mother's dreams, with windows in each room. His dreams were no match to Anna's dreams of finding the baby that was ripped from her arms. Oddly, never, when either of them spoke of their future, did that future include them together. He thought back to a story his mother had told about her and his papa wanting to be together enough to forsake her own father. He wondered if his mother were alive if he would do the same to be with Anna.

While he enjoyed the girl's company, he doubted he would choose her over his mother.

"You're quiet tonight," she said, finishing her song. "What's on your mind?"

"My momma and papa." She stiffened beside him and he instantly knew the reason. "I knew him. He died when I was but a small boy."

"You lied?"

"I didn't know you then and was afraid of saying too much."

"And what you told me about your mother?"

"All true."

"I lied too. I found out before I left that the man who married my mother was not my father. My momma had a secret lover and I am of his seed."

"I guess we both are guilty of untruths." Unfortunately, he still had one to tell, one that could change everything. He'd met with Mouse earlier in the play yard, and though he tried to keep her out of it, Mouse had insisted she meet with him, further insisting it was the only way he could be sure Mileta would be safe if sent to the asylum.

She turned back to the keyboard and began playing another tune. "What is it?" she asked when she finished and turned toward him once more.

He smiled. "Am I that easy to read?"

"Your legs are a dead giveaway."

"I need to tell you something."

"I'm ready."

"I lied to you. I didn't do it to hurt you. I guess I thought to protect you from further pain.

That day in the stairwell. The first time, when you'd hurt your ankle, I told you that you do not know my friend on the outside. That was a lie. You know him, and he wishes to meet with you."

She jumped to her feet. "You told me it wasn't my papa."

"It isn't. As far as I know, your father's dead," he said, speaking of the man who she'd just admitted wasn't her true father. "Tobias said his brother killed the man."

"Ezra killed Papa? Why?"

"Mouse said it was because your papa killed your momma," he said softly.

Anastasia sank onto the piano bench and Percival placed his hand on her back to soothe her.

"I guess I should have let Mouse tell you himself," Slim said after a time.

"He asked you to call him Mouse?"

"Sure, it's what everyone calls him. I'm not sure how he came by the name. Maybe it's because he's so quiet. He can sneak up on a person, and you don't know he's there until it's too late. He taught me a little, but I'm not nearly as good as he is. That boy is like a ghost sometimes," he replied.

"Where is Tobias now?"

"He wants to meet with you."

"He wants to meet with me?" Her voice sounded hopeful.

"Sure, I told him you've agreed to look after his girl, but he wants to make sure. He said he needs to talk to you and see the look on your face when you agree."

He watched the internal battle as her mind processed all he'd said. When she spoke, her words sounded resigned. "Who takes care of Tobias now?"

"Why, he's Mouse. Mouse doesn't need anyone to take care of him. It's he who takes care of everyone else," Slim replied.

"He's doing all right for himself, then?"

Slim grinned, hoping to reassure her. "He's doing better than okay."

"What have you told him about me?"

"Not a lot. We haven't really talked about you since you

and I became friends. You told me not to tell anyone how nice you are. I figured that meant Mouse too."

"Thank you, Slim," she said calmly. "When does he wish to meet?"

"Tonight. He's probably out there now," Slim replied, knowing it was true. He watched as she struggled with her emotions then finally pushed away from the piano. He followed as she walked without speaking through the back hallway that led to the rear of the building, gathered her cloak, and went outside, stopping to place a rock in the opening to prevent the door from closing. She needn't have bothered, as he wasn't leaving until she returned. He stood just inside the doorway, his breath catching as her vile and seemingly unfeeling words drifted in through the narrow opening. This was not the Anna he'd come to know and care about; this was the Anastasia everyone feared. Her words were as ugly as the inflection in her tone. He ached to open the door and beg her to stop, if not for her, for Mouse, as he knew his friend had to be as stunned as he upon hearing them. She loved her brothers—she'd told him as much many times over the last few months—and yet she'd just told Mouse she hated him. Was it possible for a person to love and hate at the same time? It grew quiet, then the door opened, and she blinked her surprise at seeing him.

"Why?" It was all he could muster as he gathered her into his arms.

"Because I love him," she sobbed. "It's the only way I know to keep him safe."

Safe from what? The question went unasked as he knew it would go unanswered. While he'd thought he'd broken through the wall she'd built around herself, it was obvious she barely let him in.

Chapter Thirty-One

January 1921

Percival stood with Paddy and a few other boys, waiting for the girls to enter the Common room. The door opened, and the girls filed in, breaking into groups, as was the daily ritual. He smiled when he saw Anastasia. He needn't bothered, as she walked past without looking up, heading straight to the piano, where she began beating aimlessly at the keys. It had been that way in the weeks since her conversation with Mouse. Though he continued to visit her after hours, the light in her eyes seemed to have dimmed—even her harassment of the younger kids seemed to have lost its vigor.

"There she is," Paddy said, elbowing him in the ribs.

The *she* Paddy spoke of was Mileta, who'd arrived earlier that day. Percival frowned. It was obvious by the grin on the boy's face, time had not eased the crush he had on Mouse's girl. "Remember, you're not to let on we know who she is."

"Yeah, yeah," Paddy grumbled as they walked to where the others stood.

Percival studied the girl as Mary made the introductions, both she and Paddy touting Mileta's boldness at having one-upped Anastasia by licking her mush during the meal. Mileta blushed, and even with her freshly chopped hair, it was easy to see why both Mouse and Paddy were smitten with her. Though her eyes were tinted with fear, she had a confidence about her. Not the false bravado of children plucked from the street, but the confidence of a child who'd never not known a mother's love. Percival searched his memory, trying to remember how it felt to have his mother's arms around him, only to find he had difficulty remembering her face. He rubbed at the chill that ran the length of his arms and wondered how long it would take before Mileta forgot.

Mileta's dark brows knitted together. She spun around, facing Anastasia, who was still punishing the keys at the piano. Mary's eyes grew wide as Mileta started toward Anastasia. Percival thought to warn Mileta away, but Anastasia had promised to go easy on the girl, so he let her go. He and everyone else in the room held their breath as she walked straight to the piano and asked to play. Since its arrival, no one had dared interrupt Anastasia's playing, much less asked if they could join in.

Anastasia glared at the girl for a second, then caught him looking and nodded her consent. Though she'd agreed to look after Mileta, Percival hadn't expected her to take it this far. Mileta slid onto the bench, thanked Anastasia for her kindness, and began to play. Only instead of pounding the keys, her fingers moved with incredible speed, producing such beautiful music that everyone in the room gravitated toward the piano. Anastasia's mouth fell open and—in an astonishing show of vulnerability—began to weep.

Percival looked about the room to see if anyone noticed, only to find nearly everyone else watching with tears streaming down their faces. He relaxed, allowing himself to fully enjoy the song that lasted many times over the simple tunes Anastasia played. He closed his eyes, instantly transformed back to the single-room apartment he'd shared with his momma. A phonograph played a similar song, and in his mind, his mother smiled as she moved around the room with an eloquence equal to the melody. When at last the music stopped, he too had to wipe away tears.

***

Percival entered the Common room to find Anastasia sitting in her usual spot on the bench in front of the piano. Only instead of playing, she sat staring at the keys. He slid in next to her and lifted a finger toward the ivory keys.

"No, don't," Anastasia said, stopping him.

"You don't feel like playing?" he asked, placing his hand on his legs to steady them.

"Oh, but I do, only I don't wish to do so until I can play like your friend."

My friend? "Mileta isn't my friend; she's Mouse's," he said and instantly regretted mentioning her brother.

"She promised to teach me to play like she does," Anastasia said, unfazed by his comment.

Percival wasn't sure anyone could ever play as good as Mileta, but he smiled his encouragement just the same.

"Why didn't you tell me she could play?"

"I didn't know. Why did Mileta agree to teach you?"

"Why wouldn't she?" Anastasia said tersely. "Do you not think I can learn?"

"It's not that at all. I just meant you weren't very welcoming in the dining room."

"I did what I had to do," Anastasia replied.

"Why, Anna? What has happened to you that you have to be so mean to everyone?"

"I have my reasons," she said, narrowing her eyes.

"Then tell me." He tucked a wayward strand of hair behind her ear.

"Do you really think I can learn to play as well as she?"

Percival sighed. "Remember the boxer I told you about?"

"The one that was friends with your mother?"

Percival felt a pang of guilt, as he'd never trusted her enough to tell her the truth. "Yes."

"I remember. What about him?"

"He taught me how to move so that I wouldn't get hit, but it didn't happen overnight. I had to practice and practice, then one day, it just clicked into place and I could move. I'm telling you this so you know it's going to take a lot of hard work. You'll have to keep trying until it clicks. Maybe you can ask the headmistress if you and Mileta can practice in the evenings."

"Maybe. It will mean you and I can't see each other as much."

"That's okay."

"It is?" She sounded hurt.

"You're smiling. Well, not at the moment, but today is the first time I've seen you smile in a long time."

"From the moment I heard Caleb play, I knew it was what I wanted to do. He taught me to play, but he could only play simple songs, not anything that sounded like what I heard today. She played so beautifully. Until today, I never knew anything could sound so beautiful."

"I tried to remember my momma's face today, only to realize I'd forgotten what she looked like. I knew she was tall and thin and had dark hair and eyes. But I couldn't picture her face anymore. When Mileta started playing, I closed my eyes, and through her music, I could see momma's face again," Percival said, choking up.

"It was the same for me," she said, taking his hand in hers. "As she played, I saw Caleb, my baby, and everything I have ever loved."

"It must have been that way for most, as everyone was crying when she finished," Percival noted.

"I want to make people cry," Anastasia said, squeezing his hand.

He thought to remind her she'd made a lot of people cry but

knew that wasn't the kind of tears of which she was speaking.

***

April 1921

Percival stood outside the headmistress' office waiting to be called in. He'd tried pressing his ear to the door to no avail— it was much too thick to hear through. Dr. Todd had told him he'd found him a job but reminded him he still had to seek approval from the headmistress and was currently speaking with her behind the closed door.

Hearing footsteps, he looked to see Clara walking toward him, followed by a small boy dressed in rags. The kid's eyes darted back and forth, reminding him of a small puppy who didn't know whether to explore his bright new surroundings or tuck his tail and hide in the corner.

"Another new ward for the asylum?" Percival eyed the boy with a sigh. "I expect the headmistress will want to see him before I go in."

Clara shook her head and wrinkled her nose. "The boy's covered with bugs—I saw them crawling on him the moment he entered. I'm taking him to the washroom and will bring him to see the headmistress once he's able to sit in her office without scratching."

Percival crouched to where he could look the boy in the eye. "I expect you won't like the washroom none but hold your tongue, and you'll get through it well enough. When they are finished scrubbing on you, they'll give you a new set of clothes and shoes to wear. You'd like that, wouldn't you?"

The boy's eyes widened as he nodded his answer.

Percival jerked his thumb to his chest. "My name's Slim. If you need anything, you come see me. Got it?"

This time, a smile accompanied the nod.

Clara raised a brow. "Trying to take over Mary's job?"

"Nah, just thought the kid looked like he needed a friend,"

Percival said, pulling himself up to full height.

"You're good at that," Clara said.

"Being a friend?"

Clara laughed. "Helping people. Look what you did for Anastasia."

Percival knew what Clara was talking about. In the months since Mileta's arrival, the transformation in Anastasia had been remarkable. While the two girls were far from friends, they'd spent most of their free time together with Mileta patiently teaching Anastasia how to properly play the piano. Anastasia was soaking up everything, and though it had only been a short time, was already playing full tunes without missing any keys. "I didn't do nothing; that was all Mileta's doing."

"You're the one who got her inside."

Percival shook his head. "That wasn't me."

"You had a hand in it. Not to worry—your secret's safe with me. I'm just glad to see Anastasia happy again. Though her happiness means a lack of enthusiasm in tormenting the new arrivals. I worry if she keeps it up, I'll have to find someone else to help me greet the children."

During one of his evening chats with Anastasia, she'd finally confessed as to why she still tormented the new children—telling him it was Clara's idea to intimidate them in order to get them to reach out to other kids. Brilliant in the inception, however, still scary for the kids being targeted and not knowing the reason. "You'll not have to worry. Anastasia's a great actress."

"And you're her biggest fan," Clara teased.

Feeling a blush creep over his face, he lowered his gaze. The boy stared up at him, his eyes full of wonder as he scratched furiously at his scalp. "I think you'd better get him to the washroom before we all need a dunk."

Clara looked down, wrinkled her nose, and set out toward

the washroom holding on to the child's hand with only two fingers of her right hand.

Percival placed his ear to the door once more, nearly toppling over when it opened. Dr. Todd caught hold of his arm and shot him an exasperated look as he helped right him.

"There now, Slim, you should know better than to lean against the door," Dr. Todd said, covering for him.

"Yes, sir, I'll not do it again," Percival promised.

"Good lad." Dr. Todd stepped to the side to allow him entrance. "I was just telling Headmistress the same thing—that you're a good lad, that is. Such is the case. I told her I found a proper job for you, and she's agreed to allow you to partake of this grand opportunity."

She said yes! It was all Percival could do not to whoop his excitement.

"Here now, Doctor, I am more than capable of speaking for myself," Headmistress said stiffly.

"Oh, yes, to be sure. I just know as to how the boy has been fretting over the decision," Dr. Todd replied.

"Yes, well, I am still of the mind that the boy would be better off learning a proper trade than reading books," she countered.

"But I love reading," Percival insisted.

Dr. Todd wrinkled his brow and gave the slightest shake of his head, warning him off. "Rest assured, Madam, the boy will not be reading for the pleasure of it. I assure you he'll be performing a great service to a man who himself has served our great city well. Why, Mr. Thornton is an esteemed lawyer who has argued many a case over the years. If it weren't for his declining eyesight, I suspect he'd be weighing in on many more. The man requires a lad who will be his second set of eyes for a few short hours each day. Someone who will be able to pronounce the words properly while reading his past cases. In doing so, the lad will help to keep the man's mind free from the clutter that comes with feeling useless."

"And you believe Mr. Barsotti will be able to read at the level required?" she asked, looking over her glasses at him.

"Indeed I do. Why, I have it on good authority that the lad acted as a teacher before coming into this very asylum."

"I did?" Percival said at the same time the headmistress questioned it.

Dr. Todd slid his foot over stealthily, nudging Percival's shoe.

"Oh, yes, I did," Percival said, changing the inflection.

"Yes, see there," Dr. Todd affirmed.

Headmistress removed her glasses and cleaned them with a cloth she pulled from the drawer. "And what kind of teaching could a child of the streets do?"

"Oh, to be sure, the boy wasn't living on the streets at the time. The teaching was done before his poor mother died; God rest her soul."

Boy, and I thought Anastasia was good at acting.

"Who did you teach? Let the boy speak," she said when Dr. Todd opened his mouth.

Percival searched Dr. Todd's face for the answer, but the man seemed to be holding his breath. He searched his own mind—nearly shrugging his shoulders for lack of an answer— then recalled showing Big Joe how to read. *Does that make me a teacher?* "Big Joe?"

Dr. Todd let out the breath he'd been holding and smiled a brilliant smile. "That's right! And allow me to remind you that Big Joe was so appreciative for what the boy had taught him that he donated a nice sum to this very asylum just to see this boy well cared for. Now you must believe that if Big Joe would donate so freely that the good Mr. Thornton would do so as well."

Headmistress must have agreed, as it was the first time Percival recalled seeing the woman smile such a wide smile.

Chapter Thirty-Two

"How come you get to go to work and I have to go to school?" Paddy grumbled.

"Why are ya so sore at me?" Percival said, trying to smooth him over. While Percival had tried to convince Dr. Todd to get his friend a job too, the man had insisted he'd used up all his favors by getting Percival his job, insisting the best he could do for Paddy was to see that he got to attend the industrial school with some of the other boys from the asylum. "Do you think I want to go to work?"

Paddy cocked his head sideways. "Don't ya?"

"Course not. You're the lucky one. They're going to teach you a trade so you can get a real job one day."

"I guess I wouldn't mind a real job one day." Paddy's face turned serious. "You just make sure you come back after work."

"Course I'll come back; where else would I go?" Actually, he'd been worried that Paddy would decide not to return.

Paddy shrugged. "I thought maybe you'd go back and find Mouse."

"Nah, I kind of like it in here. Besides, I never was good at living on the streets," Percival answered honestly.

"Swear you'll come back," Paddy said, spitting into his palm.

Percival spit into his own palm then shook Paddy's hand, bonding their agreement.

***

"Mr. Thornton lives in this building?" Percival gulped,

following Dr. Todd up the stairs to the front entrance of the massive building.

"Mr. Thornton owns the building." Dr. Todd lifted the knocker, clanging it several times. "I told you he is a very wealthy man. Did you drink your tea this morning?"

"You gave it to me yourself," Percival said, counting the windows of the four-story red brick building.

"Yes, well, do try to calm yourself. We wouldn't want Mr. Thornton to think you damaged, now would we?"

"No, sir," Percival replied.

The door opened and a man wearing a black suit greeted them. "Good day, sir."

"A fine day it is, Martin." Dr. Todd removed his hat and motioned for Percival to do the same. "Mr. Thornton is expecting us."

Martin's brows arched as he looked Percival up and down. "Indeed. I shall tell Mr. Thornton that Dr. Todd and his guest have arrived. He shall meet you in the drawing room. Would you like me to show you where it is?"

The doctor chuckled, and the man named Martin's eyes twinkled. Something had obviously passed between the two, though Percival didn't get the joke.

Dr. Todd stepped inside, and Percival followed, twisting his head back and forth to take in all the ornate wood that adorned both walls and ceiling. A stunning wood staircase wide enough to allow three adults to walk up side by side sat just inside the door. The wood wasn't limited to the stairs; rather, it seemed to be everywhere. It not only lined the walls, but rose halfway up the walls of the stairs as well. Large plate-size squares were carved into the wood, which met up with brightly printed yellow flowered paper. A thick carved wood banister trailed down from the top and looked inviting enough to slide down.

"Don't even think about it," Dr. Todd said, hanging his hat on a hook just inside the door.

"Did ya read my mind, then?" Percival whispered.

"Not in the least." Dr. Todd laughed. "You forget I was a boy of your age once upon a time."

Percival craned his neck to see where the stairs led, only to see more wood lining the upper walls. Dr. Todd motioned for Percival to follow and led him into a brightly lit room. Upon entering, Percival realized the room not to be lit at all. It only appeared so due to the lack of wood and floor-length windows that lined the outer wall. The walls in the room were white, as were the furnishings. The only bit of color came from a floor-to-ceiling fireplace, which, to his delight, was alive with a crackling fire. A large stone mantel hovered just above the opening. Above that was a creature the likes of which he'd never seen before. Looking closer, he realized he had in fact seen one in a book his mother had brought home from the library several years prior. Percival pointed to the enormous head. "It's a real moose! Its eyes are open, but surely it's dead, as it has no body."

"It better be dead," called a robust voice from the hallway.

Percival looked to see a man standing in the doorway. Short, with snow-white hair, the man wore a long red dress tied at the middle. "The man's wearing a dress," Percival whispered.

"It's not a dress; it's a robe, and at his age, he can wear whatever he wishes," Dr. Todd countered.

"That's the thing about going blind; it causes you to rely on your other senses. You'd think an old codger like me would be deaf as a doornail, but I can hear every word the two of you say. The good doctor is correct, it is a robe and I wear it because it is easier to put my arms in the sleeves than to dance around like a fool trying to put these decrepit old legs into a pair of trousers.

The last time I tried to do so by myself, I lost my balance, hit my head, and lay on the floor for hours waiting for Martin to come check on me."

"Took sixteen stitches to sew you up if I recall correctly," Dr. Todd said, watching as Mr. Thornton walked to the chair closest to the window.

"If you can't see, why not sit in the chair closest to the door?" Percival asked.

"Mind your manners, Percival," Dr. Todd warned.

"Leave the boy be, doctor. I've spent my life waiting for the opposition to ask pertinent questions. I'm glad to hear the boy has a logical head attached to that long neck of his."

Percival lifted a hand to his neck. "I thought you couldn't see."

"I see mostly shadows, which is why I prefer this room. It's nice and bright most days, and I sit in this particular chair because its position offers me the most light. I shot that moose up there from a distance such as this years ago when I had better eyesight than sense. I happened upon him and the missus having a discussion and waited for them to finish their talk," he smiled a devious smile, "then shot him dead."

Percival couldn't figure out why someone would want the head of a dead animal on their wall, but Mr. Thornton seemed happy with it staring out at him. He, on the other hand, felt a bit uneasy with the thing looking down at him.

"What's wrong with your legs, son?" Mr. Thornton asked.

"There's nothing wrong with my legs, sir. It's my head that's messed up," Percival said.

"Percival had a little mishap when he was younger. A head injury that left his legs a little mis-wired. He is in good health. Just a bit jittery is all," Dr. Todd added. "You have my assurance that his legs will not interfere with the work you require."

"Quit selling the boy, Robert—I don't have any plans of turning him away. I just asked a simple question. Now, if you'll leave us be, the lad and I will begin."

"I'll take my leave now; I have some patients to see. I'll come collect you when I'm finished." He turned his attention to Mr. Thornton. "If he gives you any trouble, have him sit on the porch until I arrive."

"There'll be no need of that, will there, boy?"

"No, sir, I promised Headmistress I'd be on my best behavior. She said I should be on account of she thinks you're going to give her a donation."

Dr. Todd's eyes bugged, and his face turned crimson.

Mr. Thornton chuckled. "Boy, look at the good doctor's face and tell me if he looks like he swallowed a bug."

As a matter of fact, Dr. Todd looked like he'd swallowed a whole mess of bugs. "Yes, sir, he does."

Mr. Thornton slapped his knee. "Oh, what I wouldn't give to see that. The good doctor is an excellent litigator. Too bad he's wasting all those skills playing doctor."

Percival wasn't sure what a litigator was, but it didn't sound good. He also didn't like the way the man had said he shouldn't be a doctor; why, if not for him, his legs would be jumping even more than they were.

"He's not playing doctor," Percival said, shaking his head. "He's a very good doctor. He fixed up my friend Mouse so he didn't die, and he's fixed my legs so they don't jump so much."

"It's okay, Percival," Dr. Todd said, patting him on the head. "My uncle here knows I'm very good at what I do. He's just sore that I didn't follow in his footsteps."

"On second thought, you would make a lousy litigator. One must stay in character if one plans to win the case."

"Good day, Uncle." Dr. Todd winked at Percival.

"Good day, Robert. I expect you can show yourself out."

"I expect so," Dr. Todd said, leaving the room.

"Is he gone?" Mr. Thornton asked after a moment of silence.

"Yes, sir," Percival replied.

"I suppose we'd better get to it, then. My office is through those doors." He pointed to a room that adjoined the room they were in. "On the desk is a stack of papers sitting under a glass paperweight. Bring them here and we'll get started."

Opening the door to the room, he saw the walls were lined with the same wood as in the front hallway and stairs.

"Turn on the overhead light so you can see," Mr. Thornton called from his chair.

Percival did as he was told and sucked in his breath. While the walls were indeed wood, they turned out to be shelves filled with books. *The man has his own library!* While he wished to run to the shelves and see what mysteries they held, he didn't want to get chastened for dawdling. He hurried to the large wooden desk where the papers sat on the corner of the desk under a paperweight just as Mr. Thornton had said. Beside the pile of papers sat a brown leather wallet, folded in half and filled with paper money. Next to the wallet was a silver tray filled to the brim with coins of the same color. As he reached for the papers, he thought of his time on the streets and imagined Mouse's voice urging him to pocket the wallet. He shook off the image. *At least take a few coins to line your pocket*, the voice in his head persisted. Once again, he shook it off, gathered up the papers, and hurried from the room. As he walked toward Mr. Thornton, he realized the man to be sitting in line with the desk—not that it mattered, since the man couldn't see.

"You struggled with your conscience," the man said when he approached.

"I did?"

"Did you not think about taking some of the money?"

"I didn't take any!"

"Calm down. I know you didn't take any. I merely said you thought about it. Did you not?"

"I looked at it knowing that if my friends were with me, they would have wanted me to take some." Percival sighed. "That's not true—they would have taken it themselves since I never was good at stealing anything, on account of my legs."

"What do your legs have to do with stealing?"

"They move too much, not so much now because of the tea Dr. Todd gives me to drink. They get worse when I'm nervous, so anytime I went to dip pockets, they would jump around, and the mark would see me."

"Ah, so you're saying picking pockets made you nervous. Did any of your friends get nervous dipping pockets?"

Percival thought about that for a moment, picturing Mouse and the others dipping pockets with ease then smiling when showing off their loot. "No, sir, I don't think so."

"Then one could argue the point that it was not your legs that stopped you, but your conscience. Good scruples is a sign of a good upbringing."

"It is?"

"Why, I have won many a case on lesser evidence," Mr. Thornton said, crossing his legs. "The legal system could do with more men with good morals. Have you given any thought to being an attorney when you grow up?"

"No, sir, I guess I just thought I'd be a boxer like my friend Big Joe on account of he told me my legs would keep me from getting hit."

"Yes, I suppose they would serve you well in the ring. However, I'm not sure your conscience would agree."

"Big Joe never mentioned my conscience when he was teaching me to fight."

"Perhaps that's because he didn't know you had one."

"Don't everyone have one?"

"You'd think that to be the case, but I'm here to tell you it isn't so. Tell me, if you saw a fellow lying on the floor right there, and say the fellow is bleeding and looking at you with fear in his eyes. What would you do?"

"I suppose I'd call for Dr. Todd."

"Now, what if that guy got up and you knew it was you who'd hurt him so badly but also knew that now you had to hurt him some more. Could you do it?"

Percival looked at the spot when Mr. Thornton pointed, and gulped. "No, sir, I guess I wouldn't want to hurt him no more."

Mr. Thornton uncrossed his legs then crossed them in the other direction. "That, son, is what boxing is about. Beating and punching your opponent until they are incapable of getting up from the floor. Now, don't go thinking bad about your friend. The men he fights know what they are getting themselves into before they climb into the ring—Big Joe didn't do anything wrong. He's a good man and he's done right by you."

Percival stared at the man. "You know Big Joe?"

"I've had the privilege of meeting him a time or two," Mr. Thornton replied. "I know he taught you how to defend yourself and that he gave me some money he set aside for you."

"You mean the money from my momma," Percival corrected.

"No, I have that and more," Mr. Thornton said, uncrossing his legs and leaning back in his chair. "It will be yours when you are old enough to manage it."

"Why did he give you my money?"

"Because Big Joe and I are of the same mind when it comes to banks. Neither of us believe in letting someone else hold all our money."

"Then I should be worried that you have my money,"

Percival deducted.

Thornton laughed. "I guess it should appear so, but I assure you most of your money is secure in my safe and will be turned over to you when the time comes."

"Most of it?"

"Big Joe has the money you gave him. Since it is not his to withhold, he will give it to you anytime you ask. I will hold on to the other money."

"Why would Big Joe give me more?"

"I suppose he saw something in you. Just as Robert—Dr. Todd—and I see potential in you."

"You've only just met me."

"Yes, but I see it in your actions. I saw you looking at that money on the desk and saw you walk away without taking any."

"Dr. Todd said you couldn't see."

He laughed. "No, son, he said I'm going blind. If you're going to be a good defense attorney, you'll need to learn to listen."

"I never said I was going to be one of those," Percival replied.

"True, but you didn't say you weren't." Mr. Thornton smiled. "Drag that chair over here so we can begin your lessons."

"I thought I was going to read to you," Percival said with a sigh.

"Reading is learning, dear boy. Today, I'm going to introduce you to a whole new way of fighting."

"You mean there is more than one way to fight?"

Thornton smiled. "With words comes knowledge, with knowledge, you can take on the world."

Percival wasn't sure exactly what Thornton meant by that, but the smile on his face told him it was a good thing.

Chapter Thirty-Three

October 1924

As summer changed to fall, Percival found it harder and harder to return to the building at the end of each day. Even his occasional conversation with Anna failed to lift his spirits. The only bright spot of his day was taking the trolley to West 71st Street to meet with Mr. Thornton. He jumped from the trolley the moment it came to a stop. Two boys jumped onto the spot he'd just vacated—giggling and gawking in his direction—perhaps contemplating if he'd be an easy mark. This was not their neighborhood; he could tell from the rags that covered their bodies. A small part of him yearned to join them—to race through the streets free from rules, iron gates, and cold stone walls. One of the boys lifted a hand, scratching furiously at his head, reminding him that life on the street wasn't all fun and games.

Turning from the boys, Percival headed toward Mr. Thornton's townhouse. Life wasn't all that bad, he reminded himself as he took the stairs to the building three at a time and lifted the iron knocker, clanging it to announce his arrival. It didn't take long before the door opened and Martin stepped aside, allowing entrance.

"Good morning, Martin," Percival said, securing his hat on the hook. "You're looking extra chipper today."

"Indeed," came the man's usual stiff greeting.

Percival shook his head. Martin performed his job to the highest quality and, in doing so, totally lacked emotion. "One of these days, I will see you smile."

"Highly unlikely," Martin said dryly. "Mr. Thornton is in his office."

"Mr. Thornton is always in his office," Percival replied. While they used to do their work in the drawing room, once Mr. Thornton's eyesight permanently faded, he'd insisted on conducting their meetings in his office. Though it was a nice room, it was much too dark for Percival's liking; heavy and depressing, it reminded him of a tomb.

"Good morning, Percival," Mr. Thornton said before he announced his arrival. "Are you having a bad morning? Your step seems to be off today."

It was no surprise the man had picked up on his mood. With his eyesight gone, his hearing wasn't the only sense that'd heightened. Knowing he wouldn't let up until he'd badgered him for the truth, Percival decided to confess. "I saw some boys on the way over—they reminded me of my life long ago."

Mr. Thornton peered up from his seat behind the large wooden desk. "You miss your life on the street?"

"I miss the freedom."

Mr. Thornton pressed his fingertips together. "I was under the impression that you enjoyed your life in the asylum."

"I do, or at least I did. It's just I'm not a kid anymore. I'll be sixteen in two months. The Asylum is no place for a boy my age. It feels more like a prison than a home." The word "home" came out on a squeak.

"I do wish I were able to bring you into my home full time," Mr. Thornton said solemnly.

"I'm not asking you to," Percival said, cutting him off. They'd had this discussion before, Mr. Thornton explaining that while he had the room and means, he did not have the desire to have children underfoot every waking hour of the day. He'd gone on to divulge how he'd lost his dear wife and sons to the influenza long before agreeing to mentor Percival—further noting that the pain of the past left him incapable of opening his heart to future heartache.

Mr. Thornton tapped his fingers together. "You're at a most unfortunate age. You're not a child anymore and yet the authorities do not see fit to call you an adult."

"When Dr. Todd talked me into going into the asylum, he spoke of finding a family. While I missed my mother, I was tired of living on the streets and ready to find another home. I'm pretty easy, so I thought it would only be a matter of time before someone wished to adopt me. That was four years ago. It's not just me. My friend Paddy says it feels like we're in a cage. I maybe could sweat it out a couple more years, but Paddy and some of the others are not as old as I. My fear is they will leave the asylum and end up back on the street."

Martin appeared in the doorway and cleared his throat to announce his arrival.

"What is it, Martin?" Mr. Thornton's voice carried a note of irritation.

"Lunch is ready to be served. Would you like it brought to your study or do you prefer to eat in the dining room?" It was a daily question, one that seemed unnecessary as the man's answer was always the same. Once in his study, the man rarely left the room.

"We shall eat in the dining room today," Mr. Thornton said, causing Percival and Martin to blink their surprise. "Percival, you may go along with Martin. I wish to make a call."

"Shall I tell the cook to hold your lunch?" Martin asked.

"No, she can put it on the table. I shan't be long," Thornton said, feeling his way across the desk until he found the telephone. "Go on, Percival. I'll be in directly."

"He's acting strange," Percival said, following Martin to the center dining room.

"Indeed," Martin replied.

It was a full fifteen minutes later when Mr. Thornton joined Percival in the dining room. Strolling into the room unassisted, he took his rightful place at the head of the table. Martin signaled the housemaid, a petite matronly woman with greying black hair, who hurried into the room and placed a dome-covered plate in front of each of them before using her apron to remove the domes. Percival's mouth watered as he saw the slices of beef sitting in their own juices, potatoes covered with a rich gravy, and fresh baked rolls.

"It's still warm," she said, clicking her tongue. "Telling me to place it on the table and wait for you to make your way in indeed. I'll not have you eating cold food if I have anything to say about it."

"Tell me, young Percival, has Ms. Beverly taken it upon herself to cut up my meat?" Mr. Thornton asked, lifting his fork to the plate.

Percival paused cutting his own beef and looked at Mr. Thornton's plate. Sure enough, the man's plate held small bits of meat. "Yes, sir."

"Not only does the woman scold me, she thinks because I'm blind that I am incapable of cutting my own meat. She thinks me a child, and she my mother. I expect she would wipe my behind if I asked her to," he said, taking a bite.

Not knowing how to respond, Percival lifted his fork to his mouth and filled it.

"Good, boy," Mr. Thornton said when he failed to answer his complaint. "A good defense attorney never gets goaded into an argument. You must remain unbiased in your actions, if not your thoughts."

"Mr. Thornton, do you really think I could be an attorney?"

"You have the head for it. You've done most well in your schooling. Not only did you excel in your basic studies, you can recite laws and have pored through my cases enough to give you an adequate start. If you ever put your mind to the task, come find me—I'll vouch for you. And if you find yourself in trouble, I'll come out of retirement, travel to where you are, and defend you."

"Thank you, sir. But I doubt I will get into much trouble in the asylum."

"What if I told you I could get you out of the asylum?" he said, filling his mouth.

Percival stopped chewing mid-bite. Had the man changed his mind about adopting him? Not wanting to assume, he worked to keep his voice casual. "How would you get me out?"

"That phone call I made was to a dear friend of mine, William Vanderbilt. I told him of your plight and am pleased to say that he was highly interested. William has connections to the Children's Aid Society; I've worked with him before placing other kids whom Robert has sent my way. William has agreed to reach out to your asylum to see that you and your friends are sent out on the next train along with those from the society. They do that from time to time—reach out to other asylums. He told me there is a train leaving in just a couple of weeks, heading west to Detroit."

A train heading west—it was what his mother had always dreamed about. Only she wasn't here. He grappled with his feelings—as unhappy as he was at the asylum, it was a known entity. In the end, he had to think his mother would be happy for him to go, even if it meant going alone. *Wait, hadn't Big Joe said he was going to Detroit? Sure, he had, even saying he was going by train.* While Percival had seen trains, he'd never ridden on one. The excitement peaked once more. "A train to Detroit. Do you think I'll get to see Big Joe?"

"Detroit's a fairly big city, but if he knows you're there, I'm sure he'll find a way to see you. The details still have to be worked out. But these trains transport children such as yourself to the country where there are families that will speak for you. Some of the children get adopted, but I don't want you to get your hopes up. You're close to being a man, so you might merely get a family that wishes for you to help them with their work. It could be hard work, but I expect it would keep your mind busy."

Once again, Percival struggled with his emotions. Instantly going from the excitement of a possible family to being told he might be too old to have one. Was he willing to take the chance? And what if he said no? Would Mr. Thornton still help his friends get sent out? He had to say yes; if he didn't agree, his friends might never get the chance to find homes.

"Here, here, what's that noise?" Mr. Thornton asked, taking hold of the edge of the table.

"Sorry, sir, it's my knees. I can't seem to control my legs."

"Yes, well, do try, before you spill the milk."

Percival pushed away from the table, swinging his knees to the side. While still bouncing, there was no danger of them thumping against the table. As he continued to eat, he thought of Paddy, Mary, Anna, and the others, wondering what they would think about leaving the asylum. What if they didn't truly wish to go? Would they be angry at him for getting them sent away?

"Are you still there, boy?"

"Yes, sir."

"You've grown quiet. What's on your mind?"

"I was thinking of my friends. They tell me they wish to leave, but what if it isn't true? If they find out it's my doing? They might be mad."

"There's no reason they need to know of your involvement. What else ails you, boy?" he asked after a moment.

"I just realized I won't ever see you again."

"We shall have some time yet; besides, never is a long time. You know where I live, and how to put pencil to paper. You write and tell me your address, and I'll keep in touch." He leaned closer and kept his voice low—though since they were alone in the room, Percival didn't know who he thought would hear. "You're not to tell anyone of the money you have waiting for you. Money makes people do strange things. That money your momma left you is for you to do as you will; the rest is for your education."

His education. With all this talk of going west, he suddenly remembered his mother's dream of buying a house and maybe someday opening her own restaurant. "Sir?"

"Yes, Percival?"

"Will you be awfully mad if I don't become an attorney?"

"A bit disappointed perhaps, but not mad. Your life is yours to live as you choose. Do you have something else in mind?"

"I like cooking. I used to help my momma in the kitchen." *Before we had to move and didn't have a kitchen to cook in.* He'd never told Mr. Thornton much about his life before the asylum, so he kept that part to himself. "I thought maybe I'd like to give that a try."

"I have a friend in the business who will tell you owning a restaurant is hard work." A smile flitted across his lips, leaving as quickly as it came, but not before Percival had a chance to see it and wonder about his thoughts. "Let's get you settled first. You have a few years to decide what you wish to do with your life. So, am I correct in assuming that you'd like to go?"

"Yes, sir. I think it would make my momma very happy to know I'm leaving the city."

"What about you, son, will it make you happy?"

"I think so. At least once I stop being scared."

"It's alright to be scared of something. Just don't let that fear keep you from living your life. Take me, for example.

When I lost my vision, I could've chosen to stay in bed and feel sorry for myself, or I could do as I did and find someone to help me see. I will always be grateful to you for being my eyes over the past few years."

Percival frowned. "Who will see for you when I leave?"

"Don't you worry about that. Robert has a good track record of finding boys who could use the benefit of my wisdom."

Percival knew he'd been one of those boys. "Sir, I'm glad he chose me."

"As am I, Percival, as am I."

Chapter Thirty-Four

The dining room was a soft hum of whispered voices as the children had all finished their evening meal and waited for the mistresses to enter, gather them together, and lead them up the stairs for the evening. The door opened, the room growing quiet when the headmistress entered along with the mistresses.

"She only comes if someone is in trouble," Mary whispered loud enough for all to hear. At her words, several of the younger children in the room began to whimper.

The mistresses stood in front of their charges, clapping their hands. Percival stood, following Paddy and the others as they lined up single file, watching as Mary and the girls did the same on the other side of the room.

Headmistress summoned Clara and Anastasia, whispered something he couldn't hear, and the two girls left without a word. Headmistress waited for the door to close behind the girls before pulling a slip of paper from her pocket. "If I call your name, you are to have a seat at one of the tables. Mary, Mileta, Ruth…"

The children grew quiet once more as everyone listened for their name to be called, not knowing if being chosen was a good thing or not. As the headmistress continued singling children out, Percival's legs began to twitch. *This is it.* Mr. Thornton told him it would be soon, but it still came as a shock knowing this was the time. When at last she'd finished reading the names from the list, everyone from Mary's gang was among those singled out. Though Mr. Thornton assured him all his friends would be selected for the train, he wondered briefly how the man had managed to see it done.

Headmistress grew quiet, folded the paper she'd been reading, and returned it to her pocket before nodding to give the others their leave.

"Quiet down, children. You know there is to be no talking in the hallways," she warned as those not chosen left the room. Her stern face transformed into a rare wide smile as she turned her attention to those still in the room. "Cheer up, children. I have excellent news to share with you."

Please don't tell them it was me. Please don't tell them it was me, Percival repeated silently as her gaze landed on him. To his relief, she continued scanning the room as she spoke.

"For nearly seventy years, the Children's Aid Society has worked tirelessly to help find thousands upon thousands of children such as yourselves homes. Most of those placements took place far outside this great city and the children selected count themselves privileged. Before leaving, each child received a fresh set of clothing and were sent west via trains, where they were then placed with fine families who promised to love and cherish them. In an unprecedented turn of events, the Children's Aid Society has generously offered to allow me to select children from this establishment to join their next Placing Out Program. I am pleased to tell you that, after careful consideration, I have chosen you."

The room exploded in a mix of excited whispers and fresh new tears.

"Yes," Headmistress said when Mary raised her hand.

"I believe there's been a mistake. My mother promised to return for me one day."

The headmistress' smile faded. "I'm not in the habit of making mistakes. I assure each and every one of you, if you're in this room, your parents have relinquished all parental rights."

Percival slid a glance to Mary, who jutted her chin and stoically blinked back the tears.

"Now, if there aren't any more questions, I will continue. Yes," Headmistress sighed when Ruth, a young girl from Mary's gang, raised her hand.

"What if we do not wish to go?" she asked tearfully.

Percival could understand the girl's reluctance, as she'd spent her entire life within the sterile walls of the asylum. Once again, his stomach clenched from the guilt of being responsible for her unease.

"Don't you fret, child," Headmistress said, showing a most unusual display of compassion. "Unlike here, you will have a chance at a real family to love you and see to your needs. Why, if I were a child, I would gladly fill your shoes."

Gideon, one of the boys in Mary's gang, raised his hand then began speaking without being called upon. "I had a family once. They were mean to me. What if we don't like the family that chooses us?"

"That is a perfectly reasonable question, one I too asked. My contact at the Children's Aid Society told me that all precautions would be taken to find homes that fit each child. People called placing agents will oversee the placements and work to find you the best home possible. Once placed, the agents will check in on you from time to time to see that the home remains a good fit. If you're not happy within your home, the agent will move you to a new home that better suits you. I must also warn you that if your new family is not happy with you, they may return you to this establishment. I shan't have to tell you how unhappy I will be if any of you are returned because of misconduct on your part. I know you must have many more questions," she said, warding off more questions. "I'm told the Children's Aid Society will do everything in their power to see to it that you are each happy and well cared for.

You must see this for what it is, an opportunity to grow up outside the walls of this institution. Consider it a grand adventure, one that I expect to hear about when you write telling me of your new family."

The door opened and Clara returned with Mistress Gretchen and two women from the washroom, each of which pushed carts piled high with clothing and shoes. While Percival expected Anastasia to be with them, she was not. His heart thumped in his chest as he realized that Anastasia wasn't to be going with him. *She's too old to be adopted.* How had he not thought of that? Even if she were sent out on the trains, it was highly unlikely they'd be kept together. *None of us will.*

"Mr. Barsotti, do try and control your legs," the headmistress said, pulling him from his panic. You'll have a difficult enough time being selected at your age without potential families thinking you to be damaged."

Paddy giggled and the headmistress narrowed her eyes at him.

"That goes for you too, young man. Why I'm sending you out is a mystery to me, as I've been told it is highly unlikely a redhead such as yourself will be adopted." When her gaze settled on him for a second time, Percival shifted from side to side, knowing in that instant that it was he who would bear the blame if Paddy were not selected. He looked about the room, searching each face. As he noted the mixture of giddiness and fear, it took everything in his being not to stand up, confess his sin, and beg his friends to forgive him.

***

The next couple of hours were a blur as each child received a fresh set of clothes and shoes. Just as the mistresses finished doling out the clothing, Anastasia entered, carrying a large stack of cloth bags. She divided the pile in half, handing one section to Clara, then weaved in and around the room handing them out. Percival made his way to the edge of the room hoping to speak with her, if only for a moment. Just as she reached him, Clara, who'd been handing out bags on the other side of the room, began coughing furiously. Seeing the diversion for what it was, he pulled Anastasia aside.

"They're sending us out on the trains," he said, keeping his voice low.

"I know," she said, trying unsuccessfully to pull away.

"You knew and yet said nothing." He knew he was being unreasonable accusing her when he'd known all along.

"There's nothing to be done about it. Now let me go before someone sees."

He released her, watching as she continued to move about the room. After the bags were given out and filled, the group was then marched upstairs to a new dorm room with beds positioned on either side of the room. After selecting a bed and placing their bags underneath for safekeeping, the children were allowed to go in supervised pairs to freshen up.

Percival sighed as his stomach continued to knot. With the entire group sleeping in a combined room, they would be supervised at all times by at least one of the matrons, making it impossible to sneak away, much less allow him a chance to speak to Anastasia further.

***

Two weeks had passed since those chosen had received the news. Much of that time was spent in makeshift classrooms, getting refresher tips on manners and hygiene. The boys and the girls were cordoned off on the opposite sides of the room. Percival wasn't sure what the girls were discussing, but every now and then, they would erupt in giggles, only to be shushed by one of the mistresses. Just when he'd lost all hope of being able to speak with Anastasia at length, the door opened and Clara entered. She whispered something to the matron, who nodded and motioned Percival over.

"Headmistress wishes to see you in her office. I've been told to warn you against speaking to any of the children you may meet in the hallway," Clara said loudly enough for everyone to hear.

"Why all the secrecy?" he asked as soon as she'd closed the door.

Clara kept her voice low as she spoke. "The headmistress doesn't wish for any of the others to know about the selection as she's afraid it may hurt their feelings knowing they weren't chosen."

"You mean she has a heart." He smiled when rewarded by a giggle from the mostly stoic girl. "Does Anastasia know we're leaving tomorrow?"

"She does," Clara said, growing serious once more. "She had a meeting with the Headmistress—I'm not sure what was said, but she seemed rather upset afterward."

She's upset that I'm leaving. Maybe I should stay. It would only be for a couple more years. Percival's heart pounded at the thought of remaining at the asylum, even if it meant a nearly daily release to see Mr. Thornton. They were almost to the headmistress' office when Percival took Clara by the arm. "I need to speak with her."

She stopped, motioned toward the headmistress' door with her chin, and lowered her voice. "Go to the Common room after you're finished here. I'll meet you there in a bit and take you upstairs."

Percival closed his eyes, letting out the breath he didn't realize he was holding. He mouthed his thanks, then knocked on the door.

"Come in," Headmistress called from her desk.

Percival stepped inside, gasping the second he saw his mother's necklace and ring lying alongside his mother's book on the headmistress's desk. He reached for the book, his fingers trembling as they caressed the familiar form. Instantly, he could see his mother's face staring out at him with eyes that matched his own. He recalled helping her in the kitchen, then wrinkling his nose as she spit on her apron and used it to cleanse his face. He could easily remember her glistening silhouette sitting next to him on the floor under the window, fanning the stale air as they spoke late into the night, waiting for the heat of the day to ease. It wasn't until the headmistress reached into her drawer and handed him a handkerchief that he noticed the tears streaming down his face. He wiped them, blew his nose, and returned the cloth, which she set aside.

"Mr. Barsotti, I must say that in all my years of being Headmistress, you are the most fascinating child I've had under my supervision. I'm not just saying that because of your connections, though I must admit they are just as intriguing and most generous in their donations. When I first met you, I thought to myself, *Here is a boy I will have trouble with*. Now I must admit I will miss having you here as, despite the restlessness of your own limbs, you've been a most calming influence on those around you." Percival blinked his surprise and she smiled. "Yes, Mr. Barsotti, I do have a soft side. Can you imagine the unrest it would create if the children in this establishment knew? The only way to control so many is to instill a bit of fear, do you not agree?"

Actually, I do. "Yes, ma'am."

Her smile disappeared. "I expect you will write to me and keep me apprised of how you fare."

"Yes, ma'am," he repeated. "If it wouldn't be too much trouble, could you please have Dr. Todd see that Mr. Thornton gets my mother's jewelry for safekeeping?"

"I can do that. Now take your book and be off. The train ride will be a long one, and this could very well be the last good night's sleep you have for a while."

He thought to tell her he was thinking about staying but didn't think she'd approve. Especially after what she'd just told him—so he merely nodded and backed from the room clutching his mother's book to his chest.

***

Percival heard the music even before he got to the Common room. Once there, he stood just outside with his forehead pressed against the door—listening as the music mingled with his emotions, seemingly pulling the notes directly from his heart. He'd never seen anyone so devoted to learning anything. Her dedication showed as the level of her playing closely equaled the songs his mother played on her phonograph when attempting to teach him to dance. Anastasia knew she was good, but he often wondered if she knew just how good she actually was.

As she started in on the next song, he opened the door and quietly slipped inside. Not wishing to have to explain the book, he laid it on the table before approaching the piano.

"Sometimes, I think you play better than Mileta," he said, sliding onto the bench next to her.

"I didn't know you were here," she said, wiping the top of the piano. "I couldn't sleep, so I came down to play."

He had so many things he wished to tell her, all of which rolled around in his mind like a jumble of marbles rolling across the floor. He grasped for the most important thought. "I'm not sure I want to go."

She turned toward him once more. "Of course you want to go. Why wouldn't you?"

Her words—spoken like a mother easing the fears of a child—were like a knife to the heart. "Why wouldn't I? Why because of you. I like you."

She laughed. "You like what we do together."

"And you don't?"

"I didn't say that. But you can't stay just on account of that. You have a chance at a whole new life. Mileta is leaving. She's the reason you agreed to come here in the first place. If she's gone, there's no reason for you to stay."

If she'd meant to hurt him, she'd succeeded. "You're saying you ain't a good enough reason for me to stay?"

"That's exactly what I'm saying. They're making me a mistress. I'll have a lot more responsibilities and won't have much time to see you. Why, I'm even getting my own room. I probably won't be able to see you at all."

"You don't sound all that broken up about it." Was she acting, or had she been using him all along?

"I had my share of fun. But you didn't give me nothing I can't find anywhere else."

"Yeah, well, you weren't nothing special either. I just come onto you because I told Mouse I'd keep an eye on you," he said, wishing to hurt her as much as she'd hurt him. He pushed off the bench, retrieved his book from the table, and left without so much as a glance in her direction. Mostly because he didn't want to give her the satisfaction of seeing the tears that trailed down his cheeks. Clara was waiting for him outside the door. To her credit, she started walking without bombarding him with questions he was in no mood to answer. As she led him to the room where he'd spend his final night, any reservations he'd had at leaving were gone.

Chapter Thirty-Five

After several weeks of anticipation, departure day had finally arrived, with the previous night's confrontation with Anastasia firming his readiness to go. He didn't need Anna anyway. No, last night, she'd acted like Anastasia—the person others feared, not the Anna he'd grown to care for. What if he'd misjudged her after all? What if she truly was Anastasia and only played the part of Anna to get close to him? Why? Not that it mattered; he was leaving—good riddance to her and her lies. Still, if he was ready to leave her and everything else behind, then why were his legs about to stomp their way through the bottom of the train? So much so, the boy sitting beside him had wormed his way into an already crowded seat in front of him, leaving Percival alone in his seat.

"I thought you drank your tea," Paddy grumbled, sliding onto the bench seat beside him.

"I did," Percival replied. "They wouldn't let you move to the front car?"

"No. The conductor said I had to stay in my seat, but I'm not sitting with that baby."

The baby Paddy spoke of was a girl named Ruth, who was considerably younger than either of them. Still, Percival knew that wasn't the real reason for his friend's sour mood. Paddy was upset because Mileta was placed in a forward car and he wasn't allowed to make the switch to join her. To make matters worse, Mouse had shown up just as they'd gotten to the station. Not only had the boy found a way to get himself included in the trip, but he had secured a seat in the forward car along with Mileta.

Paddy sighed. "Are ya gonna be like that the whole trip?"

"I hope not. Dr. Todd gave me enough for a whole other month and said he'd send me more when I get settled. What about you?" Percival asked when Paddy sighed once more. "Are you going to be like that the whole way?"

"What if I am?" Paddy snapped.

"Then I guess it's going to be uncomfortable for the both of us," Percival reasoned.

Paddy sighed for a third time—this time sounding more deflated than irritated. "How does he do it? Four years since we come and he just happens to show up the day we're sent out and just happens to be on the same train car as Mileta. I ain't buying it."

Percival agreed. It couldn't be mere coincidence that Mouse had found out about their leaving. He wasn't sure how Mouse had wormed his way onto the train, but it was obvious to Percival that he wasn't the only one with friends. Even still, Percival doubted Mouse's connections had anything to do with getting him placed inside the same car as Mileta. The boy was just plain lucky that way. He shrugged. "He's Mouse. It's what he does. Not that it matters."

"Why not?"

"Cause once we get to Detroit, we're all going our separate ways anyhow."

"What if Mouse was lying about going to Detroit?"

He wasn't. "Why would he lie about that?"

"I don't know. I hate him always being right is all."

"I guess someone has to be," Percival said, watching the last of the buildings disappear.

"It don't have to always be him," Paddy mumbled. "You just don't understand what it's like on account of you've never liked a girl."

Actually, he had, and unlike Paddy, who swooned all over a girl who never seemed to look in his direction, Anastasia had given him every impression that she cared about him in return. He considered telling Paddy. After all, it was over and they'd never see Anastasia again. Would his friend cheer him for his conquest or recoil in the horrors of his touching a girl no one liked? Most likely the latter, especially if he were to find out the girl was Mouse's sister. Percival closed his eyes, recalling the look on her face when he offered to stay and how quickly she'd told him she didn't care. Opening his eyes once more, he turned to the window, staring out at a forest of trees so thick, he couldn't see between them. While he knew there were trees, he also knew there had to be something beyond. It was like the binding of his mother's book—a cover with words he couldn't pronounce—but he knew there to be more inside, and that knowledge seemed to tell him to keep his thoughts to himself. "You're right. I haven't."

"Yeah, well, someday you'll find yourself a gal, and when ya do, you'll know how much it hurts when a friend worms his way in between you."

Percival wanted to tell him that it was he who was trying to do the worming, but didn't think anything good would come of it, so he continued to peer out the window. The trees opened up exposing a vast field. In the field was an enormous herd of horses. Before he could get Paddy's attention, all the children erupted in excited jabber. Unable to speak, he grabbed Paddy by the shirt collar, pulling him to the window.

"What are they, then?" Paddy asked peering outside.

"I thought they were horses, but horses don't have antlers. They're too large to be deer. They must be elk, though I've only seen them in books, so I can't be certain."

"Maybe they are moose," Paddy replied.

"No, I've seen a moose and that's not it," Percival said, remembering the massive beast displayed over Mr. Thornton's fireplace.

"They're elk," came a voice of authority from the back of the train car. "Keep your eyes open, as one never knows what they will see along the way."

A boy with brown eyes filled with mischief popped his head up over a seat ahead of them. "Will we see Indians?"

"That's highly unlikely, as they're mostly in Indian territory. So, unless you're trouble enough not to be chosen at any of the closer stations, you'll not likely see them."

If she'd meant to scare the boy, she succeeded as his face turned sullen as he disappeared from view. Everyone in the group had been warned of the possibility of not being selected—her words reminded them the excitement they felt about finding homes could be short-lived.

"Whatcha thinking about?" Percival asked when Paddy grew quiet once again.

"Just a wondering if I'll get picked. Headmistress said I might not on account of I have red hair."

"Yeah, well, she told me I might not on account of I'm too old."

"Really?"

"Sure, and don't forget about my legs. Why, you'll get adopted before I do."

"That's true," Paddy said, nodding his head.

The door to the front of the cabin opened. Paddy stretched his head around the seat. "Just a man in a fancy suit." He pulled his head back and they both watched as the man strolled past.

"Don't even think about it," Percival warned when Paddy attempted to follow.

"I could see his wallet as he passed. It would be so easy," Paddy said, sinking into the seat once more.

Percival chanced a look over the back of their seat. "Good thing I stopped you; he's talking to one of the agents. If you'd gotten caught, you would have been sent back for sure."

"You should have let me go after him. Now that he's on the move, I'll not have a chance," Paddy griped.

"Who's on the, oh…" Percival said, seeing Mouse standing in the doorway. His focus on the man showed he'd already made him as a mark. "Maybe I should warn him the man is talking with one of the agents."

"You'll do no such thing," Paddy stretched his foot to block his way. "First Mileta, and now he's moving in on my mark. It'll serve him right if he gets caught."

"I know you have a beef with Mouse, but remember all he did for us—teaching us how to dip pockets and how to move so we wouldn't get caught. Okay, that didn't work so well on me, but it did for you and the others. You only know how to dip without getting caught because of what he taught you. That's got to account for something. If you rat him out, he'll get sent back. I know you wouldn't want that, especially over a gal you carry a torch for and probably won't see again."

Paddy blew out a sigh. "I won't cause no trouble for him."

Percival turned so Paddy couldn't see his relief. The last thing he wanted to do was to choose between the only two real friends he had.

"He's leaving," Paddy said, looking around the seat once more. "I don't know what his business was, but it must have gone well on account of the man's smiling."

"Yeah, he won't be smiling long," Percival said, watching Mouse move out of view.

"Yeah, Mouse always had it in for the do-gooders." Paddy snickered.

Before Percival could answer, someone shouted they saw a bear and the car exploded with excited squeals. Both Percival and Paddy pressed their faces to the window, gawking at the fat black bear walking casually through a field in full view of the train. As it drifted from sight, Percival wondered what his mother would have thought of seeing such a magnificent creature.

***

The train eased to a stop and Percival thought it one of the many pauses to gather water for the steam engine.

Miss Agana, one of the agents riding in their car, stood, clapping her hands. "Heads up, children. We'll be leaving the train for a spell."

"Hurray," several of the kids shouted in unison. "Let's go see what they have in the store."

"No, you'll not." The agent's tone left no room for argument. "We'll all stay together to ensure no one gets left behind. We are to gather in the grass where you'll all receive fresh bread and honey. Leave your belongings on the train, as you'll be returning to the same seat when we come back."

Percival placed his mother's book on the seat, then put his sack of clean clothes on top before following along with the rest of the children. As soon as he saw the sour expression on Paddy's face, he knew something was wrong. "Now what?"

"Mileta went into the mercantile," he said grimly.

"Maybe they didn't tell the kids in the other car," Percival offered.

"Yes, they did. The rest are coming this way." He looked at Percival as if willing him to understand. "She didn't go alone."

She hadn't gone with Mouse, as he was heading their way. From the pound of his step, Percival could tell he was also upset. Mouse stopped just beyond earshot of the others and motioned them to join, telling them how a couple from the train had set their sights on Mileta.

"That's wonderful," Mary replied.

"No, it's not," Mouse spat. "You didn't see the way the man looks at Mileta or the way his hand rested on her leg when he spoke."

"Not so wonderful, then," Mary and the others agreed.

"We have to go get her," Paddy said, pulling himself taller.

Percival didn't like the idea of being sent back, but neither did he like the idea of Mileta or any of the others going with someone who would do them harm. "I'll help," he said, pounding a fist into his palm.

Mary placed a hand on his arm. "Wait, 'tis a better way—one that shan't get any of you sent back."

"Mary's smart. We'll do it her way first," Percival said.

"I trust Mary," Paddy agreed when Mouse looked ready to object. "You'll be there to keep an eye on her. Anything goes wrong, just say the word."

"Things don't work out, we'll help, even if it means getting sent back," Percival said and was thankful when the others nodded their heads in agreement. While he had no desire to go back, he was glad if he had to, he wouldn't be going alone.

***

It was nearly dusk when Mary rose from her seat and made her way to the forward car. Percival knew he wasn't the only one praying for her to succeed. Though not everyone was in on the plan, the train car grew quiet as if everyone on board were holding their breath awaiting her return. It didn't take long until the door opened, those in the know breathing a collective sigh as Mary and Mileta entered, their faces aglow with mysterious giggles. Mary gave a nod to the girl sharing her seat, who then took her bag and crammed into another without a word. As Mileta slid onto the now vacant bench, Mary offered him and Paddy a victorious smile. While Percival returned the gesture, Paddy, who remained unusually quiet during the whole procession, closed his eyes. As blackness overtook the train, the children in the car grew quiet. Those that continued to speak spoke in whispers, a few released their fears in gentle sobs, and soon he heard the soft breathing of some lucky enough to drift into sleep. Exhausted from the day's events, yet too overcome with emotion to give in to sleep, Percival laid his head against the window, staring out into the night.

"Are you asleep?" Paddy asked.

He wasn't, but neither was he in the mood for conversation, so he remained quiet. After a moment, Paddy pulled his feet up onto the small seat and somehow managed to find a comfortable position. Only when Paddy's breathing slowed, showing he had given in to sleep, did Percival whisper into the darkness begging for a home to see him grown and promising the night that one day he would own a house with windows in every room. Closing his eyes, he finally gave in to the swaying lullaby of the train.

Chapter Thirty-Six

"Paddy, wake up. We're finally here!" Percival said, shaking the boy furiously.

"The train's still moving," Paddy grumbled.

"I know, but look out the window. We're here!"

"I don't know what you're so excited about; you said yourself that you and I probably won't find a home." Paddy sat up, wiping the sleep out of his eyes with the back of his hands.

"I didn't say that." *Well, not exactly.* "Headmistress said that, and what does she know anyway. She's stuck in New York and probably has never even been to Detroit."

"Are you sure we're in Detroit?" Paddy asked, craning his neck to look out the window.

"Yes. At least I think so," Percival replied.

"I'm not sure I'm ready," Paddy said softly. "What if we do get adopted, and you and I never see each other again?"

"We'll see each other again. You said yourself you're going to put an advert in the paper," Percival reminded him.

"Yeah, but not until we grow up."

"Don't be sad, Paddy. You're beginning to make me sad."

"Aren't you even a little scared?"

"Sure, I'm scared," Percival admitted. "But I'm even more scared of going back to New York and spending the next couple of years in the asylum. And it is only a couple; think about Gideon, Ruth, and the little ones. They have years until they grow up enough before they don't need to be cared for."

"I guess I can handle anything for a couple of years," Paddy agreed.

As the train rumbled to a stop, Miss Agana stepped in from the forward car. "Okay, children, this is our first official placing stop. Remember to gather your belongings as you exit. Even if you're not selected, we will be moving forward on another train. Once outside, you're to line up single file, where Miss Grace, Miss Tany, and I will escort you inside Central Station. There'll be no time for lollygagging—you'll need to change into your clean clothes before being presented to those who've gathered. I want to remind each of you that this is only the first stop. If, by no fault of your own, you're not chosen today, we'll press on. The Children's Aid Society's goal is to see that each and every one of you receive a home, but unfortunately, that is not always the case."

Percival raised his hand.

Miss Agana hesitated. "Yes?"

"Could you surmise the percentage of children who don't find homes?" he asked, lowering his hand.

The woman raised an eyebrow before answering. "I can surmise that if I stand here answering questions, we shall be late arriving and may jeopardize today's placements. Would you agree that we should press on, or would you prefer me to stay and answer?"

Ah, a worthy opponent. Mr. Thornton had always said a good attorney answers a question with a question. While the woman wasn't an attorney, she obviously knew better than dampen their hopes with statistics that wouldn't matter. "No, ma'am, I wouldn't wish us to be late."

She winked at him and smiled a triumphant smile. "I'll trust you're capable of waiting to the end to make sure everyone departs this car?"

"Yes, ma'am," Percival said, stepping back so that the others could pass.

"Why'd you have to go and make her mad?" Paddy asked when the woman departed. "Now we have to wait until the end."

"You don't have to stay," Percival reminded him. "I'm the one she's sore at, not you."

"Sure, I do," Paddy said, watching as others departed. "She didn't yell at ya, so maybe she's not all that sore. Could be she just thinks you sounded smart. You got to watch using all those big words you learned from Mr. Thornton, on account of they might keep you from getting a home."

"Why would the way I talk keep me from getting picked?"

"Sheesh, all that time on the street, and you still don't know nothing. You know why Mouse gets under my skin so much?"

"Because he's Mouse?" Percival replied.

"Because he always acts like he knows everything."

"Mouse knows a lot," Percival reminded him.

"Yeah, but he doesn't know everything. Only he don't say that—he just pretends that he does and that rubs some of us the wrong way. Now you go around using big words all the time, and people are gonna think you're smart."

"What's wrong with being smart?"

"I know you're okay on account of we were friends before you learnt all those words. But if I didn't know ya and heard ya using all those big words, I'd be thinking we couldn't be friends. On account of I don't like feeling dumb."

Percival liked using the words he'd learned reading Mr. Thornton's court transcripts, but he'd never considered being smart could keep him from getting a home. "Good thinking, Paddy. I guess I should try not to sound so smart."

"Yeah, sometimes it's good when people don't know you're smart on account of they don't watch you so close. They know you're smart—they figure you got to be up to something even when you're not. That's why I try to act dumb. People are already watching me because I have red hair. If they thought I was smart on top of being willful, I'd never catch a break."

The last kid stepped off the train and Percival walked through the car to make sure no one was hiding under the seats. When he returned to where his friend was standing, he clapped a hand on Paddy's shoulder. "I might know more words than you, but in some ways, you're way smarter than me."

***

Percival stood with Paddy, Mary, and the others, listening to Miss Agana work the crowd. He was impressed with her speech and the way she added just the right inflection as she walked the room pleading her case. Though he'd never seen Mr. Thornton in action, he'd spoken with the man and read enough of his case files to imagine him doing the same. While not a courtroom, the outcome would be similar—if Miss Agana were able to convince the crowd of their worthiness, they would each find a home. If she failed to adequately convince the onlookers of their need, they would not. He pressed his hands on top of his legs, praying she proved to be a worthy advocate—further hoping someone in attendance could look past his physical attributes to deem him worthy of a home.

He slid a glance to Paddy, saw the boy nervously chewing on his fingernails, and added an extra prayer for him. Surely there was one person in the group not afraid to take in a child with red hair. He remembered the first time he saw him standing on the roof of his apartment building and how he too was leery because of the color of Paddy's hair. No, that wasn't entirely true—he was leery because Paddy had appeared seemingly out of nowhere. Lending to that the boy's mischievous grin and bright red hair, no wonder he'd thought him to be a leprechaun. Percival sighed. Life was so much simpler then.

He turned his attention to Mary, watching as the normally

confident matriarch of their little gang bit the bottom of her lip to keep it from trembling. *She shouldn't be nervous. If anyone in our group has a chance of finding a home, it's Mary. Everyone likes her.*

Gideon, he thought looking toward the boy. *Now he's one that might have trouble.* Gideon was without a doubt one of the oddest boys he ever met. To prove his point, the boy currently stood with his hands crammed into the pits of his arms. What was with those hands anyway? Rarely a day went by when he hadn't seen the kid's hands twisted around his legs, bottom in the air, as he used his hands to crab-carry him across the floor. Even punishment for having done so hadn't stopped him from repeating the process anytime he had the chance. *Maybe his arms are like my legs and he can't keep them from doing strange things.* Percival stared at the boy with a renewed understanding.

He heard a slight sob, turned, and saw tears dripping from Ruth's chin. He bumped her with his shoulder and smiled an encouraging smile. She tried to return the gesture but released another sob instead. Not knowing what else to do, he turned away, his gaze settling on Dorthia, who, when focusing all her attention on the baby Miss Agana had saddled her with, looked more nurturing than annoying. Furthermore, dressed in something other than the identical garb worn within the asylum, was surprisingly attractive. In that instant, Percival knew the pairing not to be accidental—Miss Agana manipulated the onlookers to allow the oldest girl in the group to be perceived more as a caregiver than a child looking for a home. *Mr. Thornton would approve.* Still, if the woman were that good, why had she not figured out a way to draw attention away from his legs. *Maybe because even she knows there's no chance of finding me a home.*

Suddenly, the onlookers rushed toward them—a flurry of

eager people searching through the group of children seeking out the worthiest prospect. He looked to Miss Agana, who'd gone from self-assured and competent to waving her hands in a fruitless attempt of regaining control. People came from all directions, pulling at the children and asking questions. A couple approached; the man looking him up and down before focusing on his legs. Just as the woman opened her mouth to speak, the man grabbed her arm, pulling her away.

Percival swallowed and silently begged his legs to be still, his hopes dimming as one by one children got selected. A man approached Mouse, who laughed and shook his head. In that moment, Percival envied his friend, as he knew Mouse was impervious to what others thought of him. Nor did Mouse seem to need anyone in return. That was the problem: Percival did care, and he wanted someone to care in return. He spied a haggard-faced man with spectacles and a thick mustache, searching the crowd as if looking for someone. The man saw him then looked to Percival's legs. Instead of turning away, he smiled, almost as if he found the person he'd been looking for.

The man moved forward. Pushing his way through the crowd, he stopped directly in front of Percival and smiled a weary smile. "My name is Louis Gianetti, I own Gianetti's Italian Restaurant across street. I much need of someone help me work the place. You look lika' strong boy. If'a' you have no better offer, I'd lika' offer you a place. I teacha you to cook ifa you no mind."

Percival stood frozen in place. The man standing in front of him looked and sounded a great deal like his papa, at least from the little he remembered of the man. He didn't recall his papa looking quite that tired, but then again, all he had were fragments of memories.

"You no wanna come, that okay. Hard work not for everyone. I tell him I tried," the man said when he failed to answer.

"I'm not afraid of hard work," Percival said, finding his voice.

"You no afraid of woman's work?"

"Not if you're not afraid of teaching me." Percival grinned.

"I put your name on da application and we'll take it to da committee, okay?"

"Okay," Percival said, bobbing his head up and down.

"Should be no trouble. They all lika me very much," Mr. Gianetti assured him. "Most are good customers and lika my food."

It was all Percival could do not to jump for joy. He'd done it—found someone who wasn't put off by the restlessness of his legs. Not only that, but the man owned a restaurant and had promised to teach him to cook. He wasn't sure Mr. Thornton would be happy with his placement, but something told him that his mother would approve.

***

Mr. Gianetti was right; the committee had no reservations in letting him go with the man. Even Mouse had stopped him as he and Mr. Gianetti were leaving to ask if he was alright before he himself took off to places unknown.

"Slim!"

Percival turned to see Paddy heading his way, an elderly man and woman following close behind. Percival frowned; this wasn't the type of family he'd pictured for the boy. "Is this the best you could do?" Percival whispered when Paddy grew near.

"They seem alright," Paddy said with a shrug. "Besides, if I get in trouble, they'll have a devil of a time catching me. How about you?"

"I found me a home too." Percival beamed. "Mr. Gianetti owns a restaurant across the street and is going to teach me how to cook."

"You're gonna do woman's work," Paddy said, wrinkling his nose.

"Yep," Percival replied, and they both burst out laughing.

"Don't you worry," Paddy said before they parted. "Now that I know where you are, I'll find ya."

***

"Your legs," Mr. Gianetti said as they began walking. "Do they hurt much?"

"No, sir, they don't hurt at all—just get jumpy from time to time. I have a tea to drink. It helps, at least most of the time."

"Where do you get this tea?"

"Dr. Todd gave me some before I left. He said if I have trouble finding it, he would send me more."

"That's good. Tell me what it is, I'll see to it."

All this talk about his legs made him think Mr. Gianetti was having second thoughts. "Mr. Gianetti, if you've changed your mind, please tell me now while there's still time to join Miss Agana and the others. I'd rather go to the next stop and try to find a home than to have you send me back to the asylum in a few days."

"You wish go?"

"Only if you're thinking about sending me away."

"I only just found you Why you think I send away?"

"On account of my legs."

"I no want send you away. I want to help you be better. What kind of papa would I be if I no take care my son?"

Percival stopped, staring after the man as he continued to walk. "You mean to say you're gonna adopt me?"

Mr. Gianetti turned on his heels and pushed his spectacles closer to his face, shrugging his broad shoulders. "I dunno. But I no need no papers to tell me what's what. You gonna live wit' me, you gonna be my son. That okay wit' you?"

"That's okay with me," Percival said, following once more.

They crossed the street dodging cars and buggies, then walked to a small brown brick building where Mr. Gianetti pulled open the door. "It no much but it ours."

Ours?

"Come, son, I show you around."

While Gianetti was correct about the restaurant being small, he was mistaken about it not being much. The inside was perfectly delightful with the same brown brick coating the outer walls of the room. Eight tables—each with four chairs nestled beneath white linen tablecloths— were scattered around the room, some filled with men chatting over their food. A subtle aroma of tomato sauce and spices lingered in the air, reminding him he'd not eaten anything substantial since leaving New York City days earlier.

A woman with graying hair pulled high upon her head came out of the back carrying two bowls piled high with pasta. She smiled a relieved smile then hurried to place the bowls on a nearby table.

"That Ralina; she's worked here a vera long time," Gianetti said, nodding toward the woman.

Percival followed as Gianetti weaved around the tables.

"Who's the kid?" a hefty-size man sitting alone at a table asked as they neared.

"Thisa my son," Gianetti said, wrapping an arm around Percival and pulling him close. "He's been staying wit' my sister in New York."

Percival stiffened at the lie.

"Ah yes, I can see the resemblance." The man studied Percival's legs for a moment then stuffed half a large meatball in his mouth.

The resemblance? Percival slid a glance toward Gianetti, who was beaming under the compliment. While the man had reminded him of his father, it didn't dawn on him to think he looked like the man—but it was true.

"Everything okay wit' your meal?" Gianetti asked, maintaining his hold on Percival.

"Yes, good, as always," the man said, waving him away.

It wasn't until he'd pulled him away from the table that Gianetti released his hold on Percival. "You stay away from him. He needs sumptin, you tell me."

"Who is he?" Percival asked, looking over his shoulder. "And why did you lie to him about me?"

"Who he is no concern you. We have all kinds come here, some good. Others not so much. Someone ask you question, keep it simple," he said firmly then slackened the lines in his face. "I do my best keepa you safe. They no be getting their mitts on my boy."

Percival had so many questions. Who was the big guy and why was Mr. Gianetti afraid of him? He said he'd lied to protect him; just who was he trying to protect him from? Remembering what Paddy had said about not coming across as too smart, he kept his questions to himself.

The moment they entered the kitchen, Percival's senses were bombarded with a mixture of tomato sauce, garlic, and fresh baked bread.

Closing his eyes, he breathed in the aroma as his stomach rumbled its eagerness. "And I thought the dining room smelled good."

"You hungry?" Gianetti asked, reaching for an apron.

Percival's mouth watered. "Boy, am I!"

"I fixa' food jus lika my momma." He pushed out his stomach and patted the fluff. "You eat and you no look so thin. Soon no one question you my son."

Chapter Thirty-Seven

"Slim, come taka bite and tell me what you think," Gianetti said, removing the lid from a large pot.

Percival dipped a spoon into the pot and blew briefly before tasting, closing his eyes as the sauce slid down his throat.

"It good, no?"

"Good yes, but it could use more garlic."

Gianetti grabbed a spoon, took a taste, and smiled. "Ah, yes, never go wrong wit' more garlic."

"That's what my momma always said," Percival said, watching as Gianetti pulled some garlic from the overhead basket, removed a few cloves, and peeled the outer lining, smashing them onto the counter using the blade of a large knife before throwing them into the pot.

"We let that simmer a bit. It be vera good. You gonna maka good cook," Gianetti said, wiping the remnants from the wooden counter.

"Maybe someday I can use one of my mother's recipes." Percival went to the stool where he'd set his bag and pulled the book out for Gianetti to see.

"It's a vera nice book, but I no can read," Gianetti said, glancing at the cover.

"I can't read it either. My mother's notes are in the margins inside. See?" he said, opening the book to show him.

"No can read," Gianetti repeated.

Percival was about to show him again when he realized it wasn't that the man couldn't read what his mother had written.

He couldn't read anything. Percival nodded his understanding then read the recipe his mother had used to make caponata aloud.

"Yes," Gianetti said, bobbing his head. "We make tomorrow."

Percival closed the book, hugging it to his chest briefly before returning it to the bag. He was about to ask what to do next then decided to start in on the dishes that were piling up in the sink. As he dipped his hands in the sudsy water, Gianetti moved up beside him, humming a familiar tune as they worked together to clear the dishes.

***

Percival finished washing the last supper pot and set it on the rack to dry.

"You empty trash, and I go lock up," Gianetti said, drying his hands.

Percival stepped outside, breathing the cool evening air deep into his lungs.

Mouse appeared from the shadows, laughing when Percival jumped. "He didn't waste any time putting you to work."

"It's not so bad," Percival said, emptying the can. "It's lots of work, but I don't mind being busy."

"I need you to ask around about a friend of mine," Mouse said, handing him a slip of paper.

Percival read the note. "Who's Big Mike?"

"I told you he's a friend of mine. Told me to look him up if I ever made it to town, only I don't know where he lives. Ask around and see if you know anyone who knows how to find him."

The back door opened; Mr. Gianetti stuck his head out, then stepped into the back alley. "Who this?"

"I was just leaving," Mouse said, holding his hands up. "I'll see you later, Slim."

Gianetti's brow furrowed. "He seem like he wanting you go wit' him."

"Nah, he just wanted to make sure I was doing okay," Percival said, leaving out the part about Mouse asking for help finding his friend. "He rode the train with me."

"You coming in?" Gianetti asked, reaching for the door. "We go upstairs—I show you your room."

"Sure, I need to grab my bag from the kitchen," Percival said, following him inside. As he reached for the bag, he saw a shadow out of the corner of his eye. Turning, he saw the silhouette of a man. Percival doubled his hand into a fist. "Who are you?"

"I'm nobody, kid," the man said before opening the basement door and disappearing down the stairs.

"There was a man in the kitchen," Percival said the second he saw Gianetti. "He went into the basement."

Gianetti walked to the basement door and locked it. "We go up now."

"What about the man?" Percival asked, looking over his shoulder.

"You must learn no ask so many questions."

Don't ask questions? Earlier in the day, he'd seen two guys walking through the basement. When he'd turned to ask what they were doing, the men were nowhere to be found. Now a guy was in their restaurant after hours, and he wasn't supposed to ask about it. Mr. Thornton had taught him to question everything, but Gianetti, who he'd only just met, wanted him to question nothing. Remembering his conversation with Paddy, Percival held his tongue.

***

October 31, 1924

Percival bit the end of the pencil, gathering his thoughts. It had been nearly a month since he'd arrived on the train and he'd yet to write Mr. Thornton. Mainly because he still wasn't sure what to tell the man about his placement. He liked Mr. Gianetti—Pop, as the man preferred him to call him—but there was something about the man that caused him pause. Perhaps it was just that Gianetti was trying too hard to fill the fatherly role he thought missing in Percival's life. Or perhaps it was the years spent reading over Mr. Thornton's case files that made him feel as if Gianetti was hiding something. Something more than the reason why he allowed men to come and go without explaining why they were there or where they disappeared to. More than once, Percival had crept down the basement stairs hoping to finally learn what the secrecy was about, only to find himself alone. The men weren't spirits, as he had heard their footsteps and he'd spoken to one on the day of his arrival.

Ghosts don't speak. But neither do grown men disappear. It just didn't make sense.

A shadow fell over him. Percival looked up to see Gianetti standing in the doorway. "You okay, Pop?"

"I saw you talk that boy today. Is same boy from trains, no?"

"Yes, sir," Percival answered truthfully. It was the third time since he'd arrived that Mouse had come by asking for information. Today, he'd brought a friend, though he hadn't seen fit to introduce them.

"Ralina said you ask 'bout guy name Big Mike. Then she tell me you ask about someone else."

"Yes, sir," Percival replied.

"Remember I tell you there are some no good people who come here?"

"Yes, sir."

"Big Mike one those guys. He big trouble. The boy your friend wit', he big trouble. If your friend know him, your friend big trouble too."

"Mouse isn't trouble."

Gianetti lowered his voice as though even saying the words would bring trouble. "Those men are wit' the Purple Gang. Bad people. Vera bad. I no want you talk to him. This Mouse."

"But…"

"I say no. You live in my house now, and I say no talk this Mouse. He no good for you. He come in here again, you tell him I say go. He no listen, I tell him myself."

Percival wanted to tell him he was wrong about Mouse, but the truth was Gianetti was right. Mouse hadn't acted like himself and the guy he was with seemed shady. Mouse was hiding something. The problem was he wasn't the only one. He looked up at Gianetti, "Mouse is my friend, but I'll keep my distance if it will make you happy. But you of all people shouldn't talk bad about people when I know you're keeping secrets."

Gianetti started to leave, then hesitated. Instead, he pulled a chair around and sat wringing his hands.

"Something on your mind, sir?"

"I don't know what to say."

Percival lowered the pencil to the table and pivoted toward the man. "Just tell me the truth. You call me your son, but I know there are things going on that you're not telling me."

Gianetti hung his head. "Some time ago, a man came see me—told me about the trains—said be a boy with wandering legs and say how I to give you a home."

Percival gulped. He thought Gianetti was going to tell him about the men in the basement.

"I tell man I know not about taking care of boy, but he say how you were nearly a man—say how you wan' learn cook.

Man offers to pay me for my troubles—I need money and know much about cooking, so I agree. I say you my son that day so you be happy to stay. But until you came, I never know how lonely I am. We laugh and work together and I lika you just like my own son. I feel it here," he said, bringing a fist to his chest. "Money no maka you my son; my heart maka it true. I canna tell you to trust me if I don't trust you."

Percival felt the hit just as sure as if he'd been physically punched. "So you only picked me on account of someone paid you?"

Gianetti's eyes grew wide. "You no understand. I only know about you because the man told me. If he no come to me, you no be here. I was sad man, now much joy in my life. I would gladly send da money back if I still had it to send."

"Who was the man?" Percival knew the answer, the one man capable of seeing to such a feat.

"I dunna know name. He was sent by your Mr. Thornton," Gianetti said, confirming his suspicion. "You no be mad at Mr. Thornton. He good man. He care about you a great deal. He know he could not help you, so asked me to do so. Only he didn't know of company I keep. I do my best keepa you safe, but I need you to trust my judgment. I know these men and they know I kill them if dey touch my son."

Percival pushed from the chair. "I'm not your son. I'm just a boy who sleeps in your house."

"Dat's not true," Gianetti said, wrapping his arms around him. "You my son as much as if you born of my seed. I no tell you all this to hurt you. I tell you so you will know I love you. We good together. You need me as much I need you and I no let you go until you tell me you'll stay."

Percival did care about the man and he was happy—happier than he'd been in a long time—but there were things that didn't add up. "What's going on in the basement?"

Gianetti released him and slumped in the chair once more. "I no wan' tell you."

"You said no more secrets," Percival reminded him.

"I have debt. Man come to me and say I can break legs or we can make deal. I no can cook if he break legs, so I make deal."

The thought of someone threatening Gianetti angered him. "What kind of deal?"

"They make a blind pig; drinking, gambling, started working dat vera night. Cutting into the dirt and making a room."

"A blind pig; the guy I saw going down to the basement the first night. He was going to the blind pig. But where did he come from?" Percival remembered the guys he saw disappear. At least he hadn't imagined it, but where had they come from? "There must be a tunnel."

"From the church," Gianetti whispered.

"You really are afraid of those guys, aren't you?"

"Purples are vera bad men," Gianetti said solemnly. "You wan' go, I no stop you."

Go where? While he wasn't happy that Thornton paid Gianetti to take him in, he couldn't complain about how he'd been treated since arriving. He had his own bedroom with a bed and desk and, in all truthfulness, had felt very much like Gianetti's son. Never had the man asked more of him than he required from himself. Besides, he wouldn't mind sticking around to make sure the man remained safe. "I'm not going anywhere."

At his words, Gianetti burst into tears. "You such a good boy, Slim. I happy you my son."

Percival embraced the man briefly, as had been their nightly routine since the day he'd arrived. "I'll stay. Go to bed, Pop, you look tired."

Gianetti released him and nodded to the paper. "You writing Mr. Thornton?"

That had been the plan before all this started. "Yes, Pop."

"You gonna tell him what I say?"

"I don't know," Percival answered truthfully.

"If you do, tell him I happy he gave me a son."

As soon as Gianetti left the room, Percival picked up the pencil. This time, when he touched the lead to paper, he knew what he was going to write.

Mr. Thornton,

I wanted to let you know I arrived safely in Detroit. I am placed with Mr. Gianetti, who, as chance has it, owns a fine Italian restaurant. It shall come as no surprise that it is hard work but helps the day pass quickly and keeps me from trouble. I had intended to share the address at which I stay; however, since it was you who saw to my placement, I believe it is safe to assume that you are already aware of my location.

Pop, as Mr. Gianetti wishes me to call him, sends his regards and wishes me to tell you he is grateful to have found a son.

Respectfully yours,
Percival Barsotti

He thought to include the part about the blind pig in the basement just to raise his ire but knew if he told Mr. Thornton of the possible danger, the man would find a way to remove him from his home. He folded the paper, put it in the envelope, and addressed it to Mr. Thornton's home. His hand hovered over the paper once more before finally putting lead to paper once again.

Dear Anastasia,

Percival crumpled the paper and began again.

Dear Anna,

I wanted to write to let you know that I have found a home in Detroit with a kind man by the name of Mr. Gianetti. Though he has not formally adopted me, he calls me his son and asks that I refer to him as Pop. The man is kind, so I see no reason not to fulfill the request. He owns an Italian restaurant and makes the kind of food my mother once made. I've shown him the recipes written in my mother's hand, and he has taken to using some to offer to those who come to eat. I do not mind, as when I eat, I can clearly recall my mother's face.

I do not like the way things were between us when I went away. I hope that when we see each other again, the meeting will be filled with smiles instead of tears. I will include my address in this post in case you wish to write.

Yours,
Slim

He pulled out a third piece of paper.

Headmistress,

I hope this letter finds you well. I'm writing to let you know that I've found a most agreeable home with a man who thinks me his son. He treats me well and I enjoy working in his restaurant.

I hope none of the children are being difficult, as I know I am not there to keep them calm.

Respectfully yours,
Percival Barsotti

Percival folded the letter and placed it in its envelope. Addressing them all, he placed them in a neat pile on the desk before shutting off the light and slipping into bed. Unable to sleep, he recalled his days since arriving in Detroit, remembering his fear of not finding a home, his relief at having been picked, and recalling how pleased he'd been at hearing that Mr. Gianetti owned a restaurant. Odd, since he had thought one day he too would like to own one. He recalled Mr. Thornton's face when he told him he didn't wish to be an attorney and that he'd like to own a restaurant instead. He remembered Mr. Thornton warning him of the work involved and the quickest of smiles that crossed the man's face. *That's when he planned it. He wasn't trying to hurt me, nor did he think I couldn't find a home on my own. He wanted to give me a chance to see for myself how difficult it was to own a restaurant so I could see if it was truly what I wished to do. I don't. Not really.* While he didn't mind working in the restaurant and enjoyed cooking, it wasn't what he pictured himself doing forever. The restaurant was his mother's dream, not his. He enjoyed books and even enjoyed reading through Mr. Thornton's case files.

Percival got out of bed, went to the desk, turned on the lamp, and rifled through the letters he'd just written. He pulled out Mr. Thornton's letter and added, *p.s. Thank you for seeing that I was sent to live with Mr. Gianetti. He's a nice man, and I couldn't have asked for a better home. Your plan worked, while I don't mind hard work, I no longer wish to open my own restaurant.*

Percival refolded the letter and slid it back into the envelope. He smiled and removed the letter from the headmistress's envelope. Picking up the pencil he added, *I thought one day to own my own restaurant; however, I think I'm meant for greater things. As you know, I enjoy books. Having spent time reading over Mr. Thornton's case files, I may one day wish to study law. I shan't tell Mr. Thornton that just yet as I do not wish to see his hopes dashed should I change my mind.*

Returning the paper to the envelope, he reached to turn off

the lamp, nearly turning it over in the process.

"Everything okay, son?" Gianetti called from the next room.

"Just fine, Pop."

"Good night, son."

"Good night, Pop."

Chapter Thirty-Eight

October 14, 1926

"You read dat letter so much, you gonna wear a hole in da paper," Gianetti said, sticking his head around the corner of Percival's bedroom door. "Dat the girl in New York you keep posting letters to?"

Percival nodded without answering. The letter had come a few days prior. Though he'd written to Anna on numerous occasions telling of his life in Detroit and sometimes letting her know he'd seen Mouse—though never telling her of the company her brother ran with—it was the first time she'd answered him. He refolded the letter from Anastasia and slid it back into the envelope with the one she'd asked him to give to her brother, sitting them on his desk.

"Glad she finally write you back. She say she sweet on you?" Gianetti asked, glancing at the envelope.

"She's not sweet on me, and I'm sure not sweet on her," Percival said. He retrieved the envelope, not that there was much of anything to read even if Gianetti knew how. Two years since his departure, and though he'd written her often, this was the first time she'd answered. Not that he would even call it an answer; the only thing she'd written was telling of her son and asking if he would give Mouse a letter for her. She'd told him not to read it, and he hadn't, though he'd started to on several occasions. It wasn't that he was nosey. He just wished to know if what she'd written to Mouse was as impersonal as the one she'd written to him.

"Dis girl, she pretty?"

"Very much so," Percival replied. Even her scar, which others thought so menacing, made him smile. *At least it used to.*

"You no boy anymore. You should go to her see if she feels da same about you."

"I told you I don't have any feelings for her," Percival replied.

"Your mouth say no, your legs say otherwise," Gianetti said softly.

"My legs are jumping because I have yet to have my morning tea," Percival said, placing the letters in his pocket. "Come on, Pop; I'll fix us some breakfast."

***

October 15, 1926

Percival was in the basement organizing the storeroom when he heard muffled voices coming from upstairs—odd, since the restaurant had not yet opened its doors for the day. Setting the pot he'd been holding aside, he quietly made his way up the stairs. Stopping at the top, he pressed his ear to the door, hoping to hear. While he couldn't make out what was being said, he could tell by the tone the conversation was not friendly. He pulled open the door, expecting to see his pop and whoever he was speaking with, but was surprised when he saw nothing. A moment later, he heard coughing, then silence once more. Hurrying into the kitchen, he saw a man pushing Gianetti's head into a sink full of water. Furious, Percival grabbed hold of the guy, shoving him against the wall as he helped Gianetti to a chair. He saw the man lunge for him, ducked out of the way, then sent him to the floor with a single punch.

"No, son, you no get involved," Gianetti cried between coughs.

"I'm not going to stand back and let them hurt you," Percival said through clenched teeth.

The man pushed to his feet, worried his jaw with his hand, and glowered at Percival. "Harry isn't going to be happy about this."

Percival wished Gianetti wasn't there, as he wanted nothing more than to mop the floor with the guy. "You tell Harry if he wants to talk, he knows where to find me."

Gianetti's face turned white and he followed the man down the hall dripping water as he went. "No, my boy no responsible for my debt. You tell Harry his beef with me, not my boy!"

Percival followed them outside, pushing his fingernails into his palm as the man left without so much as a backward glance. As soon as the guy drove off, Percival whirled on Gianetti. "What was that about, Pop?"

"Jus' a little misunderstanding. It no concern you," Gianetti said, brushing his wet hair from his eyes with his fingers.

"Don't concern me? DON'T CONCERN ME? The man was trying to kill you."

"He no drown; he just wan' maka sure I listen."

"If he wanted you to listen, he should have been talking, not pushing your head in a sink full of water," Percival fumed. "What does he want from you?"

"I owe his boss a bit of money," Gianetti said, waving him off.

"How much?"

"It no matter. I no have dat kinda dough," Gianetti said, thrusting his hands up in the air.

"How much, Pop?" Percival pressed.

"Over ten," Gianetti said, staring at his shoes.

"All that over ten bucks?"

"Ten big ones," Gianetti corrected.

Percival's mouth went dry. "You borrowed ten thousand

dollars?"

"I borrow more but paid some back with the money I got from Mr. Thornton."

"That was two years ago. What did you do with the money you borrowed?"

"The blind pig," Gianetti said, shrugging his shoulders. "At first, Harry told me come down. Tell me I drink for free. Then I roll a few dice and they said I good. Then one day it no good and they wan' me pay. I try stop, but I lika it too much."

Percival eyed Gianetti. "I've never even seen you drink."

"Da drinking not so bad. I lika the dice." He rolled the tips of his fingers around in his right hand. "I lika da way day feel."

Percival ran his hands through his hair. "Don't worry, Pop. I'll figure something out."

"No, this no your problem."

Percival turned and saw Mouse sitting on the steps of the Presbyterian Church and wondered how much his friend had overheard. "Go on in and finish getting ready for the lunch crowd. I'll be in in a minute."

"You no gonna do anything stupid?"

"No, Pop, I just need to calm down for a minute. I'm okay. Go on in; I'll be in soon." Percival waited for Gianetti to go inside then walked to the church, taking a seat beside his friend.

"Trouble?" Mouse asked.

"The man's up to his ears in debt, and yet he won't let me help him," Percival replied.

"How'd you propose to help him?" Mouse asked.

I can't. Even if he'd been good at dipping pockets, there was no way he could come up with the kind of dough Gianetti needed. *But Mouse is not dipping pockets anymore.* "I told him I could go to work with you."

"The man barely tolerates me in his establishment. Why'd you think he'd want you to work with me?"

"It's not you, it's what you represent," Percival said.

"And yet he has a blind pig in his basement."

"You've got it all wrong. He doesn't have a problem with that. Heck, sometimes he's downstairs more than he's in the kitchen. That's where his money goes."

"Then what's his problem?"

"He knows I knew you before, in New York. It reminds him that I'm not his true son." Okay, it wasn't the total truth, but he needed to get Mouse to agree to let him work with him.

"Has he offered to adopt you?"

"Not officially, but he calls me 'son.'"

"And the fight just now?"

Percival looked toward the brown brick building. *The guy is in serious trouble.* "Not a fight, just a father looking out for his son."

"I wouldn't let you."

"Wouldn't let me what?"

"Work with me."

"You didn't have a problem with me working with you in the city."

"That was different. You worked for me."

"What's the difference?"

"I'm not working for myself, Slim. The guys I work for are into a lot of stuff."

"I've been downstairs. I know about the gambling and drinking," Percival assured him. *And the Purples and the fact they kill people just for mentioning their name.*

"That doesn't begin to cover it," Mouse whispered. "These guys kidnap people. They cut off body parts and send them in nice little packages to get people to pay the ransom."

"And if they don't pay?" Percival asked, trying to keep his voice even.

"Then they kill them," Mouse said, meeting his stare.

Percival's legs increased their tempo. Gianetti was in bigger trouble than he'd let on. If he didn't find a way to help the man, they'd off him and toss his body in the river. "You work for them. Have you ever killed anyone?"

They sat in silence for several moments before Percival got up the nerve to ask the question he already knew the answer to. "So you're in the Purple Gang."

Mouse didn't answer.

"Word on the street is if you're in with the Purples, you are never to tell anyone. Word is if you admit to being a Purple, they take you for a ride and you never come back," Percival said, repeating some of what Gianetti told him.

Mouse gave the slightest of nods and Percival blinked his understanding.

"I have someone I want you to meet," Mouse said, changing the subject. "He used to be a boxer. Pretty good too. Name's Knuckles. I told him about you."

"You did?" He wondered if Big Joe had heard about the guy. Big Joe, Percival sighed. It had been two years since he'd arrived in Detroit, and still no word from the guy.

"Yeah, I told him you showed me how to throw a punch and asked if he'd give you some pointers. That's if you're interested."

"Sure I am." Not that he thought he needed any pointers. But Mouse didn't know that, as he'd never told him the full story of how he'd learned to fight. Still, it might be a way to get some dough to help out his Pop.

"Okay, I'll introduce you under one condition. Just boxing. Anything else and you have to clear it through me."

Percival laughed. "You know I'm older than you, right?"

Mouse turned to him. "I know you're not a kid. You're my friend, the only person I can really count on."

Percival was touched. This was the Mouse he remembered

and trusted.

"Don't you go all baby on me," Mouse said.

"Mouse, I've got something to tell you."

Mouse took in a slow breath. "Go on, then."

"I got a letter from Anastasia." He held his breath, waiting for his friend to explode.

Mouse's eyes grew wide. "Why would Anastasia send you a letter?"

"We were kind of close before I got sent out."

"How close?"

"We're friends." *At least we used to be.*

"That's not what I asked."

"I guess about as close as two people can be."

Mouse turned toward him, his nostrils flaring.

"You're not gonna say anything?"

Mouse leaned back against the stoop. "Sheesh, Slim, here I've been trying to protect you from the hornets, and you've been lying with the honey bees."

"She told me you're her brother," Percival said, ignoring the comment.

"I don't have any family."

"Did you know she had a son?"

"Is he yours?" Mouse asked coolly.

"No, and I don't know who the father is. Anna didn't like to speak about it." It was a lie, but she'd told him about Caleb in confidence. She'd also told him not to read the letter she'd sent to Mouse, but in the end, he'd read it several times before folding it neatly and returning it to the envelope he now had in his pocket.

"Anna?"

"It's what she asked me to call her. Anyway, about the kid, his name's Franky and he's six."

"Why are you telling me this?"

"Cause she asked me to. Said the kid went out on the trains last month. I guess a letter from the placing agent came in and it said he'd been placed in Chicago. She asked me to give you this and told me not to read it. I didn't." He handed Mouse the envelope and watched as he shoved it into his pocket without a word. "You told me you went to Chicago a few months ago. You didn't say why, but now that I know about... well, I guess I figure you'll go again, someday. I thought that if you did, you could maybe check on the boy."

"Why would I do that?" Mouse snapped.

"I figure it wouldn't hurt to look in on him, since he's your family."

"Yeah, well, I don't have any plans to go to Chicago."

Percival got up, walked a few steps, then reconsidered.

"Forget something?" Mouse asked tersely.

"We grew up on the streets. That kid grew up in the asylum. If things aren't good, I'm not sure he'd know how to handle it. Besides, wouldn't it have been nice if someone would've cared enough to check on us?" Percival turned and left without waiting for a reply. As he walked back to the restaurant, anger fueled his steps. The problem was he wasn't sure which bothered him more, that Gianetti was in trouble and he wasn't sure he'd be able to help the man or that Anna needed help and hadn't even considered asking him.

Chapter Thirty-Nine

January 1927

"I'm going out for a bit," Percival said, pulling his coat from the hook.

"Where you going dis late?" Gianetti asked, looking at the clock.

"It's not late, Pop. I'm just going out for a bit. Don't wait up. I have my key." He pulled his coat on, hurrying outside before Gianetti could ask any more questions. Bracing against the wind, he trampled through the snow-covered lot, hurrying to Mouse's car, which idled in front of the church.

"Old man give you grief about going out with me?" Mouse asked when he opened the door.

"Nah, I just told him I was going out, not who I was going with," Percival said, kicking his shoes against the running board of the Ford.

Mouse waited for him to close the door then pulled away from the curb. "You know you're plenty old enough to move out."

"I know, but I never know when Harry's goons are going to come around."

"It's been months since you decked the guy. What makes you think it's safe to leave him tonight?"

"I never think it's safe, but I need to see about making some dough to get him out of that mess."

"Word on the street is dough's not gonna be enough. Little Harry's not used to being made a fool of. I still haven't figured out why he hasn't sent his guys after you. Something about it don't smell right."

Percival grunted his agreement. He'd expected trouble straight away, and yet there'd been nothing but crickets. "You'd tell me if you knew anything, wouldn't you, Mouse?"

"Of course I would; you're the only true friend I've got," Mouse replied. "I haven't heard anything. I even asked Big Mike if he'd heard any rumblings. He did some checking and got nothing. If Harry was going to bump off someone, Big Mike would've heard something."

Percival shook off an imaginary shiver. "It doesn't add up. I hit the guy pretty hard, but not enough to scare them off."

"Maybe you should relax a bit and be glad you're not in the East River," Mouse said, turning a corner.

"Would you relax if you were in my shoes?"

"Your legs haven't relaxed in years," Mouse quipped, then grew serious once more. "Not even for a second. I was you, I'd sleep with one eye open, which is why we're going to see my friend, Knuckles. He said he'd give you some pointers."

"Do I need to remind you that I knocked out Harry's guy with only one punch?"

"I know you're good, but it doesn't hurt to learn more," Mouse said, pulling into the parking lot of the gym. He gunned the engine to get over a snowdrift and parked close to the building. They both got out, plunging shin deep into the snow. Mouse looked to the sky. "We might have to dig our way out."

Percival followed his gaze and got a face full of snow. "You got a shovel?"

"Nope."

"So much for digging our way out."

"The Ford got in on her own, she'll get out on her own," Mouse said with a shrug.

Entering the building through the side entrance, Percival

scanned the large room, noting two separate roped-off sections, each with men sparring inside the ring. Various bags hung from the ceiling, most with men standing in front of them, pounding the bags with gloved hands. The sweaty stench of the gym instantly reminded him of Big Joe. Percival automatically searched the room, hoping to see the man—a pang gripped his heart when he did not. Big Joe had been a comfort when he lost his mother, and he wished nothing more than to see the man about now.

"What's got into them?" Mouse said when the room grew quiet, all eyes staring in their direction.

Percival nodded to his legs, which were currently dancing as if they too were in the ring. "The same thing everyone always stares at."

"I'd ask you to stop, but I know better," Mouse replied. "Heads up; here comes Knuckles."

The man in question was heading in their direction, the downward curve of his mouth showing he wasn't overly pleased to see them. Knuckles was a solid mass of muscle, long arms, and a nose that looked as if it had been broken on more than one occasion. Percival moved close to Mouse and lowered his voice. "I thought you said he was expecting us."

"He is. I spoke with him just this afternoon," Mouse whispered in return.

"This the guy you were telling me about?" Knuckles asked without waiting for introductions.

"It is," Mouse said, pulling himself taller.

"You didn't tell me about his legs. I can't do nothing with him," Knuckles said, turning away.

"His legs don't have nothing to do with nothing," Mouse called after him.

"You afraid I'll show you up, old man?" Percival said, goading the man. Though he didn't fancy hitting someone that looked to be triple his age, he needed the money and would gladly step into the ring if it meant helping his Pop.

Knuckles turned and narrowed his eyes at Percival. "Don't test me, boy."

"Come on, Slim, you don't need to prove anything to this old man," Mouse said, pulling at his coat.

"This old man could take both of you at the same time. I didn't say I couldn't take you. I said I couldn't train you." Knuckles' nostrils flared, showing Percival had touched a nerve.

"I don't need training. I'll step into the ring with anyone in the place," Percival said, looking around the room.

"Take it easy," Knuckles said when several in the room called him out. He turned back to Percival. "There's a difference between knowing how to fight and being conditioned to withstand the time in the ring. You'd do good to remember that. Ain't no one in here going to fight you; no one in the town wants that kind of trouble. You've been blackballed, kid. You may as well go home."

Mouse lifted a hand to Percival's chest to calm him then questioned Knuckles. "Blackballed by who?"

"Don't matter. What matters is anyone wants to live, they ain't gonna work with your boy."

Wants to live? Who would threaten anyone for working with me? Is that how Little Harry is getting his revenge? "It's got to be Little Harry," Percival said, voicing the thought aloud. "He knew I'd be looking to make some dough."

"Don't be a fool. Just 'cause you whale on one of his goons don't mean he knows you know how to fight."

Mouse was right; even though he knocked the guy down with one punch wasn't proof he knew how to fight. He could have just gotten lucky. *Mr. Thornton?* No, for all he knew, Percival was happily working at his pop's restaurant. Who else knew he could… "Big Joe?"

Knuckles took a step backward, and Percival knew he'd guessed right.

"Who's Big Joe?" Mouse asked.

"A friend of mine," Percival said, wondering why the guy had turned on him.

"You need to learn how to pick your friends," Mouse replied.

"You're one to talk," Percival said, then leveled a look at Knuckles. "Where is he?"

"You might as well tell him," Mouse said, "We ain't leaving here until he gets his answer."

"Big Joe didn't say not to tell him," Knuckles replied. "He owns a gym over on Woodward. You want the phone number?"

Percival shook his head. "I want the address. Mouse and I are going to pay him a visit."

***

"Why haven't you ever mentioned this guy?" Mouse asked once they were back on the road.

"It's not like either of us has talked a lot about our family," Percival replied.

"This Big Joe, he got a reason not to want you to fight," Mouse said, ignoring the dig.

"If he does, I don't know what it is. It don't make sense 'cause he's the one that taught me how to fight in the first place."

"Knuckles said the guy owns a gym. Maybe he wants you to himself. He didn't know where to find you and knew you'd show up at some point."

"Maybe." The same thought had already crossed his mind, but it didn't fit Big Joe's personality. Then again, people can change—Mouse sure had. While he still felt he could trust the guy, there was no doubt he had changed since arriving in

Detroit. "We'll find out soon enough."

They rode the rest of the way in silence, Percival's mind swirling just as much as the snow outside the motorcar's window.

It was just after nine when they entered the building, which was considerably smaller than the one they'd just left. There was a ring in the front near the window, which was as empty as the rest of the building appeared to be. A large punching bag that Percival recognized as the one that used to hang in the makeshift shed on the roof of Big Joe's building hung from the ceiling. Percival walked to it, running his hand down the length of it, remembering simpler times.

"You'd get in trouble caressing a man's woman that way," came a familiar voice from above.

"If this is your woman, you have more troubles than I," Percival said, looking toward the voice.

Big Joe stood by the rail of the upper floor, smiling the instant Percival lifted his gaze in his direction. "I'm smarter than to leave a woman alone in a place like this."

"I thought you said this guy was family?" Mouse whispered.

"What, you don't see the family resemblance?" Percival laughed.

"Come on up, Slim," Big Joe called from above.

"My friend too?" Percival asked with a nod to Mouse.

"He packing?"

Percival looked to Mouse, who gave a subtle nod. He turned to Big Joe. "You got a problem if he is?"

"You trust him?"

Percival smiled. "As much as I trust you."

Big Joe chuckled and waved them both up.

"It's good to see you, Slim," Big Joe said, leading them into his office and pointing toward the chairs.

"If it's so good, then why didn't you come see me?" Percival asked, forgoing formalities.

The smile vanished. "Because I was asked not to."

"Who would've told you not to come see me? The only one who knew I was here was Mr. Thornton. Did he tell you to stay away?"

"No. Thornton sent me to have a conversation with Mr. Gianetti before you showed up. Seems he wanted you to see what it would be like to work in a restaurant," Big Joe said, settling in an oversized chair behind a wooden desk.

"If not Mr. Thornton, then who? No one else knew I was here," Percival replied.

"Your pop knew," Mouse said. "Makes sense since he don't like me coming around either."

Percival looked to Big Joe, who nodded his head in answer.

"Why wouldn't Pop want you around? Didn't you tell him we're friends?"

"I wanted to, but I wasn't actually there on friendly terms. Gianetti didn't want to take in a kid and I kind of had to lean on him a little. I've had people check in on you from time to time just to see how you were getting along. Even talked to Ralina, told her to call me should anything happen."

"That sounds like a load of bull. If you would've truly wanted to see me, you'd have found a way."

"I understand you feel betrayed. But think of Gianetti. You called the man your pop, so you obviously care about him. He agreed to take you in and doesn't hesitate to tell everyone you're his son. The man wanted to believe it and wanted others to believe it as well. It wasn't me or your friend here that your pop wanted to keep you from. It was your previous life. He told everyone you'd been living with his sister in New York to keep up the charade."

It was true; Percival remembered hearing him tell that to a

man when he first arrived. "Okay, so you stayed away to appease my pop. Why blackball me from the gyms?"

"I couldn't watch over you like I wanted, knew if you got in trouble that you'd either go to Thornton or fall back on the skills I taught you. So, I contacted all the gyms in the area and told them if a kid with wandering legs were to come in, they were to send you away. I knew you wouldn't let them turn you away without reason, so I sat back and waited for you to show up. So, tell me what kind of trouble you're in."

"I'm not in any trouble," Percival lied. "Just looking to do a little fighting."

Big Joe caught Mouse's attention. "See those legs?"

Mouse nodded.

"They tell me he's lying. Want to take that bet?"

Mouse shook his head.

Big Joe leaned back in his chair and put his hands behind his head, his arms showing the man didn't miss many days in the gym. "You can tell me now or come back when you get desperate. Big Joe's a very patient man."

"You might as well tell him," Mouse agreed.

Percival sighed. "My Pop—Mr. Gianetti—is in trouble. Gambling. He owes big money to a guy named Little Harry. A few months ago, I caught one of Little Harry's goons pushing Pops' head into a sink full of water, so I clocked him. Took him down with one punch."

"I've heard of this Little Harry," he said, lowering his arms. "The man's not one to let something like that go. The fact that he hasn't sent his henchmen after you is worrisome."

"I've checked and even had my friend Big Mike look into it," Mouse said. "No one's heard anything."

"You run with a bad crowd," Big Joe said, eyeing Mouse. He turned his attention to Percival. "Are you with them too?"

"NO!" Mouse answered for him. "And he won't be

neither."

Big Joe must have believed him because the lines in his jaw slackened. "You know what's good for you, you'll get out before it's too late."

"Already is," Mouse said softly. "Don't you worry about Slim—I'm not letting him anywhere near them."

"I have connections," he said without elaborating. "Let me do some asking. I'll have you some answers tomorrow."

"Tomorrow?" Mouse laughed.

"Some connections are better than others," Big Joe said with a wink.

Chapter Forty

January 15, 1927

"You no going out tonight?" Gianetti asked when they'd finished cleaning up for the night.

"No, Pop, I'm not going out." Big Joe had promised to come by as soon as he found out anything. The second Percival flipped the light off, the back door creaked open, followed by the distinct sound of feet stomping in the back hallway. *Big Joe?* Not likely; though the man had promised word today, Mouse had warned him not to expect news so soon. "You expecting anyone, Pop?"

"No, who I expect?" Gianetti asked.

"I don't know, but someone just came in through the back door." Percival pulled the man behind him, grabbed a knife from the drawer, and crept toward the hallway. Common sense told him it was someone they could trust. If it were one of Harry's guys, they would've been quieter in their entrance, but since neither of them was expecting anyone, he wanted to be safe. "Leave the light off, Pop."

"I go too."

"No, wait here. I'm sure it's okay, but I want to make sure," Percival said, feeling his way along the wall. Just as he reached the hallway, he saw the silhouette of a man cautiously making his way down the hall. Percival raised the knife.

"Don't you have any lights in this place?"

"Turn on the lights, Pop." Percival lowered the knife. "Sheesh, Big Joe, what are you doing sneaking around this late?

I could've killed you."

"I figured you were expecting me since you left the back door unlocked. You went and turned the lights off, so I thought there might be trouble. Just so you know, when your life is in danger, you shouldn't leave the back door unlocked."

"It's a restaurant. The doors are always unlocked," Percival reminded him.

"Are you open?"

"No."

Percival sighed when Big Joe leveled a look at him.

"You okay, son?" Gianetti asked from the other room.

"I'm good, Pop. Put some coffee on—we have a visitor." Percival led Big Joe into the freshly mopped dining room, took the chairs off the top of one of the tables, and placed them on the floor. "Mouse didn't think you'd have anything for us this soon."

"I told you both I have different connections," Big Joe said, joining Percival at the table.

Percival raised an eyebrow. "Better than the Purples? Maybe I should be worried about you as well."

Big Joe raised his arm, turning his hand back and forth. "There are great advantages to having skin this color. I have friends placed in establishments where people like to talk freely and don't pay attention to those they think too simple-minded to take notice."

Percival smiled. "I do believe you to be one of the smartest men I know."

Big Joe placed a finger to his lips. "Please keep that thought to yourself, my friend."

"I bring coffee," Gianetti said, coming into the room with a tray. He stopped the moment he recognized Big Joe. "You!"

Percival jumped up, taking the tray from him. "It's okay, Pop. Big Joe's my friend."

"He no friend of mine! He bad man! Say vera bad things me."

Big Joe looked at Percival and shrugged. "Told you I wasn't there to make friends."

"Pop, I need you to sit down. I asked Big Joe to look into Little Harry to see if we should be worried. He's come to tell us what he found out." Percival turned to Big Joe. "That is why you came, isn't it?"

Big Joe nodded.

Gianetti pulled up a chair next to Percival and poured them each a cup of coffee.

"It's not good," Big Joe said, getting to the point.

"He no gonna hurt my boy, is he?" Gianetti asked.

"It depends on Slim here."

"Meaning?" Percival asked.

"You are into them for a great deal of dough," Big Joe directed his comment to Gianetti. "Little Harry isn't happy Slim here laid out one of his goons, but he has his eye on a bigger piece of the pie, which is the reason he hasn't retaliated. He knows he has you over a barrel because of the paper you signed."

"What paper?" Percival asked Gianetti.

Gianetti swallowed. "They maka me sign. Said they'd break my fingers I no sign. I no cook with broken fingers."

Percival didn't like what he was hearing. "What did the paper say, Pop?"

"It okay—dey tell me it say I pay dem back."

Percival exchanged glances with Big Joe. "Where's the paper?"

"In da kitchen. I go get," Gianetti said, pushing away from the table.

"He can't read," Percival said when Gianetti was out of earshot.

"I figured as much."

Gianetti rushed back into the room waving the paper. "It say I pay back, yes?"

The contract was short and to the point—Gianetti was to make regular payments against the debt. If there were any monies due on the loan on the term date, Gianetti would relinquish ownership of the building and its contents at 624 Third St. to one Harry Weitzman. Percival felt a knot forming in the pit of his stomach. That explained why they hadn't leaned on Gianetti too much and didn't make a fuss when Percival confronted the guy who did show up. They didn't want the money, which would have bought the place several times over—they knew Gianetti wouldn't sell—so they figured out a way to take it from him. The contract term ended at six pm on January 15, 1927. Percival looked at the clock on the wall, noting they were three hours past the deadline.

"What is it, son?" Gianetti asked, looking at Percival's legs.

Unfortunately, there was no easy way to break the news. "You've lost everything, Pop."

"No, I pay back," Gianetti said, shaking his head. "I give money every month."

"It doesn't matter, Pop," Percival said, holding up the paper showing Gianetti's mark. "You signed a paper saying you would give up the building and everything in it if the loan was not paid in full by the due date."

"Then I get another loan and pay dis," Gianetti replied.

"Pop, you don't understand. Today was the last day. I'm surprised they aren't breaking down the door telling us to leave," Percival told him. "They're going to take everything and there's nothing we can do to fight it."

"Do you think your friend Mouse would help babysit the place tonight?" Big Joe asked.

"I'll give him a call," Percival said, struggling to keep his emotions under control. "Pop, you need to go upstairs and get everything you want to keep. We have to get it out of the building before they come. I'll bring up some crates from the basement."

"Must be some mistake." Gianetti turned to Big Joe on the verge of tears. "You big man, you stop them, yes? You gave me money to take in my son. You give them more money to stay away. I pay you back."

Big Joe shook his head.

"Pop, even if we had the money to give them, Little Harry won't let us stay. He could be on the way here right now. You need to get what you want to keep."

"I want keep all." This time, Gianetti was unable to hold back his tears.

Percival wanted to tell him it was his own fault. That he shouldn't have gambled everything away, but the man was already broken. "It's okay, Pop. We'll figure something out."

"We'll figure out how to keep restaurant?" Gianetti's voice was hopeful.

Percival shook his head then wrapped his arms around the man—holding on to him while he shed his tears and then released him—turning him to the stairs and giving him a slight push as one would do with a child reluctant to do as told.

"If I'd met him earlier, I may have been able to teach him to read," Percival said, watching Gianetti trudge up the stairs.

"Little Harry wanted the building. He'd of found another way," Big Joe replied. "Call your friend. Have him watch the front of the building. I'll take the back."

"I have to bring up some crates from the basement, and then I'll need help pushing this cabinet in front of the basement door. There's a speakeasy down there and a tunnel from the church," Percival said when Big Joe cocked his head.

"Explains why the man wanted the building so bad," Big

Joe said. "Get your crates and I will call some guys to help move you out."

"What if Little Harry forgot about the deadline. Maybe they won't come," Percival said, knowing the answer.

Big Joe chuckled. "Do you really think they're going to pass up this opportunity?"

Percival shook his head.

"Then it'd be best to be gone when they get here. Your pop gives them any grief and things could get out of hand. Little Harry's got enough connections he'd be able to say your pop started it and no one would question him. At least not publicly."

"Slim," Big Joe said when he started downstairs. "For what it's worth, I'm sorry it turned out this way. I know you like the guy."

Unable to speak, Percival gave a half smile then continued growing angrier with each step. As he reached the bottom, he'd become so furious that he pounded his fists against the dirt wall. When that didn't relieve his frustration, he walked through the storeroom, sweeping everything to the floor before grabbing the shelves and sending them tumbling on top the mess. When at last he finished, he rooted through the muddle, fishing out several crates.

"Feel better?" Big Joe asked when he returned.

"How'd you know I wasn't tangling with someone from the speakeasy?" Percival asked.

"I would've been more worried about them than you," he said with a nod to Percival's battered knuckles.

"I had to settle for the wall."

"Probably best. You might have killed a man. Something like that stays with a guy for a long time."

"Is that why you didn't return to New York?"

Big Joe shook his head. "Can't run from something like that."

"Then why didn't you come back?"

"It was easier to stay away than to look you in the eye again and tell you I couldn't help you, couldn't give you a home."

"You did help me—with your donations to the asylum."

"That was only money."

"It was enough," Percival said honestly. "They treated me better because of it."

"Make sure to soap up those knuckles; you'll feel them in the morning." Big Joe's lips quivered when he spoke.

"I'll call Mouse," Percival said, leaving the man to compose himself.

***

March 1927

Percival stared at the large trunk as the men loaded it onto the train car. A lifetime of living condensed into a single box. *It's of Pop's own doing,* Percival kept reminding himself. *You did everything in your power to help.* He knew this to be true, but it didn't ease the pain of seeing his pop so distraught. The trunk disappeared from sight, and Percival walked to the end of the platform and waved for Gianetti to join him. The man moved forward, though there was no joy in his step.

"It's time for you to board," Percival said when he neared.

"You sure you no come?" Gianetti asked for the hundredth time since making the decision to return to New York to live with his sister and help in her restaurant.

"No, Pop. We've discussed this. It's time I make my own way," Percival said, standing his ground.

"You promise your pop you no get involved with those Purples," Gianetti said then quickly looked to make sure no one had overheard.

"Do you think Big Joe would allow me to mix it up with the wrong people?" Percival asked.

Gianetti smiled for the first time since arriving at Detroit's

336

Grand Central Station. "Big Joe a good man. Made me a promise to look out for you."

"Big Joe's been looking out for me for a long time," Percival agreed. "He's not going to stop now."

"You come see me one day."

"Yes, Pop, I'll come to see you." Percival looked over his shoulder when the conductor yelled for final boarding. "It's time to get on the train—remember to keep your eyes open for bears."

"You a good son. Slim," Gianetti said, embracing him.

"And you're the best pop a boy could wish for," Percival said, patting him on the back.

"Not true. I let you down."

"No, Pop, you let yourself down, but you were always there for me."

Chapter Forty-One

June 1928

Percival was enjoying an early dinner at Fox & Hounds when he saw Mac standing in the doorway. He lowered his head, hoping the guy wouldn't see him, but when he chanced a glance, Mac was heading in his direction. Percival sighed as Mac pulled out a chair and sat without being invited. If only the man knew how much he loathed him.

"What brings you here?" Percival asked, not caring about the answer.

"Bringing in a little flavor," Mac said, keeping his voice low. "The boys are bringing it in through the tunnel as we speak. You want some special coffee? I can arrange it."

"Thanks, but I'll pass," Percival answered.

"I don't know why Mouse thinks so highly of you. You always act like you're better than him," Mac said, leaning back in the chair. "Seriously, you're such a killjoy."

"If you dislike me so much, why are you here?" The guy was up to something, he was sure of it.

"I didn't say I dislike you. I said I don't trust you," Mac corrected.

"I assure you the feeling's mutual," Percival told him.

"See there, just like that, we got something in common."

"Who would have thought," Percival said dryly.

"Have you talked to Mouse lately?" Mac asked.

"Been a few weeks."

"Then he hasn't filled you in on our trip to Chicago," Mac

said, meeting his eye.

The guy was obviously fishing. *Maybe Mouse is in trouble and someone sent Mac to see what I know.* "Mouse never discusses his business with me."

"Nah, this wasn't business. I mean, the trip was business, but the kid wasn't part of it."

Kid? Franky? Though he'd given Mouse the letter from Anastasia, he never expected him to follow through and check on the boy. Mac seemed in a mood to talk, so Percival tried to keep his voice casual. "What kid would that be?"

"Name's Franky. Mouse calls him Little Man. I'm not sure of all the details, but there was a big to-do in Chicago and Mouse ended up with this kid. Mouse don't seem like much of a father figure to me, so I might have to step in and show him the ropes." Mac laughed as if he'd said something funny. "Anyhow, you enjoy your dinner. I've got to see a man about a dog."

So, Mouse has Franky and hasn't bothered to call. Percival pushed his plate away and waved a hand toward the waiter, motioning him to bring the bill. He had to get to Mouse and convince him to send the boy back to his mother.

***

Arriving at Mouse's apartment, Percival tried the door, found it unlocked, and entered without knocking.

"Leave the light off," Mouse whispered when he reached for the light switch.

"How's the kid?" he asked looking toward the bedroom.

"He had a nightmare, but he's sleeping now. How'd you know he was here?"

Percival sat on the arm of the chair and silently chastised his leg for giving away his nervousness. "I ran into Mac. He told me there was some trouble in Chicago and you brought back a kid. Said the kid was pretty messed up. You going to tell his mother?"

"No."

"She has a right to know. Have you told the kid about her? He has a right to know too." Percival got up, pacing the room and trying to put himself in Mr. Thornton's place. *Don't ask him if he's sending him back. Make him think it's his idea.* "Maybe if he knew, he'd take going back to the asylum a little easier."

"What makes you think I'm sending him back?" Mouse asked tersely.

Percival laughed. "Don't tell me you're planning on keeping him. He's not a stray pup you found on the street. He's a kid. And he has a mom who's worried about him." Percival could tell Mouse was getting defensive and purposely refrained from mentioning Anastasia.

"My sister was never a mother to him," Mouse said firmly.

"She cares about him, Mouse. You have to know that. If not for her asking you to go, you never would have found the kid in the first place."

"The kid has a name. And you're proving my point. She didn't ask me to look for him. She told you to ask me. And when I said no, she didn't give it another thought."

"You don't know that to be true."

"Don't I? Did she ask you to go? She's old enough to leave the asylum. Did she bother to go herself? If she was so worried about the boy, why didn't she check on him? She knew the address."

No, she hadn't asked him, not originally and not in any of her follow-up letters. Nor had she seen fit to go check on him herself. Percival shook his head. "I don't know. Maybe Anastasia…"

"Maybe nothing," Mouse said, cutting him off. "Anna doesn't care about anyone but herself. She never did and never will. She knew what our father was doing to my family and me, and yet she left anyway. Because of her, our mother is dead. I ended up on the streets and Ezra... I'll never know what happened to him. You don't know her like I do, Slim. She lies and manipulates everyone around her just to get her way. The last time I saw my sister, her tongue held the venom of a snake, and yet the letter you gave me purred like a kitten. Anna's not to be trusted. She's not fit to be a mother and I'll not send Franky to her."

Realizing he was losing his argument, Percival cast a glance toward the bedroom. "How many times have you told me not to get involved with the Purples? And yet you think he's better off being brought up in your world?"

"He won't be working for the Purples; he'll be working for me," Mouse said. "I can guard the kid."

"And just how do you propose to do that?" Percival asked, pacing the floor once more.

"With your help."

"My help? You want me to be his bodyguard?"

Mouse laughed. "Only if it comes to that. For now, I just want you to keep your mouth shut. No one is to know who the kid is to me, not even Franky. People find out and they will use the boy to get to me."

"So we make up a lie?"

"No, his story is legit. No one will blame me for taking him away from that. But that is where the story stops."

"Seems a shame the kid's never going to know you're his Uncle Tobias," Percival said sarcastically.

"It's for his own good."

"What do I tell Anastasia?"

"Tell her I was too late. Tell her when I found him, the boy was already dead," Mouse said coolly.

"To what purpose?" Percival asked, unable to keep the

anger from his voice, knowing news like that would destroy Anna.

"She had plenty of time to come clean with the kid and never did. Tell her what you want, but if she ever mentions the kid, well, you'd better make sure that doesn't happen," Mouse said tersely.

"Don't worry, Mouse. Your secret is safe with me." Percival started toward the door and hesitated. "Oh, and keep the kid away from Mac. There's something about him that sets my neck hairs on end."

"Mac's all right."

Percival held firm to the door. "You asked me for a favor and I'll do it. Now I'm asking for this from you. Keep him away from Mac or no deal."

Mouse nodded his agreement and Percival left. It was all he could do not to slam the door on his way out.

All the way back, he rolled over in his mind what he should tell Anastasia. If he told her Mouse had found the boy, she'd insist he bring him home. But what Mouse had said struck a nerve, if she was so worried about the boy, why hadn't she gone looking for him? She had a job and knew the boy's address. She had proof that the boy was hers and could have easily taken him. She also knew he himself would have done anything she asked, and yet knowing that, had never once even hinted that he should. He'd even sent her flowers on multiple occasions professing his love and yet she'd never once mentioned receiving them. Mouse was right: she didn't care about the kid, or anyone else but herself. While he'd tried to get close to her, she'd continuously pushed him away. Mouse, on the other hand, had been the one person, other than Big Joe and Paddy, that had always been there for him. He realized in that moment he would have to do what Mouse asked. Mouse had promised to keep the kid away from Mac and the Purples, and he would be there to make sure his friend kept his promise. *I'll keep the kid safe. I'll see to it myself,* Percival vowed.

Arriving at the gym, he went straight to his room and pulled out a piece of paper.

Dear Anna,

I'm afraid I have some terrible news to tell you. Mouse traveled to Chicago just this month and while there decided to check in on your son. There's no easy way to tell you this, but I'm afraid Franky is dead. Mouse is beside himself with grief having not checked in on the boy sooner. I cannot imagine your anguish at having lost your son yet again, but I know you also care about Mouse. It is for that reason that I ask that if you ever write to him again, please do not mention Franky, for I'm afraid the guilt of not having saved him would cause him considerably more pain.

My heart goes out to you in your moment of sorrow.

Love, Slim

As he wrote that last line, he knew it to be untrue. While a part of him would always care for what they had together, he no longer felt the urgent need for her approval. *Her approval? Why would he care if she approved of him?* As he pondered the question, he knew the answer as clearly as if someone had whispered it in his ear. He didn't love her. He never had. It was her vulnerability that had drawn him to her, hoping to protect her the way he never could protect the other woman in his life. Percival read over the letter once more. While it would hit her hard, it was the only way. Mouse said that Anastasia should never mention the boy again or there would be consequences, and he knew his friend to be a man of his word. He thought the letter enough to do the trick. While he hated upsetting her, he knew thinking her son dead would be easier than knowing him alive and being kept from her.

***

Cindy stared at the page she'd just read, her heart aching to find Anastasia and tell her the truth. "Why?" she said when she realized Linda was watching her.

"It explains why Anastasia never mentioned Franky in her letters," Linda mused.

"Can you imagine going through life thinking your child to be dead?"

"No, I can't," Linda said, shaking her head. "But I guess I can see why he did it."

"Was he protecting Uncle Frank or Tobias?"

"All three."

"How do you figure?"

"Tobias and Anastasia didn't actually part on friendly terms, and by this time, they'd both changed. Tobias had seen and done things that we can only imagine. Anastasia comes in like a momma bear trying to get her cub back, and Tobias is going on the defensive. He's angry at her, protective over the kid, and someone's going to get hurt, maybe even worse," Linda said, explaining her logic.

"Then you think what Slim did was right?"

"I think he did the only thing he could've done at this point. Tobias considers him a friend, but that's because Slim has never crossed him. So, this way, the only one who gets hurt is Anastasia."

"I'm not sure I agree. I think they've all lost something. I just wish someone would've gathered them all together and made them hash out their differences."

Linda crossed her arms, placing her hands on the opposite shoulders. "Would you have them sing 'Kumbaya' while you're at it?"

"Now you're just mocking me," Cindy retorted.

"I think you're letting this all get to you. If you want to cast blame, then let's start with Tobias' father for causing him to be on the street in the first place. Their mother for not being able to protect any of her kids. The fire for destroying the best chance Anastasia ever had at true happiness. Percival's mom for stepping off that curb and leaving the boy alone. Or Louis Gianetti for gambling away his business. Fate dealt them all a bum hand—they were all kids living on the streets at one point or another, trying to survive any way they could. Sending them out on trains might not have been the perfect solution, but it was better than anything else available at the time. Did Percival screw up in not telling Mouse the truth about Anastasia? You're darn right he did, but what's done is done. You might as well go shake your fist at the sky for what good it'll do you."

Cindy closed her eyes and took in a calming breath. "You're right. I guess I should give them all credit for putting the ugly stuff in their journals and not trying to tidy it all up in a bow."

"They didn't put it all in," Linda reminded her.

"What do you mean?"

"The missing pages in Anastasia's journal."

Cindy felt her eyes grow wide. "That's right. The ones telling who Dad's real father was. You don't think it was Slim?"

"There's only one way to find out," Linda said, handing her another stack.

Chapter Forty-Two

1931

"You're hitting the books more than you're hitting the bag these days," Big Joe said, coming into the office. Percival began gathering his books, and Big Joe waved him off. "You stay where you are. I'm happy to see the desk being put to proper use."

"Just because I'm on break doesn't mean I can slack off. Law school is serious stuff." With Thornton's help, Percival had gotten into Brooklyn Law School, only returning to Detroit during breaks from the school. Thornton had told him he'd chosen Brooklyn Law School as he knew the Dean, but Percival knew the man was pleased he'd moved back to New York, so much so, Percival now lived on the upper floor of Thornton's expansive townhome.

"Little Slim's going to be a hotshot lawyer. Makes me very proud to say I helped you, even if it's just letting you use my desk."

"You helped a lot more than that," Percival said, rolling his neck from side to side.

"Speaking of helping, those boys are looking good in the gym. I wouldn't be surprised to see one of them in the ring someday. Franky looks a lot like your friend Mouse. Acts like him too; won't be long before people start putting two and two together."

Percival had told Big Joe Franky's story so the big man could help keep an eye on the kid while he was away. Big Joe had also brought a few of his friends into the know to help watch over the boy. There weren't many places Franky could go without someone reporting back to Big Joe. "Mouse sees it too. I tried to have Mouse let Franky come stay here, but he feels responsible for him and won't listen to reason."

"It's a darn shame he didn't send him back to his momma," Big Joe said, shaking his head.

Percival felt a pang of guilt. While he'd told Big Joe about Mouse refusing to send Franky home, he'd left out the grievous wrong he'd committed, which helped keep mother and son apart. Rarely a day passed that Percival didn't feel the guilt of telling Anastasia Franky was dead. So guilty that he'd taken to writing the occasional letter and signing Mouse's name. Not only did he enjoy reading her responses, he hoped that in some small way, it helped ease the pain of losing her son. "He had his reasons."

"Between him and his maker, I suppose."

"We've all got to pay the price of our wrongs at some point," Percival agreed.

***

June 1932

Percival leaned against the wall in New York's Grand Central Station, people watching. A long line of people came in from the terminal, and he knew them to be passengers from the train that had just arrived from Detroit. A woman leaned to embrace a child, and when she did, Percival saw the man he was waiting for. He waved and was greeted with a relieved smile.

"You haven't changed a bit," Paddy said, embracing him briefly. "Although you dress pretty snazzy these days."

Percival returned the man's embrace. "And you still look like a leprechaun, especially with the red beard."

"This place hasn't changed much," Paddy said, looking

around. "I swear the second I got off the train, I had the urge to step in line and keep my mouth shut."

"Children are to be seen, not heard," Percival said and they both laughed. "You got any luggage?"

"Just this bag." Paddy hoisted it over his shoulder. "Hey, thanks for meeting me. I don't think I'd want to do this by myself."

"I never figured you for a scaredy baby," Percival teased as he led the way through Grand Central Station.

"Hey, you live here. You've had time to walk through our old haunts and deal with any demons that linger. I've been living up in the frozen north where most people still take horses and buggies to town."

"Small town, huh?"

"Everything in our town could fit inside this building."

"Has it been hit hard by the Depression?"

"What Depression?" Paddy quipped.

"You're kidding, right?"

"I mean, I've read about it in the paper and listened to the news on the radio, but living in a small town where the main industry is farming does have its advantages. The farmers are feeling it in crop prices. People don't trust the banks and we don't get many visitors, not that we ever did. Still, it helps when people know how to grow their own food and women can make and mend the family's clothes." When they reached the street, Paddy stopped taking it all in.

Percival scanned the street, noting the noise as people pushed their way to their location, the rumble of the vehicles, shouts from vendors hocking their wares to those new to the city, "Just as you remember it?" Percival asked.

"And then some," Paddy replied.

"Better keep your wallet in your front pocket," Percival said as they began walking. "People are desperate."

Paddy laughed. "I know. I used to be one of them."

"This is different. If we hadn't got out when we did, we'd probably be dead or living in Hooverville with hundreds of other Hard-luck Harrys."

Paddy's face turned serious. "Is it really as bad as the papers say?"

"Worse. You have Hardlucksville at the end of 10th Street with nearly eighty shacks. Hoover City has men, women, and children, and Camp Thomas Paine is full of veterans of the Great War. That one is a bit more organized: fifty-plus shacks along with a clubroom and mess hall. Central Park is now known as Hoover Valley, and they've named the main walkthrough between the huts Depression Street. They make houses out of anything they can find, from bricks to cardboard to tarps. It's different than when we were kids."

"How's that?"

"Most in the city seem to tolerate the homeless and look the other way when they set up close by."

"Wish they would've tolerated us kids when we lived on the streets. I can't tell you how many times I was chased with a broom just for stopping and trying to warm my hands over a grate," Paddy replied, and Percival nodded his head in agreement.

Percival started toward the trolley as it rolled to a stop a few feet away. "I thought we'd go straight to the asylum then grab some dinner, unless you'd like a tour of one of the Hoovervilles."

"Dinner I can do. I don't need to see the homeless. I lived it," Paddy said, sliding onto the seat next to him. He leaned in, lowering his voice. "Any chance at getting a drink?"

"Why, Howard, you must be behind the times. Haven't you heard of Prohibition?" Percival said dryly. Paddy raised an eyebrow. Percival smiled and gave a subtle nod.

Paddy leaned back against the seat. "You know, I do believe this is the first time I've actually paid to ride this thing. If I close my eyes, I'm ten again and we're holding on to the back, hoping no one sees us hitching a ride."

"They frown upon that a bit more at our age," Percival told him, but his friend was right; from the moment he'd seen Paddy in the terminal, it was like time had evaporated. "I'm glad you followed through in placing the advert in the papers. Have you heard from anyone else?"

"A few," Paddy said without divulging names. "It's only been a few weeks. If I don't hear from the others, I'll place the advert again."

Percival had penned a letter to Paddy the moment he'd seen the advert, letting him know of his return to New York, telling of his decision to become a lawyer and that he was staying with Mr. Thornton while going to law school. To his surprise, he'd received a return letter a couple of weeks later telling him he was coming for a visit, as he had business to attend to at the asylum. What that particular business was Paddy hadn't said. "You were vague in your letter. Exactly what business do you have with the asylum?"

Paddy brushed some dust off his hat and rubbed the tip of his shoe on the back of his pants leg. "I'm impressed. You've not yet graduated and yet you already sound like an attorney."

"I don't have to have a law degree to know when my friend is withholding information."

"Not withholding; simply don't want to come across as a fool just yet. You'll think that of me soon enough."

Percival crossed his legs and folded his hands over his knees. "Now I'm truly intrigued."

"So am I," Paddy said with a nod to Percival's legs. "They're close to being still."

"A doctor friend sent me to a most intriguing little man who is using me as a pincushion. He takes great pleasure in placing little needles all around my body once a week. As you can see, the results have been most agreeable."

"Needles, you say. That doesn't sound like fun."

"One gets used to them, I suppose."

"I don't know if I'd ever get used to a person jabbing needles into me," Paddy replied.

"About this business you're here to tend to," Percival said, returning to the original question.

"It's not that I don't want to tell you. It's just I don't want you to think I've gone off my rocker."

"Even if I thought it, I assure you I have no authority to have you committed." Percival chuckled.

"I'm going to the asylum to convince the headmistress to sell me the piano," Paddy blurted.

Percival wasn't sure what he expected, but it wasn't that. "You know they have pianos in Michigan, right?"

"Now, don't be making fun of me," Paddy said. "Do you know how hard it was for me to tell you that? Heck, if it weren't for me sending you a letter, you'd never have known. I'd already decided to come here, and I thought wouldn't it be great if I could see my old pal Slim."

"So why did you tell me?" Percival asked.

Paddy shrugged. "I guess I thought maybe you'd talk some sense into me. You know why I want it, don't you?"

"I have a pretty good idea." It was no secret Paddy had been infatuated with Mileta from the moment he'd seen her.

"You know Anastasia played it more than Mileta, right?"

"Anastasia," Paddy gulped. "Do you think she'd still be there?"

"No, she left years ago," Percival assured him, then continued before Paddy could question how he knew. "If I told you not to buy it, would you listen?"

"Doubtful. I've been telling myself the same thing ever since I got on the train in Sandusky."

"Then I guess we'd better see to it. This here's our stop," Percival said, standing and motioning him forward.

***

"Here's to a productive day," Paddy said, lifting his glass of illegal spirits. "Not only did I buy myself a piano, I get to drink something that wasn't made in someone's washtub."

"Go easy on that stuff. You don't want to have to explain where it came from."

"Waiter, another round," Paddy said, ignoring him. "I get the chance to drink, I'm gonna drink. Now lift your glass and drink a toast to my wife."

"You never said anything about being married," Percival said, raising his glass.

"I'm not. Not yet anyway. But as soon as I find Mileta, that piano will seal the deal."

Percival started to lower his glass, then drained it, deciding he needed a shot of liquid courage. "I hate to break it to you, pal, but Mileta is married."

"Married?" Paddy repeated.

"To Mouse."

"Why that…"

"Easy, Paddy," Percival warned.

"Yeah, I forgot you and he are friends."

"We are, as are you and I. They've been married a few years."

"A few years? What? Did he marry her right out of high school?"

"Pretty much. Her family—she found a good one—died. Mouse was afraid she'd be sent back, so he married her."

"Pretty convenient. They got any kids?" Paddy asked, taking the fresh glass from the waiter the moment he arrived.

Percival started to wave his glass away then reconsidered. He took a swallow before continuing. "They had one. A daughter, she died."

"Must have been hard on them," Paddy said into his glass.

"About destroyed Mildred—that's the name she goes by now. That or Millie. But she has Franky. I guess it's a good thing Mouse wanted him to stay." Percival knew he should quit talking but was feeling the effects of the alcohol, and it felt so good to finally get his secret out in the open. Who better to tell than someone he could trust? "I was feeling bad about telling Anastasia her son was dead, but if it wasn't for Franky, I don't think Mileta would've ever found her way back. She plays piano in a rooftop speakeasy over on 43rd Street."

Paddy jerked his head up. "Mileta is here?"

"What? No, Anastasia."

Paddy ran a hand through his hair. "How come you know so much about Anastasia? You have a thing for her or what?"

"Not anymore," Percival said, finishing his drink. Paddy was leaving in the morning, so what harm would it do to tell him? "We had a thing back at the asylum, but that's all over now."

"That girl was a... I can't even think of anything bad enough to call her. She was mean to everyone. Wait. Are you telling me this Franky is your kid?"

"No, she had him before she arrived at the asylum."

"If it's her kid, why does Mouse have him?"

"Because she's Mouse's sister."

Paddy's eyes rounded. "That's why he wanted Mileta to go there. He knew his sister would protect her."

"There's more to it than that, but yes, that was his intent."

"So what's all this about telling her the kid was dead?"

Percival suddenly felt as if he was under examination. "I've already said too much."

"Oh no, you don't. You're not going to clam up on me now. Besides, who am I going to tell?"

The guy had a point. Besides, it felt as if a weight had been lifted off his shoulders. He took another drink, then told Paddy the whole story of how Franky came to be living with Mouse and Mileta and unburdened himself of the guilt of keeping Anastasia from her son.

Chapter Forty-Three

December 1, 1933

Percival was sitting at the desk in Thornton's study when the telephone rang. "Hello," he said, answering on the second ring.

"Slim, it's Mouse."

Something in his friend's tone told him this was not a casual call. "Hey, Mouse, how are things in Detroit?"

"Detroit's heating up, so I took a trip to Indiana to see my Ma."

I thought your papa killed your momma. "You told me your mother's dead."

"My momma is dead. I came to visit Ma, the woman who took me in the first time they sent me out on the trains. I've been thinking a lot about her of late and wanted to come down and check on her. Listen, it's a long story, but I did some thinking on the way down to Noblesville. I want out."

Percival gripped the handpiece tighter. "Out of Indiana or away from the Purples?"

"The second one," Mouse replied, letting Percival know he couldn't talk freely. "As soon as I'm done here, I'm going back to the city to get Millie and Franky. I'm not sure where we'll go yet. Florida or maybe even California, someplace far away from the people I work for. Slim, just so you know, you're welcome to join us."

"I can't move away. Not just yet anyway."

"How's the judge?"

Sherry A. Burton

"Mr. Thornton isn't a judge; he was an attorney." Percival's hands fiddled with the phone cord. "His mind is still sharp, but his body's failing him. He rarely comes downstairs these days, and when he does, he doesn't stay long."

Mouse whistled into the phone. "So you're going to have the place all to yourself after he croaks."

"When Mr. Thornton expires, his house will be sold and monies donated to his designated charities," Percival informed him.

Mouse laughed. "Give the boy an education, and he starts sounding like one of those do-gooders."

"There's nothing wrong with an education. You should see that Franky gets one," Percival said tersely.

"I will," Mouse said, sounding contrite. "Trust me. Everything is going to change. I want to be able to walk down the street with my wife without having to worry. I want them both to have a normal life, which is why I called. I can't leave without your help—just for a few days. I need someone I can trust to have my back when we leave. Can you do that, Slim? Can you help me to see that my family's safe? I've already lost Fannie. I don't want to lose Millie and Franky too."

Percival thought of Mr. Thornton and knew the man not to be long for this world, but he had months, not days, and Mouse was right, he wouldn't be able to simply walk away without help. He let out a breath, firming his decision. "I'll come."

"I knew I could count on you." Mouse's voice was full of relief. "Slim, forget about what I said about you sounding like a do-gooder. You are and always have been the most loyal friend I've ever had. Mac's going to pick me up. It was arranged before I made my decision, and I don't want him getting wise. I have a few things to finish up here before I leave. I'll see you when I get to Detroit."

Martin entered the study as Percival placed the handset on

356

the cradle. "An upsetting telephone call, sir?"

"A friend in Detroit is in trouble," Percival said, checking the time. "If I leave soon, I can still make today's train."

"Shall I tell Mr. Thornton you're leaving?" Martin asked, casting a glance toward the ceiling.

Percival knew Martin disapproved of his decision. He was unhappy about it as well, but if Mouse was serious about leaving, he would need all the help he could get. "No, I'll tell him myself."

"He'll be sorry to see you go," Martin replied.

"I wouldn't leave if it could be helped," Percival snapped. "I'm sorry, Martin. I understand your concern. I'll telephone Dr. Todd to let him know I'm going so he can arrange a nurse to stay with him, and I do promise to come back as soon as I can."

"I'll ask the cook to prepare you a bag for the train," Martin replied.

"Have her put it in a lunch bucket. I don't want to draw any unnecessary attention on the train. And thank you, Martin," Percival said, then hurried upstairs to Mr. Thornton's room, entering without knocking.

"Ah, Percival, my boy, what's got you in such a hurry?" Thornton asked the moment he entered.

Percival pulled the chair close to Thornton's bed. "How is it you always know it's me?"

"I can hear the way you walk," Thornton said by way of explanation. "Now, to my question."

"I need to go to Detroit for a few days," Percival replied.

Thornton frowned. "I heard the telephone. Is something wrong?"

The man might be ailing, but he rarely missed a thing. "My friend Mouse is in trouble."

"With the law?" Thornton asked, struggling to pull himself

up in the bed. "Is that why he's calling you?"

"No, sir, he's not in trouble with the law." Percival took hold of Thornton's elbow, helping him get comfortable. "There's no need to trouble yourself. I'm going as a friend, not an attorney."

"I don't like you messing around in Purple Gang business."

"I won't be gone long," Percival replied, knowing travel to and from alone would take several days. He thought to ease his mind and tell him his trip did not involve the Purples but knew the man would see through his lie. Though his eyesight left him years earlier, Thornton had no problem gauging the truth.

"I'll telephone Big Joe and let him know you are on your way," Thornton said, patting the nightstand in search of the telephone.

Percival had expected nothing less. Rising from the chair, he handed Thornton the phone and leaned in, kissing him on top of his head. "Thanks for looking out for me."

"I'll see you when you return," Thornton said as his fingers searched out the numbers.

"If you need anything, ring for Martin." Percival slid the small handbell closer to the edge of the nightstand. Taking one last look at Thornton, he rushed to his room to change and gather his things. He was nearly to the door when he returned and added Anastasia's letters to the bag.

***

Percival climbed on board the train just as the conductor was shouting last call. Removing his hat, he walked through the cabin searching for an empty seat. Not having any luck, he pushed through to the next car and the one after that until, at last, he spied an open seat. Had he'd bothered to look before sitting, he might have gone on to the next car, as he wasn't in the mood for talking. The girl sitting next to him had hair so vibrant, he instantly thought of Paddy, who was never at a loss for words. He nodded a polite hello, and she lowered her eyes and quickly turned away, pretending to be fascinated by something on the other side of the window. *Obviously, I've misjudged the girl, and the ride won't be all that bad after all. Perhaps being born with the gift of gab isn't a redhead thing— maybe it's just a Paddy thing.*

Percival bent, setting the lunch bucket the cook prepared for him beside his seat. As he slid his case underneath, he caught a glimpse of the girl's cloth bag crammed beneath hers. Something about it looked familiar. He thought to ask her about it, but she kept her face pressed against the window—odd, since there was nothing to see within the underground train yard. Not wishing to interrupt her thoughts, Percival placed his hat under his seat, then leaned back and closed his eyes as the train jerked to a start. A few moments later, he heard the girl gasp and opened his eyes to see the city landscape now replaced by a forest of trees.

"First time on a train?" he asked.

She turned to him, green eyes bright with wonder. "Yes. Never in my life have I seen so many trees."

He closed his eyes once more, recalling his first time riding the train and remembering the mixture of excitement and fear that had gripped him. He'd since traveled by train so many times, it seemed routine, and he wondered when he'd outgrown the magic of childhood—further wondering if he'd ever really felt it. Maybe. He thought to the days before his mother became aware of him slipping out of the apartment and how much he'd enjoyed those small escapes.

"I don't know how you can sleep with so much to see. I can't imagine I could ever bore of traveling."

He opened his eyes, saw her staring at him, and nodded toward the window. "Keep an eye out for bears."

Her eyes grew wider. "Are there really bears out there?"

"Yes, ma'am," Percival was surprised when his comment elicited a giggle. While initially wanting to be left alone, the girl's naive manner intrigued him. In her blue and white polka dot dress and matching hat, she presented as a mature woman but giggled with the innocence of a child, complete with a rosy-cheeked face full of freckles that had lingered from childhood. Her face, he realized was plain. Not that she wasn't attractive.

On the contrary, he thought her to be quite pretty, but the thing that made her stand out most was that she wore no makeup. Most of the women in the city wouldn't think of leaving the house without having their faces painted—some to excess. Why, a fellow couldn't kiss a girl without having to reach for his handkerchief to remove the paint she'd left behind. He thought of his own mother and lifted a hand to his cheek. Wishing to attract the girl's attention, he counterfeited a sneeze.

"Bless you," she said, turning from the window.

"Thank you. Percival Barsotti; a pleasure to make your acquaintance," he said before she had a chance to look away.

Her eyes darted from side to side as if deciding if she should give him her name. Finally, her shoulders relaxed, and she offered her hand. "Delia Gallagher."

Delia, what a lovely name. "Well, Miss Gallagher, where, may I ask, are you running off to?"

"I'm not running away. I have every right to be on this train. I have a ticket and everything." She opened her mouth as if to say more and then reconsidered. As she jerked her hand away, he noticed her eyes, once bright with excitement, were now shrouded with fear.

"I didn't say you were running away. I asked where you were running off to. Let me begin again; what great adventure are you off to?"

She hesitated before speaking, then jutted her chin. "I'm going to visit my grandmother. She's been quite ill. I'm going to take care of her."

Percival instantly thought of Thornton. "Oh dear, what's wrong with her?"

She swallowed before speaking. "She's ill; did you not hear?"

It was apparent the girl was hiding something. Why he cared, he did not know. "I heard. I was only curious as to what ailed her."

"I'd say that was none of your business," she said, firming her chin.

"Of course, forgive me for being so forward." He chastised himself for acting like a lawyer. Even if she were hiding something, it was none of his concern. It wasn't as if the girl sitting beside him was on trial.

"What about you?" she asked.

"I assure you I'm quite well," Percival answered.

She giggled. "No, I meant to ask where you're going."

Her question reminded him of the seriousness of his trip. "I'm going to help a friend who's in trouble."

"What kind of trouble?"

"Nothing that concerns you," Percival said, then realized he'd sounded short. "I'm sorry. It's just that I'm not at liberty to divulge that information."

"I guess we both have our secrets," she replied.

"It appears so," he agreed.

She turned back toward the window, and he found himself wishing he'd made up his own story if only to keep her talking.

"Why are we stopping?" she asked when the train slowed sometime later.

"A water stop," Percival said without glancing out the window. "They need water to produce the steam for the engine."

"You've traveled this way so many times, you know this

without looking?" she asked, sounding amazed by the prospect.

"I've spent a great deal of time on the trains," he agreed.

"You say that as if it's a bad thing."

Percival smiled. "When you reach your destination, weary and covered with grime, you too may feel the same way."

"Dirt will wash off, but the memories will remain forever."

"Ah, an optimist—always looking on the bright side," he said when she furrowed her brow.

"Sometimes clinging to hope is all a person has," she said, turning toward the window once more.

"See, you're tired already," he said when she yawned.

"A little. I didn't sleep much last night."

"Anticipation for your trip?"

"What? Oh, yes, I was terribly anxious about leaving."

"Your family. Were they sad to see you go?"

She stiffened, and he could tell he'd touched on another nerve. "I doubt anyone will miss me much."

He wished to ask more but didn't want to take a chance at scaring her off. As the train picked up speed once more, they settled into comfortable silence. Shortly after that, her easy breathing told him she'd fallen asleep.

Chapter Forty-Four

The cabin was growing colder. At first, Percival thought he was the only one feeling it but watched as, one by one, the inhabitants within the cabin donned their coats. Several travelers pulled blankets around them, and he wished he were among those better prepared. The train slowed, Percival pulled his coat together as the cabin grew cooler still. Delia slept atop her coat with her head pressed against the window. He debated waking her—a decision he didn't have to make when the door to the cabin opened, sending a blast of cold air swirling around the cabin. Delia woke as the conductor came in blowing on his hands to warm them.

"Another water stop," she asked, struggling into her coat.

"No, something's wrong," Percival said with a nod to the conductor. "I expect he's here to tell us the heat has gone out."

"He doesn't think we're smart enough to know that already?" Delia asked, rubbing her arms.

A lady in the seat in front of them waved the man closer. "Turn up the heat. It's freezing in here."

"I'm sorry, madam, I'm afraid there is an issue in the engine compartment, and we are making an unscheduled stop to fix it. The engineer assures me it won't take too long, but the train cannot be in motion while being fixed."

"Here? In the middle of nowhere? At least have the decency to stop in a town so we can stay warm?" the woman scolded.

"If we wait until the nearest town, you would have frostbite by the time we arrive," the conductor said, continuing to the next cabin.

"Still enjoying your adventure?" Percival asked.

Delia smiled a wide smile. "It wouldn't be a true adventure if everything went as planned, now would it?"

"No, I suppose it would not," Percival agreed. "I guess we should have a bit to eat to bide the time."

Delia nodded her agreement. Pulling a cloth from her coat pocket, she unfolded it and stared unblinking at what was left of a cheese biscuit. "I must have sat on it," she surmised, picking at the crumbs.

Percival lifted his lunch bucket from beside his chair, opened it, and pulled out his Globe thermos, gripping it with his knees. He peered inside and sent a silent thank you to the cook, who worried over his weight and always packed way too much food for him to eat. He pulled out a tightly wrapped sandwich, unwrapped it, and offered half to Delia.

Her lips trembled as she shook her head.

"You don't like roast beef," he asked, keeping his voice low so as not to invite unwelcomed beggars.

"I cannot take your food," she whispered, eying the sandwich.

"I assure you I have enough food in this box to last us this trip and the next," Percival said, pushing it into her hand.

"Thank you." She took a bite, then quickly choked down the rest. Either the girl was extremely hungry or was used to fighting for her food.

He thought about offering her his half of the sandwich, but two things stopped him. First, he was hungry, and second, he worried about her getting motion sickness after getting too much in her stomach too quickly. "Do you have any siblings?"

"What?"

"I was wondering if you have any brothers or sisters." *A large family would explain why she felt the need to scarf down her food.*

"I have a younger brother," she said with a shiver.

So much for my theory. Percival placed his half of the sandwich in his lap and unscrewed the yellow plastic cap from the thermos. Uncorking the lid, he poured some of the contents into the cap and handed it to her. She smelled it, took a sip, then coughed.

"I take it you don't like black coffee. I'd offer you some sugar, but I don't have any. If you can stomach it, then it will help keep you warm."

"I wasn't expecting it to be so warm," she said, taking another sip. This time, she managed without coughing.

"It's the thermos. A great invention for us traveling folks." He held up a finger, reached into his lunch bucket, and pulled out another wrapped parcel, handing it to her. "Nothing goes better with coffee than cake."

This time, she took the offering without hesitation. Percival watched as she unwrapped it, studied it for a moment, then dipped a finger to the icing, touching it to the tip of her tongue. She gasped, then picked up the cake and took a bite. Instead of inhaling it the way she had the sandwich, she finished it with slow, deliberate bites. Not wishing to stare, he ate his sandwich, allowing her to finish her cake in silence. When at last he turned to her, he saw tears rolling down her face.

"Is something wrong, Miss Gallagher?"

"It's just that you've been so kind to me."

He pulled his handkerchief from his pocket and handed it to her.

"See, there you go again." She blew her nose and handed it back to him.

"Are you not used to people being nice to you?" he asked, folding it and returning it to his pocket.

"They told me not to talk to anyone on the train. They said

people would not think too kindly of me." She sniffed.

"Who told you? Your parents?" If they were mean to her, it would explain why she'd said she wouldn't be missed.

"I lied to you," she said, staring at the back of the seat in front of her. "Well, not everything. This is my first time on a train, but I'm not going to visit my grandmother."

"Where are you going?"

"I'm going out west for work."

"Work?"

"Yes." The excitement had returned to her voice. "I'm going to get paid $17.50 a month. I have a contract and everything."

"A contract?"

"Yes, they told me it was a good thing for a girl like me. They said if I stayed in New York, bad things would happen to me. They showed me the paper and told me where I should sign my name. Then they put me on this train."

Percival had an uneasy feeling in his stomach. Everything was starting to make sense, from her naivety to scarfing down food. She wasn't starving. She was afraid someone was going to take it from her. "Delia, who are the 'they' you speak of?"

"The mistresses at the asylum. As soon as I reached my eighteenth birthday, they told me I had to leave. I told them I did not wish to leave my little brother, and they said I was too old to stay. I then told them I wished to take him with me, but they said I could not take him because I didn't have a job." The train had started moving again. If she noticed, she did not say. She absently touched her coat pocket. "Then they showed me the paper and told me it would be a way for me to work and earn enough money to one day send for him."

"Do you remember what the advert said? Or what kind of work you'll be doing?"

"I'm going to be a waitress," she said unapologetically. "A

Harvey Girl, to be precise. They will give me a salary, a place to sleep, and feed me food as good as what I just ate. I won't have to spend my money, so I can save it and one day have enough to bring my brother to live with me."

Percival had heard about the Harvey Girls. They were to be clean, pure of heart, and obey strict rules while under contract. The problem was many of the girls left before their one-year contract was up—primarily to get married. Delia was a very pretty girl and would no doubt gain the interest of many suitors. Why, if he were looking to get married, he too would throw his hat in the ring. "What if your brother gets adopted before..."

"Oh, he won't," she said, cutting him off. "He has red hair just like me. People don't like people with red hair."

Percival started to tell her about Paddy but decided that his friend's adoption would only give her something else to worry about. He poured himself a cap full of coffee and drank it down, wishing for something stronger. Delia had a respectable job lined up, and she was getting out of the city. He should be happy for her. Instead, his mind was scrambling for ways of getting her to return to New York so that he could spend more time with her.

"I hope they place me on a train," she said, pulling him from his thoughts.

"You don't know where you're going yet?" he asked, corking the thermos and returning the cap.

"I'm going to Chicago to train, and then they'll place me where best suits me."

"Where best suits them is more like it."

"You don't approve?"

"It sounds like a wonderful opportunity," Percival said, forcing a smile. He had no claim to her and no reason to dampen her hopes for the future. Still, he might be of service to her brother. "How old is your brother?"

"Peter is nine."

"Peter Pan rears his head yet again," Percival mumbled. *There has to be hundreds of Peter Gallaghers in the system.* There were at least ten in his dorm room at the asylum. He'd have to press to get more information.

"Excuse me?"

"Sorry, the name just reminded me of the book *Peter Pan*. Have you read it?"

"Hundreds of times. It's Peter's favorite. I think he likes to pretend it is written about him. I even caught him dangling out the window once." She closed her eyes as if remembering. "I swear if I hadn't grabbed hold of him, he would've plummeted to his death. I'm still not sure he's convinced he can't fly."

"I think all boys think they're invincible. I've been known to dangle out a window or two in my day. He'll grow out of it," Percival assured her. "Did you both grow up in the asylum?"

"We were there long enough, and now Peter will have to bear it longer." Her voice broke, and she stood. "If you'll excuse me, I need to go to the facility."

"Of course," he said, stepping into the aisle to let her out. He made a show of swaying with the motion of the train and bumped into her as she passed. The moment she stepped through the door to the forward cabin, he unfolded the papers he lifted from the pocket of her coat. Among them was the contact information for the Harvey House facility in Chicago, an original newspaper advert seeking women to work in the restaurants, and the information he'd been looking for—a small piece of paper with the address of the asylum that still held her brother. Percival pulled a pencil and paper from his jacket and wrote down the address, glad that the boy was at the Children's Aid Society instead of one of the smaller institutions such as the one he came from. Delia was correct: the boy's hair color aside, he would have little chance at adoption when there were so many children to choose from. He heard the door to the cabin slide open, and folded the papers, easily slipping them back into her pocket when she returned.

"I passed a couple empty seats if you'd like to move," Delia said once seated.

"You wish us to change cars?"

"Not us, you," she replied.

"Why? Did I say or do something to offend you?"

"You don't have to stay with me just because you feel sorry for me," she said, meeting his eyes.

"The only thing I'm sorry about is that we don't have much time to get better acquainted," he replied.

A lovely rose crept over her cheeks. "The mistress told me that if I were to tell anyone of my upbringing, they would think poorly of me."

"What if roles were reversed?"

"What do you mean?"

"What if I told you that my mother died when I was young, and I lived on the streets until finally going to live in an asylum? What if I told you that the asylum sent me out on a train to Detroit, where I found a home? Would that appall you?"

"Now you're just making fun of me," she said, looking away.

He took hold of her chin, turning her toward him once again. "You didn't answer my question."

"No, it wouldn't bother me."

"Then why should I allow your story to bother me?" he asked, releasing his hold on her.

She lowered her eyes. "Because my story is true."

"So is mine."

Her mouth fell open briefly, then she quickly recovered. "You were at the Children's Aid Society?"

"No, but I was at an asylum." Percival could tell she was struggling to believe him. Yes, he could have moved to another seat and left her to her own devices, but something inside him needed her to know how much they had in common, so he continued. "You have no trunk filled with traveling clothes. That bag under your seat holds everything you own. They gave it to you before you left, along with the clothes you're wearing."

Her face brightened. "It's true. You were sent out on the trains."

"Yes, nine years ago."

"You've done fairly well for yourself, then," she said, looking him over.

"I had help, but yes, I manage rather well."

"I have help too." The relief was evident in her voice. "I have a job and a contract that says they must keep me for a year as long as I do as they say. That shouldn't be hard, since I'm used to strict rules. If I'd like, I can renew my contract for another year and a year after that."

Percival tried to smile his encouragement, but it wouldn't come. The thought of never seeing this girl again filled him with a sadness he couldn't figure out. The look of determination on her face let him know there would be no changing her mind about continuing on her journey. Still, if he could find a way to help her, then maybe…"I'll be returning to New York soon after my business in Detroit is finished. I'd be happy to check in on your brother if that would be alright with you."

She burst into tears, laughing at the same time. "I'm sorry. I'm not usually this emotional. Yes, I would very much like you checking in on Peter."

"I could write you and tell you how he's doing." Percival's heart sank when she shook her head.

"Oh, it's not that I don't wish to hear from you. I just don't know where they are sending me after my training. Would it be unladylike if I were to request your address so that I can write you?"

"No, not at all," Percival didn't bother to hide his excitement. He pulled out his notepad, hurriedly flipping the page so she couldn't see he'd already procured her brother's information, then wrote down his address, handing it to her. "I'm staying with a friend."

Delia folded the paper without looking at the address, then tilted her head as she reached into her pocket—the expression on her face told him he'd returned her belongings to the wrong pouch. Still watching him, she searched the opposite side, found what she was looking for, winking as she returned everything to the correct pocket.

Chapter Forty-Five

December 4, 1933

Even though Percival stayed with Delia in Detroit's Grand Central Station until her connecting train arrived, he still made it to the apartment before Mouse and Mac returned, letting himself in using the key Mouse had given him when he lived there full time.

The apartment was much like he remembered it, dark and sparsely furnished. Percival went to Mouse's room, pulled a crate from the closet, and began to pack, which took all of five minutes since there were barely any personal items in the room. Percival decided it best not to be there when Mac arrived, so he left Mouse a note that simply read, *You know where to find me*, then left it unsigned on top of the crate. He was halfway to the door when he remembered Anastasia's letters. Returning to Mouse's room, he added them to the crate with the rest of his belongings—hoping if Mouse were serious about making a fresh start, maybe he would open his heart enough to make room for his sister as well.

Pretending to be Mouse, Percival had written to Anastasia, trying to fill a void in his life. Though he no longer felt the same way about her, he enjoyed reading the letters she wrote. He knew it was time to end the charade, further hoping to fill the void with a new pen pal. He thought of Delia and sighed. Though he'd only known her a matter of hours, she'd stolen his heart.

Leaving the apartment, he made his way to Big Joe's gym

and wasn't the least surprised to find the man pacing the room.

"Your train was due hours ago. I was getting worried," he said when Percival entered.

"The train was delayed, and then I had to go by Mouse's apartment," Percival said, leaving out the more personal stuff.

"Big Joe don't like you going to that place on your own."

"I'm a big boy now, remember?"

"Fists don't trump guns. Now tell me what's going on."

"Not here," Percival said with a nod to the stairs.

Big Joe took the hint and led the way to his office, closing the door behind them. Sitting behind the desk, he waited for Percival to speak.

"Mouse wants out."

"Out out?"

"Yes, he's going to take Mileta and Franky and start fresh."

Big Joe sat up in his chair. "Purples don't take too kindly to one of their own skipping out on them."

"He knows. That's why he called me."

"You should've stayed in New York." Big Joe's nostrils flared when he spoke.

"He's my friend."

"Not a very good one," Big Joe said evenly.

"If Mouse tries to leave without someone having his back, he's liable to get killed. The Purples wouldn't care if Mileta and Franky are with him. I owe it to Franky to make sure he gets a chance to grow up and make something of himself."

"Is there something Big Joe should know about why you've taken such an interest in the boy?"

Percival thought about it for a moment, then nodded his head. "The short of it is I told his mother he was dead, so she didn't come looking for him."

Big Joe sat back in his chair. "Maybe if you told me the whole story, I'd be inclined to help your friend leave town."

Percival pulled up a chair and turned it around, leaning over the back as he told Big Joe the truth about Mouse paying him to go into the asylum to keep an eye on Mileta. He told him about falling for Anastasia, only to discover she was cold and heartless. He told about Anastasia asking Mouse to go check on Franky and how it hurt that she hadn't asked him. He told about how Mouse threatened unknowns if she should come looking for the kid. Of his decision to agree to Mouse's demands that he tell Anastasia her son was dead and how the guilt of that decision had been eating at him ever since. "I got him into this mess. I need to help him get free of it before they claim him too."

"Big Joe will agree to help you under one condition," he said after hearing him out.

"Which is?"

"You are not to get involved."

"What do you mean I'm not to get involved? I'm already involved."

"Not with the leaving. The Purples know you, Slim. You won't be any safer than the rest of the family. I've got guys that can blend in. Got a new guy been coming around. Name's Hoffa, goes by Jimmy. Smart kid, seems to have a good head on his shoulders—I'll give him and some of the others a call. But you got to stay here. You can sleep on the sofa over there. When your friend Mouse calls to let you know he's ready, we'll put things in motion."

Percival didn't like twiddling his thumbs, but Big Joe had a point. Mac and the others knew him and would know it was he who helped them disappear. "Okay."

"You stay inside. You need something, you tell me and I'll see that you get it. Word on the street is some guy named Butch just got out of the joint and has it out for your friend Mouse."

"What's his beef with Mouse?"

"Claims Mouse and that Mac guy are the ones that got him sent up. From what Big Joe hears, the Purples want to have a chat with them, so that might be the reason for your friend's sudden interest in leaving."

"It makes sense," Percival agreed.

"You talk to your friend, you tell him I'm not happy about him pulling you into this. You tell him you get hurt, he better watch his back."

Percival smiled. "I think he already knows."

The telephone phone rang. Big Joe answered it then held the handset out to Percival. "It's your guy."

"Yeah, Mouse?" Percival said, talking into the mouthpiece. "Okay, just let me know when you're ready. Big Joe's got some guys who'll help see you all safe. Better get that arm looked at."

"What's the word?" Big Joe asked the moment he replaced the handset.

"Mouse pretty much said what we already know. The street's too hot to go tonight. He's going to try for tomorrow. He said if anything happens to him, he'll send Franky here."

"What was the business with his arm?"

"It's nothing. Said he got into a tussle with a guy on the train and the guy knifed him. Said it's only a nick."

"What'd he do to the guy?"

"Said the guy decided to walk home."

"I can see where a fellow might be inclined to leave the train early," Big Joe said, rising from the chair. "You need anything?"

"I could use something to eat. I left my lunch bucket on the train." Actually, he'd had it refilled at the station and sent it on with Delia, but Big Joe didn't need to know that. *Delia.* He caught Big Joe looking and erased the smile that had appeared just at the thought of her.

***

December 6, 1933

"What's the word?" Percival asked when Big Joe came into the room. The lack of a smile told him it wasn't good news.

"I don't know how to tell you this, but your friend Mouse is dead."

"Dead? You mean I've been sitting here doing nothing and..."

"It wasn't the Purples," Big Joe said, shaking his head. "It was that scratch he told you about. It poisoned his blood."

Percival felt his whole body begin to tremble. After everything Mouse had been through, he'd got taken out by a dirty blade. *Franky!* "I've got to go get Franky."

"And what would you do with him?" Big Joe asked.

"What do you mean? Why, I'd take him home, of course."

Big Joe placed his hand on Percival's chest to stop him. "What happened before wasn't right, but that boy's been through enough. From what you've told me, Mileta has become somewhat of a mother to him. She lost her parents, her baby, and her husband, and you want to take the boy away. A person can only take so much pain."

Big Joe was right. While taking Franky back to Anastasia would ease his conscience, doing so would do more harm than good. He looked at Big Joe. "Now what?"

"Now we wait. There are things in motion—the less you know, the better off everyone will be. The boy will come to you. When he does, you call for Jimmy. He's staying in the building, and he knows what to do."

"But..."

"It will be up to them where they decide to go. My guys will help get them out of the city."

Percival had never felt so helpless. "Do you still have that money you were holding for me?"

" It's in the safe."

"Give it to them."

Big Joe started to object and Percival raised his hand. "They need it more than I do."

"I'll see that they get it."

"Then what?"

"Then you'll go home."

"Not until I see Mouse properly buried."

"Already arranged. They're doing it tonight."

"I'm going to. That's not open for discussion."

Big Joe nodded. "After you talk to Franky, you'll go home. You've got other friends to look after."

"Thornton."

"He called as I was coming to find you. He's ready to have you home."

Percival's heart had been stretched in so many directions in the last few days. He looked at Big Joe, suddenly feeling like that little boy who'd lost everything he ever held dear. When he spoke, his voice showed his vulnerability. "I don't even know where home is anymore."

Big Joe clamped an arm around him and pulled him close. "You take care of this and then go be with Mr. Thornton. He's not long for this world. After he goes, you'll have plenty of time to find yourself."

***

December 12, 1933

"Hey, buddy, we've been here five minutes. You going to get out or not?" the cab driver asked.

"Yeah, I'm getting out," Percival said, sliding across the seat. He handed the man a bill, made his way into the restaurant, and took a seat at the table nearest the door. Though he'd driven past often, this was the first time he'd bothered to enter, preferring to meet with Gianetti at his sister's house. As he waited, he watched a waitress flutter about the room, moving from table to table, smiling and speaking with the customers. She was young and laughed easily at what a gentleman at one of the tables said. Percival could easily see Delia in the same role and for a moment wanted to call out to the girl. The waitress turned, he saw her face painted brightly, and the moment was gone.

She saw him watching and made her way to his table, handing him a menu.

Percival started to open it then hesitated. "Do you have caponata?"

"Yes, we do. Would you like a glass of wine to go with it?" She smiled. "I'm so happy I can ask that again."

He shook his head.

"Caponata, it is."

"Would you please tell Gianetti that his son is here?" Percival asked and watched as her mouth fell open. She recovered then left, hurrying to the back of the room.

So much had happened over the last few days, Percival had completely forgotten they'd recalled Prohibition, and wondered what that would mean for the bootleggers. He instantly thought about Mouse lying in an unmarked grave next to the couple who'd taken Mileta in. *It's not a pauper's grave*, he reminded himself. *At least he is with his daughter—so much death.* Percival rubbed at his temples as a deep sadness pulled at his heart.

"Slim! My boy," Gianetti called from across the room. He hurried to Percival's table, wiping his hands on his apron as he crossed the floor. "You come see your pop."

"How ya doing, Pop?" Percival asked. He stood and embraced the man, hanging on just a little longer as Gianetti clapped him on the back.

"You okay, Slim? You no look so good," Gianetti asked

when Percival released him.

"I'm okay, Pop, just tired. I just came in from Detroit and didn't get any sleep on the train." It wasn't the whole truth, but it wasn't a lie either. He'd not been able to stop thinking long enough to sleep. He'd thought about Mouse, wondering if he could have done more to help his friend. Maybe if he'd gone by the apartment, he would've seen how ill he was and gotten him to a doctor in time. He thought about Mileta and Franky, wondering where they'd gone. And he thought about Delia; never had a girl gotten under his skin such as she. "So how are you, Pop? Things going alright with you?"

"Yes. Yes. My sister, she taka good care of me." He looked from side to side and lowered his voice. "She no let me do dumb t'ings; no more bets."

"That's good, Pop. That's really good."

"I be a good pop. You be proud of me too, yes?"

"Yes, Pop. I'm proud. I couldn't have asked for better. Actually, that's why I'm here. I have a friend whose brother needs looking after. I want to talk to her about having him come and help you around the restaurant. You don't have to pay him. I'll take care of that. I just want to find something that will keep him busy so he doesn't get in trouble on the streets." He'd thought of it on the train on the way home and hoped he could get everyone to agree.

"You bring me another son?"

"He'll go to live with his sister when she gets settled, but he'll need people to look out for him while he's here."

"Your pop gonna look after him very good," Gianetti said, bobbing his head.

"I know you will, Pop," Percival said. "Listen, Pop. I'm tired. Can you put my meal in a container for me so I can get home?"

"Yes, of course. I get it now," Gianetti said, hurrying to the back. He returned moments later with two bags. "I give you extra. For Mr. Thornton."

"Thanks, Pop," Percival said, taking the bags. "I'll be in touch soon. And, Pop?"

"Yes, Slim."

"I love you."

"I love you too, my boy." Gianetti said, blinking back tears.

Chapter Forty-Six

Thornton was in the keeping room, sitting in a wingback chair with a wool blanket over his lap when Percival arrived. Seeing the man dressed and sitting on the lower level lifted one of the weights that seemed to have settled over Percival's heart. So much had gone wrong in the last week that he'd been afraid Thornton wouldn't be there when he returned. He didn't bother to announce his arrival, as the man's face lit up the moment he stepped into the room.

"Ah, Percival. Glad to see you've made it back to us," Thornton said. "The house has been much too quiet with you gone."

"It's good to see you up and about," Percival said, sinking into a chair.

"You've seen far too much misery of late. I did not wish to add to your troubles."

"I do admit to worrying that you wouldn't be here when I returned," Percival replied.

"Don't bury me just yet, dear boy. Robert is scouring the world, writing letters to colleagues, unearthing every concoction known to man. He even convinced me to allow that little man of yours to poke some of his needles in me."

"Did it work?"

"I put up a fuss, but here I am sitting in this chair. Made it down of my own accord." He laughed. "About did Martin in when he came into the room and found me sitting here. Of course, that may have been because I'd neglected to put on my trousers. Still can't seem to put my legs in them without help."

"And your robe?" Percival asked.

"Felt around the bed, but I couldn't find the thing. Serves him right to see me in my underdrawers." Thornton went silent for a moment. "You're quiet. Big Joe told me about your friend. How are you holding up?"

"I spent most of the trip back wondering if I could've done more."

"You're a thinker. There won't be many things in life that you won't revisit to see if you made the right decision. I get the feeling that isn't the only thing that's troubling you."

Percival knew better than to lie to the man. "There's a boy I'd like to help. He's in the asylum, and I'd like to get him out."

"You wish to adopt someone?"

"Only if I must. I stopped to see Pop on the way home and asked if he would allow Peter— that's the boy's name—if he would help keep an eye on him."

"You'd ask him over me?"

"To be honest, I wasn't sure what kind of shape you'd be in. But if you are up for it, I'd appreciate it if you could help me see that he gets an education. His sister tells me he can read."

"This sister you speak of, you seem to think highly of her."

"Yes, sir, I met her on the train and plan to make her my wife one day." Though he'd thought it many times over the last few days, this was the first time he'd said it out loud.

"Then I suppose we should do everything in our power to see to it that happens," Thornton agreed. "It'll be nice having a boy in the house again. Now, tell me all about this girl and how you came to meet her."

Percival leaned back in the chair, recounting every step of his trip in vivid detail so the man—who was just as much a father to him as Gianetti—could see through his eyes. While he still had to reach out to Delia to ask her permission to set things in motion to get Peter out of the asylum, he knew his life was about to change. He also knew himself to be ready for whatever lay ahead.

***

Cindy finished the last page of the journal and placed it onto the stack with the others. While she would have liked to have read more, she was happy to see Percival end up in a better place.

"I think I have your final page," Linda said, handing it to her. "It was stuck to my final page."

"Oh good, I was hoping there'd be more," Cindy said. Taking the paper, she began to read.

I stopped journaling after that trip to Detroit. I don't know if it was because I wanted to leave my old life behind or because my new life was so busy after Peter came to live with us. I was going to send these off to Paddy since he asked, but I supposed whoever would be reading them would like to know whatever became of me. I worked in a law firm in Brooklyn from thirty-four to forty-one when I got drafted to serve in WWII. Being a lawyer, I ended up serving my country behind a desk. While I didn't see any combat, I saw my share of atrocities, as just when I was to return home, the Army sent me to Nuremberg, Germany, to help with the trials. I wasn't sent as a lawyer. However, I was inside the Palace of Justice and, on more than one occasion, came within feet of the men on trial. On the outside, they looked like ordinary men. I guess you never know the ugliness within a man's soul.

I, along with hundreds of others, was responsible for sifting through thousands of pounds of documents to help prosecute the accused. With the exception of a few trips stateside, I stayed in Nuremberg until after the last trial concluded in October of forty-eight.

In case you're wondering, I did end up marrying Delia. She proved to be a fine and loving wife and provided me with four sturdy sons. We left New York upon my return to the states. Thornton was long gone, and Gianetti had passed during my time in Nuremberg. Big Joe is still alive and I visit him from time to time. I asked Delia where she'd like to go, and she told me she enjoyed seeing the rolling hills. So I bought her a large house with windows in nearly every room just outside of Gettysburg, Pennsylvania, where I continue to practice law.

"Wow, to be part of history like that," Cindy said when she finished reading.

"If you think about it, his whole life was nothing but history. From the train rides to the trials to everything in between," Linda replied.

"He bought her his mother's house," Cindy said with a sigh. "I love that he wrote that he continues to practice law. That way, I can pretend he's still there doing what he loves."

The doorbell rang, and Cindy looked to Linda. "Whoever it is doesn't know we don't use the front door."

"Probably a solicitor."

"If it is, they're selling flowers," Cindy said, looking out the window. She opened the door to a man she'd never seen before, standing on the front stoop holding a vase of yellow roses mixed with maroon flowers. "I believe you have the wrong house."

"You Cindy Moore?"

"Yes." *But I don't know anyone that would send me flowers.*

"Right house," he said, pushing the flowers into her hand. "Have a nice day."

Cindy lifted the small envelope from the plastic holder, opened the flap, and pulled the card free.

Thank you for the nice letter. Apology accepted.
I would love to have dinner with you.
David.

David? I don't know any David. Not any old enough to send me flowers. The only David she could recall was the man whose daughter she'd frightened in the cemetery. She reread the note, focusing on the part about the apology. Her mouth went dry as she looked up to see Linda slinking from the living room. "Mother?" she said, trying to keep her voice steady. "What have you done?"

A Note from the Author

I often hear comments about how poorly the children who rode the orphan trains were treated. Some feel the people who took the children in worked them and treated them as slaves.

The truth of the matter is the children were sent out to the heartland and most taken in by families who owned farms. In return, the families expected the children to pull their weight. Did some go too far? I think that is a reasonable assumption. Still, I ask you to consider the era in which the placing out program existed. The trains ran from 1854 to 1929. There were no fast-food establishments, no expansive grocery stores. If a person was to eat, they would more than likely grow and cultivate their own crops. Families would hunt, raise, and butcher meat for the table and purchase or barter for the rest. More often than not, women would sew and mend what the family wore and wash those items from water collected from a well or nearby stream. Families, adults, and children alike worked in the fields, did household chores, and tended to the babies—there was no birth control. They did these tasks from sun up to sun down with little time to rest.

Most of the families that took children in were not rich. They did not have the luxury of taking in a child simply to give them a happy home. Another child meant another mouth to feed, and each family member was expected to help earn their keep.

It would be an erroneous leap for me to declare the Placing Out Program to be perfect. I know all too well that some people are capable of taking things to the extreme. I merely wish to point out that the children sent west came from cities where death and disease were rampant. Children were pushed from their homes because their families could not care for them. They ran away because the homes they had were too intolerable to bear.

Children as young as four and five roamed the streets, begging, stealing, and prostituting themselves in order to survive. Children who ran afoul of the law were not put into juvenile institutions. They were thrown into adult jails with rapists and murderers.

There were no child labor laws at the time, so children lucky enough to find work were often locked in sweat factories where they worked until they either died or were lucky enough to break free.

I am not condoning abuse, especially physical abuse. If any of the children were truly harmed, that is wrong—shame on the person(s) who wronged them.

My goal is to point out it was a different time, and sometimes it helps to look at things from a different perspective. The bottom line—Reverend Charles Loring Brace observed an atrocity and made it his mission to correct it. The Children's Aid Society Reverend Brace founded helped relocate over a quarter of a million children who may have otherwise perished.

Whether true orphans or simply a product of the times in which they lived, my heart goes out to the children who rode the trains. Furthermore, I am grateful to those families who opened their homes to the children when so many who encountered them on the street treated them with disdain.

Since I began writing and speaking about the orphan trains, I have had the pleasure of meeting many people with connections to someone who rode the trains. So far, the stories they have related have been favorable. I am grateful to share my journey with you. I hope you enjoy it as much as I do.

~Sherry

A special thanks to:

My editor, Beth, for allowing me to keep my voice.

My cover artist and media design guru, Laura Prevost, thanks for keeping me current.

My proofreader, Latisha Rich, for that extra set of eyes.

To my amazing team of beta readers, thank you for helping take a final look.

To my husband, thank you for your endless hours of researching, your help with all things genealogy, and for allowing me to bounce story ideas off of you.

Please find it in your heart to take a moment and go to Amazon to leave a review. Reviews are also welcomed at Barnes & Noble, Bookbub, and Goodreads as well. If you purchased the book at a signing or from my website, please begin your review by including that information. If not, Amazon may not allow the review.

Most importantly, please tell EVERYONE and share in the reading groups! As an indie author, word of mouth is the best publicity I can get.
Thank you for taking this journey with me.

Sherry A. Burton

Please remember to follow me on Amazon and sign up for my newsletter on my website to keep up to date with all new releases.

For more information on the author and her works, please see
www.SherryABurton.com
Follow Sherry on social media:
https://www.facebook.com/SherryABurtonauthor
https://www.amazon.com/Sherry-A.-
Burton/e/B005PM6QFG?ref=dbs_m_mng_rwt_auth
https://www.bookbub.com/profile/sherry-a-burton
https://www.instagram.com/authorsherryaburton

About the Author

Born in Kentucky, Sherry married a Navy man at the age of eighteen. She and her now-retired Navy husband have three children and ten grandchildren.

After moving around the country and living in nine different states, Sherry and her husband now live in Michigan's thumb, with their three rescue cats and a standard poodle named Murdoc.

Sherry writes full time and is currently hard at work on the next novel in her Orphan Train Saga, an eighteen-book historical fiction series that revolves around the orphan trains.

When Sherry is not writing, she enjoys traveling to lectures and signing events, where she shares her books and speaks about the history of the Orphan Trains.

Coming in 2022

Howard's (AKA Paddy) Story

Made in the USA
Columbia, SC
24 November 2021